I0608908

THE HONOR OF
THE NAME

THE HONOR
OF THE NAME

Translated from the French of

EMILE GABORIAU

WILDSIDE PRESS: MMIII

Published by
Wildside Press, LLC
P.O. Box 301
Holicong, PA 18928-0301 USA
www.wildsidepress.com

Wildside Press Edition: MMIII

He hung suspended over the abyss into which the baron had
just fallen

From a drawing by Bayard Jones

THE HONOR OF THE NAME

CHAPTER I

On the first Sunday in the month of August, 1815, at ten o'clock precisely—as on every Sunday morning—the sacristan of the parish church at Sairmeuse sounded the three strokes of the bell which warn the faithful that the priest is ascending the steps of the altar to celebrate high mass.

The church was already more than half full, and from every side little groups of peasants were hurrying into the church-yard. The women were all in their bravest attire, with cunning little *fichus* crossed upon their breasts, broad-striped, brightly colored skirts, and large white *coifs*.

Being as economical as they were coquettish, they came barefooted, bringing their shoes in their hands, but put them on reverentially before entering the house of God.

But few of the men entered the church. They remained outside to talk, seating themselves in the porch, or standing about the yard, in the shade of the century-old elms.

For such was the custom in the hamlet of Sairmeuse.

The two hours which the women consecrated to prayer the men employed in discussing the news, the success or the failure of the crops; and, before the service ended, they could generally be found, glass in hand, in the bar-room of the village inn.

For the farmers for a league around, the Sunday mass was only an excuse for a reunion, a sort of weekly bourse.

All the *curés* who had been successively stationed at Sairmeuse had endeavored to put an end to this scandalous habit, as they termed it; but all their efforts had made no impression upon country obstinacy.

They had succeeded in gaining only one concession. At the moment of the elevation of the Host, voices were hushed, heads uncovered, and a few even bowed the knee, and made the sign of the cross.

But this was the affair of an instant only, and conversation was immediately resumed with increased vivacity.

But to-day the usual animation was wanting.

No sounds came from the little knots of men gathered here and there, not an oath, not a laugh. Between buyers and sellers, one did not overhear a single one of those interminable discussions, punctuated with the popular oaths, such as: "By my faith in God!" or "May the devil burn me!"

They were not talking, they were whispering together. A gloomy sadness was visible upon each face; lips were placed cautiously at the listener's ear; anxiety could be read in every eye.

One scented misfortune in the very air.

Only a month had elapsed since Louis XVIII. had been, for the second time, installed in the Tuileries by a triumphant coalition.

The earth had not yet had time to swallow the sea of blood that flowed at Waterloo; twelve hundred thousand foreign soldiers desecrated the soil of France; the Prussian General Muffling was Governor of Paris.

And the peasantry of Sairmeuse trembled with indignation and fear.

This king, brought back by the allies, was no less to be dreaded than the allies themselves.

To them this great name of Bourbon signified only a terrible burden of taxation and oppression.

Above all, it signified ruin—for there was scarcely one among them who had not purchased some morsel of government land; and they were assured now that all estates were to be returned to the former proprietors, who had emigrated after the overthrow of the Bourbons.

Hence, it was with a feverish curiosity that most of them clustered around a young man who, only two days before, had returned from the army.

With tears of rage in his eyes, he was recounting the shame and the misery of the invasion.

He told of the pillage at Versailles, the exactions at Orleans, and the pitiless requisitions that had stripped the people of everything.

"And these accursed foreigners to whom the traitors have delivered us, will not go so long as a shilling or a bottle of wine is left in France!" he exclaimed.

As he said this he shook his clinched fist menacingly at a white flag that floated from the tower.

His generous anger won the close attention of his auditors, and they were still listening to him with undiminished interest, when the sound of a horse's hoofs resounded upon the stones of the only street in Sairmeuse.

A shudder traversed the crowd. The same fear stopped the beating of every heart.

Who could say that this rider was not some English or Prussian officer? He had come, perhaps, to an-

nounce the arrival of his regiment, and imperiously
demand money, clothing, and food for his soldiers.

But the suspense was not of long duration.

The rider proved to be a fellow-countryman, clad in
a torn and dirty blue linen blouse. He was urging forward, with repeated blows, a little, bony, nervous mare,
covered with foam.

"Ah! it is Father Chupin," murmured one of the
peasants, with a sigh of relief.

"The same," observed another. "He seems to be
in a terrible hurry."

"The old rascal has probably stolen the horse he is
riding."

This last remark disclosed the reputation Father
Chupin enjoyed among his neighbors.

He was, indeed, one of those thieves who are the
scourge and the terror of the rural districts. He pretended to be a day-laborer, but the truth was, that he
held all work in holy horror, and spent all his time in
sleeping and idling about his hovel. Hence, stealing
was the only means of support for himself, his wife,
and two sons—terrible youths, who, somehow, had escaped the conscription.

They consumed nothing that was not stolen.
Wheat, wine, fuel, fruits—all were the rightful property
of others. Hunting and fishing at all seasons, and
with forbidden appliances, furnished them with ready
money.

Everyone in the neighborhood knew this; and yet
when Father Chupin was pursued and captured, as he
was occasionally, no witness could be found to testify
against him.

"He is a hard case," men said; "and if he had a
grudge against anyone, he would be quite capable of

lying in ambush and shooting him as he would a squirrel."

Meanwhile the rider had drawn rein at the inn of the Bœuf Couronne.

He alighted from his horse, and, crossing the square, approached the church.

He was a large man, about fifty years of age, as gnarled and sinewy as the stem of an old grape-vine. At the first glance one would not have taken him for a scoundrel. His manner was humble, and even gentle; but the restlessness of his eye and the expression of his thin lips betrayed diabolical cunning and the coolest calculation.

At any other time this despised and dreaded individual would have been avoided; but curiosity and anxiety led the crowd toward him.

"Ah, well, Father Chupin!" they cried, as soon as he was within the sound of their voices; "whence do you come in such haste?"

"From the city."

To the inhabitants of Sairmeuse and its environs, "the city" meant the country town of the *arrondissement*, Montaignac, a charming sub-prefecture of eight thousand souls, about four leagues distant.

"And was it at Montaignac that you bought the horse you were riding just now?"

"I did not buy it; it was loaned to me."

This was such a strange assertion that his listeners could not repress a smile. He did not seem to notice it, however.

"It was loaned me," he continued, "in order that I might bring some great news here the quicker."

Fear resumed possession of the peasantry.

"Is the enemy in the city?" anxiously inquired some of the more timid.

" Yes; but not the enemy you refer to. This is the former lord of the manor, the Duc de Sairmeuse."

" Ah! they said he was dead."

" They were mistaken."

" Have you seen him? "

" No, *I* have not seen him, but someone else has seen him for me, and has spoken to him. And this someone is Monsieur Laugeron, the proprietor of the Hôtel de France at Montaignac. I was passing the house this morning, when he called me. ' Here, old man,' he said, ' do you wish to do me a favor? ' Naturally I replied: ' Yes.' Whereupon he placed a coin in my hand and said: ' Well! go and tell them to saddle a horse for you, then gallop to Sairmeuse, and tell my friend Lacheneur that the Duc de Sairmeuse arrived here last night in a post-chaise, with his son, Monsieur Martial, and two servants."

Here, in the midst of these peasants, who were listening to him with pale cheeks and set teeth, Father Chupin preserved the subdued mien appropriate to a messenger of misfortune.

But if one had observed him carefully, one would have detected an ironical smile upon his lips and a gleam of malicious joy in his eyes.

He was, in fact, inwardly jubilant. At that moment he had his revenge for all the slights and all the scorn he had been forced to endure. And what a revenge!

And if his words seemed to fall slowly and reluctantly from his lips, it was only because he was trying to prolong the sufferings of his auditors as much as possible.

But a robust young fellow, with an intelligent face, who, perhaps, read Father Chupin's secret heart, brusquely interrupted him:

"What does the presence of the Duc de Sairmeuse at Montaignac matter to us?" he exclaimed. "Let him remain at the Hôtel de France as long as he chooses; we shall not go in search of him."

"No! we shall not go in search of him," echoed the other peasants, approvingly.

The old rogue shook his head with affected commiseration.

"Monsieur le Duc will not put you to that trouble," he replied; "he will be here in less than two hours."

"How do you know?"

"I know it through Monsieur Laugeron, who, when I mounted his horse, said to me: ' Above all, old man, explain to my friend Lacheneur that the duke has ordered horses to be in readiness to convey him to Sairmeuse at eleven o'clock.' "

With a common movement, all the peasants who had watches consulted them.

"And what does he want here?" demanded the same young farmer.

"Pardon! he did not tell me," replied Father Chupin; "but one need not be very cunning to guess. He comes to revisit his former estates, and to take them from those who have purchased them, if possible. From you, Rousselet, he will claim the meadows upon the Oiselle, which always yield two crops; from you, Father Gauchais, the ground upon which the Croix-Brulee stands; from you, Chanlouineau, the vineyards on the Borderie——"

Chanlouineau was the impetuous young man who had interrupted Father Chupin twice already.

"Claim the Borderie!" he exclaimed, with even greater violence; "let him try, and we will see. It was waste land when my father bought it—covered with briers ; even a goat could not have found pasture there. We have cleared it of stones, we have scratched up the soil with our very nails, we have watered it with our sweat, and now they would try to take it from us! Ah! they shall have my last drop of blood first! "

" I do not say but——"

" But what ? Is it any fault of ours that the nobles fled to foreign lands? We have not stolen their lands, have we ? The government offered them for sale ; we bought them, and paid for them; they are lawfully ours."

" That is true; but Monsieur de Sairmeuse is the great friend of the king."

The young soldier, whose voice had aroused the most noble sentiments only a moment before, was forgotten.

Invaded France, the threatening enemy, were alike forgotten. The all-powerful instinct of avarice was suddenly aroused.

" In my opinion," resumed Chanlouineau, " we should do well to consult the Baron d'Escorval."

" Yes, yes! " exclaimed the peasants ; " let us go at once! "

They were starting, when a villager who sometimes read the papers, checked them by saying :

" Take care what you do. Do you not know that since the return of the Bourbons Monsieur d'Escorval is of no account whatever ? Fouché has him upon the proscription list, and he is under the surveillance of the police."

This objection dampened the enthusiasm.

" That is true," murmured some of the older men ; " a visit to Monsieur d'Escorval would, perhaps, do us more harm than good. And, besides, what advice could he give us ? "

Chanlouineau had forgotten all prudence.

" What of that? " he exclaimed. " If Monsieur d'Escorval has no counsel to give us about this matter, he can, perhaps, teach us how to resist and to defend ourselves."

For some moments Father Chupin had been studying, with an impassive countenance, the storm of anger he had aroused. In his secret heart he experienced the satisfaction of the incendiary at the sight of the flames he has kindled.

Perhaps he already had a presentiment of the infamous part he would play a few months later.

Satisfied with his experiment, he assumed, for the time, the *rôle* of moderator.

" Wait a little. Do not cry before you are hurt," he exclaimed, in an ironical tone. " Who told you that the Duc de Sairmeuse would trouble you? How much of his former domain do you all own between you? Almost nothing. A few fields and meadows and a hill on the Borderie. All these together did not in former times yield him an income of five thousand francs a year."

" Yet, that is true," replied Chanlouineau ; " and if the revenue you mention is quadrupled, it is only because the land is now in the hands of forty proprietors who cultivate it themselves."

" Another reason why the duke will not say a word ; he will not wish to set the whole district in commotion. In my opinion, he will dispossess only one of the owners of his former estates, and that is our worthy ex-mayor—Monsieur Lacheneur, in short."

Ah! he knew only too well the egotism of his compatriots. He knew with what complacency and eagerness they would accept an expiatory victim whose sacrifice should be their salvation.

"That is a fact," remarked an old man; "Monsieur Lacheneur owns nearly all the Sairmeuse property."

"Say all, while you are about it," rejoined Father Chupin. "Where does Monsieur Lacheneur live? In that beautiful Château de Sairmeuse whose gable we can see there through the trees. He hunts in the forests which once belonged to the Ducs de Sairmeuse; he fishes in their lakes; he drives the horses which once belonged to them, in the carriages upon which one could now see their coat-of-arms, if it had not been painted out.

"Twenty years ago, Lacheneur was a poor devil like myself; now, he is a grand gentleman with fifty thousand livres a year. He wears the finest broadcloth and top-boots like the Baron d'Escorval. He no longer works; he makes others work; and when he passes, everyone must bow to the earth. If you kill so much as a sparrow upon his lands, as he says, he will cast you into prison. Ah, he has been fortunate. The emperor made him mayor. The Bourbons deprived him of his office; but what does that matter to him? He is still the real master here, as the Sairmeuse were in other days. His son is pursuing his studies in Paris, intending to become a notary. As for his daughter, Mademoiselle Marie-Anne——"

"Not a word against her!" exclaimed Chanlouineau; "if she were mistress, there would not be a poor man in the country; and yet, how some of her pensioners abuse her bounty. Ask your wife if this is not so, Father Chupin."

Undoubtedly the impetuous young man spoke at the peril of his life.

But the wicked old Chupin swallowed this affront which he would never forget, and humbly continued:

"I do not say that Mademoiselle Marie-Anne is not generous; but after all her charitable work she has plenty of money left for her fine dresses and her fallals. I think that Monsieur Lacheneur ought to be very well content, even after he has restored to its former owner one-half or even three-quarters of the property he has acquired—no one can tell how. He would have enough left then to grind the poor under foot."

After his appeal to selfishness, Father Chupin appealed to envy. There could be no doubt of his success.

But he had not time to pursue his advantage. The services were over, and the worshippers were leaving the church.

Soon there appeared upon the porch the man in question, with a young girl of dazzling beauty leaning upon his arm.

Father Chupin walked straight toward him, and brusquely delivered his message.

M. Lacheneur staggered beneath the blow. He turned first so red, then so frightfully pale, that those around him thought he was about to fall.

But he quickly recovered his self-possession, and without a word to the messenger, he walked rapidly away, leading his daughter.

Some minutes later an old post-chaise, drawn by four horses, dashed through the village at a gallop, and paused before the house of the village *curé*.

Then one might have witnessed a singular spectacle.

Father Chupin had gathered his wife and his children together, and the four surrounded the carriage, shouting, with all the power of their lungs:

"Long live the Duc de Sairmeuse!"

CHAPTER II

A gently ascending road, more than two miles in length, shaded by a quadruple row of venerable elms, led from the village to the Château de Sairmeuse.

Nothing could be more beautiful than this avenue, a fit approach to a palace; and the stranger who beheld it could understand the naïvely vain proverb of the country: "He does not know the real beauty of France, who has never seen Sairmeuse nor the Oiselle."

The Oiselle is the little river which one crosses by means of a wooden bridge on leaving the village, and whose clear and rapid waters give a delicious freshness to the valley.

At every step, as one ascends, the view changes. It is as if an enchanting panorama were being slowly unrolled before one.

On the right you can see the saw-mills of Fereol. On the left, like an ocean of verdure, the forest of Dolomien trembles in the breeze. Those imposing ruins on the other side of the river are all that remain of the feudal manor of the house of Breulh. That red brick mansion, with granite trimmings, half concealed by a bend in the river, belongs to the Baron d'Escorval.

And if the day is clear, one can easily distinguish the spires of Montaignac in the distance.

This was the path traversed by M. Lacheneur after Chupin had delivered his message.

But what did he care for the beauties of the landscape!

Upon the church porch he had received his death-wound; and now, with a tottering and dragging step, he dragged himself along like one of those poor soldiers, mortally wounded upon the field of battle, who go back, seeking a ditch or quiet spot where they can lie down and die.

He seemed to have lost all thought of his surroundings—all consciousness of previous events. He pursued his way, lost in his reflections, guided only by force of habit.

Two or three times his daughter, Marie-Anne, who was walking by his side, addressed him; but an " Ah! let me alone!" uttered in a harsh tone, was the only response she could draw from him.

Evidently he had received a terrible blow; and undoubtedly, as often happens under such circumstances, the unfortunate man was reviewing all the different phases of his life.

At twenty Lacheneur was only a poor ploughboy in the service of the Sairmeuse family.

His ambition was modest then. When stretched beneath a tree at the hour of noonday rest, his dreams were as simple as those of an infant.

" If I could but amass a hundred pistoles," he thought, " I would ask Father Barrois for the hand of his daughter Martha; and he would not refuse me."

A hundred pistoles! A thousand francs!—an enormous sum for him who, in two years of toil and privation had only laid by eleven louis, which he had placed carefully in a tiny box and hidden in the depths of his straw mattress.

Still he did not despair. He had read in Martha's eyes that she would wait.

And Mlle. Armande de Sairmeuse, a rich old maid, was his god-mother; and he thought, if he attacked her adroitly, that he might, perhaps, interest her in his love-affair.

Then the terrible storm of the revolution burst over France.

With the fall of the first thunder-bolts, the Duke of Sairmeuse left France with the Count d'Artois. They took refuge in foreign lands as a passer-by seeks shelter in a doorway from a summer shower, saying to himself: " This will not last long."

The storm did last, however; and the following year Mlle. Armande, who had remained at Sairmeuse, died.

The château was then closed, the president of the district took possession of the keys in the name of the government, and the servants were scattered.

Lacheneur took up his residence in Montaignac.

Young, daring, and personally attractive, blessed with an energetic face, and an intelligence far above his station, it was not long before he became well known in the political clubs.

For three months Lacheneur was the tyrant of Montaignac.

But this *métier* of public speaker is by no means lucrative, so the surprise throughout the district was immense, when it was ascertained that the former ploughboy had purchased the château, and almost all the land belonging to his old master.

It is true that the nation had sold this princely domain for scarcely a twentieth part of its real value. The appraisement was sixty-nine thousand francs. It was giving the property away.

And yet, it was necessary to have this amount, and Lacheneur possessed it, since he had poured it in a flood of beautiful louis d'or into the hands of the receiver of the district.

From that moment his popularity waned. The patriots who had applauded the ploughboy, cursed the capitalist. He discreetly left them to recover from their rage as best they could, and returned to Sairmeuse. There everyone bowed low before Citoyen Lacheneur.

Unlike most people, he did not forget his past hopes at the moment when they might be realized.

He married Martha Barrois, and, leaving the country to work out its own salvation without his assistance, he gave his time and attention to agriculture.

Any close observer, in those days, would have felt certain that the man was bewildered by the sudden change in his situation.

His manner was so troubled and anxious that one, to see him, would have supposed him a servant in constant fear of being detected in some indiscretion.

He did not open the château, but installed himself and his young wife in the cottage formerly occupied by the head game-keeper, near the entrance of the park.

But, little by little, with the habit of possession, came assurance.

The Consulate had succeeded the Directory, the Empire succeeded the Consulate, Citoyen Lacheneur became M. Lacheneur.

Appointed mayor two years later, he left the cottage and took possession of the château.

The former ploughboy slumbered in the bed of the Ducs de Sairmeuse; he ate from the massive plate, graven with their coat-of-arms; he received his visitors in the magnificent *salon* in which the Ducs de Sairmeuse had received their friends in years gone by.

To those who had known him in former days, M. Lacheneur had become unrecognizable. He had adapted himself to his lofty station. Blushing at his own ignorance, he had found the courage—wonderful in one of his age—to acquire the education which he lacked.

Then, all his undertakings were successful to such a degree that his good fortune had become proverbial. That he took any part in an enterprise, sufficed to make it turn out well.

His wife had given him two lovely children, a son and a daughter.

His property, managed with a shrewdness and sagacity which the former owners had not possessed, yielded him an income of at least sixty thousand francs.

How many, under similar circumstances, would have lost their heads! But he, M. Lacheneur, had been wise enough to retain his *sang-froid*.

In spite of the princely luxury that surrounded him, his own habits were simple and frugal. He had never had an attendant for his own person. His large income he consecrated almost entirely to the improvement of his estate or to the purchase of more land. And yet, he was not avaricious. In all that concerned his wife or children, he did not count the cost. His son, Jean, had been educated in Paris; he wished him to be fitted for any position. Unwilling to consent to a separation from his daughter, he had procured a governess to take charge of her education.

Sometimes his friends accused him of an inordinate ambition for his children; but he always shook his head sadly, as he replied:

" If I can only insure them a modest and comfortable future! But what folly it is to count upon the future. Thirty years ago, who could have foreseen that the Sairmeuse family would be deprived of their estates ? "

With such opinions he should have been a good master; he was, but no one thought the better of him on that account.   His former comrades could not forgive him for his sudden elevation.

They seldom spoke of him without wishing his ruin in ambiguous words.

Alas! the evil days came.   Toward the close of the year 1812, he lost his wife; the disasters of the year 1813 swept away a large portion of his personal fortune, which had been invested in a manufacturing enterprise. Compromised by the first Restoration, he was obliged to conceal himself for a time; and to cap the climax, the conduct of his son, who was still in Paris, caused him serious disquietude.

Only the evening before, he had thought himself the most unfortunate of men.

But here was another misfortune menacing him; a misfortune so terrible that all the others were forgotten.

From the day on which he had purchased Sairmeuse to this fatal Sunday in August, 1815, was an interval of twenty years.

Twenty years!   And it seemed to him only yesterday that, blushing and trembling, he had laid those piles of louis d'or upon the desk of the receiver of the district.

Had he dreamed it?

He had not dreamed it.   His entire life, with its struggles and its miseries, its hopes and its fears, its unexpected joys and its blighted hopes, all passed before him.

Lost in these memories, he had quite forgotten the present situation, when a commonplace incident, more powerful than the voice of his daughter, brought him back to the terrible reality.

The gate leading to the Château de Sairmeuse, to *his* château, was found to be locked.

He shook it with a sort of rage; and, being unable to break the fastening, he found some relief in breaking the bell.

On hearing the noise, the gardener came running to the scene of action.

"Why is this gate closed?" demanded M. Lacheneur, with unwonted violence of manner. "By what right do you barricade my house when I, the master, am without?"

The gardener tried to make some excuse.

"Hold your tongue!" interrupted M. Lacheneur. "I dismiss you; you are no longer in my service."

He passed on, leaving the gardener petrified with astonishment, crossed the court-yard—a court-yard worthy of the mansion, bordered with velvet turf, with flowers, and with dense shrubbery.

In the vestibule, inlaid with marble, three of his tenants sat awaiting him, for it was on Sunday that he always received the workmen who desired to confer with him.

They rose at his approach, and removed their hats deferentially. But he did not give them time to utter a word.

"Who permitted you to enter here?" he said, savagely, "and what do you desire? They sent you to play the spy on me, did they? Leave, I tell you!"

The three farmers were even more bewildered and dismayed than the gardener had been, and their remarks must have been interesting.

But M. Lacheneur could not hear them. He had opened the door of the grand *salon*, and dashed in, followed by his frightened daughter.

Never had Marie-Anne seen her father in such a mood; and she trembled, her heart torn by the most frightful presentiments.

She had heard it said that oftentimes, under the influence of some dire calamity, unfortunate men have suddenly lost their reason entirely; and she was wondering if her father had become insane.

It would seem, indeed, that such was the case. His eyes flashed, convulsive shudders shook his whole body, a white foam gathered on his lips.

He made the circuit of the room as a wild beast makes the circuit of his cage, uttering harsh imprecations and making frenzied gestures.

His actions were strange, incomprehensible. Sometimes he seemed to be trying the thickness of the carpet with the toe of his boot; sometimes he threw himself upon a sofa or a chair, as if to test its softness.

Occasionally, he paused abruptly before some one of the valuable pictures that covered the walls, or before a bronze. One might have supposed that he was taking an inventory, and appraising all the magnificent and costly articles which decorated this apartment, the most sumptuous in the château.

"And I must renounce all this!" he exclaimed, at last.

These words explained everything.

"No, never!" he resumed, in a transport of rage; "never! never! I cannot! I will not!"

Now Marie-Anne understood it all. But what was passing in her father's mind? She wished to know; and, leaving the low chair in which she had been seated, she went to her father's side.

"Are you ill, father?" she asked, in her sweet voice; "what is the matter? What do you fear? Why do

you not confide in me? Am I not your daughter?
Do you no longer love me?"

At the sound of this dear voice, M. Lacheneur trembled like a sleeper suddenly aroused from the terrors
of a nightmare, and he cast an indescribable glance
upon his daughter.

"Did you not hear what Chupin said to me?" he
replied, slowly. "The Duc de Sairmeuse is at Montaignac; he will soon be here; and we are dwelling in
the château of his fathers, and his domain has become
ours!"

The vexed question regarding the national lands,
which agitated France for thirty years, Marie understood, for she had heard it discussed a thousand times.

"Ah, well, dear father," said she, "what does that
matter, even if we do hold the property? You have
bought it and paid for it, have you not? So it is rightfully and lawfully ours."

M. Lacheneur hesitated a moment before replying.

But his secret suffocated him. He was in one of
those crises in which a man, however strong he may
be, totters and seeks some support, however fragile.

"You would be right, my daughter," he murmured,
with drooping head, "if the money that I gave in exchange for Sairmeuse had really belonged to me."

At this strange avowal the young girl turned pale
and recoiled a step.

"What?" she faltered; "this gold was not yours,
my father? To whom did it belong? From whence
did it come?"

The unhappy man had gone too far to retract.

"I will tell you all, my daughter," he replied, "and
you shall judge. You shall decide. When the Sairmeuse family fled from France, I had only my hands to

depend upon, and as it was almost impossible to obtain work, I wondered if starvation were not near at hand.

"Such was my condition when someone came after me one evening to tell me that Mademoiselle Armande de Sairmeuse, my godmother, was dying, and wished to speak with me. I ran to the château.

"The messenger had told the truth. Mademoiselle Armande was sick unto death. I felt this on seeing her upon her bed, whiter than wax.

"Ah! if I were to live a hundred years, never should I forget her face as it looked at that moment. It was expressive of a strength of will and an energy that would hold death at bay until the task upon which she had determined was performed.

"When I entered the room I saw a look of relief appear upon her countenance.

"'How long you were in coming!' she murmured faintly.

"I was about to make some excuse, when she motioned me to pause, and ordered the women who surrounded her to leave the room.

"As soon as we were alone:

"'You are an honest boy,' said she, 'and I am about to give you a proof of my confidence. People believe me to be poor, but they are mistaken. While my relatives were gayly ruining themselves, I was saving the five hundred louis which the duke, my brother, gave me each year.'

"She motioned me to come nearer, and to kneel beside her bed.

"I obeyed, and Mademoiselle Armande leaned toward me, almost glued her lips to my ear, and added:

"'I possess eighty thousand francs.'

"I felt a sudden giddiness, but my godmother did not notice it.

" ' This amount,' she continued, ' is not a quarter part of the former income from our family estates. But now, who knows but it will, one day, be the only resource of the Sairmeuse? I am going to place it in your charge, Lacheneur. I confide it to your honor and to your devotion. The estates belonging to the emigrants are to be sold, I hear. If such an act of injustice is committed, you will probably be able to purchase our property for seventy thousand francs. If the property is sold by the government, purchase it; if the lands belonging to the emigrants are not sold, take that amount to the duke, my brother, who is with the Count d'Artois. The surplus, that is to say, the ten thousand francs remaining, I give to you— they are yours.'

" She seemed to recover her strength. She raised herself in bed, and, holding the crucifix attached to her rosary to my lips, she said:

" ' Swear by the image of our Saviour, that you will faithfully execute the last will of your dying godmother.'

" I took the required oath, and an expression of satisfaction overspread her features.

" ' That is well,' she said; ' I shall die content. You will have a protector on high. But this is not all. In times like these in which we live, this gold will not be safe in your hands unless those about you are ignorant that you possess it. I have been endeavoring to discover some way by which you could remove it from my room, and from the château, without the knowledge of anyone; and I have found a way. The gold is here in this cupboard, at the head of my bed, in a stout oaken chest. You must find strength to move the chest—you must. You can fasten a sheet around it, and let it down gently from the window into the garden.   You will then leave the house as you entered it, and as soon as you are outside, you must take the chest and carry it to your home.   The night is very dark, and no one will see you, if you are careful.   But make haste; my strength is nearly gone.'

"The chest was heavy, but I was very strong.

"In less than ten minutes the task of removing the chest from the château was accomplished, without a single sound that would betray us.   As I closed the window, I said:

"'It is done, godmother.'

"'God be praised!' she whispered; 'Sairmeuse is saved!'

"I heard a deep sigh.   I turned; she was dead."

This scene that M. Lacheneur was relating rose vividly before him.

To feign, to disguise the truth, or to conceal any portion of it was an impossibility.

He forgot himself and his daughter; he thought only of the dead woman, of Mlle. Armande de Sairmeuse.

And he shuddered on pronouncing the words: "She was dead."   It seemed to him that she was about to speak, and to insist upon the fulfilment of his pledge.

After a moment's silence, he resumed, in a hollow voice:

"I called for aid; it came.   Mademoiselle Armande was adored by everyone; there was great lamentation, and a half hour of indescribable confusion followed her death.   I was able to withdraw, unnoticed, to run into· the garden, and to carry away the oaken chest.   An hour later, it was concealed in the miserable hovel in which I dwelt.   The following year I purchased Sairmeuse."

He had confessed all; and he paused, trembling, trying to read his sentence in the eyes of his daughter.

"And can you hesitate?" she demanded.

"Ah! you do not know——"

"I know that Sairmeuse must be given up."

This was the decree of his own conscience, that faint voice which speaks only in a whisper, but which all the tumult on earth cannot overpower.

"No one saw me take away the chest," he faltered. "If anyone suspected it, there is not a single proof against me. But no one does suspect it."

Marie-Anne rose, her eyes flashed with generous indignation.

"My father!" she exclaimed; "oh! my father!"

Then, in a calmer tone, she added:

"If others know nothing of this, can *you* forget it?"

M. Lacheneur appeared almost ready to succumb to the torture of the terrible conflict raging in his soul.

"Return!" he exclaimed. "What shall I return? That which I have received? So be it. I consent. I will give the duke the eighty thousand francs; to this amount I will add the interest on this sum since I have had it, and—we shall be free of all obligation."

The girl sadly shook her head.

"Why do you resort to subterfuges which are so unworthy of you?" she asked, gently. "You know perfectly well that it was Sairmeuse which Mademoiselle Armande intended to intrust to the servant of her house. And it is Sairmeuse which must be returned."

The word "servant" was revolting to a man, who, at least, while the empire endured, had been a power in the land.

"Ah! you are cruel, my daughter," he said, with intense bitterness; "as cruel as a child who has never suffered—as cruel as one who, having never himself been tempted, is without mercy for those who have yielded to temptation.

" It is one of those acts which God alone can judge, since God alone can read the depths of one's secret soul.

" I am only a depositary, you tell me. It was, indeed, in this light that I formerly regarded myself.

" If your poor sainted mother was still alive, she would tell you the anxiety and anguish I felt on being made the master of riches which were not mine. I trembled lest I should yield to their seductions; I was afraid of myself. I felt as a gambler might feel who had the winnings of others confided to his care; as a drunkard might feel who had been placed in charge of a quantity of the most delicious wines.

" Your mother would tell you that I moved heaven and earth to find the Duc de Sairmeuse. But he had left the Count d'Artois, and no one knew where he had gone or what had become of him. Ten years passed before I could make up my mind to inhabit the château —yes, ten years—during which I had the furniture dusted each morning as if the master was to return that evening.

" At last I ventured. I had heard Monsieur d'Escorval declare that the duke had been killed in battle. I took up my abode here. And from day to day, in proportion as the domain of Sairmeuse became more beautiful and extensive beneath my care, I felt myself more and more its rightful owner."

But this despairing pleading in behalf of a bad cause produced no impression upon Marie-Anne's loyal heart.

" Restitution must be made," she repeated.

M. Lacheneur wrung his hands.

"Implacable!" he exclaimed; "she is implacable. Unfortunate girl! does she not understand that it is for her sake I wish to remain where I am? I am old, and I am familiar with toil and poverty; idleness has not removed the callosities from my hands. What do I require to keep me alive until the day comes for me to take my place in the graveyard? A crust of bread and an onion in the morning, a porringer of soup in the evening, and for the night a bundle of straw. I could easily earn that. But you, unhappy child! and your brother, what will become of you?"

"We must not discuss nor haggle with duty, my father. I think, however, that you are needlessly alarmed. I believe the duke is too noble-hearted ever to allow you to suffer want after the immense service you have rendered him."

The old servitor of the house of Sairmeuse laughed a loud, bitter laugh.

"You believe that!" said he; "then you do not know the nobles who have been our masters for ages. 'A., you are a worthy fellow!'—very coldly said—will be the only recompense I shall receive; and you will see us, me, at my plough; you, out at service. And if I venture to speak of the ten thousand francs that were given me, I shall be treated as an impostor, as an impudent fool. By the holy name of God this shall not be!"

"Oh, my father!"

"No! this shall not be. And I realize—as you cannot realize—the disgrace of such a fall. You think you are beloved in Sairmeuse? You are mistaken. We have been too fortunate not to be the victims of hatred and jealousy. If I fall to-morrow, you will see

all who kissed your hands to-day fall upon you to tear
you to pieces!"

His eye glittered; he believed he had found a victorious argument.

"And then you, yourself, will realize the horror of
the disgrace. It will cost you the deadly anguish of
a separation from him whom your heart has chosen."

He had spoken truly, for Marie-Anne's beautiful
eyes filled with tears.

"If what you say proves true, father," she murmured, in an altered voice, "I may, perhaps, die of
sorrow; but I cannot fail to realize that my confidence
and my love has been misplaced."

"And you still insist upon my returning Sairmeuse
to its former owner?"

"Honor speaks, my father."

M. Lacheneur made the arm-chair in which he was
seated tremble by a violent blow of his fist.

"And if *I* am just as obstinate," he exclaimed—"if
I keep the property—what will you do?"

"I shall say to myself, father, that honest poverty is
better than stolen wealth. I shall leave this château,
which belongs to the Duc de Sairmeuse, and I shall
seek a situation as a servant in the neighborhood."

M. Lacheneur sank back in his arm-chair sobbing.
He knew his daughter's nature well enough to be assured that what she said, that she would do.

But he was conquered; his daughter had won the
battle. He had decided to make the heroic sacrifice.

"I will relinquish Sairmeuse," he faltered, "come
what may——"

He paused suddenly; a visitor was entering the
room.

It was a young man about twenty years of age, of

distinguished appearance, but with a rather melancholy and gentle manner.

His eyes when he entered the apartment encountered those of Marie-Anne; he blushed slightly, and the girl half turned away, crimsoning to the roots of her hair.

" Monsieur," said the young man, " my father sends me to inform you that the Duc de Sairmeuse and his son have just arrived. They have asked the hospitality of our *curé*."

M. Lacheneur rose, unable to conceal his frightful agitation.

" You will thank the Baron d'Escorval for his attention, my dear Maurice," he responded. " I shall have the honor of seeing him to-day, after a very momentous step which we are about to take, my daughter and I."

Young D'Escorval had seen, at the first glance, that his presence was inopportune, so he remained only a few moments.

But as he was taking leave, Marie-Anne found time to say, in a low voice:

" I think I know your heart, Maurice; this evening I shall know it certainly."

CHAPTER III

Few of the inhabitants of Sairmeuse knew, except by name, the terrible duke whose arrival had thrown the whole village into commotion.

Some of the oldest residents had a faint recollection of having seen him long ago, before '89 indeed, when he came to visit his aunt, Mlle. Armande.

His duties, then, had seldom permitted him to leave the court.

If he had given no sign of life during the empire, it was because he had not been compelled to submit to the humiliations and suffering which so many of the emigrants were obliged to endure in their exile.

On the contrary, he had received, in exchange for the wealth of which he had been deprived by the revolution, a princely fortune.

Taking refuge in London after the defeat of the army of Condé, he had been so fortunate as to please the only daughter of Lord Holland, one of the richest peers in England, and he had married her.

She possessed a fortune of two hundred and fifty thousand pounds sterling, more than six million francs.

Still the marriage was not a happy one. The chosen companion of the dissipated and licentious Count d'Artois was not likely to prove a very good husband.

The young duchess was contemplating a separation when she died, in giving birth to a boy, who was baptized under the names of Anne-Marie-Martial.

The loss of his wife did not render the Duc de Sairmeuse inconsolable.

He was free and richer than he had ever been.

As soon as *les convenances* permitted, he confided his son to the care of a relative of his wife, and began his roving life again.

Rumor had told the truth. He had fought, and that furiously, against France in the Austrian, and then in the Russian ranks.

And he took no pains to conceal the fact; convinced that he had only performed his duty. He considered that he had honestly and loyally gained the rank of general which the Emperor of all the Russias had bestowed upon him.

He had not returned to France during the first Restoration; but his absence had been involuntary. His
father-in-law, Lord Holland, had just died, and the
duke was detained in London by business connected
with his son's immense inheritance.

Then followed the " Hundred Days." They exasperated him.

But " the good cause," as he styled it, having triumphed anew, he hastened to France.

Alas! Lacheneur judged the character of his former
master correctly, when he resisted the entreaties of his
daughter.

This man, who had been compelled to conceal himself during the first Restoration, knew only too well,
that the returned *émigrés* had learned nothing and forgotten nothing.

The Duc de Sairmeuse was no exception to the
rule.

He thought, and nothing could be more sadly absurd, that a mere act of authority would suffice to suppress forever all the events of the Revolution and of
the empire.

When he said: " I do not admit that! " he firmly believed that there was nothing more to be said; that
controversy was ended; and that what *had* been was
as if it had never been.

If some, who had seen Louis XVII. at the helm in
1814, assured the duke that France had changed in
many respects since 1789, he responded with a shrug
of the shoulders:

" Nonsense! As soon as we assert ourselves, all
these rascals, whose rebellion alarms you, will quietly
sink out of sight."

Such was really his opinion.

On the way from Montaignac to Sairmeuse, the duke, comfortably ensconced in his berlin, unfolded his theories for the benefit of his son.

" The King has been poorly advised," he said, in conclusion. " Besides, I am disposed to believe that he inclines too much to Jacobinism. If he would listen to my advice, he would make use of the twelve hundred thousand soldiers which our friends have placed at his disposal, to bring his subjects to a sense of their duty. Twelve hundred thousand bayonets have far more eloquence than the articles of a charter."

He continued his remarks on this subject until the carriage approached Sairmeuse.

Though but little given to sentiment, he was really affected by the sight of the country in which he was born—where he had played as a child, and of which he had heard nothing since the death of his aunt.

Everything was changed: still the outlines of the landscape remained the same; the valley of the Oiselle was as bright and laughing as in days gone by.

" I recognize it ! " he exclaimed, with a delight that made him forget politics. " I recognize it ! "

Soon the changes became more striking.

The carriage entered Sairmeuse, and rattled over the stones of the only street in the village.

This street, in former years, had been unpaved, and had always been rendered impassable by wet weather.

" Ah, ha ! " murmured the duke, " this is an improvement ! "

It was not long before he noticed others. The dilapidated, thatched hovels had given place to pretty and comfortable white cottages with green blinds, and a vine hanging gracefully over the door.

As the carriage passed the public square in front of

the church, Martial observed the groups of peasants who were still talking there.

"What do you think of all these peasants?" he inquired of his father. "Do they have the appearance of people who are preparing a triumphal reception for their old masters?"

M. de Sairmeuse shrugged his shoulders. He was not the man to renounce an illusion for such a trifle.

"They do not know that I am in this post-chaise," he replied. "When they know——"

Shouts of "Vive Monsieur le Duc de Sairmeuse!" interrupted him.

"Do you hear that, Marquis?" he exclaimed.

And pleased by these cries that proved him in the right, he leaned from the carriage-window, waving his hand to the honest Chupin family, who were running after the vehicle with noisy shouts.

The old rascal, his wife, and his children, all possessed powerful voices; and it was not strange that the duke believed the whole village was welcoming him. He was convinced of it; and when the berlin stopped before the house of the *curé*, M. de Sairmeuse was persuaded that the *prestige* of the nobility was greater than ever.

Upon the threshold of the parsonage, Bibiaine, the old housekeeper, was standing. She knew who these guests must be, for the *curé's* servants always know what is going on.

"Monsieur has not yet returned from church," she said, in response to the duke's inquiry; "but if the gentlemen wish to wait, it will not be long before he comes, for the poor, dear man has not breakfasted yet."

"Let us go in," the duke said to his son.

And guided by the housekeeper, they entered a sort of drawing-room, where the table was spread.

M. de Sairmeuse took an inventory of the apartment in a single glance. The habits of a house reveal those of its master. This was clean, poor, and bare. The walls were whitewashed; a dozen chairs composed the entire furniture; upon the table, laid with monastic simplicity, were only tin dishes.

This was either the abode of an ambitious man or a saint.

" Will these gentlemen take any refreshments ? " inquired Bibiaine.

" Upon my word," replied Martial, " I must confess that the drive has whetted my appetite amazingly."

" Blessed Jesus ! " exclaimed the old housekeeper, in evident despair. " What am I to do? I, who have nothing ! That is to say—yes—I have an old hen left in the coop. Give me time to wring its neck, to pick it, and clean it——"

She paused to listen, and they heard a step in the passage.

" Ah ! " she exclaimed, " here is Monsieur le Curé now ! "

The son of a poor farmer in the environs of Montaignac, he owed his Latin and tonsure to the privations of his family.

Tall, angular, and solemn, he was as cold and impassive as the stones of his church.

By what immense efforts of will, at the cost of what torture, had he made himself what he was ? One could form some idea of the terrible restraint to which he had subjected himself by looking at his eyes, which occasionally emitted the lightnings of an impassioned soul.

Was he old or young ? The most subtle observer

would have hesitated to say on seeing this pallid and emaciated face, cut in two by an immense nose—a real eagle's beak—as thin as the edge of a razor.

He wore a white cassock, which had been patched and darned in numberless places, but which was a marvel of cleanliness, and which hung about his tall, attenuated body like the sails of a disabled vessel.

He was known as the Abbé Midon.

At the sight of the two strangers seated in his drawing-room, he manifested some slight surprise.

The carriage standing before the door had announced the presence of a visitor; but he had expected to find one of his parishioners.

No one had warned him or the sacristan, and he was wondering with whom he had to deal, and what they desired of him.

Mechanically, he turned to Bibiaine, but the old servant had taken flight.

The duke understood his host's astonishment.

" Upon my word, Abbé! " he said, with the impertinent ease of a *grand seigneur* who makes himself at home everywhere, " we have taken your house by storm, and hold the position, as you see. I am the Duc de Sairmeuse, and this is my son, the Marquis."

The priest bowed, but he did not seem very greatly impressed by the exalted rank of his guests.

" It is a great honor for me," he replied, in a more than reserved tone " to receive a visit from the former master of this place."

He emphasized this word " former " in such a manner that it was impossible to doubt his sentiments and his opinions.

" Unfortunately," he continued, " you will not find here the comforts to which you are accustomed, and I fear——"

" Nonsense! " interrupted the duke. " An old soldier is not fastidious, and what suffices for you, Monsieur Abbé, will suffice for us. And rest assured that
we shall amply repay you in one way or another for any
inconvenience we may cause you."

The priest's eye flashed. This want of tact, this
disagreeable familiarity, this last insulting remark,
kindled the anger of the man concealed beneath the
priest.

" Besides," added Martial, gayly, " we have been
vastly amused by Bibiaine's anxieties, we already
know that there is a chicken in the coop——"

" That is to say there was one, Monsieur le Marquis."

The old housekeeper, who suddenly reappeared, explained her master's response. She seemed overwhelmed with despair.

" Blessed Virgin! Monsieur, what shall I do? " she
clamored. " The chicken has disappeared. Someone has certainly stolen it, for the coop is securely
closed! "

" Do not accuse your neighbor hastily," interrupted
the *curé;* " no one has stolen it from us. Bertrande
was here this morning to ask alms in the name of her
sick daughter. I had no money, and I gave her this
fowl that she might make a good *bouillon* for the sick
girl."

This explanation changed Bibiaine's consternation
to fury.

Planting herself in the centre of the room, one hand
upon her hip, and gesticulating wildly with the other,
she exclaimed, pointing to her master:

" That is just the sort of man he is; he has less
sense than a baby! Any miserable peasant who meets

him can make him believe anything he wishes. Any
great falsehood brings tears to his eyes, and then they
can do what they like with him. In that way they take
the very shoes off his feet and the bread from his
mouth. Bertrande's daughter, messieurs, is no more
ill than you or I!"

"Enough," said the priest, sternly, "enough."
Then, knowing by experience that his voice had not
the power to check her flood of reproaches, he took her
by the arm and led her out into the passage.

M. de Sairmeuse and his son exchanged a glance of
consternation.

Was this a comedy that had been prepared for their
benefit? Evidently not, since their arrival had not
been expected.

But the priest, whose character had been so plainly
revealed by this quarrel with his domestic, was not a
man to their taste.

At least, he was evidently not the man they had
hoped to find—not the auxiliary whose assistance was
indispensable to the success of their plans.

Yet they did not exchange a word; they listened.

They heard the sound as of a discussion in the passage. The master spoke in low tones, but with an unmistakable accent of command; the servant uttered an
astonished exclamation.

But the listeners could not distinguish a word.

Soon the priest re-entered the apartment.

"I hope, gentlemen," he said, with a dignity that
could not fail to check any attempt at raillery, "that
you will excuse this ridiculous scene. The *curé* of
Sairmeuse, thank God! is not so poor as she says."

Neither the duke nor Martial made any response.

Even their remarkable assurance was very sensibly

diminished; and M. de Sairmeuse deemed it advisable
to change the subject.

This he did, by relating the events which he had just
witnessed in Paris, and by insisting that His Majesty,
Louis XVIII., had been welcomed with enthusiasm
and transports of affection.

Fortunately, the old housekeeper interrupted this
recital.

She entered, loaded with china, silver, and bottles,
and behind her came a large man in a white apron,
bearing three or four covered dishes in his hands.

It was the order to go and obtain this repast from
the village inn which had drawn from Bibiaine so many
exclamations of wonder and dismay in the passage.

A moment later the *curé* and his guests took their
places at the table.

Had the much-lamented chicken constituted the dinner the rations would have been "short." This the
worthy woman was obliged to confess, on seeing the
terrible appetite evinced by M. de Sairmeuse and his
son.

"One would have sworn that they had eaten nothing for a fortnight," she told her friends, the next day.

Abbé Midon was not hungry, though it was two
o'clock, and he had eaten nothing since the previous
evening.

The sudden arrival of the former masters of Sairmeuse filled his heart with gloomy forebodings. Their
coming, he believed, presaged the greatest misfortunes.

So while he played with his knife and fork, pretending to eat, he was really occupied in watching his
guests, and in studying them with all the penetration
of a priest, which, by the way, is generally far superior
to that of a physician or of a magistrate.

The Duc de Sairmeuse was fifty-seven, but looked considerably younger.

The storms of his youth, the dissipation of his riper years, the great excesses of every kind in which he had indulged, had not impaired his iron constitution in the least.

Of herculean build, he was extremely proud of his strength, and of his hands, which were well-formed, but large, firmly knit and powerful, such hands as rightly belonged to a gentleman whose ancestors had given many a crushing blow with ponderous battle-axe in the crusades.

His face revealed his character. He possessed all the graces and all the vices of a courtier.

He was, at the same time *spirituel* and ignorant, sceptical and violently imbued with the prejudices of his class.

Though less robust than his father, Martial was a no less distinguished-looking cavalier. It was not strange that women raved over his blue eyes, and the beautiful blond hair which he inherited from his mother.

To his father he owed energy, courage, and, it must also be added, perversity. But he was his superior in education and in intellect. If he shared his father's prejudices, he had not adopted them without weighing them carefully. What the father might do in a moment of excitement, the son was capable of doing in cold blood.

It was thus that the *abbé*, with rare sagacity, read the character of his guests.

So it was with great sorrow, but without surprise, that he heard the duke advance, on the questions of the day, the impossible ideas shared by nearly all the *émigrés*.

Knowing the condition of the country, and the state of public opinion, the *curé* endeavored to convince the obstinate man of his mistake; but upon this subject the duke would not permit contradiction, or even raillery; and he was fast losing his temper, when Bibiaine appeared at the parlor door.

"Monsieur le Duc," said she, "Monsieur Lacheneur and his daughter are without and desire to speak to you."

CHAPTER IV.

This name Lacheneur awakened no recollection in the mind of the duke.

First, he had never lived at Sairmeuse.

And even if he had, what courtier of the *ancien régime* ever troubled himself about the individual names of the peasants, whom he regarded with such profound indifference.

When a *grand seigneur* addressed these people, he said: "Halloo! hi, there! friend, my worthy fellow!"

So it was with the air of a man who is making an effort of memory that the Duc de Sairmeuse repeated:

"Lacheneur—Monsieur Lacheneur——"

But Martial, a closer observer than his father, had noticed that the priest's glance wavered at the sound of this name.

"Who is this person, Abbé?" demanded the duke, lightly.

"Monsieur Lacheneur," replied the priest, with very evident hesitation, "is the present owner of the Château de Sairmeuse."

Martial, the precocious diplomat, could not repress

a smile on hearing this response, which he had foreseen. But the duke bounded from his chair.

"Ah!" he exclaimed, "it is the rascal who has had
the impudence— Let him come in, old woman, let
him come in."

Bibiaine retired, and the priest's uneasiness increased.

"Permit me, Monsieur le Duc," he said, hastily, "to
remark that Monsieur Lacheneur exercises a great influence in this region—to offend him would be impolitic——"

"I understand—you advise me to be conciliatory.
Such sentiments are purely Jacobin. If His Majesty
listens to the advice of such as you, all these sales of
confiscated estates will be ratified. Zounds! our interests are the same. If the Revolution has deprived
the nobility of their property, it has also impoverished
the clergy."

"The possessions of a priest are not of this world,
Monsieur," said the *curé*, coldly.

M. de Sairmeuse was about to make some impertinent response, when M. Lacheneur appeared, followed
by his daughter.

The wretched man was ghastly pale, great drops of
perspiration stood out upon his temples, his restless,
haggard eyes revealed his distress of mind.

Marie-Anne was as pale as her father, but her attitude and the light that burned in her eyes told of in-
vincible energy and determination.

"Ah, well! friend," said the duke, "so we are the
owner of Sairmeuse, it seems."

This was said with such a careless insolence of manner that the *curé* blushed that they should thus treat, in
his own house, a man whom he considered his equal.

He rose and offered the visitors chairs.

" Will you take a seat, dear Monsieur Lacheneur? " said he, with a politeness intended as a lesson for the duke; " and you, also, Mademoiselle, do me the honor ——"

But the father and the daughter both refused the proffered civility with a motion of the head.

" Monsieur le Duc," continued Lacheneur, " I am an old servant of your house——"

" Ah! indeed! "

" Mademoiselle Armande, your aunt, accorded my poor mother the honor of acting as my god-mother ——"

"Ah, yes," interrupted the duke. " I remember you now. Our family has shown great goodness to you and yours. And it was to prove your gratitude, prob-ably, that you made haste to purchase our estate! "

The former ploughboy was of humble origin, but his heart and his character had developed with his fort-unes; he understood his own worth.

Much as he was disliked, and even detested, by his neighbors, everyone respected him.

And here was a man who treated him with undis-guised scorn. Why? By what right?

Indignant at the outrage, he made a movement as if to retire.

No one, save his daughter, knew the truth; he had only to keep silence and Sairmeuse remained his.

Yes, he had still the power to keep Sairmeuse, and he knew it, for he did not share the fears of the igno-rant rustics. He was too well informed not to be able to distinguish between the hopes of the *émigrés* and the possible. He knew that an abyss separated the dream from the reality.

A beseeching word uttered in a low tone by his daughter, made him turn again to the duke.

" If I purchased Sairmeuse," he answered, in a voice husky with emotion, " it was in obedience to the command of your dying aunt, and with the money which she gave me for that purpose. If you see me here, it is only beca•ıse I come to restore to you the deposit confided to my keeping."

Anyone not belonging to that class of spoiled fools which surround a throne would have been deeply touched.

But the duke thought this grand act of honesty and of generosity the most simple and natural thing in the world.

" That is very well, so far as the principal is concerned," said he. " Let us speak now of the interest. Sairmeuse, if I remember rightly, yielded an average income of one thousand louis per year. These revenues, well invested, should have amounted to a very considerable amount. Where is this ? "

This claim, thus advanced and at such a moment, was so outrageous, that Martial, disgusted, made a sign to his father, which the latter did not see.

But the *curé* hoping to recall the extortioner to something like a sense of shame, exclaimed :

" Monsieur le Duc ! Oh, Monsieur le Duc ! "

Lacheneur shrugged his shoulders with an air of resignation.

" The income I have used for my own living expenses, and in educating my children ; but most of it has been expended in improving the estate, which to-day yields an income twice as large as in former years."

" That is to say, for twenty years, Monsieur Lacheneur has played the part of lord of the manor. A delightful comedy. You are rich now, I suppose."

" I possess nothing. But I hope you will allow me to take ten thousand francs, which your aunt gave to me."

" Ah! she gave you ten thousand francs? And ' when ? "

" On the same evening that she gave me the eighty thousand francs intended for the purchase of the estate."

" Perfect! What proof can you furnish that she gave you this sum ? "

Lacheneur stood -motionless and speechless. He tried to reply, but he could not. If he opened his lips it would only be to pour forth a torrent of menaces, insults, and invectives.

Marie-Anne stepped quickly forward.

" The proof, Monsieur," said she,.in a clear, ringing voice, " is the word of this man, who, of his own free will, comes to return to you—to give you a fortune."

As she sprang forward her beautiful dark hair escaped from its confinement, the rich blood crimsoned her cheeks, her dark eyes flashed brilliantly, and sorrow, anger, horror at the humiliation, imparted a sublime expression to her face.

She was so beautiful that Martial regarded her with wonder.

" Lovely ! " he murmured, in English ; " beautiful as an angel ! "

These words, which she understood, abashed Marie-Anne. But she had said enough ; her father felt that he was avenged.

He drew from his pocket a roll of papers, and throwing them upon the table:

" Here are your titles," he said, addressing the duke in a tone full of implacable hatred. " Keep the legacy that your aunt gave me, I wish nothing of yours. I shall never set foot in Sairmeuse again. Penniless I entered it, penniless I will leave it! "

He quitted the room with head proudly erect, and when they were outside, he said but one word to his daughter:

" Well! "

" You have done your duty," she replied; " it is those who have not done it, who are to be pitied! "

She had no opportunity to say more. Martial came running after them, anxious for another chance of seeing this young girl whose beauty had made such an impression upon him.

" I hastened after you," he said, addressing Marie-Anne, rather than M. Lacheneur, " to reassure you. All this will be ·arranged, Mademoiselle. Eyes so beautiful as yours should never know tears. I will be your advocate with my father——"

" Mademoiselle Lacheneur has no need of an advocate! " a harsh voice interrupted.

Martial turned, and saw the young man, who, that morning, went to warn M. Lacheneur of the duke's arrival.

" I am the Marquis de Sairmeuse," he said, insolently.

" And I," said the other, quietly, " am Maurice d'Escorval."

They surveyed each other for a moment; each expecting, perhaps, an insult from the other. Instinctively, they felt that they were to be enemies; and the bitterest animosity spoke in the glances they exchanged. Perhaps they felt a presentiment that they were to be champions of two different principles, as well as rivals.

Martial, remembering his father, yielded.

" We shall meet again, Monsieur d'Escorval," he said, as he retired. At this threat, Maurice shrugged his shoulders, and said:

" You had better not desire it."

CHAPTER V

The abode of the Baron d'Escorval, that brick structure with stone trimmings which was visible from the superb avenue leading to Sairmeuse, was small and unpretentious.

Its chief attraction was a pretty lawn that extended to the banks of the Oiselle, and a small but beautifully shaded park.

It was known as the Château d'Escorval, but that appellation was gross flattery. Any petty manufacturer who had amassed a small fortune would have desired a larger, handsomer, and more imposing establishment.

M. d'Escorval—and it will be an eternal honor to him in history—was not rich.

Although he had been intrusted with several of those missions from which generals and diplomats often return laden with millions, M. d'Escorval's worldly possessions consisted only of the little patrimony bequeathed him by his father: a property which yielded an income of from twenty to twenty-five thousand francs a year.

This modest dwelling, situated about a mile from Sairmeuse, represented the savings of ten years.

He had built it in 1806, from a plan drawn by his own hand; and it was the dearest spot on earth to him.

He always hastened to this retreat when his work allowed him a few days of rest.

But this time he had not come to Escorval of his own free will.

He had been compelled to leave Paris by the proscribed list of the 24th of July—that fatal list which summoned the enthusiastic Labedoyère and the honest and virtuous Drouot before a court-martial.

And even in this solitude, M. d'Escorval's situation was not without danger.

He was one of those who, some days before the disaster of Waterloo, had strongly urged the Emperor to order the execution of Fouché, the former minister of police.

Now, Fouché knew this counsel; and he was powerful.

"Take care!" M. d'Escorval's friends wrote him from Paris.

But he put his trust in Providence, and faced the future, threatening though it was, with the unalterable serenity of a pure conscience.

The baron was still young; he was not yet fifty, but anxiety, work, and long nights passed in struggling with the most arduous difficulties of the imperial policy, had made him old before his time.

He was tall, slightly inclined to *embonpoint*, and stooped a little.

His calm eyes, his serious mouth, his broad, furrowed forehead, and his austere manners inspired respect.

"He must be stern and inflexible," said those who saw him for the first time.

But they were mistaken.

If, in the exercise of his official duties, this truly great man had the strength to resist all temptations to swerve from the path of right; if, when duty was at stake, he was as rigid as iron, in private life he was as unassuming as a child, and kind and gentle even to the verge of weakness.

To this nobility of character he owed his domestic happiness, that rare and precious happiness which fills one's existence with a celestial perfume.

During the bloodiest epoch of the Reign of Terror, M. d'Escorval had wrested from the guillotine a young girl named Victoire-Laure d'Alleu, a distant cousin of the Rhetaus of Commarin, as beautiful as an angel, and only three years younger than himself.

He loved her—and though she was an orphan, destitute of fortune, he married her, considering the treasure of her virgin heart of far greater value than the most magnificent dowry.

She was an honest woman, as her husband was an honest man, in the most strict and vigorous sense of the word.

She was seldom seen at the Tuileries, where M. d'Escorval's worth made him eagerly welcomed. The splendors of the Imperial Court, which at that time surpassed all the pomp of the time of Louis XIV., had no attractions for her.

Grace, beauty, youth and accomplishments—she reserved them all for the adornment of her home.

Her husband was her God. She lived in him and through him. She had not a thought which did not belong to him.

The short time that he could spare from his arduous labors to devote to her were her happiest hours.

And when, in the evening, they sat beside the fire in their modest drawing-room, with their son Maurice playing on the rug at their feet, it seemed to them that they had nothing to wish for here below.

The overthrow of the empire surprised them in the heydey of their happiness.

Surprised them? No. For a long time M. d'Escorval had seen the prodigious edifice erected by the genius whom he had made his idol totter as if about to fall.

Certainly, he felt intense chagrin at this fall, but he was heart-broken at the sight of all the treason and cowardice which followed it. He was indignant and horrified at the rising *en masse* of the avaricious, who hastened to gorge themselves with the spoil.

Under these circumstances, exile from Paris seemed an actual blessing.

"Besides," as he remarked to the baroness, "we shall soon be forgotten here."

But even while he said this he felt many misgivings. Still, by his side, his noble wife presented a tranquil face, even while she trembled for the safety of her adored husband.

On this first Sunday in August, M. d'Escorval and his wife had been unusually sad. A vague presentiment of approaching misfortune weighed heavily upon their hearts.

At the same hour that Lacheneur presented himself at the house of the Abbé Midon, they were seated upon the terrace in front of the house, gazing anxiously at the two roads leading from Escorval to the château, and to the village of Sairmeuse.

Warned, that same morning, by his friends in Montaignac of the arrival of the duke, the baron had sent his son to inform M. Lacheneur.

He had requested him to be absent as short a time as possible; but in spite of this fact, the hours were rolling by, and Maurice had not returned.

"What if something has happened to him!" both father and mother were thinking.

No; nothing had happened to him. Only a word from Mlle. Lacheneur had sufficed to make him forget his usual deference to his father's wishes.

"This evening," she had said, "I shall certainly know your heart."

What could this mean? Could she doubt him?

Tortured by the most cruel anxieties, the poor youth could not resolve to go away without an explanation, and he hung around the château hoping that Marie-Anne would reappear.

She did reappear at last, but leaning upon the arm of her father.

Young D'Escorval followed them at a distance, and soon saw them enter the parsonage. What were they going to do there? He knew that the duke and his son were within.

The time that they remained there, and which he passed in the public square, seemed more than a century long.

They emerged at last, however, and he was about to join them when he was prevented by the appearance of Martial, whose promises he overheard.

Maurice knew nothing of life; he was as innocent as a child, but he could not mistake the intentions that dictated this step on the part of the Marquis de Sairmeuse.

At the thought that a libertine's caprice should dare rest for an instant upon the pure and beautiful girl whom he loved with all the strength of his being—

whom he had sworn should be his wife—all his blood mounted madly to his brain.

He felt a wild longing to chastise the insolent wretch.

Fortunately—unfortunately, perhaps—his hand was arrested by the recollection of a phrase which he had heard his father repeat a thousand times:

"Calmness and irony are the only weapons worthy of the strong."

And he possessed sufficient strength of will to appear calm, while, in reality, he was beside himself with passion. It was Martial who lost his self-control, and who threatened him.

"Ah! yes, I will find you again, upstart!" repeated Maurice, through his set teeth as he watched his enemy move away.

For Martial had turned and discovered that Marie-Anne and her father had left him. He saw them standing about a hundred paces from him. Although he was surprised at their indifference, he made haste to join them, and addressed M. Lacheneur.

"We are just going to your father's house," was the response he received, in an almost ferocious tone.

A glance from Marie-Anne commanded silence. He obeyed, and walked a few steps behind them, with his head bowed upon his breast, terribly anxious, and seeking vainly to explain what had passed.

His attitude betrayed such intense sorrow that his mother divined it as soon as she caught sight of him.

All the anguish which this courageous woman had hidden for a month, found utterance in a single cry.

"Ah! here is misfortune!" said she: "we shall not escape it."

It was, indeed, misfortune. One could not doubt it when one saw M. Lacheneur enter the drawing-room.

He advanced with the heavy, uncertain step of a drunken man, his eye void of expression, his features distorted, his lips pale and trembling.

"What has happened?" asked the baron, eagerly.

But the other did not seem to hear him.

"Ah! I warned her," he murmured, continuing a monologue which had begun before he entered the room. "I told my daughter so."

Mme. d'Escorval, after kissing Marie-Anne, drew the girl toward her.

"What has happened? For God's sake, tell me what has happened!" she exclaimed.

With a gesture expressive of the most sorrowful resignation, the girl motioned her to look and to listen to M. Lacheneur.

He had recovered from that stupor—that gift of God —which follows cries that are too terrible for human endurance. Like a sleeper who, on waking, finds his miseries forgotten during his slumber, lying in wait for him, he regained with consciousness the capacity to suffer.

"It is only this, Monsieur le Baron," replied the unfortunate man in a harsh, unnatural voice: "I rose this morning the richest proprietor in the country, and I shall lay down to-night poorer than the poorest beggar in this commune. I had everything; I no longer have anything—nothing but my two hands. They earned me my bread for twenty-five years; they will earn it for me now until the day of my death. I had a beautiful dream; it is ended."

Before this outburst of despair, M. d'Escorval turned pale.

"You must exaggerate your misfortune," he faltered; "explain what has happened."

Unconscious of what he was doing, M. Lacheneur threw his hat upon a chair, and flinging back his long, gray hair, he said:

" To you I will tell all. I came here for that purpose. I know you: I know your heart. And have you not done me the honor to call me your friend? "

Then, with the cruel exactness of the living, breathing truth, he related the scene which had just taken place at the presbytery.

The baron listened petrified with astonishment, almost doubting the evidence of his own senses. Mme. d'Escorval's indignant and sorrowful exclamations showed that every noble sentiment in her soul revolted against such injustice.

But there was one auditor, whom Marie-Anne alone observed, who was moved to his very entrails by this recital. This auditor was Maurice.

Leaning against the door, pale as death, he tried most energetically, but in vain, to repress the tears of rage and of sorrow which swelled up in his eyes.

To insult Lacheneur was to insult Marie-Anne— that is to say, to injure, to strike, to outrage him in all that he held most dear in the world.

Ah! it is certain that Martial, had he been within his reach, would have paid dearly for these insults to the father of the girl Maurice loved.

But he swore that this chastisement was only deferred—that it should surely come.

And it was not mere angry boasting. This young man, though so modest and so gentle in manner, had a heart that was inaccessible to fear. His beautiful, dark eyes, which had the trembling timidity of the eyes of a young girl, met the gaze of an enemy without flinching.

When M. Lacheneur had repeated the last words which he had addressed to the Duc de Sairmeuse, M. d'Escorval offered him his hand.

"I have told you already that I was your friend," he said, in a voice faltering with emotion; "but I must tell you to-day that I am proud of having such a friend as you."

The unfortunate man trembled at the touch of that loyal hand which clasped his so warmly, and his face betrayed an ineffable satisfaction.

"If my father had not returned it," murmured the obstinate Marie-Anne, "my father would have been an unfaithful guardian—a thief. He has done only his duty."

M. d'Escorval turned to the young girl, a little surprised.

"You speak the truth, Mademoiselle," he said, reproachfully; "but when you are as old as I am, and have had my experience, you will know that the accomplishment of a duty is, under certain circumstances, a heroism of which few persons are capable."

M. Lacheneur turned to his friend.

"Ah! your words do me good, Monsieur," said he. "Now, I am content with what I have done."

The baroness rose, too much the woman to know how to resist the generous dictates of her heart.

"And I, also, Monsieur Lacheneur," she said, "desire to press your hand. I wish to tell you that I esteem you as much as I despise the ingrates who have sought to humiliate you, when they should have fallen at your feet. They are heartless monsters, the like of whom certainly cannot be found upon the earth."

"Alas!" sighed the baron, "the allies have brought back others who, like these men, think the world created exclusively for their benefit."

" And these people wish to be our masters," growled Lacheneur.

By some strange fatality no one chanced to hear the remark made by M. Lacheneur. Had they overheard and questioned him, he would probably have disclosed some of the projects which were as yet in embryo in his own mind; and in that case what disastrous consequences might have been averted.

M. d'Escorval had regained his usual coolness.

" Now, my dear friend," he inquired, " what course do you propose to pursue with these members of the Sairmeuse family? "

" They will hear nothing more from me—for some time, at least."

" What! Shall you not claim the ten thousand francs that they owe you? "

" I shall ask them for nothing."

" You will be compelled to do so. Since you have alluded to the legacy, your own honor will demand that you insist upon its payment by all legal methods. There are still judges in France."

M. Lacheneur shook his head.

" The judges will not accord me the justice I desire. I shall not apply to them."

" But——"

" No, Monsieur, no. I wish to have nothing to do with these men. I shall not even go to the château to remove my clothing nor that of my daughter. If they send it to us—very well. If it pleases them to keep it, so much the better. The more shameful, infamous and odious their conduct appears, the better I shall be satisfied."

The baron made no reply; but his wife spoke, believing she had a sure means of conquering this incomprehensible obstinacy.

"I should understand your determination if you were alone in the world," said she, "but you have children."

"My son is eighteen, Madame; he possesses good health and an excellent education. He can make his own way in Paris, if he chooses to remain there."

"But your daughter?"

"Marie-Anne will remain with me."

M. d'Escorval thought it his duty to interfere.

"Take care, my dear friend, that your grief does not overthrow your reason," said he. "Reflect! What will become of you—your daughter and yourself?"

The wretched man smiled sadly.

"Oh," he replied, "we are not as destitute as I said. I exaggerated our misfortune. We are still landed proprietors. Last year an old cousin, whom I could never induce to come and live at Sairmeuse, died, bequeathing all her property to Marie-Anne. This property consisted of a poor little cottage near the Reche, with a little garden and a few acres of sterile land. In compliance with my daughter's entreaties, I repaired the cottage, and sent there a few articles of furniture—a table, some chairs, and a couple of beds. My daughter designed it as a home for old Father Guvat and his wife. And I, surrounded by wealth and luxury, said to myself: 'How comfortable those two old people will be there. They will live as snug as a bug in a rug!' Well, what I thought so comfortable for others, will be good enough for me. I will raise vegetables, and Marie-Anne shall sell them."

Was he speaking seriously?

Maurice must have supposed so, for he sprang forward.

"This shall not be, Monsieur Lacheneur!" he exclaimed.

"Oh——"

"No, this shall not be, for I love Marie-Anne, and I ask you to give her to me for my wife."

CHAPTER VI

Maurice and Marie-Anne had loved each other for many years.

As children, they had played together in the magnificent grounds surrounding the Château de Sairmeuse, and in the park at Escorval.

Together they chased the brilliant butterflies, searched for pebbles on the banks of the river, or rolled in the hay while their mothers sauntered through the meadows bordering the Oiselle.

For their mothers were friends.

Mme. Lacheneur had been reared like other poor peasant girls; that is to say, on the day of her marriage it was only with great difficulty she succeeded in inscribing her name upon the register.

But from the example of her husband she had learned that prosperity, as well as *noblesse*, entails certain obligations upon one, and with rare courage, crowned with still rarer success, she had undertaken to acquire an education in keeping with her fortune and her new rank.

And the baroness had made no effort to resist the sympathy that attracted her to this meritorious young woman, in whom she had discerned a really superior mind and a truly refined nature.

When Mme. Lacheneur died, Mme. d'Escorval

mourned for her as she would have mourned for a favorite sister.

From that moment Maurice's attachment assumed a more serious character.

Educated in a Parisian lyceum, his teachers sometimes had occasion to complain of his want of application.

" If your professors are not satisfied with you," said his mother, " you shall not accompany me to Escorval on the coming of your vacation, and you will not see your little friend."

And this simple threat was always sufficient to make the school-boy resume his studies with redoubled diligence.

So each year, as it passed, strengthened the *grande passion* which preserved Maurice from the restlessness and the errors of adolescence.

The two children were equally timid and artless, and equally infatuated with each other.

Long walks in the twilight under the eyes of their parents, a glance that revealed their delight at meeting each other, flowers exchanged between them—which were religiously preserved—such were their simple pleasures.

But that magical and sublime word, love—so sweet to utter, and so sweet to hear—had never once dropped from their lips.

The audacity of Maurice had never gone beyond a furtive pressure of the hand.

The parents could not be ignorant of this mutual affection ; and if they pretended to shut their eyes, it was only because it did not displease them nor disturb their plans.

M. and Mme. d'Escorval saw no objection to their

son's marriage with a young girl whose nobility of character they appreciated, and who was as beautiful as she was good. That she was the richest heiress in all the country round about was naturally no objection.

So far as M. Lacheneur was concerned, he was delighted at the prospect of a marriage which would ally him, a former ploughboy, with an old family whose head was universally respected.

So, although no direct allusion to the subject had ever escaped the lips of the baron or of M. Lacheneur, there was a tacit agreement between the two families.

Yes, the marriage was considered a foregone conclusion.

And yet this impetuous and unexpected declaration by Maurice struck everyone dumb.

In spite of his agitation, the young man perceived the effect produced by his words, and frightened by his own boldness, he turned and looked questioningly at his father.

The baron's face was grave, even sad; but his attitude expressed no displeasure.

This gave renewed courage to the anxious lover.

" You will excuse me, Monsieur," he said, addressing Lacheneur, " for presenting my request in such a manner, and at such a time. But surely, when fate glowers ominously upon you, that is the time when your friends should declare themselves—and deem themselves fortunate if their devotion can make you forget the infamous treatment to which you have been subjected."

As he spoke, he was watching Marie-Anne.

Blushing and embarrassed, she turned away her head, perhaps to conceal the tears which inundated her face—tears of joy and of gratitude.

The love of the man she adored came forth victorious from a test which it would not be prudent for many heiresses to impose.

Now she could truly say that she knew Maurice's heart.

He, however, continued:

" I have not consulted my father, sir; but I know his affection for me and his esteem for you. When the happiness of my life is at stake, he will not oppose me. He, who married my dear mother without a dowry, must understand my feelings."

He was silent, awaiting the verdict.

" I approve your course, my son," said M. d'Escorval, deeply affected; " you have conducted yourself like an honorable man. Certainly you are very young to become the head of a family; but, as you say, circumstances demand it."

He turned to M. Lacheneur, and added:

" My dear friend, I, in my son's behalf, ask the hand of your daughter in marriage."

Maurice had not expected so little opposition.

In his delight he was almost tempted to bless the hateful Duc de Sairmeuse, to whom he would owe his approaching happiness.

He sprang toward his father, and seizing his hands, he raised them to his lips, faltering:

" Thanks ! you are so good ! I love you ! Oh, how happy I am ! "

Alas ! the poor boy was in too much haste to rejoice.

A gleam of pride flashed in M. Lacheneur's eyes; but his face soon resumed its gloomy expression.

" Believe me, Monsieur le Baron, I am deeply touched by your grandeur of soul—yes, deeply touched. You wish to make me forget my humiliation; but, for this very reason, I should be the most contemptible of men if I did not refuse the great honor you desire to confer upon my daughter."

"What!" exclaimed the baron, in utter astonishment; "you refuse?"

"I am compelled to do so."

Thunderstruck at first, Maurice afterward renewed the attack with an energy which no one had ever suspected in his character before.

"Do you, then, wish to ruin my life, Monsieur?" he exclaimed; "to ruin *our* life; for if I love Marie-Anne, she also loves me."

It was easy to see that he spoke the truth. The unhappy girl, crimson with happy blushes the moment before, had suddenly become whiter than marble, as she looked imploringly at her father.

"It cannot be," repeated M. Lacheneur; "and the day will come when you will bless the decision I make known at this moment."

Alarmed by her son's evident agony, Mme. d'Escorval interposed:

"You must have reasons for this refusal."

"None that I can disclose, Madame. But never while I live shall my daughter be your son's wife!"

"Ah! it will kill my child!" exclaimed the baroness.

M. Lacheneur shook his head.

"Monsieur Maurice," said he, "is young; he will console himself—he will forget."

"Never!" interrupted the unhappy lover— "never!"

"And your daughter?" inquired the baroness.

Ah! this was the weak spot in his armor; the instinct of a mother was not mistaken. M. Lacheneur hesitated a moment; but he finally conquered the weakness that had threatened to master him.

"Marie-Anne," he replied, slowly, "knows her duty too well not to obey when I command. When I tell her the motive that governs my conduct, she will become resigned; and if she suffers, she will know how to conceal her sufferings."

He paused suddenly. They heard in the distance a firing of musketry, the discharge of rifles, whose sharp ring overpowered even the sullen roar of cannon.

Every face grew pale. Circumstances imparted to these sounds an ominous significance.

With the same anguish clutching the hearts of both, M. d'Escorval and Lacheneur sprang out upon the terrace.

But all was still again. Extended as was the horizon, the eye could discern nothing unusual. The sky was blue; not a particle of smoke hung over the trees.

"It is the enemy," muttered M. Lacheneur, in a tone which told how gladly he would have shouldered his gun, and, with five hundred others, marched against the united allies.

He paused. The explosions were repeated with still greater violence, and for a period of five minutes succeeded each other without cessation.

M. d'Escorval listened with knitted brows.

"That is not the fire of an engagement," he murmured.

To remain long in such a state of uncertainty was out of the question.

"If you will permit me, father," ventured Maurice, "I will go and ascertain——"

"Go," replied the baron, quietly; "but if it is anything, which I doubt, do not expose yourself to danger; return."

"Oh! be prudent!" insisted Mme. d'Escorval, who already saw her son exposed to the most frightful peril.

"Be prudent!" entreated Marie-Anne, who alone understood what attractions danger might have for a despairing and unhappy man.

These precautions were unnecessary. As Maurice was rushing to the door, his father stopped him.

"Wait," said he; "here is someone who can probably give us information."

A man had just appeared around a turn of the road leading to Sairmeuse.

He was advancing bareheaded in the middle of the dusty road, with hurried strides, and occasionally brandishing his stick, as if threatening an enemy visible to himself alone.

Soon they were able to distinguish his features.

"It is Chanlouineau!" exclaimed M. Lacheneur.

"The owner of the vineyards on the Borderie?"

"The same! The handsomest young farmer in the country, and the best also. Ah! he has good blood in his veins; we may well be proud of him."

"Ask him to stop," said M. d'Escorval.

Lacheneur leaned over the balustrade, and, forming a trumpet out of his two hands, he called:

"Oh! Chanlouineau!"

The robust young farmer raised his head.

"Come up," shouted Lacheneur; "the baron wishes to speak with you."

Chanlouineau responded by a gesture of assent. They saw him enter the gate, cross the garden, and at last appear at the door of the drawing-room.

His features were distorted with fury, his disordered clothing gave evidence of a serious conflict. His cravat was gone, and his torn shirt-collar revealed his muscular throat.

"Where is this fighting?" demanded Lacheneur eagerly; "and with whom?"

Chanlouineau gave a nervous laugh which resembled a roar of rage.

"They are not fighting," he replied; "they are amusing themselves. This firing which you hear is in honor of Monsieur le Duc de Sairmeuse."

"Impossible!"

"I know it very well; and yet, what I have told you is the truth. It is the work of that miserable wretch and thief, Chupin. Ah, *canaille!* If I ever find him within reach of my arm he will never steal again."

M. Lacheneur was confounded.

"Tell us what has happened," he said, excitedly.

"Oh, it is as clear as daylight. When the duke arrived at Sairmeuse, Chupin, the old scoundrel, with his two rascally boys, and that old hag, his wife, ran after the carriage like beggars after a diligence, crying, 'Vive Monsieur le Duc!' The duke was enchanted, for he doubtless expected a volley of stones, and he placed a six-franc piece in the hand of each of the wretches. This money gave Chupin an appetite for more, so he took it into his head to give this old noble a reception like that which was given to the Emperor. Having learned through Bibiaine, whose tongue is as long as a viper's, all that has passed at the presbytery, between you, Monsieur Lacheneur, and the duke, he came and proclaimed it in the market-place. When they heard it, all who had purchased national lands were frightened. Chupin had counted on this, and soon he began telling the poor fools that they must burn powder under the duke's nose if they wished him to confirm their titles to their property."

"And did they believe him?"

"Implicitly. It did not take them long to make their preparations. They went to the town hall and took the firemen's rifles, and the guns used for firing a salute on *fête* days; the mayor gave them the powder, and you heard——

"When I left Sairmeuse there were more than two hundred idiots before the presbytery, shouting:

"*Vive Monseigneur! Vive le Duc de Sairmeuse!*"

It was as D'Escorval had thought.

"The same pitiful farce that was played in Paris, only on a smaller scale," he murmured. "Avarice and human cowardice are the same the world over!"

Meanwhile, Chanlouineau was going on with his recital.

"To make the *fête* complete, the devil must have warned all the nobility in the neighborhood, for they all came running. They say that Monsieur de Sairmeuse is a favorite with the King, and that he can get anything he wishes. So you can imagine how they all greeted him! I am only a poor peasant, but never would I lie down in the dust before any man as these old nobles who are so haughty with us, did before the duke. They kissed his hands, and he allowed them to do it. He walked about the square with the Marquis de Courtornieu——"

"And his son?" interrupted Maurice.

"The Marquis Martial, is it not? He is also walking before the church with Mademoiselle Blanche de Courtornieu upon his arm. Ah! I do not understand how people can call her pretty—a little bit of a thing, so blond that one might suppose her hair was gray. Ah! how those two laughed and made fun of the peasants. They say they are going to marry each other.

And even this evening there is to be a banquet at the
Château de Courtornieu in honor of the duke."

He had told all he knew. He paused.

"You have forgotten only one thing," said M.
Lacheneur; "that is, to tell us how your clothing
happened to be torn, as if you had been fighting."

The young farmer hesitated for a moment, then replied, somewhat brusquely:

"I can tell you, all the same. While Chupin was
preaching, I also preached, but not in the same strain.
The scoundrel reported me. So, in crossing the
square, the duke paused before me and remarked:
'So you are an evil-disposed person?' I said no, but
that I knew my rights. Then he took me by the coat
and shook me, and told me that he would cure me, and
that he would take possession of *his* vineyard again.
Saint Dieu! When I felt the old rascal's hand upon
me my blood boiled. I pinioned him. Fortunately,
six or seven men fell upon me, and compelled me to
let him go. But he had better make up his mind not
to come prowling around my vineyard!"

He clinched his hands, his eyes blazed ominously,
his whole person breathed an intense desire for vengeance.

And M. d'Escorval was silent, fearing to aggravate
this hatred, so imprudently kindled, and whose explosion, he believed, would be terrible.

M. Lacheneur had risen from his chair.

"I must go and take possession of my cottage," he
remarked to Chanlouineau; "you will accompany me;
I have a proposition to make to you."

M. and Mme. d'Escorval endeavored to detain him,
but he would not allow himself to be persuaded, and
he departed with his daughter.

But Maurice did not despair; Marie-Anne had promised to meet him the following day in the pine-grove near the Reche.

CHAPTER VII

The demonstrations which had greeted the Duc de Sairmeuse had been correctly reported by Chanlouineau.

Chupin had found the secret of kindling to a white heat the enthusiasm of the cold and calculating peasants who were his neighbors.

He was a dangerous rascal, the old robber, shrewd and cautious; bold, as those who possess nothing can afford to be; as patient as a savage; in short, one of the most consummate scoundrels that ever existed.

The peasants feared him, and yet they had no conception of his real character.

All his resources of mind had, until now, been expended in evading the precipice of the rural code.

To save himself from falling into the hands of the *gendarmes*, and to steal a few sacks of wheat, he had expended treasures of intrigue which would have made the fortunes of twenty diplomats.

Circumstances, as he always said, had been against him.

So he desperately caught at the first and only opportunity worthy of his talent, which had ever presented itself.

Of course, the wily rustic had said nothing of the true circumstances which attended the restoration of Sairmeuse to its former owner.

From him, the peasants learned only the bare fact;
and the news spread rapidly from group to group.

"Monsieur Lacheneur has given up Sairmeuse,"
said he. " Château, forests, vineyards, fields—he sur-
renders everything."

This was enough, and more than enough to terrify
every land-owner in the village.

If Lacheneur, this man who was so powerful in their
eyes, considered the danger so threatening that he
deemed it necessary or advisable to make a complete
surrender, what was to become of them—poor devils—
without aid, without counsel, without defence?

They were told that the government was about to
betray their interests; that a decree was in process of
preparation which would render their title-deeds
worthless. They could see no hope of salvation, except through the duke's generosity—that generosity
which Chupin painted with the glowing colors of the
rainbow.

When one is not strong enough to weather the gale,
one must bow like the reed before it and rise again
after the storm has passed; such was their conclusion.

And they bowed. And their apparent enthusiasm
was all the more vociferous on account of the rage
and fear that filled their hearts.

A close observer would have detected an undercur-
rent of anger and menace in their shouts.

Each man also said to himself:

"What do we risk by crying, 'Vive le Duc?'
Nothing; absolutely nothing. If he is contented with
that as a compensation for his lost property—good!
If he is not content, we shall have time afterward to
adopt other measures."

So they shouted themselves hoarse.

And while the duke was sipping his coffee in the little drawing-room of the presbytery, he expressed his lively satisfaction at the scene without.

He, this *grand seigneur* of times gone by, this man of absurd prejudices and obstinate illusions; the unconquerable, and the incorrigible—he took these acclamations, "truly spurious coin," as Châteaubriand says, for ready money.

"How you have deceived me, sure," he was saying to Abbé Midon. "How could you declare that your people were unfavorably disposed toward us? One is compelled to believe that these evil intentions exist only in your own mind and in your own heart."

Abbé Midon was silent. What could he reply?

He could not understand this sudden revolution in public opinion—this abrupt change from gloom and discontent to excessive gayety.

There is somebody at the bottom of all this, he thought.

It was not long before it became apparent who that somebody was.

Emboldened by his success without, Chupin ventured to present himself at the presbytery.

He entered the drawing-room with his back rounded into a circle, scraping and cringing, an obsequious smile upon his lips.

And through the half-open door one could discern, in the shadows of the passage, the far from reassuring faces of his two sons.

He came as an ambassador, he declared, after an interminable litany of protestations—he came to implore "monseigneur" to show himself upon the public square.

"Ah, well—yes," exclaimed the duke, rising; "yes,

I will yield to the wishes of these good people. Follow me, Marquis!"

As he appeared at the door of the presbytery, a loud shout rent the air; the rifles were discharged, the guns belched forth their smoke and fire. Never had Sairmeuse heard such a salvo of artillery. Three windows in the Bœf Couronne were shattered.

A veritable *grand seigneur*, the Duc de Sairmeuse knew how to preserve an appearance of haughtiness and indifference. Any display of emotion was, in his opinion, vulgar; but, in reality, he was delighted, charmed.

So delighted that he desired to reward his welcomers.

A glance over the deeds handed him by Lacheneur had shown him that Sairmeuse had been restored to him intact.

The portions of the immense domain which had been detached and sold separately were of relatively minor importance.

The duke thought it would be politic, and, at the same time, inexpensive, to abandon all claim to these few acres, which were now shared by forty or fifty peasants.

"My friends," he exclaimed, in a loud voice, "I renounce, for myself and for my descendants, all claim to the lands belonging to my house which you have purchased. They are yours—I give them to you!"

By this absurd pretence of a gift, M. de Sairmeuse thought to add the finishing touch to his popularity. A great mistake! It simply assured the popularity of Chupin, the organizer of the farce.

And while the duke was promenading through the crowd with a proud and self-satisfied air, the peasants were secretly laughing and jeering at him.

And if they promptly took sides with him against
Chanlouineau, it was only because his gift was still
fresh in their minds; except for this——

But the duke had not time to think much about this
encounter, which produced a vivid impression upon
his son.

One of his former companions in exile, the Marquis
de Courtornieu, whom he had informed of his arrival,
hastened to welcome him, accompanied by his daughter, Mlle. Blanche.

Martial could do no less than offer his arm to the
daughter of his father's friend; and they took a leisurely promenade in the shade of the lofty trees, while
the duke renewed his acquaintance with all the nobility
of the neighborhood.

There was not a single nobleman who did not hast-
en to press the hand of the Duc de Sairmeuse. First,
he possessed, it was said, a property of more than
twenty millions in England. Then, he was the friend
of the King, and each neighbor had some favor to ask
for himself, for his relatives, or for his friends.

Poor king! He should have had entire France to
divide like a cake between these cormorants, whose
voracious appetites it was impossible to satisfy.

That evening, after a grand banquet at the Château
de Courtornieu, the duke slept in the Château de Sairmeuse, in the room which had been occupied by Lacheneur, "like Louis XVIII.," he laughingly said, "in
the chamber of Bonaparte."

He was gay, chatty, and full of confidence in the
future.

"Ah! it is good to be in one's own house!" he remarked to his son again and again.

But Martial responded only mechanically. His

mind was occupied with thoughts of two women who had made a profound impression upon his by no means susceptible heart that day. He was thinking of those two young girls, so utterly unlike.

Blanche de Courtornieu—Marie-Anne Lacheneur.

CHAPTER VIII

Only those who, in the bright springtime of life, have loved, have been loved in return, and have suddenly seen an impassable gulf open between them and happiness, can realize Maurice d'Escorval's disappointment.

All the dreams of his life, all his future plans, were based upon his love for Marie-Anne.

If this love failed him, the enchanted castle which hope had erected would crumble and fall, burying him in the ruins.

Without Marie-Anne he saw neither aim nor motive in his existence. Still he did not suffer himself to be deluded by false hopes. Although at first, his appointed meeting with Marie-Anne on the following day seemed salvation itself, on reflection he was forced to admit that this interview would change nothing, since everything depended upon the will of another party—the will of M. Lacheneur.

The remainder of the day he passed in mournful silence. The dinner-hour came; he took his seat at the table, but it was impossible for him to swallow a morsel, and he soon requested his parents' permission to withdraw.

M. d'Escorval and the baroness exchanged a sorrowful glance, but did not allow themselves to offer any comment.

They respected his grief. They knew that his was one of those sorrows which are only aggravated by any attempt at consolation.

"Poor Maurice!" murmured Mme. d'Escorval, as soon as her son had left the room. And, as her husband made no reply: "Perhaps," she added, hesitatingly, "perhaps it will not be prudent for us to leave him too entirely to the dictates of his despair."

The baron shuddered. He divined only too well the terrible apprehensions of his wife.

"We have nothing to fear," he replied, quickly; "I heard Marie-Anne promise to meet Maurice to-morrow in the grove on the Reche."

The anxious mother breathed more freely. Her blood had frozen with horror at the thought that her son might, perhaps, be contemplating suicide; but she was a mother, and her husband's assurances did not satisfy her.

She hastily ascended the stairs leading to her son's room, softly opened the door, and looked in. He was so engrossed in his gloomy revery that he had heard nothing, and did not even suspect the presence of the anxious mother who was watching over him.

He was sitting at the window, his elbows resting upon the sill, his head supported by his hands, looking out into the night.

There was no moon, but the night was clear, and over beyond the light fog that indicated the course of the Oiselle one could discern the imposing mass of the Château de Sairmeuse, with its towers and fanciful turrets.

More than once he had sat thus silently gazing at this château, which sheltered what was dearest and most precious in all the world to him.

From his windows he could see those of the room occupied by Marie-Anne; and his heart always quickened its throbbing when he saw them illuminated.

" She is there," he thought, " in her virgin chamber. She is kneeling to say her prayers. She murmurs my name after that of her father, imploring God's blessing upon us both."

But this evening he was not waiting for a light to gleam through the panes of that dear window.

Marie-Anne was no longer at Sairmeuse—she had been driven away.

Where was she now? She, accustomed to all the luxury that wealth could procure, no longer had any home except a poor thatch-covered hovel, whose walls were not even whitewashed, whose only floor was the earth itself, dusty as the public highway in summer, frozen or muddy in winter.

She was reduced to the necessity of occupying herself the humble abode she, in her charitable heart, had intended as an asylum for one of her pensioners.

What was she doing now? Doubtless she was weeping.

At this thought poor Maurice was heartbroken.

What was his surprise, a little after midnight, to see the château brilliantly illuminated.

The duke and his son had repaired to the château after the banquet given by the Marquis de Courtornieu was over; and, before going to bed, they made a tour of inspection through this magnificent abode in which their ancestors had lived. They, therefore, might be said to have taken possession of the mansion whose threshold M. de Sairmeuse had not crossed for twenty-two years, and which Martial had never seen.

Maurice saw the lights leap from story to story, from

casement to casement, until at last even the windows of Marie-Anne's room were illuminated.

At this sight the unhappy youth could not restrain a cry of rage.

These men, these strangers, dared enter this virgin bower, which he, even in thought, scarcely dared to penetrate.

They trampled carelessly over the delicate carpet with their heavy boots. Maurice trembled in thinking of the liberties which they, in their insolent familiarity, might venture upon. He fancied he could see them examining and handling the thousand petty trifles with which young girls love to surround themselves; they opened the presses, perhaps they were reading an unfinished letter lying upon her writing-desk.

Never until this evening had Martial supposed he could hate another as he hated these men.

At last, in despair, he threw himself upon his bed, and passed the remainder of the night in thinking over what he should say to Marie-Anne on the morrow, and in seeking some issue from this inextricable labyrinth.

He rose before daybreak, and wandered about the park like a soul in distress, fearing, yet longing, for the hour that would decide his fate. Mme. d'Escorval was obliged to exert all her authority to make him take some nourishment. He had quite forgotten that he had passed twenty-four hours without eating.

When eleven o'clock sounded he left the house.

The lands of the Reche are situated on the other side of the Oiselle. Maurice, to reach his destination, was obliged to cross the river at a ferry only a short distance from his home. When he reached the river-

bank he found six or seven peasants who were waiting to cross.

These people did not observe Maurice. They were
talking earnestly, and he listened.

"It is certainly true," said one of the men. "I
heard it from Chanlouineau himself only last evening.
He was wild with delight. 'I invite you all to the
wedding!' he cried. 'I am betrothed to Monsieur
Lacheneur's daughter; the affair is decided.'"

This astounding news positively stunned Maurice.
He was actually unable to think or to move.

"Besides, he has been in love with her for a long
time. Everyone knows that. One had only to see his
eyes when he met her—coals of fire were nothing to
them. But while her father was so rich he did not
dare to speak. Now that the old man has met with
these reverses, he ventures to offer himself, and is accepted."

"An unfortunate thing for him," remarked a little
old man.

"Why so?"

"If Monsieur Lacheneur is ruined, as they say——"

The others laughed heartily.

"Ruined—Monsieur Lacheneur!" they exclaimed
in chorus. "How absurd! He is richer than all of
us together. Do you suppose that he has been stupid
enough not to have laid anything aside during all these
years? He has put this money not in grounds, as he
pretends, but somewhere else."

"You are saying what is untrue!" interrupted Maurice, indignantly. "Monsieur Lacheneur left Sairmeuse as poor as he entered it."

On recognizing M. d'Escorval's son, the peasants
became extremely cautious. He questioned them, but

could obtain only vague and unsatisfactory answers. A peasant, when interrogated, will never give a response which he thinks will be displeasing to his questioner; he is afraid of compromising himself.

The news he had heard, however, caused Maurice to hasten on still more rapidly after crossing the Oiselle.

" Marie-Anne marry Chanlouineau ! " he repeated; " it is impossible ! it is impossible ! "

CHAPTER IX

The Reche, literally translated the " Waste," where Marie-Anne had promised to meet Maurice, owed its name to the rebellious and sterile character of the soil.

Nature seemed to have laid her curse upon it. Nothing would grow there. The ground was covered with stones, and the sandy soil defied all attempts to enrich it.

A few stunted oaks rose here and there above the thorns and broom-plant.

But on the lowlands of the Reche is a flourishing grove. The firs are straight and strong, for the floods of winter have deposited in some of the clifts of the rock sufficient soil to sustain them and the wild clematis and honeysuckle that cling to their branches.

On reaching this grove, Maurice consulted his watch. It marked the hour of mid-day. He had supposed that he was late, but he was more than an hour in advance of the appointed time.

He seated himself upon a high rock, from which he could survey the entire Reche, and waited.

The day was magnificent; the air intensely hot. The rays of the August sun fell with scorching vio-

lence upon the sandy soil, and withered the few plants
which had sprung up since the last rain.

The stillness was profound, almost terrible. Not a
sound broke the silence, not even the buzzing of an in-
sect, nor a whisper of breeze in the trees. All nature
seemed sleeping. And on no side was there anything
to remind one of life, motion, or mankind.

This repose of nature, which contrasted so vividly
with the tumult raging in his own heart, exerted a
beneficial effect upon Maurice. These few moments
of solitude afforded him an opportunity to regain his
composure, to collect his thoughts scattered by the
storm of passion which had swept over his soul, as
leaves are scattered by the fierce November gale.

With sorrow comes experience, and that cruel
knowledge of life which teaches one to guard one's
self against one's hopes.

It was not until he heard the conversation of these
peasants that Maurice fully realized the horror of
Lacheneur's position. Suddenly precipitated from the
social eminence which he had attained, he found, in
the valley of humiliations into which he was cast,
only hatred, distrust, and scorn. Both factions despised and denied him. Traitor, cried one; thief, cried
the other. He no longer held any social status. He
was the fallen man, the man who *had* been, and who
was no more.

Was not the excessive misery of such a position a
sufficient explanation of the strangest and wildest
resolutions?

This thought made Maurice tremble. Connecting
the stories of the peasants with the words addressed
to Chanlouineau at Escorval by M. Lacheneur on the
preceding evening, he arrived at the conclusion that

this report of Marie-Anne's approaching marriage to the young farmer was not so improbable as he had at first supposed.

But why should M. Lacheneur give his daughter to an uncultured peasant? From mercenary motives? Certainly not, since he had just refused an alliance of which he had been proud in his days of prosperity. Could it be in order to satisfy his wounded pride, then? Perhaps he did not wish it to be said that he owed anything to a son-in-law.

Maurice was exhausting all his ingenuity and penetration in endeavoring to solve this mystery, when at last, on a foot-path which crosses the waste, a woman appeared—Marie-Anne.

He rose, but fearing observation, did not venture to leave the shelter of the grove.

Marie-Anne must have felt a similar fear, for she hurried on, casting anxious glances on every side as she ran. Maurice remarked, not without surprise, that she was bare-headed, and that she had neither shawl nor scarf about her shoulders.

As she reached the edge of the wood, he sprang toward her, and catching her hand raised it to his lips.

But this hand, which she had so often yielded to him, was now gently withdrawn, with so sad a gesture that he could not help feeling there was no hope.

"I came, Maurice," she began, "because I could not endure the thought of your anxiety. By doing so I have betrayed my father's confidence—he was obliged to leave home. I hastened here. And yet I promised him, only two hours ago, that I would never see you again. You hear me—never!"

She spoke hurriedly, but Maurice was appalled by the firmness of her accent.

Had he been less agitated, he would have seen what a terrible effort this semblance of calmness cost the young girl. He would have understood it from her pallor, from the contraction of her lips, from the redness of the eyelids which she had vainly bathed with fresh water, and which betrayed the tears that had fallen during the night.

"If I have come," she continued, "it is only to tell you that, for your own sake, as well as for mine, there must not remain in the secret recesses of your heart even the slightest shadow of a hope. All is over; we are separated forever! Only weak natures revolt against a destiny which they cannot alter. Let us accept our fate uncomplainingly. I wished to see you once more, and to say this: Have courage, Maurice. Go away—leave Escorval—forget me!"

"Forget you, Marie-Anne!" exclaimed the wretched young man, "forget you!"

His eyes met hers, and in a husky voice he added:

"Will you then forget me?"

"I am a woman, Maurice——"

But he interrupted her:

"Ah! I did not expect this," he said, despondently. "Poor fool that I was! I believed that you would find a way to touch your father's heart."

She blushed slightly, hesitated, and said:

"I have thrown myself at my father's feet; he repulsed me."

Maurice was thunderstruck, but recovering himself:

"It was because you did not know how to speak to him!" he exclaimed in a passion of fury; "but I shall know—I will present such arguments that he will be forced to yield. What right has he to ruin my happiness with his caprices? I love you—by right of this love, you are mine—mine rather than his! I will make him understand this, you shall see. Where is he? Where can I find him?"

Already he was starting to go, he knew not where. Marie-Anne caught him by the arm.

"Remain," she commanded, "remain! So you have failed to understand me, Maurice. Ah, well! you must know the truth. I am acquainted now with the reasons of my father's refusal; and though his decision should cost me my life, I approve it. Do not go to find my father. If, moved by your prayers, he gave his consent, I should have the courage to refuse mine!"

Maurice was so beside himself that this reply did not enlighten him. Crazed with anger and despair, and with no remorse for the insult he addressed to this woman whom he loved so deeply, he exclaimed:

"Is it for Chanlouineau, then, that you are reserving your consent? He believes so since he goes about everywhere saying that you will soon be his wife."

Marie-Anne shuddered as if a knife had entered her very heart; and yet there was more sorrow than anger in the glance she cast upon Maurice.

"Must I stoop so low as to defend myself from such an imputation?" she asked, sadly. "Must I declare that if even I suspect such an arrangement between Chanlouineau and my father, I have not been consulted? Must I tell you that there are some sacrifices which are beyond the strength of poor human nature? Understand this: I have found strength to renounce the man I love—I shall never be able to accept another in his place!"

Maurice hung his head, abashed by her earnest words, dazzled by the sublime expression of her face.

Reason returned; he realized the enormity of his suspicions, and was horrified with himself for having dared to give utterance to them.

"Oh! pardon!" he faltered, "pardon!"

What did the mysterious causes of all these events which had so rapidly succeeded each other, or M. Lacheneur's secrets, or Marie-Anne's reticence, matter to him now?

He was seeking some chance of salvation; he believed that he had found it.

"We must fly!" he exclaimed: "fly at once without pausing to look back. Before night we shall have passed the frontier."

He sprang toward her with outstretched arms, as if to seize her and bear her away; but she checked him by a single look.

"Fly!" said she, reproachfully: "fly! and is it you, Maurice, who counsel me thus? What! while misfortune is crushing my poor father to the earth, shall I add despair and shame to his sorrows? His friends have deserted him; shall I, his daughter, also abandon him? Ah! if I did that, I should be the vilest, the most cowardly of creatures! If my father, yesterday, when I believed him the owner of Sairmeuse, had demanded the sacrifice to which I consented last evening, I might, perhaps, have resolved upon the extreme measure you have counselled. In broad daylight I might have left Sairmeuse on the arm of my lover. It is not the world that I fear! But if one might consent to fly from the château of a rich and happy father, one *cannot* consent to desert the poor abode of a despairing and penniless parent. Leave me, Maurice, where honor holds me. It will not be difficult for me, who am the daughter of generations of peasants, to become a peasant. Go ! I cannot endure more! Go! and remember that one cannot be utterly wretched if one's conscience is clean, and one's duty fulfilled ! "

Maurice was about to reply, when a crackling of dry branches made him turn his head.

Scarcely ten paces off, Martial de Sairmeuse was standing motionless, leaning upon his gun.

CHAPTER X

The Duc de Sairmeuse had slept little and poorly on the night following his return, or his restoration, as he styled it.

Inaccessible, as he pretended to be, to the emotions which agitate the common herd, the scenes of the day had greatly excited him.

He could not help reviewing them, although he made it the rule of his life never to reflect.

While exposed to the scrutiny of the peasants and of his acquaintances at the Château de Courtornieu, he felt that his honor required him to appear cold and indifferent, but as soon as he had retired to the privacy of his own chamber, he gave free vent to his excessive joy.

For his joy *was* intense, almost verging on delirium.

Now he was forced to admit to himself the immense service Lacheneur had rendered him in restoring Sairmeuse.

This poor man to whom he had displayed the blackest ingratitude, this man, honest to heroism, whom he had treated as an unfaithful servant, had just relieved him of an anxiety which had poisoned his life.

Lacheneur had just placed the Duc de Sairmeuse beyond the reach of a not probable, but very possible calamity which he had dreaded for some time.

If his secret anxiety had been made known, it would have created much merriment.

"Nonsense!" people would have exclaimed, "everyone knows that the Sairmeuse possesses property to the amount of at least eight or ten millions, in England."

This was true. Only these millions, which had accrued from the estate of the duchess and of Lord Holland, had not been bequeathed to the duke.

He enjoyed absolute control of this enormous fortune; he disposed of the capital and of the immense revenues to please himself; but it all belonged to his son—to his only son.

The duke possessed nothing—a pitiful income of twelve hundred francs, perhaps; but, strictly speaking, not even the means of subsistence.

Martial, certainly, had never said a word which would lead him to suspect that he had any intention of removing his property from his father's control; but he might possibly utter this word.

Had he not good reason to believe that sooner or later this fatal word would be uttered?

And even at the thought of such a contingency he shuddered with horror.

He saw himself reduced to a pension, a very handsome pension, undoubtedly, but still a fixed, immutable, regular pension, by which he would be obliged to regulate his expenditures.

He would be obliged to calculate that two ends might meet—he, who had been accustomed to inexhaustible coffers.

" And this will necessarily happen sooner or later," he thought. " If Martial should marry, or if he should become ambitious, or meet with evil counsellors, that will be the end of my reign."

He watched and studied his son as a jealous woman studies and watches the lover she mistrusts. He thought he read in his eyes many thoughts which were not there; and according as he saw him, gay or sad, careless or preoccupied, he was reassured or still more alarmed.

Sometimes he imagined the worst. " If I should quarrel with Martial," he thought, " he would take possession of his entire fortune, and I should be left without bread."

These torturing apprehensions were, to a man who judged the sentiments of others by his own, a terrible chastisement.

Ah! no one would have wished his existence at the price he paid for it—not even the poor wretches who envied his lot and his apparent happiness, as they saw him roll by in his magnificent carriage.

There were days when he almost went mad.

"What am I?" he exclaimed, foaming with rage. " A mere plaything in the hands of a child. My son owns me. If I displease him, he casts me aside. Yes, he can dismiss me as he would a lackey. If I enjoy his fortune, it is only because he is willing that I should do so. I owe my very existence, as well as my luxuries, to his charity. But a moment of anger, even a caprice, may deprive me of everything."

With such ideas in his brain, the duke could not love his son.

He hated him.

He passionately envied him all the advantages he

possessed—his youth, his millions, his physical beauty, and his talents, which were really of a superior order.

We meet every day mothers who are jealous of their daughters, and some fathers!

This was one of those cases.

The duke, however, showed no sign of mental disquietude; and if Martial had possessed less penetration, he would have believed that his father adored him. But if he had detected the duke's secret, he did not allow him to discover it, nor did he abuse his power.

Their manner toward each other was perfect. The duke was kind even to weakness; Martial full of deference. But their relations were not those of father and son. One was in constant fear of displeasing the other; the other was a little too sure of his power. They lived on a footing of perfect equality, like two companions of the same age.

From this trying situation, Lacheneur had rescued the duke.

The owner of Sairmeuse, an estate worth more than a million, the duke was free from his son's tyranny; he had recovered his liberty.

What brilliant projects flitted through his brain that night!

He beheld himself the richest landowner in that locality; he was the chosen friend of the King; had he not a right to aspire to anything?

Such a prospect enchanted him. He felt twenty years younger—the twenty years that had been passed in exile.

So, rising before nine o'clock, he went to awaken Martial.

On returning from dining with the Marquis de

Courtornieu, the evening before, the duke had gone through the château; but this hasty examination by candle-light had not satisfied his curiosity. He wished to see it in detail by daylight.

Followed by his son, he explored one after another of the rooms of the princely abode; and, with every step, the recollections of his infancy crowded upon him.

Lacheneur had respected everything. The duke found articles as old as himself, religiously preserved, occupying the old familiar places from which they had never been removed.

When his inspection was concluded:

" Decidedly, Marquis," he exclaimed, " this Lacheneur was not such a rascal as I supposed. I am disposed to forgive him a great deal, on account of the care which he has taken of our house in our absence."

Martial seemed engrossed in thought.

" I think, Monsieur," he said, at last, " that we should testify our gratitude to this man by paying him. a large indemnity."

This word excited the duke's anger.

" An indemnity!" he exclaimed. " Are you mad, Marquis? Think of the income that he has received from my estate. Have you forgotten the calculation made for us last evening by the Chevalier de la Livandière? "

" The chevalier is a fool !" declared Martial promptly. " He forgot that Lacheneur has trebled the value of Sairmeuse. I think that our family honor requires us to bestow upon this man an indemnity of at least one hundred thousand francs. This would, moreover, be a good stroke of policy in the present state of public sentiment, and His Majesty would, I am sure, be much pleased."

"Stroke of policy"—"public sentiment"—"His Majesty." One might have obtained almost anything from M. de Sairmeuse by these arguments.

"Heavenly powers!" he exclaimed; "a hundred thousand francs! how you talk! It is all very well for you, with your fortune! Still, if you really think so ——"

"Ah! my dear sir, is not my fortune yours? Yes, such is really my opinion. So much so, indeed, that if you will allow me to do so, I will see Lacheneur myself, and arrange the matter in such a way that his pride will not be wounded. His is a devotion which it would be well to retain."

The duke opened his eyes to their widest extent.

"Lacheneur's pride!" he murmured. "Devotion which it would be well to retain! Why do you sing in this strain? Whence comes this extraordinary interest?"

He paused, enlightened by a sudden recollection.

"I understand!" he exclaimed; "I understand. He has a pretty daughter."

Martial smiled without replying.

"Yes, pretty as a rose," continued the duke; "but one hundred thousand francs! Zounds! That is a round sum to pay for such a whim. But, if you insist upon it——"

Armed with this authorization, Martial, two hours later, started on his mission.

The first peasant he met told him the way to the cottage which M. Lacheneur now occupied.

"Follow the river," said the man, "and when you see a pine-grove upon your left, cross it."

Martial was crossing it, when he heard the sound of voices. He approached, recognized Marie-Anne and Maurice d'Escorval, and obeying an angry impulse, he paused.

CHAPTER XI

During the decisive moments of life, when one's entire future depends upon a word, or a gesture, twenty contradictory inspirations can traverse the mind in the time occupied by a flash of lightning.

On the sudden apparition of the young Marquis de Sairmeuse, Maurice d'Escorval's first thought was this:

" How long has he been there? Has he been playing the spy? Has he been listening to us? What did he hear? "

His first impulse was to spring upon his enemy, to strike him in the face, and compel him to engage in a hand-to-hand struggle.

The thought of Anne-Marie checked him.

He reflected upon the possible, even probable results of a quarrel born of such circumstances. The combat which would ensue would cost this pure young girl her reputation. Martial would talk of it; and country people are pitiless. He saw this girl, whom he looked so devotedly upon, become the talk of the neighborhood; saw the finger of scorn pointed at her, and possessed sufficient self-control to master his anger. All these reflections had occupied only half a second.

Then, politely touching his hat, and stepping toward Martial:

" You are a stranger, Monsieur," said he, in a voice which was frightfully altered, " and you have doubtless lost your way? "

His words were ill-chosen, and defeated his prudent intentions. A curt " Mind your own business " would have been less wounding. He forgot that this word " stranger " was the most deadly insult that one could cast in the face of the former *émigrés*, who had returned with the allied armies.

Still the young marquis did not change his insolently nonchalant attitude.

He touched the visor of his hunting cap with his finger, and replied:

" It is true—I have lost my way."

Agitated as Marie-Anne was, she could not fail to understand that her presence was all that restrained the hatred of these two young men. Their attitude, the glance with which they measured each other, did not leave the shadow of a doubt on that score. If one was ready to spring upon the other, the other was on the alert, ready to defend himself.

The silence of nearly a moment which followed was as threatening as the profound calm which precedes the storm.

Martial was the first to break it.

" A peasant's directions are not generally remarkable for their clearness," he said, lightly; " and for more than an hour I have been seeking the house to which Monsieur Lacheneur has retired."

" Ah!"

" I am sent to him by the Duc de Sairmeuse, my father."

Knowing what he did, Maurice supposed that these strangely rapacious individuals had some new demand to make.

" I thought," said he, " that all relations between Monsieur Lacheneur and Monsieur de Sairmeuse were broken off last evening at the house of the *abbé*."

This was said in the most provoking manner, and yet Martial never so much as frowned. He had sworn that he would remain calm, and he had strength enough to keep his word.

"If these relations—as God forbid—have been broken off," he replied, "believe me, Monsieur d'Escorval, it is no fault of ours."

"Then it is not as people say ? "

"What people? Who ? "

"The people here in the neighborhood."

"Ah! And what do these people say? "

"The truth. That you have been guilty of an offence which a man of honor could never forgive nor forget."

The young marquis shook his head gravely.

"You are quick to condemn, sir," he said, coldly. " Permit me to hope that Monsieur Lacheneur will be less severe than yourself; and that his resentment—just, I confess, will vanish before "—he hesitated—" before a truthful explanation."

Such an expression from the lips of this haughty young aristocrat! Was it possible?

Martial profited by the effect he had produced to advance toward Marie-Anne, and, addressing himself exclusively to her, seemed after that to ignore the presence of Maurice completely.

"For there has been a mistake—a misunderstanding, Mademoiselle," he continued. " Do not doubt it. The Sairmeuse are not ingrates. How could anyone have supposed that we would intentionally give offense to a—devoted friend of our family, and that at a moment when he had rendered us a most signal service ! A true gentleman like my father, and a hero of probity like yours, cannot fail to esteem each other. I admit that in the scene of yesterday, Monsieur de Sairmeuse did not appear to advantage; but the step he takes to-day proves his sincere regret."

Certainly this was not the cavalier tone which he had employed in addressing Marie-Anne, for the first time, on the square in front of the church.

He had removed his hat, he remained half inclined before her, and he spoke in a tone of profound respect, as though it were a haughty duchess, and not the humble daughter of that " rascal " Lacheneur whom he was addressing.

Was it only a *roue's* manœuvre ? Or had he also involuntarily submitted to the power of this beautiful girl? It was both; and it would have been difficult for him to say where the voluntary ended, and where the involuntary began.

He continued:

" My father is an old man who has suffered cruelly. Exile is hard to bear. But if sorrows and deceptions have embittered his character, they have not changed his heart. His apparent imperiousness and arrogance conceal a kindness of heart which I have often seen degenerate into positive weakness. And—why should I not confess it ?—the Duc de Sairmeuse, with his white hair, still retains the illusions of a child. He refuses to believe that the world has progressed during the past twenty years. Moreover, people had deceived him by the most absurd fabrications. To speak plainly, even while we were in Montaignac, Monsieur Lacheneur's enemies succeeded in prejudicing my father against him."

One would have sworn that he was speaking the truth, so persuasive was his voice, so entirely did the expression of his face, his glance, and his gestures accord with his words.

And Maurice, who felt—who was certain that the young man was lying, impudently lying, was abashed by this scientific prevarication which is so universally practised in good society, and of which he was entirely ignorant.

But what did the marquis desire here—and why this farce ?

" Need I tell you, Mademoiselle," he resumed, " all that I suffered last evening in the little drawing-room in the presbytery?   No, never in my whole life can I recollect such a cruel moment.   I understood, and I did honor to Monsieur Lacheneur's heroism. Hearing of our arrival, he, without hesitation, without delay, hastened to voluntarily surrender a princely fortune— and he was insulted.   This excessive injustice horri- fied me.   And if I did not openly protest against it— if I did not show my indignation—it was only because contradiction drives my father to the verge of frenzy. And what good would it have done for me to protest? The filial love and piety which you displayed were far more powerful in their effect than any words of mine would have been.   You were scarcely out of the vil- lage before Monsieur de Sairmeuse, already ashamed of his injustice, said to me: ' I have been wrong, but I am an old man ; it is hard for me to decide to make the first advance ; you, Marquis, go and find Monsieur Lacheneur, and obtain his forgiveness.' "

Marie-Anne, redder than a peony, and terribly em- barrassed, lowered her eyes.

" I thank you, Monsieur," she faltered, " in the name of my father——"

" Oh! do not thank me," interrupted Martial, ear- nestly ; " it will be my duty, on the contrary, to render you thanks, if you can induce Monsieur Lacheneur to accept the reparation which is due him—and he will accept it, if you will only condescend to plead our cause. Who could resist your sweet voice, your beautiful, beseeching eyes?"

However inexperienced Maurice might be, he could no longer fail to comprehend Martial's intentions. This man whom he mortally hated already, dared to speak of love to Marie-Anne, and before him, Maurice. In other words, the marquis, not content with having ignored and insulted him, presumed to take an insolent advantage of his supposed simplicity.

The certainty of this insult sent all his blood in a boiling torrent to his brain.

He seized Martial by the arm, and with irresistible power whirled him twice around, then threw him more than ten feet, exclaiming:

"This last is too much, Marquis de Sairmeuse!"

Maurice's attitude was so threatening that Martial fully expected another attack. The violence of the shock had thrown him down upon one knee; without rising, he lifted his gun, ready to take aim.

It was not from anything like cowardice on the part of the Marquis de Sairmeuse that he decided to fire upon an unarmed foe; but the affront which he had received was so deadly and so ignoble in his opinion, that he would have shot Maurice like a dog, rather than feel the weight of his finger upon him again.

This explosion of anger from Maurice Marie-Anne had been expecting and hoping for every moment.

She was even more inexperienced than her lover; but she was a woman, and could not fail to understand the meaning of the young marquis.

He was evidently "paying his court to her." And with what intentions! It was only too easy to divine.

Her agitation, while the marquis spoke in a more and more tender voice, changed first to stupor, then to indignation, as she realized his marvellous audacity.

After that, how could she help blessing the violence which put an end to a situation which was so insulting for her, and so humiliating for Maurice?

An ordinary woman would have thrown herself between the two men who were ready to kill each other. Marie-Anne did not move a muscle.

Was it not the duty of Maurice to protect her when she was insulted? Who, then, if not he, should defend her from the insolent gallantry of this libertine? She would have blushed, she who was energy personified, to love a weak and pusillanimous man.

But any intervention was unnecessary. Maurice comprehended that this was one of those affronts which the person insulted must not seem to suspect, under penalty of giving the offending party the advantage.

He felt that Marie-Anne must not be regarded as the cause of the quarrel!

His instant recognition of the situation produced a powerful reaction in his mind; and he recovered, as if by magic, his coolness and the free exercise of his faculties.

"Yes," he resumed, defiantly, "this is hypocrisy enough. To dare to prate of reparation after the insults that you and yours have inflicted, is adding intentional humiliation to insult—and I will not permit it."

Martial had thrown aside his gun; he now rose and brushed the knee of his pantaloons, to which a few particles of dust had adhered, with a phlegm whose secret he had learned in England.

He was too discerning not to perceive that Maurice

had disguised the true cause of his outburst of passion; but what did it matter to him? Had he avowed it, the marquis would not have been displeased.

Yet it was necessary to make some response, and to preserve the superiority which he imagined he had maintained up to that time.

" You will never know, Monsieur," he said, glancing alternately at his gun and at Marie-Anne, " all that you owe to Mademoiselle Lacheneur. We shall meet again, I hope——"

" You have made that remark before," Maurice interrupted, tauntingly. " Nothing is easier than to find me. The first peasant you meet will point out the house of Baron d'Escorval."

" *Eh bien!* sir, I cannot promise that you will not see two of my friends."

" Oh ! whenever it may please you ! "

" Certainly; but it would gratify me to know by what right you make yourself the judge of Monsieur Lacheneur's honor, and take it upon yourself to defend what has not been attacked. Who has given you this right? "

From Martial's sneering tone, Maurice was certain that he had overheard, at least a part of, his conversation with Marie-Anne.

" My right," he replied, " is that of friendship. If I tell you that your advances are unwelcome, it is because I know that Monsieur Lacheneur will accept nothing from you. No, nothing, under whatever guise you may offer these alms which you tender merely to appease your own conscience. He will never forgive the affront which is his honor and your shame. Ah! you thought to degrade him, Messieurs de Sairmeuse! and you have lifted him far above your mock

grandeur. *He* receive anything from you! Go; learn
that your millions will never give you a pleasure equal
to the ineffable joy he will feel, when seeing you roll
by in your carriage, he says to himself: ' Those people owe everything to me ! ' "

His burning words vibrated with such intensity of
feeling that Marie-Anne could not resist the impulse
to press his hand; and this gesture was his revenge
upon Martial, who turned pale with passion.

" But I have still another right," continued Maurice.
" My father yesterday had the honor of asking of Monsieur Lacheneur the hand of his daughter——"

" And I refused it ! " cried a terrible voice.

Marie-Anne and both young men turned with the
same movement of alarm and surprise.

M. Lacheneur stood before them, and by his side
was Chanlouineau, who surveyed the group with
threatening eyes.

" Yes, I refused it," resumed M. Lacheneur, " and
I do not believe that my daughter will marry anyone
without my consent. What did you promise me this
morning, Marie-Anne? Can it be you, you who grant
a rendezvous to gallants in the forest? Return to the
house, instantly——"

" But father——"

" Return ! " he repeated with an oath; " return, I
command you."

She obeyed and departed, not without giving Maurice a look in which he read a farewell that she believed would be eternal.

As soon as she had gone, perhaps twenty paces, M.
Lacheneur, with folded arms, confronted Maurice.

" As for you, Monsieur d'Escorval," said he, rudely,
" I hope that you will no longer undertake to prowl
around my daughter——"

" I swear to you, Monsieur——"

" Oh, no oaths, if you please. It is an evil action
to endeavor to turn a young girl from her duty, which
is obedience. You have broken forever all relations
between your family and mine."

The poor youth tried to excuse himself, but M.
Lacheneur interrupted him.

" Enough! enough! " said he; " go back to your
home."

And as Maurice hesitated, he seized him by the collar and dragged him to the little footpath leading
through the grove.

It was the work of scarcely ten seconds, and yet, he
found time to whisper in the young man's ear, in his
formerly friendly tones:

" Go, you little wretch! do you wish to render all my
precautions useless? "

He watched Maurice as he disappeared, bewildered
by the scene he had just witnessed, and stupefied by
what he had just heard; and it was not until he saw
that young D'Escorval was out of hearing that he
turned to Martial.

" As I have had the honor of meeting you, Monsieur
le Marquis," said he, " I deem it my duty to inform
you that Chupin and his sons are searching for you
everywhere. It is at the instance of the duke, your
father, who is anxious for you to repair at once to the
Château de Courtornieu."

He turned to Chanlouineau, and added:

" We will now proceed on our way."

But Martial detained him with a gesture.

" I am much surprised to hear that they are seeking
me," said he. " My father knows very well where he

sent me; I was going to your house, Monsieur, and at his request."

" To my house? "

" To your house, yes, Monsieur, to express our sincere regret at the scene which took place at the presbytery last evening."

And without waiting for any response, Martial, with wonderful cleverness and felicity of expression, began to repeat to the father the story which he had just related to the daughter.

According to his version, his father and himself were in despair. How could M. Lacheneur suppose them guilty of such black ingratitude? Why had he retired so precipitately? The Duc de Sairmeuse held at M. Lacheneur's disposal any amount which it might please him to mention—sixty, a hundred thousand francs, even more.

But M. Lacheneur did not appear to be dazzled in the least; and when Martial had concluded, he replied, respectfully, but coldly, that he would consider the matter.

This coldness amazed Chanlouineau; he did not conceal the fact when the marquis, after many earnest protestations, at last wended his way homeward.

" We have misjudged these people," he declared.

But M. Lacheneur shrugged his shoulders.

" And so you are foolish enough to suppose that it was to me that he offered all that money? "

" Zounds! I have ears."

" Ah, well! my poor boy, you must not believe all they hear, if you have. The truth is, that these large sums were intended to win the favor of my daughter. She has pleased this coxcomb of a marquis; and—he wishes to make her his mistress——"

Chanlouineau stopped short, with eyes flashing, and hands clinched.

"Good God!" he exclaimed; "prove that, and I am yours, body and soul—to do anything you desire."

CHAPTER XII

"No, never in my whole life have I met a woman who can compare with this Marie-Anne! What grace and what dignity! Ah! her beauty is divine!"

So Martial was thinking while returning to Sairmeuse after his proposals to M. Lacheneur.

At the risk of losing his way he took the shortest course, which led across the fields and over ditches, which he leaped with the aid of his gun.

He found a pleasure, entirely novel and very delightful, in picturing Marie-Anne as he had just seen her, blushing and paling, about to swoon, then lifting her head haughtily in her pride and disdain.

Who would have suspected that such indomitable energy and such an impassioned soul was hidden beneath such girlish artlessness and apparent coldness? What an adorable expression illumined her face, what passion shone in those great black eyes when she looked at that little fool D'Escorval! What would not one give to be regarded thus, even for a moment? How could the boy help being crazy about her?

He himself loved her, without being, as yet, willing to confess it. What other name could be given to this passion which had overpowered reason, and to the furious desires which agitated him?

"Ah!" he exclaimed, "she shall be mine. Yes, she shall be mine; I will have her!"

Consequently he began to study the strategic side of the undertaking which this resolution involved with the sagacity of one who had not been without an extended experience in such matters.

His *début*, he was forced to admit, had been neither fortunate nor adroit. Conveyed compliments and money had both been rejected. If Marie-Anne had heard his covert insinuations with evident horror, M. Lacheneur had received, with even more than coldness, his advances and his offers of actual wealth.

Moreover, he remembered Chanlouineau's terrible eyes.

" How he measured me, that magnificent rustic ! " he growled. " At a sign from Marie-Anne he would have crushed me like an eggshell, without a thought of my ancestors. Ah ! does he also love her ? There will be three rivals in that case."

But the more difficult and even perilous the undertaking seemed, the more his passions were inflamed.

" My failures can be repaired," he thought. " Occasions of meeting shall not be wanting. Will it not be necessary to hold frequent interviews with Monsieur Lacheneur in effecting a formal transfer of Sairmeuse ? I will win him over to my side. With the daughter my course is plain. Profiting by my unfortunate experience, I will, in the future, be as timid as I have been bold ; and she will be hard to please if she is not flattered by this triumph of her beauty. D'Escorval remains to be disposed of——"

But this was the point upon which Martial was most exercised.

He had, it is true, seen this rival rudely dismissed by M. Lacheneur ; and yet the anger of the latter had seemed to him too great to be absolutely real.

He suspected a comedy, but for whose benefit? For his, or for Chanlouineau's? And yet, what could possibly be the motive?

"And yet," he reflected, " my hands are tied; and I cannot call this little D'Escorval to account for his insolence. To swallow such an affront in silence is hard. Still, he is brave, there is no denying that; perhaps I can find some other way to provoke his anger. But even then, what could I do? If I harmed a hair of his head, Marie-Anne would never forgive me. Ah! I would give a handsome sum in exchange for some little device to send him out of the country."

Revolving in his mind these plans, whose frightful consequences he could neither calculate nor foresee, Martial was walking up the avenue leading to the château, when he heard hurried footsteps behind him.

He turned, and seeing two men running after him and motioning him to stop, he paused.

It was Chupin, accompanied by one of his sons.

This old rascal had been enrolled among the servants charged with preparing Sairmeuse for the reception of the duke; and he had already discovered the secret of making himself useful to his master, which was by seeming to be indispensable.

" Ah, Monsieur," he cried, " we have been searching for you everywhere, my son and I. It was Monsieur le Duc——"

" Very well," said Martial, dryly. " I am returning——"

But Chupin was not sensitive; and although he had not been very favorably received, he ventured to follow the marquis at a little distance, but sufficiently near to make himself heard. He also had his schemes; for it was not long before he began a long recital of the cal-

umnies which had been spread about the neighborhood in regard to the Lacheneur affair. Why did he
choose this subject in preference to any other? Did
he suspect the young marquis's passion for Marie-
Anne?

According to this report, Lacheneur—he no longer
said " monsieur "—was unquestionably a rascal; the
complete surrender of Sairmeuse was only a farce, as
he must possess thousands, and hundreds of thousands
of francs, since he was about to marry his daughter.

If the scoundrel had felt only suspicions, they were
changed into certainty by the eagerness with which
Martial demanded:

" How! is Mademoiselle Lacheneur to be married? "

" Yes, Monsieur."

" And to whom? "

" To Chanlouineau, the fellow whom the peasants
wished to kill yesterday upon the square, because he
was disrespectful to the duke. He is an avaricious
man; and if Marie-Anne does not bring him a good
round sum as a dowry, he will never marry her, no
matter how beautiful she may be."

" Are you sure of what you say? "

" It is true. My eldest son heard from Chanlouineau and from Lacheneur that the wedding would
take place within a month."

And turning to his son:

" Is it not true, boy? "

" Yes," promptly replied the youth, who had heard
nothing of the kind.

Martial was silent, ashamed, perhaps, of allowing
himself to listen to the gossip, but glad to have been
informed of such an important circumstance

If Chupin was not telling a falsehood—and what reason could he have for doing so—it became evident that M. Lacheneur's conduct concealed some great mystery. Why, without some potent motive, should he have refused to give his daughter to Maurice d'Escorval whom she loved, to bestow her upon a peasant?

As he reached Sairmeuse, he was swearing that he would discover this motive. A strange scene awaited him. In the broad open space extending from the front of the château to the *parterre* lay a huge pile of all kinds of clothing, linen, plate, and furniture. One might have supposed that the occupants of the château were moving. A half dozen men were running to and fro, and standing in the centre of the rubbish was the Duc de Sairmeuse, giving orders.

Martial did not understand the whole meaning of the scene at first. He went to his father, and after saluting him respectfully, inquired:

" What is all this? "

M. de Sairmeuse laughed heartily.

" What! can you not guess? " he replied. " It is very simple, however. When the lawful master, on his return, sleeps beneath the bed-coverings of the usurper, it is delightful, the first night, not so pleasant on the second. Everything here reminds me too forcibly of Monsieur Lacheneur. It seems to me that I am in his house; and the thought is unendurable. So I have had them collect everything belonging to him and to his daughter—everything, in fact, which did not belong to the château in former years. The servants will put it all into a cart and carry it to him."

The young marquis gave fervent thanks to Heaven that he had arrived before it was too late. Had his father's project been executed, he would have been obliged to bid farewell to all his hopes.

" You surely will not do this, Monsieur le Duc? "
said he, earnestly.

" And why, pray? Who will prevent me from doing it? "

" No one, most assuredly. But you will decide, on
reflection, that a man who has not conducted himself
too badly has a right to some consideration."

The duke seemed greatly astonished.

" Consideration! " he exclaimed. " This rascal has
a right to some consideration! Well, this is one of
the poorest of jokes. What! I give him—that is to
say—you give him a hundred thousand francs, and
that will not content him! He is entitled to consideration! You, who are after the daughter, may give it
to him if you like, but *I* shall do as I like! "

" Very well; but, Monsieur, I would think twice, if
I were in your place. Lacheneur has surrendered
Sairmeuse. That is all very well; but how can you
authenticate your claim to the property? What would
you do if, in case you imprudently irritated him, he
should change his mind? What would become of
your right to the estate? "

M. Sairmeuse actually turned green.

" Zounds! " he exclaimed. " I had not thought of
that. Here, you fellows, take all these things back
again, and that quickly! "

And as they were obeying his order:

" Now," he remarked, " let us hasten to Courtornieu. They have already sent for us twice. It must
be business of the utmost importance which demands
our attention."

CHAPTER XIII

The Château de Courtornieu is, next to Sairmeuse, the most magnificent habitation in the *arrondissement* of Montaignac.

The approach to the castle was by a long and narrow road, badly paved. When the carriage containing Martial and his father turned from the public highway into this rough road, the jolting aroused the duke from the profound revery into which he had fallen on leaving Sairmeuse.

The marquis thought that he had caused this unusual fit of abstraction.

"It is the result of my adroit manœuvre," he said to himself, not without secret satisfaction. "Until the restitution of Sairmeuse is legalized, I can make my father do anything I wish; yes, anything. And if it is necessary, he will even invite Lacheneur and Marie-Anne to his table."

He was mistaken. The duke had already forgotten the affair; his most vivid impressions lasted no longer than an indentation in the sand.

He lowered the glass in front of the carriage, and, after ordering the coachman to drive more slowly:

"Now," said he to his son, "let us talk a little. Are you really in love with that little Lacheneur?"

Martial could not repress a start. "Oh! in love," said he, lightly, "that would perhaps be saying too much. Let me say that she has taken my fancy; that will be sufficient."

The duke regarded his son with a bantering air.

"Really, you delight me!" he exclaimed. "I feared

that this love-affair might derange, at least for the moment, certain plans that I have formed—for I have formed certain plans for you."

" The devil! "

" Yes, I have my plans, and I will communicate them to you later in detail. I will content myself today by recommending you to examine Mademoiselle Blanche de Courtornieu."

Martial made no reply. This recommendation was entirely unnecessary. If Mlle. Lacheneur had made him forget Mlle. de Courtornieu that morning for some moments, the remembrance of Marie-Anne was now effaced by the radiant image of Blanche.

" Before discussing the daughter," resumed the duke, " let us speak of the father. He is one of my strongest friends; and I know him thoroughly. You have heard men reproach me for what they style my prejudices, have you not? Well, in comparison with the Marquise de Courtornieu, I am only a Jacobin."

" Oh! my father! "

" Really, nothing could be more true. If I am behind the age in which I live, he belongs to the reign of Louis XIV. Only—for there is an only—the principles which I openly avow, he keeps locked up in his snuff-box—and trust him for not forgetting to open it at the opportune moment. He has suffered cruelly for his opinions, in the sense of having so often been obliged to conceal them. He concealed them, first, under the consulate, when he returned from exile. He dissimulated them even more courageously under the Empire—for he played the part of a kind of chamberlain to Bonaparte, this dear marquis. But, chut! do not remind him of that proof of heroism; he has deplored it bitterly since the battle of Lutzen."

This was the tone in which M. de Sairmeuse was accustomed to speak of his best friends.

" The history of his fortune," he continued, " is the history of his marriages—I say *marriages*, because he has married a number of times, and always advantageously. Yes, in a period of fifteen years he has had the misfortune of losing three wives, each richer than the other. His daughter is the child of his third and last wife, a Cisse Blossac—she died in 1809. He comforted himself after each bereavement by purchasing a quantity of lands or bonds. So that now he is as rich as you are, Marquis, and his influence is powerful and widespread. I forgot one detail, however : he believes, they tell me, in the growing power of the clergy, and has become very devout."

He checked himself; the carriage had stopped before the entrance of the Château de Courtornieu, and the marquis came forward to receive his guests in person. A flattering distinction, which he seldom lavished upon his visitors. The marquis was long rather than tall, and very solemn in deportment. The head that surmounted his angular form was remarkably small, a characteristic of his race, and covered with thin, glossy black hair, and lighted by cold, round black eyes.

The pride that becomes a gentleman, and the humility that befits a Christian, were continually at war with each other in his countenance.

He pressed the hands of M. de Sairmeuse and Martial, overwhelming them with compliments uttered in a thin, rather nasal voice, which, issuing from his immense body, was as astonishing as the sound of a flute issuing from the pipes of an orphicleide would be.

" At last you have come," he said; " we were waiting for you before beginning our deliberations upon a very grave, and also very delicate matter. We are thinking of addressing a petition to His Majesty. The nobility, who have suffered so much during the Revolution, have a right to expect ample compensation. Our neighbors, to the number of sixteen, are now assembled in my cabinet, transformed for the time into a council chamber."

Martial shuddered at the thought of all the ridiculous and tiresome conversation he would probably be obliged to hear; and his father's recommendation occurred to him.

" Shall we not have the honor of paying our respects to Mademoiselle de Courtornieu? "

" My daughter must be in the drawing-room with our cousin," replied the marquis, in an indifferent tone; " at least, if she is not in the garden."

This might be construed into, " Go and look for her if you choose." At least Martial understood it in that way; and when they entered the hall, he allowed his father and the marquis to go upstairs without him.

A servant opened the door of the drawing-room for him—but it was empty.

" Very well," said he; " I know my way to the garden."

But he explored it in vain; no one was to be found.

He decided to return to the house and march bravely into the presence of the dreaded enemy. He had turned to retrace his steps when, through the foliage of a bower of jasmine, he thought he could distinguish a white dress.

He advanced softly, and his heart quickened its throbbing when he saw that he was right.

Mlle. Blanche de Courtornieu was seated on a bench

beside an old lady, and was engaged in reading a letter
in a low voice.

She must have been greatly preoccupied, since she
had not heard Martial's footsteps approaching.

He was only ten paces from her, so near that he
could distinguish the shadow of her long eyelashes.

He paused, holding his breath, in a delicious ecstasy.

"Ah! how beautiful she is!" he thought.   Beautiful? no.   But pretty, yes; as pretty as heart could desire, with her great velvety blue eyes and her pouting
lips.   She was a blonde, but one of those dazzling and
radiant blondes found only in the countries of the sun;
and from her hair, drawn high upon the top of her
head, escaped a profusion of ravishing, glittering ring-
lets, which seemed almost to sparkle in the play of the
light breeze.

One might, perhaps, have wished her a trifle larger.
But she had the winning charm of all delicate and
mignonnes women; and her figure was of exquisite
roundness, and her dimpled hands were those of an infant.

Alas! these attractive exteriors are often deceitful, as
much and even more so, than the appearances of a
man like the Marquis de Courtornieu.

The apparently innocent and artless young girl possessed the parched, hollow soul of an experienced
woman of the world, or of an old courtier.   She had
been so petted at the convent, in the capacity of only
daughter of a *grand seigneur* and millionnaire; she had
been surrounded by so much adulation, that all her
good qualities had been blighted in the bud by the
poisonous breath of flattery.

She was only nineteen; and still it was impossible
for any person to have been more susceptible to the

charms of wealth and of satisfied ambition. She
dreamed of a position at court as a school-girl dreams
of a lover.

If she had deigned to notice Martial—for she had remarked him—it was only because her father had told
her that this young man would lift his wife to the highest sphere of power. Thereupon she had uttered a
" very well, we will see!" that would have changed an
enamoured suitor's love into disgust.

Martial advanced a few steps, and Mlle. Blanche, on
seeing him, sprang up with a pretty affectation of intense timidity.

Bowing low before her, he said, gently, and with
profound deference:

" Monsieur de Courtornieu, Mademoiselle, was so
kind as to tell me where I might have the honor of
finding you. I had not courage to brave those formidable discussions inside; but——"

He pointed to the letter the young girl held in her
hand, and added:

" But I fear that I am *de trop*."

" Oh! not in the least, Monsieur le Marquis, although this letter which I have just been reading has,
I confess, interested me deeply. It was written by a
poor child in whom I have taken a great interest—
whom I have sent for sometimes when I was lonely—
Marie-Anne Lacheneur."

Accustomed from his infancy to the hypocrisy of
drawing-rooms, the young marquis had taught his
face not to betray his feelings.

He could have laughed gayly with anguish at his
heart; he could have preserved the sternest gravity
when inwardly convulsed with merriment.

And yet, this name of Marie-Anne upon the lips of
Mlle. de Courtornieu, caused his glance to waver.

" They know each other ! " he thought.

In an instant he was himself again ; but Mlle
Blanche had perceived his momentary agitation.

" What can it mean ? " she wondered, much disturbed.

Still, it was with the perfect assumption of innocence
that she continued :

" In fact, you must have seen her, this poor Marie-
Anne, Monsieur le Marquis, since her father was the
guardian of Sairmeuse ? "

" Yes, I have seen her, Mademoiselle," replied Martial, quietly.

" Is she not remarkably beautiful ?   Her beauty is
of an unusual type, it quite takes one by surprise."

A fool would have protested.   The marquis was not
guilty of this folly.

" Yes, she is very beautiful," said he.

This apparent frankness disconcerted Mlle. Blanche
a trifle ; and it was with an air of hypocritical compassion that she murmured :

" Poor girl !   What will become of her ?   Here is
her father, reduced to delving in the ground."

" Oh ! you exaggerate, Mademoiselle ; my father
will always preserve Lacheneur from anything of that
kind."

" Of course—I might have known that—but where
will he find a husband for Marie-Anne ? "

" One has been found already.   I understand that
she is to marry a youth in the neighborhood, who has
some property—a certain Chanlouineau."

The artless school-girl was more cunning than the
marquis.   She had satisfied herself that she had just
grounds for her suspicions ; and she experienced a
certain anger on finding him so well informed in regard
to everything that concerned Mlle. Lacheneur.

"And do you believe that this is the husband of whom she had dreamed? Ah, well! God grant that she may be happy; for we were very fond of her, very—were we not, Aunt Medea?"

Aunt Medea was the old lady seated beside Mlle. Blanche.

"Yes, very," she replied.

This aunt, or cousin, rather, was a poor relation whom M. de Courtornieu had sheltered, and who was forced to pay dearly for her bread; since Mlle. Blanche compelled her to play the part of echo.

"It grieves me to see these friendly relations, which were so dear to me, broken," resumed Mlle. de Courtornieu. "But listen to what Marie-Anne has written."

She drew from her belt where she had placed it, Mlle. Lacheneur's letter and read:

"'MY DEAR BLANCHE—You know that the Duc de Sairmeuse has returned. The news fell upon us like a thunder-bolt. My father and I had become too much accustomed to regard as our own the deposit which had been intrusted to our fidelity; we have been punished for it. At least, we have done our duty, and now all is ended. She whom you have called your friend, will be, hereafter, only a poor peasant girl, as her mother was before her.'"

The most subtle observer would have supposed that Mlle. Blanche was experiencing the keenest emotion. One would have sworn that it was only by intense effort that she succeeded in restraining her tears—that they were even trembling behind her long lashes.

The truth was, that she was thinking only of discovering, upon Martial's face, some indication of his feelings. But now that he was on guard, his features might have been marble for any sign of emotion they betrayed.

So she continued:

" ' I should utter an untruth if I said that I have not suffered on account of this sudden change. But I have courage; I shall learn how to submit. I shall, I hope, have strength to forget, for I *must* forget ! The remembrances of past felicity would render my present misery intolerable.' "

Mlle. de Courtornieu suddenly folded up the letter.

" You have heard it, Monsieur," said she. " Can you understand such pride as that ? And they accuse us, daughters of the nobility, of being proud ! "

Martial made no response. He felt that his altered voice would betray him. How much more would he have been moved, if he had been allowed to read the concluding lines :

" One must live, my dear Blanche," added Marie-Anne, " and I feel no false shame in asking you to aid me. I sew very nicely, as you know, and I could earn my livelihood by embroidery if I knew more people. I will call to-day at Courtornieu to ask you to give me a list of ladies to whom I can present myself on your recommendation."

But Mlle. de Courtornieu had taken good care not to allude to the touching request. She had read the letter to Martial as a test. She had not succeeded; so much the worse. She rose and accepted his arm to return to the house.

She seemed to have forgotten her friend, and she was chatting gayly. When they approached the château, she was interrupted by a sound of voices raised to the highest pitch.

It was the address to the King which was agitating the council convened in M. de Courtornieu's cabinet.

Mlle. Blanche paused.

"I am trespassing upon your kindness, Monsieur. I am boring you with my silly chat when you should undoubtedly be up there."

"Certainly not," he replied, laughing. "What should I do there? The *rôle* of men of action does not begin until the orators have concluded."

He spoke so energetically, in spite of his jesting tone, that Mlle. de Courtornieu was fascinated. She saw before her, she believed, a man who, as her father had said, would rise to the highest position in the political world.

Unfortunately, her admiration was disturbed by a ring of the great bell that always announces visitors.

She trembled, let go her hold on Martial's arm, and said, very earnestly:

"Ah, no matter. I wish very much to know what is going on up there. If I ask my father, he will laugh at my curiosity, while you, Monsieur, if you are present at the conference, you will tell me all."

A wish thus expressed was a command. The marquis bowed and obeyed.

"She dismisses me," he said to himself as he ascended the staircase, "nothing could be more evident; and that without much ceremony. Why the devil does she wish to get rid of me?"

Why? Because a single peal of the bell announced a visitor for Mlle. Blanche; because she was expecting a visit from her friend; and because she wished at any cost to prevent a meeting between Martial and Marie-Anne.

She did not love him, and yet an agony of jealousy was torturing her. Such was her nature.

Her presentiments were realized. It was, indeed, Mlle. Lacheneur who was awaiting her in the drawing-room.

The poor girl was paler than usual; but nothing in her manner betrayed the frightful anguish she had suffered during the past two or three days.

And her voice, in asking from her former friend a list of " customers," was as calm and as natural as in other days, when she was asking her to come and spend an afternoon at Sairmeuse.

So, when the two girls embraced each other, their *rôles* were reversed.

It was Marie-Anne who had been crushed by misfortune; it was Mlle. Blanche who wept.

But, while writing a list of the names of persons in the neighborhood with whom she was acquainted, Mlle. de Courtornieu did not neglect this favorable opportunity for verifying the suspicions which had been aroused by Martial's momentary agitation.

" It is inconceivable," she remarked to her friend, " that the Duc de Sairmeuse should allow you to be reduced to such an extremity."

Marie-Anne's nature was so royal, that she did not wish an unjust accusation to rest even upon the man who had treated her father so cruelly.

" The duke is not to blame," she replied, gently; " he offered us a very considerable sum, this morning, through his son."

Mlle. Blanche started as if a viper had stung her.

" So you have seen the marquis, Marie-Anne ? "

" Yes."

" Has he been to your house? "

" He was going there, when he met me in the grove on the waste."

She blushed as she spoke; she turned crimson at the thought of Martial's impertinent gallantry.

This girl who had just emerged from a convent was terribly experienced; but she misunderstood the cause of Marie-Anne's confusion. She could dissimulate, however, and when Marie-Anne went away, Mlle. Blanche embraced her with every sign of the most ardent affection. But she was almost suffocated with rage.

" What ! " she thought; " they have met but once, and yet they are so strongly impressed with each other! Do they love each other already ?"

CHAPTER XIV

If Martial had faithfully reported to Mlle. Blanche all that he heard in the Marquis de Courtornieu's cabinet, he would probably have astonished her a little.

He, himself, if he had sincerely confessed his impressions and his reflections, would have been obliged to admit that he was greatly amazed.

But this unfortunate man, who, in days to come, would be compelled to reproach himself bitterly for the excess of his fanaticism, refused to confess this truth even to himself. His life was to be spent in defending prejudices which his own reason condemned.

Forced by Mlle. Blanche's will into the midst of a discussion, he was really disgusted with the ridiculous and intense greediness of M. de Courtornieu's noble guests.

Decorations, fortune, honors, power—they desired everything.

They were satisfied that their pure devotion deserved the most munificent rewards. It was only the most modest who declared that he would be content with the epaulets of a lieutenant-general.

Many were the recriminations, stinging words, and bitter reproaches.

The Marquis de Courtornieu, who acted as president of the council, was nearly exhausted with exclaiming:

"Be calm, gentlemen, be calm! A little moderation, if you please!"

"All these men are mad," thought Martial, with difficulty restraining an intense desire to laugh; "they are insane enough to be placed in a mad-house."

But he was not obliged to render a report of the *séance*. The deliberations were soon fortunately interrupted by a summons to dinner.

Mlle. Blanche, when the young marquis rejoined her, quite forgot to question him about the doings of the council.

In fact, what did the hopes and plans of these people matter to her.

She cared very little about them or about the people themselves, since they were below her father in rank, and most of them were not as rich.

An absorbing thought—a thought of her future, and of her happiness, filled her mind to the exclusion of all other subjects.

The few moments that she had passed alone, after Marie-Anne's departure, she had spent in grave reflection.

Martial's mind and person pleased her. In him were combined all the qualifications which any ambitious woman would desire in a husband—and she decided that he should be *her* husband. Probably she would not have arrived at this conclusion so quickly, had it not been for the feeling of jealousy aroused in her heart. But from the very moment that she could believe or suspect that another woman was likely to dispute the possession of Martial with her, she desired him.

From that moment she was completely controlled by one of those strange passions in which the heart has no part, but which take entire possession of the brain and lead to the worst of follies.

Let the woman whose pulse has never quickened its beating under the influence of this counterfeit of love, cast the first stone.

That she could be vanquished in this struggle for supremacy; that there could be any doubt of the result, were thoughts which never once entered the mind of Mlle. Blanche.

She had been told so often, it had been repeated again and again, that the man whom she would choose must esteem himself fortunate above all others.

She had seen her father besieged by so many suitors for her hand.

" Besides," she thought, smiling proudly, as she surveyed her reflection in the large mirrors; " am I not as pretty as Marie-Anne? "

" Far prettier! " murmured the voice of vanity; " and you possess what your rival does not: birth, wit, the genius of coquetry! "

She did, indeed, possess sufficient cleverness and patience to assume and to sustain the character which seemed most likely to dazzle and to fascinate Martial.

As to maintaining this character *after* marriage, if it did not please her to do so, that was another matter!

The result of all this was that during dinner Mlle. Blanche exercised all her powers of fascination upon the young marquis.

She was so evidently desirous of pleasing him that several of the guests remarked it.

Some were even shocked by such a breach of conventionality. But Blanche de Courtornieu could do as she chose; she was well aware of that. Was she not the richest heiress for miles and miles around? No slander can tarnish the brilliancy of a fortune of more than a million in hard cash.

"Do you know that those two young people will have a joint income of between seven and eight hundred thousand francs!" said one old viscount to his neighbor.

Martial yielded unresistingly to the charm of his position.

How could he suspect unworthy motives in a young girl whose eyes were so pure, whose laugh rang out with the crystalline clearness of childhood!

Involuntarily he compared her with the grave and thoughtful Marie-Anne, and his imagination floated from one to the other, inflamed by the strangeness of the contrast.

He occupied a seat beside Mlle. Blanche at table; and they chatted gayly, amusing themselves at the expense of the other guests, who were again conversing upon political matters, and whose enthusiasm waxed warmer and warmer as course succeeded course.

Champagne was served with the dessert; and the company drank to the allies whose victorious bayonets had forced a passage for the King to return to Paris;

they drank to the English, to the Prussians, and to the Russians, whose horses were trampling the crops under foot.

The name of D'Escorval heard, above the clink of the glasses, suddenly aroused Martial from his dream of enchantment.

An old gentleman had just risen, and proposed that active measures should be taken to rid the neighborhood of the Baron d'Escorval.

"The presence of such a man dishonors our country," said he, " he is a frantic Jacobin, and admitted to be dangerous, since Monsieur Fouché has him upon his list of suspected persons; and he is even now under the surveillance of the police."

This discourse could not have failed to arouse intense anxiety in M. d'Escorval's breast had he seen the ferocity expressed on almost every face.

Still no one spoke: hesitation could be read in every eye.

Martial, too, had turned so white that Mlle. Blanche remarked his pallor and thought he was ill.

In fact, a terrible struggle was going on in the soul of the young marquis; a conflict between his honor and passion.

Had he not longed only a few hours before to find some way of driving Maurice from the country?

Ah, well! the opportunity he so ardently desired now presented itself. It was impossible to imagine a better one. If the proposed step was taken the Baron d'Escorval and his family would be forced to leave France forever!

The company hesitated; Martial saw it, and felt that a single word from him, for or against, would decide the matter.

After a few minutes of frightful uncertainty, honor triumphed.

He rose and declared that the proposed measure was bad—impolitic.

"Monsieur d'Escorval," he remarked, "is one of those men who diffuse around them a perfume of honesty and justice. Have the good sense to respect the consideration which is justly his."

As he had foreseen, his words decided the matter. The cold and haughty manner which he knew so well how to assume, his few but incisive words, produced a great effect.

"It would evidently be a great mistake!" was the general cry.

Martial reseated himself; Mlle. Blanche leaned toward him.

"You have done well," she murmured; "you know how to defend your friends."

"Monsieur d'Escorval is not my friend," replied Martial, in a voice which revealed the struggle through which he had passed. "The injustice of the proposed measure incensed me, that is all."

Mlle. de Courtornieu was not to be deceived by an explanation like this. Still she added:

"Then your conduct is all the more grand, Monsieur."

But such was not the opinion of the Duc de Sairmeuse. On returning to the château some hours later he reproached his son for his intervention.

"Why the devil did you meddle with the matter?" inquired the duke. "I would not have liked to take upon myself the odium of the proposition, but since it had been made——"

"I was anxious to prevent such an act of useless folly!"

" Useless folly! Zounds! Marquis, you carry matters with a high hand. Do you think that this d——d baron adores you? What would you say if you heard that he was conspiring against us? "

" I should answer with a shrug of the shoulders."

" You would! Very well; do me the favor to question Chupin."

CHAPTER XV

It was only two weeks since the Duc de Sairmeuse had returned to France; he had not yet had time to shake the dust of exile from his feet, and already his imagination saw enemies on every side.

He had been at Sairmeuse only two days, and yet he unhesitatingly accepted the venomous reports which Chupin poured into his ears.

The suspicions which he was endeavoring to make Martial share were cruelly unjust.

At the moment when the duke accused the baron of conspiring against the house of Sairmeuse, that unfortunate man was weeping at the bedside of his son, who was, he believed, at the point of death.

Maurice was indeed dangerously ill.

His excessively nervous organization had succumbed before the rude assaults of destiny.

When, in obedience to M. Lacheneur's imperative order, he left the grove on the Reche, he lost the power of reflecting calmly and deliberately upon the situation.

Marie-Anne's incomprehensible obstinacy, the insults he had received from the marquis, and Lacheneur's feigned anger were mingled in inextricable confusion, forming one immense, intolerable misfortune, too crushing for his powers of resistance.

The peasants who met him on his homeward way were struck by his singular demeanor, and felt convinced that some great catastrophe had just befallen the house of the Baron d'Escorval.

Some bowed; others spoke to him, but he did not see or hear them.

Force of habit—that physical memory which mounts guard when the mind is far away—brought him back to his home.

His features were so distorted with suffering that Mme. d'Escorval, on seeing him,.was seized with a most sinister presentiment, and dared not address him.

He spoke first.

"All is over!" he said, hoarsely, " but do not be worried, mother; I have some courage, as you shall see."

He did, in fact, seat himself at the table with a resolute air. He ate even more than usual; and his father noticed, without alluding to it, that he drank much more wine than usual.

He was very pale, his eyes glittered, his gestures were excited, and his voice was husky. He talked a great deal, and even jested.

" Why will he not weep," thought Mme. d'Escorval; " then I should not be so much alarmed, and I could try to comfort him."

This was Maurice's last effort. When dinner was over he went to his room, and when his mother, who had gone again and again to listen at his door, finally decided to enter his chamber, she found him lying upon the bed, muttering incoherently.

She approached him. He did not appear to recognize or even to see her. She spoke to him. He did not seem to hear. His face was scarlet, his lips were parched. She took his hand; it was burning; and still he was shivering, and his teeth were chattering as if with cold.

A mist swam before the eyes of the poor woman; she feared she was about to faint; but, summoning all her strength, she conquered her weakness and, dragging herself to the staircase, she cried:

" Help! help! My son is dying!"

With a bound M. d'Escorval reached his son's chamber, looked at him and dashed out again, summoned a servant, and ordered him to gallop to Montaignac and bring a physician without a moment's delay.

There was, indeed, a doctor at Sairmeuse, but he was the most stupid of men—a former surgeon in the army, who had been dismissed for incompetency. The peasants shunned him as they would the plague; and in case of sickness always sent for the *curé*. M. d'Escorval followed their example, knowing that the physician from Montaignac could not arrive until nearly morning.

Abbé Midon had never frequented the medical schools, but since he had been a priest the poor so often asked advice of him that he applied himself to the study of medicine, and, aided by experience, he had acquired a knowledge of the art which would have won him a diploma from the faculty anywhere.

At whatever hour of the day or night parishioners came to ask his assistance, he was always ready—his only answer: " Let us go at once."

And when the people of the neighborhood met him on the road with his little box of medicine slung over his shoulder, they took off their hats respectfully and stood aside to let him pass. Those who did not respect the priest honored the man.

For M. d'Escorval, above all others, Abbé Midon would make haste. The baron was his friend; and a terrible apprehension seized him when he saw Mme. d'Escorval at the gate watching for him. By the way in which she rushed to meet him, he thought she was about to announce some irreparable misfortune. But no—she took his hand, and, without uttering a word, she led him to her son's chamber.

The condition of the poor youth was really very critical; the *abbé* perceived this at a glance, but it was not hopeless.

" We will get him out of this," he said, with a smile that reawakened hope.

And with the coolness of an old practitioner, he bled him freely, and ordered applications of ice to his head.

In a moment all the household were busied in fulfilling the *curé's* orders. He took advantage of the opportunity to draw the baron aside in the embrasure of a window.

" What has happened? " he asked.

" A disappointment in love," M. d'Escorval replied, with a despairing gesture. " Monsieur Lacheneur has refused the hand of his daughter, which I asked in behalf of my son. Maurice was to have seen Marie-Anne to-day. What passed between them I do not know. The result you see."

The baroness re-entered the room, and the two men said no more. A truly funereal silence pervaded the apartment, broken only by the moans of Maurice.

His excitement instead of abating had increased in violence. Delirium peopled his brain with phantoms; and the name of Marie-Anne, Martial de Sairmeuse, and Chanlouineau dropped so incoherently from his lips that it was impossible to read his thoughts.

How long that night seemed to M. d'Escorval and his wife, those only know who have counted each second beside the sick-bed of some loved one.

Certainly their confidence in the companion in their vigil was great; but he was not a regular physician like the other, the one whose coming they awaited.

Just as the light of the morning made the candles turn pale, they heard the furious gallop of a horse, and soon the doctor from Montaignac entered.

He examined Maurice carefully, and, after a short conference with the priest:

"I see no immediate danger," he declared. "All that can be done has been done. The malady must be allowed to take its course. I will return."

He did return the next day and many days after, for it was not until a week had passed that Maurice was declared out of danger.

Then he confided to his father all that had taken place in the grove on the Reche. The slightest detail of the scene had engraved itself indelibly upon his memory. When the recital was ended:

"Are you quite sure," asked his father, "that you correctly understood Marie-Anne's reply? Did she tell you that if her father gave his consent to your marriage, she would refuse hers?"

"Those were her very words."

"And still she loves you?"

"I am sure of it."

"You were not mistaken in Monsieur Lacheneur's tone when he said to you: ' Go, you little wretch! do you wish to render all my precautions useless?'"

"No."

M. d'Escorval sat for a moment in silence.

"This passes comprehension," he murmured at last.

And so low that his son could not hear him, he added:
" I will see Lacheneur to-morrow; this mystery
must be explained."

CHAPTER XVI

The cottage where M. Lacheneur had taken refuge
was situated on a hill overlooking the water.

It was, as he had said, a small and humble dwelling,
but it was rather less miserable than the abodes of most
of the peasants of the district.

It was only one story high, but it was divided into
three rooms, and the roof was covered with thatch.

In front was a tiny garden, in which a few fruit-trees,
some withered cabbages, and a vine which covered the
cottage to the roof, managed to find subsistence.

This garden was a mere nothing, but even this slight
conquest over the sterility of the soil had cost Lacheneur's deceased aunt almost unlimited courage and
patience.

For more than twenty years the poor woman had
never, for a single day, failed to throw upon her garden
three or four basketfuls of richer soil, which she was
obliged to bring more than half a league.

It had been more than a year since she died; but the
little pathway which her patient feet had worn in the
performance of this daily task was still distinctly visible.

This was the path which M. d'Escorval, faithful to
his resolution, took the following day, in the hope of
wresting from Marie-Anne's father the secret of his inexplicable conduct.

He was so engrossed in his own thoughts that he
failed to notice the overpowering heat as he climbed

the rough hill-side in the full glare of the noonday sun.

When he reached the summit, however, he paused to take breath ; and while wiping the perspiration from his brow, he turned to look back on the road which he had traversed.

It was the first time he had visited the spot, and he was surprised at the extent of the landscape which stretched before him.

From this point, which is the most elevated in the surrounding country, one can survey the entire valley of the Oiselle, and discern, in the distance, the redoubtable citadel of Montaignac, built upon an almost inaccessible rock.

This last circumstance, which the baron was afterward doomed to recall in the midst of the most terrible scenes, did not strike him then. Lacheneur's house absorbed all his attention.

His imagination pictured vividly the sufferings of this unfortunate man, who, only two days before, had relinquished the splendors of the Château de Sairmeuse to repair to this wretched abode.

He rapped at the door of the cottage.

" Come in ! " said a voice.

The baron lifted the latch and entered.

The room was small, with unwhitewashed walls, but with no other floor than the ground ; no ceiling save the thatch that formed the roof.

A bed, a table and two wooden benches constituted the entire furniture.

Seated upon a stool, near the tiny window, sat Marie-Anne, busily at work upon a piece of embroidery.

She had abandoned her former mode of dress, and her costume was that worn by the peasant girls.

When M. d'Escorval entered she rose, and for a moment they remained silently standing, face to face, she apparently calm, he visibly agitated.

He was looking at Marie-Anne; and she seemed to him transfigured. She was much paler and considerably thinner; but her beauty had a strange and touching charm—the sublime radiance of heroic resignation and of duty nobly fulfilled.

Still, remembering his son, he was astonished to see this tranquillity.

" You do not ask me for news of Maurice," he said, reproachfully.

" I had news of him this morning, Monsieur, as I have had every day. I know that he is improving; and that, since day before yesterday, he has been allowed to take a little nourishment."

" You have not forgotten him, then ? "

She trembled; a faint blush suffused throat and forehead, but it was in a calm voice that she replied:

" Maurice knows that it would be impossible for me to forget him, even if I wished to do so."

" And yet you have told him that you approve your father's decision ! "

" I told him so, Monsieur, and I shall have the courage to repeat it."

" But you have made Maurice wretched, unhappy, child; he has almost died."

She raised her head proudly, sought M. d'Escorval's eyes, and when she had found them:

" Look at me, Monsieur. Do you think that I, too, do not suffer ? "

M. d'Escorval was abashed for a moment; but recovering himself, he took Marie-Anne's hand, and pressing it affectionately, he said:

" So Maurice loves you; you love him; you suffer;
he has nearly died, and still you reject him!"

" It must be so, Monsieur."

" You say this, my dear child—you say this, and
you undoubtedly believe it. But I, who have sought
to discover the necessity of this immense sacrifice, have
failed to find it. Explain to me, then, why this must
be so, Marie-Anne. Who knows but you are frightened by chimeras, which my experience can scatter
with a breath? Have you no confidence in me? Am
I not an old friend? It may be that your father, in his
despair, has adopted extreme resolutions. Speak, let
us combat them together. Lacheneur knows how devotedly I am attached to him. I will speak to him; he
will listen to *me*."

" I can tell you nothing, Monsieur."

" What! you are so cruel as to remain inflexible
when a father entreats you on his knees—a father who
says to you: ' Marie-Anne, you hold in your hands the
happiness, the life, the reason of my son—— ' "

Tears glittered in Marie-Anne's eyes, but she drew
away her hand.

" Ah! it is you who are cruel, Monsieur; it is you
who are without pity. Do you not see what I suffer,
and that it is impossible for me to endure further torture ? No, I have nothing to tell you; there is nothing you can say to my father. Why do you seek to
impair my courage when I require it all to struggle
against my despair? Maurice must forget me; he
must never see me again. This is fate; and he must
not fight against it. It would be folly. We are parted forever. Beseech Maurice to leave the country, and
if he refuses, you, who are his father, must command
him to do so. And you, too, Monsieur, in Heaven's

name, flee from us. We shall bring misfortune upon you. Never return here; our house is accursed. The fate that overshadows us will ruin you also."

She spoke almost wildly. Her voice was so loud that it penetrated an adjoining room.

The communicating door opened and M. Lacheneur appeared upon the threshold.

At the sight of M. d'Escorval he uttered an oath. But there was more sorrow and anxiety than anger in his manner, as he said:

" You, Monsieur, you here !"

The consternation into which Marie-Anne's words had thrown M. d'Escorval was so intense that it was with great difficulty he stammered out a response.

" You have abandoned us entirely; I was anxious about you. Have you forgotten our old friendship? I come to you——"

The brow of the former master of Sairmeuse remained overcast.

" Why did you not inform me of the honor that the baron had done me, Marie-Anne ? " he said sternly.

She tried to speak, but could not; and it was the baron who replied:

" Why, I have but just come, my dear friend."

M. Lacheneur looked suspiciously, first at his daughter, then at the baron.

" What did they say to each other while they were alone? " he was evidently wondering.

But, however great may have been his disquietude, he seemed to master it; and it was with his old-time affability of manner that he invited M. d'Escorval to follow him into the adjoining room.

" It is my reception-room and my cabinet combined," he said, smiling.

This room, which was much larger than the first, was as scantily furnished; but it contained several piles of small books and an infinite number of tiny packages.

Two men were engaged in arranging and sorting these articles.

One was Chanlouineau.

M. d'Escorval did not remember that he had ever seen the other, who was a young man.

"This is my son, Jean, Monsieur," said Lacheneur. "He has changed since you last saw him ten years ago."

It was true. It had been, at least, ten years since the baron had seen Lacheneur's son.

How time flies! He had left him a boy; he found him a man.

Jean was just twenty; but his haggard features and his precocious beard made him appear much older.

He was tall and well formed, and his face indicated more than average intelligence.

Still he did not impress one favorably. His restless eyes were always invading yours; and his smile betrayed an unusual degree of shrewdness, amounting almost to cunning.

As his father presented him, he bowed profoundly; but he was very evidently out of temper.

M. Lacheneur resumed:

"Having no longer the means to maintain Jean in Paris, I have made him return. My ruin will, perhaps, be a blessing to him. The air of great cities is not good for the son of a peasant. Fools that we are, we send them there to teach them to rise above their fathers. But they do nothing of the kind. They think only of degrading themselves."

"Father," interrupted the young man; "father, wait, at least, until we are alone!"

"Monsieur d'Escorval is not a stranger."

Chanlouineau evidently sided with the son, since he made repeated signs to M. Lacheneur to be silent.

Either he did not see them, or he pretended not to see them, for he continued:

"I must have wearied you, Monsieur, by telling you again and again: 'I am pleased with my son. He has a commendable ambition; he is working faithfully; he will succeed.' Ah! I was a poor, foolish father! The friend who carried Jean the order to return has enlightened me, to my sorrow. This model young man you see here left the gaming-house only to run to public balls. He was in love with a wretched little ballet-girl in some low theatre; and to please this creature, he also went upon the stage, with his face painted red and white."

"To appear upon the stage is not a crime."

"No; but it is a crime to deceive one's father and to affect virtues which one does not possess! Have I ever refused you money? No. Notwithstanding that, you have contracted debts everywhere, and you owe at least twenty thousand francs."

Jean hung his head; he was evidently angry, but he feared his father.

"Twenty thousand francs!" repeated M. Lacheneur. "I had them a fortnight ago; now I have nothing. I can hope to obtain this sum only through the generosity of the Duc de Sairmeuse and his son."

These words from Lacheneur's lips astonished the baron.

Lacheneur perceived it, and it was with every appearance of sincerity and good faith that he resumed:

" Does what I say surprise you? I understand why. My anger at first made me give utterance to all sorts of absurd threats. But I am calm now, and I realize my injustice. What could I expect the duke to do? To make me a present of Sairmeuse? He was a trifle brusque, I confess, but that is his way; at heart he is the best of men."

" Have you seen him again? "

" No; but I have seen his son. I have even been with him to the château to designate the articles which I desire to keep. Oh! he refused me nothing. Everything was placed at my disposal—everything. I selected what I wished—furniture, clothing, linen. It is all to be brought here; and I shall be quite a *grand seigneur.*"

" Why not seek another house? This——"

" This pleases me, Monsieur. Its situation suits me perfectly."

In fact, why should not the Sairmeuse have regretted their odious conduct? Was it impossible that Lacheneur, in spite of his indignation, should conclude to accept honorable separation? Such were M. d'Escorval's reflections.

" To say that the marquis has been kind is saying too little," continued Lacheneur. " He has shown us the most delicate attentions. For example, having noticed how much Marie-Anne regrets the loss of her flowers, he has declared that he is going to send her plants to stock our small garden, and that they shall be renewed every month."

Like all passionate men, M. Lacheneur overdid his part. This last remark was too much; it awakened a sinister suspicion in M. d'Escorval's mind.

" Good God! " he thought, " does this wretched man meditate some crime? "

He glanced at Chanlouineau, and his anxiety increased. On hearing the names of the marquis and of Marie-Anne, the robust farmer had turned livid.

"It is decided," said Lacheneur, with an air of the utmost satisfaction, "that they will give me the ten thousand francs bequeathed to me by Mademoiselle Armande. Moreover, I am to fix upon such a sum as I consider a just recompense for my services. And that is not all; they have offered me the position of manager at Sairmeuse; and I was to be allowed to occupy the gamekeeper's cottage, where I lived so long. But on reflection I refused this offer. After having enjoyed for so long a time a fortune which did not belong to me, I am anxious to amass a fortune of my own."

"Would it be indiscreet in me to inquire what you intend to do?"

"Not the least in the world. I am going to turn pedler."

M. d'Escorval could not believe his ears.

"Pedler?" he repeated.

"Yes, Monsieur. Look, there is my pack in that corner."

"But this is absurd!" exclaimed M. d'Escorval. "People can scarcely earn their daily bread in this way."

"You are wrong, Monsieur. I have considered the subject carefully; the profits are thirty per cent. And besides, there will be three of us to sell goods, for I shall confide one pack to my son, and another to Chanlouineau."

"What! Chanlouineau?"

"He has become my partner in the enterprise."

"And his farm—who will take care of that?"

" He will employ day-laborers."

And then, as if wishing to make M. d'Escorval understand that his visit had lasted quite long enough, Lacheneur began arranging the little packages which were destined to fill the pack of the travelling merchant.

But the baron was not to be gotten rid of so easily, now that his suspicions had become almost a certainty.

" I must speak with you," he said, brusquely.

M. Lacheneur turned.

" I am very busy," he replied, with a very evident reluctance.

" I ask only five minutes. But if you have not the time to spare to-day, I will return to-morrow—day after to-morrow—and every day until I can see you in private."

Lacheneur saw plainly that it would be impossible to escape this interview, so, with the gesture of a man who resigns himself to a necessity, addressing his son and Chanlouineau, he said:

" Go outside for a few moments."

They obeyed, and as soon as the door had closed behind them, Lacheneur said:

" I know very well, Monsieur, the arguments you intend to advance; and the reason of your coming. You come to ask me again for Marie-Anne. I know that my refusal has nearly killed Maurice. Believe me, I have suffered cruelly at the thought; but my refusal is none the less irrevocable. There is no power in the world capable of changing my resolution. Do not ask my motives; I shall not reveal them; but rest assured that they are sufficient."

" Are we not your friends? "

" You, Monsieur! " exclaimed Lacheneur, in tones

of the most lively affection, "you! ah! you know it well! You are the best, the only friends, I have here below. I should be the basest and the most miserable of men if I did not guard the recollection of all your kindnesses until my eyes close in death. Yes, you are my friends; yes, I am devoted to you—and it is for that very reason that I answer: no, no, never!"

There could no longer be any doubt. M. d'Escorval seized Lacheneur's hands, and almost crushing them in his grasp:

"Unfortunate man!" he exclaimed, hoarsely, "what do you intend to do? Of what terrible vengeance are you dreaming?"

"I swear to you——"

"Oh! do not swear. You cannot deceive a man of my age and of my experience. I divine your intentions—you hate the Sairmeuse family more mortally than ever."

"I——"

"Yes, you; and if you pretend to forget it, it is only that they may forget it. These people have offended you too cruelly not to fear you; you understand this, and you are doing all in your power to reassure them. You accept their advances—you kneel before them— why? Because they will be more completely in your power when you have lulled their suspicions to rest, and then you can strike them more surely——"

He paused; the communicating door opened, and Marie-Anne appeared upon the threshold.

"Father," said she, "here is the Marquis de Sairmeuse."

This name, which Marie-Anne uttered in a voice of such perfect composure, in the midst of this excited discussion, possessed such a powerful significance, that M. d'Escorval stood as if petrified.

" He dares to come here ! " he thought.   " How can it be that he does not fear the walls will fall and crush him ? "

M. Lacheneur cast a withering glance at his daughter.   He suspected her of a ruse which would force him to reveal his secret.   For a second, the most furious passion contracted his features.

But, by a prodigious effort of will, he succeeded in regaining his composure.   He sprang to the door, pushed Marie-Anne aside, and leaning out, he said:

" Deign to excuse me, Monsieur, if I take the liberty of asking you to wait a moment; I am just finishing some business, and I will be with you in a moment."

Neither agitation nor anger could be detected in his voice; but, rather, a respectful deference, and a feeling of profound gratitude.

Having said this, he closed the door and turned to M. d'Escorval.

The baron, still standing with folded arms, had witnessed this scene with the air of a man who distrusts the evidence of his own senses ; and yet he understood the meaning of it only too well.

" So this young man comes here ? " he said to Lacheneur.

"Almost every day—not at this hour, usually, but a trifle later."

" And you receive him ? you welcome him ? "

" Certainly, Monsieur. How can I be insensible to the honor he confers upon me ? Moreover, we have subjects of mutual interest to discuss. We are now occupied in legalizing the restitution of Sairmeuse. I can, also, give him much useful information, and many hints regarding the management of the property."

" And do you expect to make me, your old friend,

believe that a man of your superior intelligence is deceived by the excuses the marquis makes for these frequent visits ? Look me in the eye, and then tell me, if
you dare, that you believe these visits are addressed to
you ! "

Lacheneur's eye did not waver.

" To whom else could they be addressed ? " he inquired.

This obstinate serenity disappointed the baron's expectations. He could not have received a heavier
blow.

" Take care, Lacheneur," he said, sternly. " Think
of the situation in which you place your daughter, between Chanlouineau, who wishes to make her his wife,
and Monsieur de Sairmeuse, who desires to make
her ——"

" Who desires to make her his mistress—is that
what you mean? Oh, say the word. But what does
that matter? I am sure of Marie-Anne."

M. d'Escorval shuddered.

" In other words," said he, in bitter indignation,
" you make your daughter's honor and reputation your
stake in the game you are playing."

This was too much. Lacheneur could restrain his
furious passion no longer.

" Well, yes ! " he exclaimed, with a frightful oath ;
" yes, you have spoken the truth. Marie-Anne must
be, and will be, the instrument of my plans. A man
situated as I am is free from the considerations that restrain other men. Fortune, friends, life, honor—I
have been forced to sacrifice all. Perish my daughter's
virtue—perish my daughter herself—what do they
matter, if I can but succeed ? "

He was terrible in his fanaticism ; and in his mad

excitement he clinched his hands as if he were threatening some invisible enemy; his eyes were wild and
bloodshot.

The baron seized him by the coat as if to prevent his
escape.

" You admit it, then ? " he said.   " You wish to revenge yourself on the Sairmeuse family, and you have
made Chanlouineau your accomplice ? "

But Lacheneur, with a sudden movement, freed himself.

" I admit nothing," he replied.   " And yet I wish to
reassure you——"

He raised his hand as if to take an oath, and in a
solemn voice, he said:

" Before God, who hears my words, by all that I hold
sacred in this world, by the memory of my sainted wife
who lies beneath the sod, I swear that I am plotting
nothing against the Sairmeuse family; that I had no
thought of touching a hair of their heads.   I use them
only because they are absolutely indispensable to me.
They will aid me without injuring themselves."

Lacheneur, this time, spoke the truth.   His hearer
felt it; still he pretended to doubt.   He thought by re-
taining his own self-possession, and exciting the anger
of this unfortunate man still more, he might, perhaps,
discover his real intentions.   So it was with an air of
suspicion that he said:

" How can one believe this assurance after the
avowal you have just made ? "

Lacheneur saw the snare; he regained his self-possession as if by magic.

" So be it, Monsieur, refuse to believe me.   But you
will wring from me only one more word on this subject.   I have said too much already.   I know that you

are guided solely by friendship for me; my gratitude
is great, but I cannot reply to your question. The
events of the past few days have dug a deep abyss between you and me. Do not endeavor to pass it. Why
should we ever meet again? I must say to you, what
I said only yesterday to Abbé Midon. If you are my
friend, you will never come here again—never—by
night or by day, or under any pretext whatever. Even
if they tell you that I am dying, do not come. This
house is fatal. And if you meet me, turn away; shun
me as you would a pestilence whose touch is deadly!"

The baron was silent. This was in substance what
Marie-Anne had said to him, only under another form.

"But there is still a wiser course that you might
pursue. Everything here is certain to augment the
sorrow and despair which afflicts your son. There is
not a path, nor a tree, nor a flower which does not cruelly remind him of his former happiness. Leave this
place; take him with you, and go far away."

"Ah! how can I do this? Fouché has virtually imprisoned me here."

"All the more reason why you should listen to my
advice. You were a friend of the Emperor, hence you
are regarded with suspicion; you are surrounded by
spies. Your enemies are watching for an opportunity
to ruin you. The slightest pretext would suffice to
throw you into prison—a letter, a word, an act capable
of being misconstrued. The frontier is not far off; go,
and wait in a foreign land for happier times."

"That is something which I will not do," said M.
d'Escorval, proudly.

His words and accent showed the folly of further discussion. Lacheneur understood this only too well,
and seemed to despair.

"Ah ! you are like Abbé Midon," he said, sadly; " you will not believe. Who knows how much your coming here this morning will cost you? It is said that no one can escape his destiny. But if some day the hand of the executioner is laid upon your shoulder, remember that I warned you, and do not curse me."

He paused, and seeing that even this sinister prophecy produced no impression upon the baron, he pressed his hand as if to bid him an eternal farewell, and opened the door to admit the Marquis de Sairmeuse.

Martial was, perhaps, annoyed at meeting M. d'Escorval; but he nevertheless bowed with studied politeness, and began a lively conversation with M. Lacheneur, telling him that the articles he had selected at the château were on their way.

M. d'Escorval could do no more. To speak with Marie-Anne was impossible: Chanlouineau and Jean would not let him go out of their sight.

He reluctantly departed, and oppressed by cruel forebodings, he descended the hill which he had climbed an hour before so full of hope.

What should he say to Maurice?

He had reached the little grove of pines when a hurried footstep behind him made him turn.

The Marquis de Sairmeuse was following him, and motioned him to stop. The baron paused, greatly surprised; Martial, with that air of ingenuousness which he knew so well how to assume, and in an almost brusque tone, said:

" I hope, Monsieur, that you will excuse me for having followed you, when you hear what I have to say. I am not of your party; I loathe what you adore; but I have none of the passion nor the malice of your enemies. For this reason I tell you that if I were in your place I would take a journey. The frontier is but a few miles away: a good horse, a short gallop, and you have crossed it. A word to the wise is—salvation!"

And without waiting for any response, he turned and retraced his steps.

M. d'Escorval was amazed and confounded.

"One might suppose there was a conspiracy to drive me away!" he murmured. "But I have good reason to distrust the disinterestedness of this young man."

Martial was already far off. Had he been less pre-occupied, he would have perceived two figures in the wood. Mlle. Blanche de Courtornieu, followed by the inevitable Aunt Medea, had come to play the spy.

CHAPTER XVII

The Marquis de Courtornieu idolized his daughter. Everyone spoke of that as an incontestable and uncontested fact.

When persons spoke to him of his daughter, they always said:

"You, who adore your daughter——"

And when he spoke of himself, *he* said:

"I who adore Blanche."

The truth was, that he would have given a good deal, even a third of his fortune, to be rid of her.

This smiling young girl, who seemed such an artless child, had gained an absolute control over him. She forced him to bow like a reed to her every caprice—and Heaven knows she had enough of them !

In the hope of making his escape, he had thrown her Aunt Medea; but in less than three months that poor woman had been completely subjugated, and did not

144 THE HONOR OF THE NAME

serve to divert his daughter's attention from him, even for a moment.

Sometimes the marquis revolted, but nine times out of ten he paid dearly for his attempts at rebellion. When Mlle. Blanche turned her cold and steel-like eyes upon him with a certain peculiar expression, his courage evaporated. Her weapon was irony; and knowing his weak points, she struck with wonderful precision.

It is easy to understand how devoutly he prayed and hoped that some honest young man, by speedily marrying his daughter, would free him from this cruel bondage.

But where was he to find this liberator?

The marquis had announced everywhere his intention of bestowing a dowry of a million upon his daughter. Of course this had brought a host of eager suitors, not only from the immediate neighborhood, but from parts remote.

But, unfortunately, though many of them would have suited M. de Courtornieu well enough, not a single one had been so fortunate as to please Mlle. Blanche.

Her father presented some suitor; she received him graciously, lavished all her charms upon him; but as soon as his back was turned, she disappointed all her father's hopes by rejecting him.

"He is too small," she said, "or too large. His rank is not equal to ours. I think him stupid. He is a fool—his nose is so ugly."

From these summary decisions there was no appeal. Arguments and persuasions were useless. The condemned man no longer existed.

Still, as this view of aspirants to her hand amused

her, she encouraged her father in his efforts. He was
beginning to despair, when fate dropped the Duc de
Sairmeuse and son at his very door. When he saw
Martial, he had a presentiment of his approaching release.

" He will be my son-in-law," he thought.

The marquis believed it best to strike the iron while
it was hot. So, the very next day, he broached the
subject to the duke.

His overtures were favorably received.

Possessed with the desire of transforming Sairmeuse
into a little principality, the duke could not fail to be
delighted with an alliance with one of the oldest and
wealthiest families in the neighborhood.

The conference was short.

" Martial, my son, possesses, in his own right, an income of at least six hundred thousand francs," said the
duke.

" I shall give my daughter at least—yes, at least fifteen hundred thousand francs as her marriage portion," declared the marquis.

" His Majesty is favorably disposed toward me. I
can obtain any important diplomatic position for Martial."

" In case of trouble, I have many friends among the
opposition."

The treaty was thus concluded; but M. de Courtornieu took good care not to speak of it to his daughter.
If he told her how much he desired the match, she
would be sure to oppose it. Non-interference seemed
advisable.

The correctness of his judgment was fully demon-
strated. One morning Mlle. Blanche made her appearance in his cabinet.

" Your capricious daughter has decided, papa, that she would like to become the Marquise de Sairmeuse," said she, peremptorily.

It cost M. de Courtornieu quite an effort to conceal his delight ; but he feared if she discovered his satisfaction that the game would be lost.

He presented several objections ; they were quickly disposed of ; and, at last, he ventured to say :

" Then the marriage is half decided ; one of the parties consents. It only remains to ascertain if——"

" The other will consent," declared the vain heiress.

And, in fact, for several days Mlle. Blanche had been applying herself assiduously and quite successfully to the work of fascination which was to bring Martial to her feet.

After having made an advance, with studied frankness and simplicity, sure of the effect she had produced, she now proceeded to beat a retreat—a manœuvre so simple that it was almost sure to succeed.

Until now she had been gay, *spirituelle*, and coquettish ; gradually, she became quiet and reserved. The giddy school-girl had given place to the shrinking virgin.

With what perfection she played her part in the divine comedy of first love ! Martial could not fail to be fascinated by the modest artlessness and chaste fears of the heart which seemed to be waking for him. When he appeared, Mlle. Blanche blushed and was silent. At a word from him she became confused. He could only occasionally catch a glimpse of her beautiful eyes through the shelter of their long lashes.

Who had taught her this refinement of coquetry? They say that the convent is an excellent teacher.

But what she had not learned was that the most

clever often become the dupes of their own imagination; and that great *comédiennes* generally conclude by shedding real tears.

She learned this one evening, when a laughing remark made by the Duc de Sairmeuse revealed the fact that Martial was in the habit of going to Lacheneur's house every day.

What she experienced now could not be compared with the jealousy, or rather anger, which had previously agitated her.

This was an acute, bitter, and intolerable sorrow. Before, she had been able to retain her composure; now, it was impossible.

That she might not betray herself, she left the drawing-room precipitately and hastened to her own room, where she burst into a fit of passionate sobbing.

"Can it be that he does not love me?" she murmured.

This thought made her cold with terror. For the first time this haughty heiress distrusted her own power.

She reflected that Martial's position was so exalted that he could afford to despise rank; that he was so rich that wealth had no attractions for him; and that she herself might not be so pretty and so charming as flatterers had led her to suppose.

Still Martial's conduct during the past week—and Heaven knows with what fidelity her memory recalled each incident—was well calculated to reassure her.

He had not, it is true, formally declared himself, but it was evident that he was paying his addresses to her. His manner was that of the most respectful, but the most infatuated of lovers.

Her reflections were interrupted by the entrance of

her maid, bringing a large bouquet of roses which had just been sent by Martial.

She took the flowers, and while arranging them in a large Japanese vase, she bedewed them with the first real sincere tears she had shed since her entrance into the world.

She was so pale and sad, so unlike herself when she appeared the next morning at breakfast, that Aunt Medea was alarmed.

Mlle. Blanche had prepared an excuse, and she uttered it in such sweet tones that the poor lady was as much amazed as if she had witnessed a miracle.

M. de Courtornieu was no less astonished.

" Of what new freak is this doleful face the preface ? " he wondered.

He was still more alarmed when, immediately after breakfast, his daughter asked a moment's conversation with him.

She followed him into his study, and as soon as they were alone, without giving her father time to seat himself, Mlle. Blanche entreated him to tell her all that had passed between the Duc de Sairmeuse and himself, and asked if Martial had been informed of the intended alliance, and what he had replied.

Her voice was meek, her eyes tearful; her manner indicated the most intense anxiety.

The marquis was delighted.

" My wilful daughter has been playing with fire," he thought, stroking his chin caressingly ; " and upon my word, she has burned herself."

" Yesterday, my child," he replied, " the Duc de Sairmeuse formally demanded your hand on behalf of his son; your consent is all that is lacking. So rest easy, my beautiful, lovelorn damsel—you will be a duchess."

She hid her face in her hands to conceal her blushes.

"You know my decision, father," she faltered, in an almost inaudible voice; "we must make haste."

He started back, thinking he had not heard her words aright.

"Make haste!" he repeated.

"Yes, father. I have fears."

"What fears, in Heaven's name?"

"I will tell you when everything is settled," she replied, as she made her escape from the room.

She did not doubt the reports which had reached her ears, of Martial's frequent visits to Marie-Anne, but she wished to see for herself.

So, as soon as she left her father, she obliged Aunt Medea to dress herself, and without vouchsafing a single word of explanation, took her with her to the Reche, and stationed herself where she could command a view of M. Lacheneur's house.

It chanced to be the very day on which M. d'Escorval came to ask an explanation from his friend. She saw him come; then, after a little, Martial made his appearance.

She had not been mistaken—now she could go home satisfied.

But no. She resolved to count the seconds which Martial passed with Marie-Anne.

M. d'Escorval did not remain long; she saw Martial hasten out after him, and speak to him.

She breathed again. His visit had not lasted a half hour, and doubtless he was going away. Not at all. After a moment's conversation with the baron, he returned to the house.

"What are we doing here?" demanded Aunt Medea.

"Let me alone!" replied Mlle. Blanche, angrily; "hold your tongue!"

She heard the sound of wheels, the tramp of horses' hoofs, blows of the whip, and oaths.

The wagons bearing the furniture and clothing belonging to M. Lacheneur were coming.

This noise Martial must have heard within the house, for he came out, and after him came M Lacheneur, Jean, Chanlouineau, and Marie-Anne.

Everyone was soon busy in unloading the wagons, and positively, from the movements of the young Marquis de Sairmeuse, one would have sworn that he was giving orders; he came and went, hurrying to and fro, talking to everybody, not even disdaining to lend a hand occasionally.

"He, a nobleman, makes himself at home in that wretched hovel!" Mlle. Blanche said to herself. "How horrible! Ah! this dangerous creature will do with him whatever she desires."

All this was nothing compared with what was to come. A third wagon appeared, drawn by a single horse, and laden with pots of flowers and shrubs.

This sight drew a cry of rage from Mlle. de Courtornieu which must have carried terror to Aunt Medea's heart.

"Flowers!" she exclaimed, in a voice hoarse with passion. "He sends flowers to her as he does to me —only he sends me a bouquet, while for her he despoils the gardens of Sairmeuse."

"What are you saying about flowers?" inquired the impoverished relative.

Mlle. Blanche replied that she had not made the slightest allusion to flowers. She was suffocating—and yet she compelled herself to remain there three mortal hours—all the time that was required to unload the furniture.

The wagons had been gone some time, when Martial again appeared upon the threshold.

Marie-Anne had accompanied him to the door, and they were talking together. It seemed impossible for him to make up his mind to depart.

He did so, at last, however; but he left slowly and with evident reluctance. Marie-Anne, remaining in the door, gave him a friendly gesture of farewell.

" I wish to speak to this creature ! " exclaimed Mlle. Blanche. " Come, aunt, at once ! "

Had Marie-Anne, at that moment, been within the reach of Mlle. de Courtornieu's voice, she would certainly have learned the secret of her former friend's anger and hatred.

But fate willed it otherwise. At least three hundred yards of rough ground separated the place where Mlle. Blanche had stationed herself, from the Lacheneur cottage.

It required a moment to cross this space; and that was time enough to change all the girl's intentions.

She had not traversed a quarter of the distance before she bitterly regretted having shown herself at all. But to retrace her steps now was impossible, for Marie-Anne, who was still standing upon the threshold, had seen her approaching.

There remained barely time to regain her self-control, and to compose her features. She profited by it.

She had her sweetest smile upon her lips as she greeted Marie-Anne. Still she was embarrassed; she did not know what excuse to give for her visit, and to gain time she pretended to be quite out of breath.

" Ah ! it is not very easy to reach you, dear Marie-

Anne," she said, at last; "you live upon the summit of a veritable mountain."

Mlle. Lacheneur said not a word. She was greatly surprised, and she did not attempt to conceal the fact.

"Aunt Medea pretended to know the road," continued Mlle. Blanche, "but she led me astray; did you not, aunt?"

As usual, the impecunious relative assented, and her niece resumed:

"But at last we are here. I could not, my dearest, resign myself to hearing nothing from you, especially after all your misfortunes. What have you been doing? Did my recommendation procure for you the work you desired?"

Marie-Anne could not fail to be deeply touched by this kindly interest on the part of her former friend. So, with perfect frankness, and without any false shame, she confessed that all her efforts had been fruitless. It had even seemed to her that several ladies had taken pleasure in treating her unkindly.

But Mlle. Blanche was not listening. A few steps from her stood the flowers brought from Sairmeuse; and their perfume rekindled her anger.

"At least," she interrupted, "you have here what will almost make you forget the gardens of Sairmeuse. Who sent you these beautiful flowers?"

Marie-Anne turned crimson. She did not speak for a moment, but at last she replied, or rather stammered:

"It is—an attention from the Marquis de Sairmeuse."

"So she confesses it!" thought Mlle. de Courtornieu, amazed at what she was pleased to consider an outrageous piece of impudence.

But she succeeded in concealing her rage beneath a loud burst of laughter; and it was in a tone of raillery that she said:

"Take care, my dear friend; I am going to call you to account.   It is from my *fiancé* that you are accepting flowers."

"What! the Marquis de Sairmeuse?"

"Has demanded the hand of your friend.   Yes, my darling; and my father has given it to him.   It is a secret as yet; but I see no danger in confiding in your friendship."

She believed that she had inflicted a mortal wound upon Marie-Anne's heart; but though she watched her closely, she failed to detect the slightest trace of emotion upon her face.

"What dissimulation!" she thought.   Then aloud, and with affected gayety, she resumed:

"And the country folks will see two weddings at about the same time, since you, also, are going to be married, my dear."

"I!"

"Yes, you, you little deceiver!   Everybody knows that you are engaged to a young man in the neighborhood, named—wait—I know—Chanlouineau."

Thus the report that annoyed Marie-Anne so much reached her from every side.

"Everybody is for once mistaken," said she, energetically.   "I shall never be that young man's wife."

"But why?   They speak well of him, personally, and he is quite rich."

"Because," faltered Marie-Anne, "because——"

Maurice d'Escorval's name trembled upon her lips; but unfortunately she did not utter it, prevented by a strange expression on the face of her friend.   How

often one's destiny depends upon a circumstance ap·
parently as trivial as this!

"Impudent, worthless creature!" thought Mlle.
Blanche.

Then, in cold and sneering tones, that betrayed her
hatred unmistakably, she said:

"You are wrong, believe me, to refuse this offer.
This Chanlouineau will, at all events, save you from
the painful necessity of laboring with your own hands,
and of going from door to door in quest of work which
is refused you. But, no matter; *I*—she laid great
stress upon this word—*I* will be more generous than
your old acquaintances. I have a great deal of embroidery to be done. I shall send it to you by my
maid, and you two may agree upon the price. We
must go. Good-by, my dear. Come, Aunt Medea."

She departed, leaving Marie-Anne petrified with surprise, sorrow, and indignation.

Although less experienced than Mlle. Blanche, she
comprehended that this strange visit concealed some
mystery—but what?

For more than a minute she stood motionless, gazing after her departing guests; then she started suddenly as a hand was laid gently upon her shoulder.

She trembled, and, turning quickly, found herself
face to face with her father.

Lacheneur's face was whiter than his linen, and a
sinister light glittered in his eye.

"I was there," said he, pointing to the door, "and
I heard all."

"Father!"

"What! would you try to defend her after she came
here to crush you with her insolent good fortune—after
she overwhelmed you with her ironical pity and with

her scorn? I tell you they are all like this—these girls, whose heads have been turned by flattery, and who believe that in their veins flows a different blood from ours. But patience! The day of reckoning is near at hand!"

Those whom he threatened would have shuddered had they seen him at that moment, so terrible was the rage revealed by his accent, so formidable did he appear.

"And you, my beloved daughter, my poor Marie-Anne, you did not understand the insults she heaped upon you. You are wondering why she should have treated you with such disdain. Ah, well! I will tell you: she imagines that the Marquis de Sairmeuse is your lover."

Marie-Anne tottered beneath the terrible blow, and a nervous spasm shook her from head to foot.

"Can this be possible?" she exclaimed. "Great God! what shame! what humiliation!"

"And why should this astonish you?" said Lacheneur, coldly. "Have you not expected this ever since the day when you, my devoted daughter, consented, for the sake of my plans, to submit to the attentions of this marquis, whom you loathe as much as I despise?"

"But Maurice! Maurice will despise me! I can bear anything, yes, everything but that."

M. Lacheneur made no reply. Marie-Anne's despair was heart-breaking; he felt that he could not bear to witness it, that it would shake his resolution, and he re-entered the house.

But his penetration was not at fault. While waiting to find a revenge which would be worthy of her, Mlle. Blanche armed herself with a weapon of which jealousy and hatred so often avail themselves—calumny.

Two or three abominable stories which she concocted, and which she forced Aunt Medea to circulate
everywhere, did not produce the desired effect.

Marie-Anne's reputation was, of course, ruined by
them; but Martial's visits, instead of ceasing, became
longer and more frequent. Dissatisfied with his prog
ress, and fearful that he was being duped, he even
watched the house.

So it happened that, one evening, when he was quite
sure that Lacheneur, his son, and Chanlouineau were
absent, Martial saw a man leave the house and hasten
across the fields.

He rushed after him, but the man escaped him.

He believed, however, that he recognized Maurice
d'Escorval.

CHAPTER XVIII

After his son's confession, M. d'Escorval was prudent enough to make no allusion to the hopes he, himself, entertained.

"My poor Maurice," he thought, "is heart-broken,
but resigned. It is better for him to remain without
hope than to be exposed to the danger of another disappointment."

But passion is not always blind. What the baron
concealed, Maurice divined; and he clung to this faint
hope as tenaciously as a drowning man clings to the
plank which is his only hope of salvation.

If he asked his parents no questions it was only because he was convinced that they would not tell him
the truth.

But he watched all that went on in the house with

that subtleness of penetration which fever so often imparts.

Not one of his father's movements escaped his vigilant eye and ear.

Consequently, he heard him put on his boots, ask for his hat, and select a cane from among those standing in the vestibule. He also heard the outer gate grate upon its hinges.

"My father is going out," he said to himself.

And weak as he was, he succeeded in dragging himself to the window in time to satisfy himself of the truth of his conjectures.

"If my father is going out," he thought, "it can only be to visit Monsieur Lacheneur—then he has not relinquished all hope."

An arm-chair was standing nearby; he sank into it, intending to watch for his father's return; by doing so, he might know his destiny a few moments sooner.

Three long hours passed before the baron returned.

By his father's dejected manner he plainly saw that all hope was lost. He was sure of it; as sure as the criminal who reads the fatal verdict in the solemn face of the judge.

He had need of all his energy to regain his couch. For a moment he felt that he was dying.

But he was ashamed of this weakness, which he judged unworthy of him. He determined to know what had passed—to know the details.

He rang, and told the servant that he wished to speak to his father. M. d'Escorval promptly made his appearance.

"Well?" cried Maurice.

M. d'Escorval felt that denial was useless.

"Lacheneur is deaf to my remonstrances and to my

entreaties," he replied, sadly. "Nothing remains for you but to submit, my son. I shall not tell you that time will assuage the sorrow that now seems insupportable—you would not believe me. But I do say to you, that you are a man, and that you must prove your courage. I say even more: fight against thoughts of Marie-Anne as a traveller on the verge of a precipice fights against the thought of vertigo."

"Have you seen Marie-Anne, father? Have you spoken to her?"

"I found her even more inflexible than Lacheneur."

"They reject me, and they receive Chanlouineau, perhaps."

"Chanlouineau is living there."

"My God! And Martial de Sairmeuse?"

"He is their familiar guest. I saw him there."

That each of these responses fell upon Maurice like a thunder-bolt was only too evident.

But M. d'Escorval had armed himself with the impassable courage of a surgeon who does not relax his hold on his instruments because the patient groans and writhes in agony.

M. d'Escorval wished to extinguish the last ray of hope in the heart of his son.

"It is evident that Monsieur Lacheneur has lost his reason!" exclaimed Maurice.

The baron shook his head despondently.

"I thought so myself, at first," he murmured.

"But what does he say in justification of his conduct? He must say something."

"Nothing; he refuses any explanation."

"And you, father, with all your knowledge of human nature, with all your wide experience, have not been able to fathom his intentions?"

"I have my suspicions," M. d'Escorval replied; "but only suspicions. It is possible that Lacheneur, listening to the voice of hatred, is dreaming of a terrible revenge. Who knows if he does not think of organizing some conspiracy, of which he is to be the leader? These suppositions would explain everything. Chanlouineau is his aider and abettor; and he pretends to be reconciled to the Marquis de Sairmeuse in order to get information through him——"

The blood had returned to the pale cheeks of Maurice.

"Such a conspiracy would not explain Monsieur Lacheneur's obstinate rejection of my suit."

"Alas! yes, my poor boy. It is through Marie-Anne that Lacheneur exerts such an influence over Chanlouineau and the Marquis de Sairmeuse. If she became your wife to-day, they would desert him to-morrow. Then, too, it is precisely because he loves us that he is determined we shall not be mixed up in an enterprise the success of which is extremely doubtful. But these are mere conjectures."

"Then I see that it is necessary to submit, to be resigned; forget, I cannot," faltered Maurice.

He said this because he wished to reassure his father; but he thought exactly the opposite.

"If Lacheneur is organizing a conspiracy," he said, to himself, "he must need assistance. Why should I not offer mine? If I aid him in his preparations, if I share his hopes and his dangers, it will be impossible for him to refuse me the hand of his daughter. Whatever he may desire to undertake, I can surely be of greater assistance than Chanlouineau."

From that moment Maurice thought only of doing everything possible to hasten his convalescence. This was so rapid, so extraordinarily rapid, as to astonish Abbé Midon, who had taken the place of the physician from Montaignac.

"I never would have believed that Maurice could have been thus consoled," said Mme. d'Escorval, delighted to see her son's wonderful improvement in health and spirits.

But the baron made no response. He regarded this almost miraculous recovery with distrust; he was assailed by a vague suspicion of the truth.

He questioned his son, but skilfully as he did it, he could draw nothing from him.

Maurice had decided to say nothing to his parents. What good would it do to trouble them? Besides, he feared remonstrance and opposition, and he was resolved to carry out his plans, even if he was compelled to leave the paternal roof.

In the second week of September the *abbé* declared that Maurice might resume his ordinary life, and that, as the weather was pleasant, it would be well for him to spend much of his time in the open air.

In his delight, Maurice embraced the worthy priest.

"What happiness!" he exclaimed; "then I can hunt once more!"

He really cared but little for the chase; but he deemed it expedient to pretend a great passion for it, since it would furnish him with an excuse for frequent and protracted absences.

Never had he felt more happy than on the morning when, with his gun upon his shoulder, he crossed the Oiselle and started for the abode of M. Lacheneur. On reaching the little grove on the Reche, he paused for a moment at a place which commanded a view of the cottage. While he stood there, he saw Jean La-

cheneur and Chanlouineau leave the house, each laden
with a pedler's pack.

Maurice was therefore sure that M. Lacheneur and
Marie-Anne were alone in the house.

He hastened to the cottage and entered without stopping to rap.

Marie-Anne and her father were kneeling on the
hearth, upon which a huge fire was blazing.

On hearing the door open, they turned; and at the
sight of Maurice, they both sprang up, blushing and
confused.

"What brings you here?" they exclaimed in the
same breath.

Under other circumstances, Maurice d'Escorval
would have been dismayed by such a hostile greeting,
but now he scarcely noticed it.

"You have no business to return here against my
wishes, and after what I have said to you, Monsieur
d'Escorval," said Lacheneur, rudely.

Maurice smiled, he was perfectly cool, and not a detail of the scene before him had escaped his notice.   If
he had felt any doubts before, they were now dissipated.   He saw upon the fire a large kettle of melted
lead, and several bullet-moulds stood on the hearth,
beside the andirons.

"If I venture to present myself at your house, Monsieur," said Maurice, gravely and impressively, "it is
because I know all.   I have discovered your revenge-
ful project.   You are looking for men to aid you, are
you not?   Very well! look me in the face, in the eyes,
and tell me if I am not one of those whom a leader is
glad to enroll among his followers."

M. Lacheneur was terribly agitated.

"I do not know what you mean," he faltered, for-getting his feigned anger; "I have no projects."

"Would you assert this upon oath? Why are you casting these bullets? You are clumsy conspirators. You should lock your door; someone else might have entered."

And adding example to precept, he turned and pushed the bolt.

"This is only an imprudence," he continued; "but to reject a soldier who comes to you voluntarily would be a fault for which your associate would have a right to call you to account. I have no desire, understand me, to force myself into your confidence. No, I give myself to you blindly, body and soul. Whatever your cause may be, I declare it mine; what you wish, I wish; I adopt your plans; your enemies are my enemies; command, I will obey. I ask only one favor, that of fighting, of triumphing, or of dying by your side."

"Oh! refuse, father!" exclaimed Marie-Anne; "refuse. To accept this offer would be a crime!"

"A crime! And why, if you please?"

"Because our cause is not your cause; because its success is doubtful; because dangers surround us on every side."

A scornful exclamation from Maurice interrupted her.

"And it is you who think to dissuade me by pointing out the dangers that threaten you, the dangers that you are braving——"

"Maurice!"

"So if imminent peril menaced me, instead of coming to my aid you would desert me? You would hide yourself, saying, 'Let him perish, so that I be saved!' Speak! Would you do this?"

She averted her face and made no reply. She could not force herself to utter an untruth; and she was unwilling to answer: "I would act as you are acting." She waited for her father's decision.

"If I should comply with your request, Maurice," said M. Lacheneur, "in less than three days you would curse me, and ruin us by some outburst of anger. You love Marie-Anne. Could you see, unmoved, the frightful position in which she is placed? Remember, she must not discourage the addresses either of Chanlouineau or of the Marquis de Sairmeuse. You regard me—oh, I know as well as you do that it is a shameful and odious *rôle* that I impose upon her— that she is compelled to play a part in which she will lose a young girl's most precious possession—her reputation."

Maurice did not wince. "So be it," he said, calmly. "Marie-Anne's fate will be that of all women who have devoted themselves to the political advancement of the man whom they love, be he father, brother, or lover. She will be slandered, insulted, calumniated. What does it matter? She may continue her task. I consent to it, for I shall never doubt her, and I shall know how to hold my peace. If we succeed, she shall be my wife; if we fail——"

The gesture which concluded the sentence said more strongly than any protestations, that he was ready, resigned to anything.

M. Lacheneur was greatly moved.

"At least give me time for reflection," said he.

"There is no necessity for further reflection, Monsieur."

"But you are only a child, Maurice; and your father is my friend."

" What of that ? "

" Rash boy ! do you not understand that by compromising yourself you also compromise Baron d'Escorval?   You think you are risking only your own
head ; you are endangering your father's life——"

But Maurice violently interrupted him.

" There has been too much parleying already ! " he
exclaimed ; " there have been too many remonstrances.
Answer me in a word !   Only understand this : if you
reject me, I will return to my father's house, and with
this gun which I hold in my hand I will blow out my
brains."

This was no idle threat.   It was evident that what
he said, that would he do.   His listeners were so convinced of this, that Marie-Anne turned to her father
with clasped hands and a look of entreaty.

" You are one of us, then," said M. Lacheneur,
sternly ; " but do not forget that you forced me to consent by threats ; and whatever may happen to you or
yours, remember that you would have it so."

But these gloomy words produced no impression
upon Maurice ; he was wild with joy.

" Now," continued M. Lacheneur, " I must tell you
my hopes, and acquaint you with the cause for which
I am laboring——"

" What does that matter to me ? " Maurice exclaimed, gayly ; and, springing toward Marie-Anne, he
seized her hand and raised it to his lips, crying, with
the joyous laugh of youth :

" My cause—here it is ! "

Lacheneur turned away.   Perhaps he recollected
that a sacrifice of his pride was all that was necessary
to assure the happiness of these poor children.

But if a feeling of remorse entered his mind, he
drove it away, and with increased sternness, he said:

"Still, Monsieur d'Escorval, it is necessary for you to understand our agreement."

"Make known your conditions, sir."

"First, your visits here—after certain rumors that I have put in circulation—would arouse suspicion. You must come here only at night, and then only at hours that have been agreed upon in advance—never when you are not expected."

The attitude of Maurice expressed his entire consent.

"Moreover, you must find some way to cross the river without having recourse to the ferryman, who is a dangerous fellow."

"We have an old skiff. I will persuade my father to have it repaired."

"Very well. Will you also promise me to avoid the Marquis de Sairmeuse?"

"I will."

"Wait a moment; we must be prepared for any emergency. It may be that, in spite of our precautions, you will meet him here. Monsieur de Sairmeuse is arrogance itself; and he hates you. You detest him, and you are very hasty. Swear to me that if he provokes you, you will ignore his insults."

"But I should be considered a coward, Monsieur."

"Probably. Will you swear?"

Maurice hesitated, but an imploring look from Marie-Anne decided him.

"I swear!" he said, gravely.

"As far as Chanlouineau is concerned, it would be better not to let him know of our agreement—but I will take care of this matter."

M. Lacheneur paused and reflected for a moment, as if striving to discover if he had forgotten anything.

" Nothing remains, Maurice," he resumed, " but to give you a last and very important piece of advice. Do you know my son? "

" Certainly; we were formerly the best of comrades during our vacations."

" Very well. When you know my secret—for I shall confide it to you without reserve—beware of Jean."

" What, sir? "

" Beware of Jean. I repeat it."

And he blushed deeply, as he added:

" Ah! it is a painful avowal for a father; but I have no confidence in my own son. He knows no more in regard to my plans than I told him on the day of his arrival. I deceive him, because I fear he might betray us. Perhaps it would be wise to send him away; but in that case, what would people say? Most assuredly they would say that I was very avaricious of my own blood, while I was very ready to risk the lives of others. Still I may be mistaken; I may misjudge him."

He sighed, and added:

" Beware! "

CHAPTER XIX

So it was really Maurice d'Escorval whom the Marquis de Sairmeuse had seen leaving Lacheneur's house.

Martial was not certain of it, but the very possibility made his heart swell with anger.

" What part am I playing here, then? " he exclaimed, indignantly.

He had been so completely blinded by passion that he would not have been likely to discover the real condition of affairs even if no pains had been taken to deceive him.

Lacheneur's formal courtesy and politeness he regarded as sincere. He believed in the studied respect shown him by Jean; and the almost servile obsequiousness of Chanlouineau did not surprise him in the least.

And since Marie-Anne welcomed him politely, he concluded that his suit was progressing favorably.

Having himself forgotten, he supposed that everyone else had ceased to remember.

Moreover, he was of the opinion that he had acted with great generosity, and that he was entitled to the deep gratitude of the Lacheneur family; for M. Lacheneur had received the legacy bequeathed him by Mlle. Armande, and an indemnity, besides all the furniture he had chosen to take from the château, a total of at least sixty thousand francs.

"He must be hard to please, if he is not satisfied!" growled the duke, enraged at such prodigality, though it did not cost him a penny.

Martial had supposed himself the only visitor at the cottage on the Reche; and when he discovered that such was not the case, he became furious.

"Am I, then, the dupe of a shameless girl?" he thought.

He was so incensed, that for more than a week he did not go to Lacheneur's house.

His father concluded that his ill-humor and gloom was caused by some misunderstanding with Marie-Anne; and he took advantage of this opportunity to gain his son's consent to an alliance with Blanche de Courtornieu.

A victim to the most cruel doubts and fears, Martial, goaded to the last extremity, exclaimed:

"Very well! I will marry Mademoiselle Blanche."

The duke did not allow such a good resolution to grow cold.

In less than forty-eight hours the engagement was made public; the marriage contract was drawn up, and it was announced that the wedding would take place early in the spring.

A grand banquet was given at Sairmeuse in honor of the betrothal—a banquet all the more brilliant since there were other victories to be celebrated.

The Duc de Sairmeuse had just received, with his brevet of lieutenant-general, a commission placing him in command of the military department of Montaignac.

The Marquis de Courtornieu had also received an appointment, making him provost-marshal of the same district.

Blanche had triumphed.   After this public betrothal Martial was bound to her.

For a fortnight, indeed, he scarcely left her side.   In her society there was a charm whose sweetness almost made him forget his love for Marie-Anne.

But unfortunately the haughty heiress could not resist the temptation to make a slighting allusion to Marie-Anne, and to the lowliness of the marquis's former tastes.   She found an opportunity to say that she furnished Marie-Anne with work to aid her in earning a living.

Martial forced himself to smile; but the indignity which Marie-Anne had received aroused his sympathy and indignation.

And the next day he went to Lacheneur's house.

In the warmth of the greeting that awaited him there, all his anger vanished, all his suspicions evaporated.   Marie-Anne's eyes beamed with joy on seeing him again; he noticed it.

"Oh! I shall win her yet!" he thought.

All the household were really delighted at his return; the son of the commander of the military forces at Montaignac, and the prospective son-in-law of the provost-marshal, Martial was a most valuable instrument.

"Through him, we shall have an eye and an ear in the enemy's camp," said Lacheneur. "The Marquis de Sairmeuse will be our spy."

He was, for he soon resumed his daily visits to the cottage. It was now December, and the roads were terrible; but neither rain, snow, nor mud could keep Martial from the cottage.

He made his appearance generally as early as ten o'clock, seated himself upon a stool in the shadow of a tall fireplace, and he and Marie-Anne talked by the hour.

She seemed greatly interested in matters at Montaignac, and he told her all that he knew in regard to affairs there.

Sometimes they were alone.

Lacheneur, Chanlouineau, and Jean were tramping about the country with their merchandise. Business was prospering so well that M. Lacheneur had purchased a horse in order to extend his journeys.

But Martial's conversation was generally interrupted by visitors. It was really surprising to see how many peasants came to the house to speak to M. Lacheneur. There was an interminable procession of them. And to each of these peasants Marie-Anne had something to say in private. Then she offered each man refreshments—the house seemed almost like a common drinking-saloon.

But what can daunt the courage of a lover? Martial endured all this without a murmur. He laughed and jested with the comers and goers; he shook hands with them; sometimes he even drank with them.

He gave many other proofs of moral courage. He offered to assist M. Lacheneur in making up his accounts; and once—it happened about the middle of February—seeing Chanlouineau worrying over the composition of a letter, he actually offered to act as his amanuensis.

"The d——d letter is not for me, but for an uncle of mine who is about to marry off his daughter," said Chanlouineau.

Martial took a seat at the table, and, at Chanlouineau's dictation, but not without many erasures, indited the following epistle:

"MY DEAR FRIEND—We are at last agreed, and the marriage has been decided upon. We are now busy with preparations for the wedding, which will take place on ——. We invite you to give us the pleasure of your company. We count upon you, and be assured that the more friends you bring with you the better we shall be pleased."

Had Martial seen the smile upon Chanlouineau's lips when he requested him to leave the date for the wedding a blank, he would certainly have suspected that he had been caught in a snare. But he was in love.

"Ah! Marquis," remarked his father one day, "Chupin tells me you are always at Lacheneur's. When will you recover from your *penchant* for that little girl?"

Martial did not reply. He felt that he was at that "little girl's" mercy. Each glance of hers made his heart throb wildly.   By her side he was a willing captive.   If she had asked him to make her his wife he would not have said no.

But Marie-Anne had not this ambition.   All her thoughts, all her wishes were for her father's success.

Maurice and Marie-Anne had become M. Lacheneur's most intrepid auxiliaries.   They were looking forward to such a magnificent reward.

Such feverish activity as Maurice displayed!   All day long he hurried from hamlet to hamlet, and in the evening, as soon as dinner was over, he made his escape from the drawing-room, sprang into his boat, and hastened to the Reche.

M. d'Escorval could not fail to remark the long and frequent absences of his son.   He watched him, and soon became absolutely certain that Lacheneur had, to use the baron's own expression, seduced him.

Greatly alarmed, he decided to go and see his former friend, and fearing another repulse, he begged Abbé Midon to accompany him.

It was on the 4th of March, at about half-past four o'clock, that M. d'Escorval and the *curé* started for the Reche.   They were so anxious and troubled in mind that they scarcely exchanged a dozen words as they wended their way onward.

A strange sight met their eyes as they emerged from the grove on the Reche.

Night was falling, but it was still light enough for them to distinguish objects only a short distance from them.

Before Lacheneur's house stood a group of about a dozen persons, and M. Lacheneur was speaking and gesticulating excitedly.

What was he saying?   Neither the baron nor the

priest could distinguish his words, but when he ceased, the most vociferous acclamations rent the air.

Suddenly a match glowed between his fingers; he set fire to a bundle of straw and tossed it upon the thatched roof of his cottage, crying out in a terrible voice:

"The die is cast! This will prove to you that I shall not draw back!"

Five minutes later the house was in flames.

In the distance the baron and his companion saw the windows of the citadel at Montaignac illuminated by a red glare, and upon every hill-side glowed the light of other incendiary fires.

The country was responding to Lacheneur's signal.

CHAPTER XX

Ah! ambition is a fine thing!

The Duc de Sairmeuse and the Marquis de Courtornieu were past middle age; their lives had been marked by many storms and vicissitudes; they were the possessors of millions, and the owners of the most sumptuous residences in the province. Under these circumstances one might have supposed that they would desire to end their days in peace and quietness.

It would have been easy for them to create a life of happiness by doing good to those around them, and by preparing for their last hours a chorus of benedictions and of regrets.

But no. They longed to have a hand in managing the ship of state; they were not content to be simply passengers.

And the duke, appointed to the command of the military forces, and the marquis, made presiding judge

of the court at Montaignac, were both obliged to leave
their beautiful homes and take up their abode in rather
dingy quarters in town.

They did not murmur at the change; their vanity
was satisfied.

Louis XVIII. was on the throne; their prejudices
were triumphant; they were happy.

It is true that dissatisfaction was rife on every side,
but had they not hundreds and thousands of allies at
hand to suppress it?

And when wise and thoughtful persons spoke of
" discontent," the duke and his associates regarded
them as visionaries.

On the 4th of March, 1816, the duke was just sitting
down to dinner when a loud noise was heard in the
vestibule.

He rose—but at that very instant the door was flung
open and a man entered, panting and breathless.

This man was Chupin, the former poacher, whom
M. de Sairmeuse had elevated to the position of head
gamekeeper.

It was evident that something extraordinary had
happened.

" What is it? " inquired the duke.

" They are coming! " cried Chupin; " they are already on the way! "

" Who? who? "

By way of response, Chupin handed the duke a copy
of the letter written by Martial under Chanlouineau's
dictation.

M. de Sairmeuse read:

" MY DEAR FRIEND—We are at last agreed, and the
marriage is decided. We are now busy in preparing

for the wedding, which will take place on the 4th of March."

The date was no longer blank; but still the duke did not comprehend.

" Well, what of it? " he demanded.

Chupin tore his hair.

" They are on the way," he repeated.   " I speak of the peasants—they intend to take possession of Montaignac, dethrone Louis XVIII., bring back the Emperor, or at least the son of the Emperor—miserable wretches ! they have deceived me.   I suspected this outbreak, but I did not think it was so near at hand."

This terrible blow, so entirely unexpected, stupefied the duke for a moment.

" How many are there? " he demanded.

" Ah! how do I know, Monsieur?   Two thousand, perhaps—perhaps ten thousand."

" All the towns-people are with us."

" No, Monsieur, no.   The rebels have accomplices here. All the retired officers stand ready to assist them."

" Who are the leaders of the movement? "

" Lacheneur, Abbé Midon, Chanlouineau, Baron d'Escorval——"

" Enough! " cried the duke.

Now that danger was certain, his coolness returned ; and his herculean form, a trifle bowed by the weight of years, rose to its full height.

He gave the bell-rope a violent pull; a valet appeared.

" My uniform," commanded M. de Sairmeuse ; " my pistols! Quick! "

The servant was about to obey, when the duke exclaimed:

"Wait! Let someone take a horse, and go and tell my son to come here without a moment's delay. Take one of the swiftest horses. The messenger ought to go to Sairmeuse and return in two hours."

Chupin endeavored to attract the duke's attention by pulling the skirt of his coat. M. de Sairmeuse turned:

"What is it?"

The old poacher put his finger on his lip, recommending silence, but as soon as the valet had left the room, he said:

"It is useless to send for the marquis."

"And why, you fool?"

"Because, Monsieur, because—excuse me—I——"

"Zounds! will you speak, or will you not?"

Chupin regretted that he had gone so far.

"Because the marquis——"

"Well?"

"He is engaged in it."

The duke overturned the table with a terrible blow of his clinched fist.

"You lie, wretch!" he thundered, with the most horrible oaths.

He was so formidable in his anger that the old poacher sprang to the door and turned the knob, ready to take flight.

"May I lose my head if I do not speak the truth," he insisted. "Ah! Lacheneur's daughter is a regular sorceress. All the gallants of the neighborhood are in the ranks; Chanlouineau, young D'Escorval, your son——"

M. de Sairmeuse was pouring forth a torrent of curses upon Marie-Anne when his valet re-entered the room.

He suddenly checked himself, put on his uniform,

and ordering Chupin to follow him, hastened from the house.

He was still hoping that Chupin had exaggerated the danger; but when he reached the Place d'Arms, which commanded an extended view of the surrounding country, his illusions were put to flight.

Signal-lights gleamed upon every side. Montaignac seemed surrounded by a circle of flame.

"These are the signals," murmured Chupin. "The rebels will be here before two o'clock in the morning."

The duke made no response, but hastened to consult M. de Courtornieu.

He was striding toward his friend's house when, on hastily turning a corner, he saw two men talking in a doorway, and on seeing the glittering of the duke's epaulets, both of them took flight.

The duke instinctively started in pursuit, overtook one man, and seizing him by the collar, he asked, sternly:

"Who are you? What is your name?"

The man was silent, and his captor shook him so roughly that two pistols, which had been hidden under his long coat, fell to the ground.

"Ah, brigand!" exclaimed M. de Sairmeuse, "so you are one of the conspirators against the King!"

Then, without another word, he dragged the man to the citadel, gave him in charge of the astonished soldiers, and again started for M. de Courtornieu's house.

He expected the marquis would be terrified; not in the least; he seemed delighted.

"At last there comes an opportunity for us to display our devotion and our zeal—and without danger! We have good walls, strong gates, and three thousand soldiers at our command. These peasants are fools!

But be grateful for their folly, my dear duke, and run
and order out the Montaignac chasseurs——"

But suddenly a cloud overspread his face; he knit
his brows, and added:

"The devil! I am expecting Blanche this evening.
She was to leave Courtornieu after dinner. Heaven
grant that she may meet with no misfortune on the
way!"

CHAPTER XXI

The Duc de Sairmeuse and the Marquis de Courtornieu had more time before them than they supposed.

The rebels were advancing, but not so rapidly as
Chupin had said.

Two circumstances, which it was impossible to foresee, disarranged Lacheneur's plans.

Standing beside his burning house, Lacheneur
counted the signal fires that blazed out in answer to his
own.

Their number corresponded to his expectations; he
uttered a cry of joy.

"All our friends keep their word!" he exclaimed.
"They are ready; they are even now on their way to
the rendezvous. Let us start at once, for we must be
there first!"

They brought him his horse, and his foot was already in the stirrup, when two men sprang from the
neighboring grove and darted toward him. One of
them seized the horse by the bridle.

"Abbé Midon!" exclaimed Lacheneur, in profound
astonishment; "Monsieur d'Escorval!"

And foreseeing, perhaps, what was to come, he
added, in a tone of concentrated fury:

"What do you two men want with me?"

"We wish to prevent the accomplishment of an act of madness!" exclaimed M. d'Escorval. "Hatred has crazed you, Lacheneur!"

"You know nothing of my projects!"

"Do you think that I do not suspect them? You hope to capture Montaignac——"

"What does that matter to you?" interrupted Lacheneur, violently.

But M. d'Escorval would not be silenced.

He seized the arm of his former friend, and in a voice loud enough to be heard distinctly by everyone present, he continued:

"Foolish man! You have forgotten that Montaignac is a fortified city, protected by deep moats and high walls! You have forgotten that behind these fortifications is a garrison commanded by a man whose energy and valor are beyond all question—the Duc de Sairmeuse."

Lacheneur struggled to free himself from his friend's grasp.

"Everything has been arranged," he replied, "and they are expecting us at Montaignac. You would be as sure of this as I am myself, if you had seen the light gleaming on the windows of the citadel. And look, you can see it yet. This light tells me that two or three hundred retired officers will come to open the gates of the city for us as soon as we make our appearance."

"And after that! If you take Montaignac, what will you do then? Do you suppose that the English will give you back your Emperor? Is not Napoleon II. the prisoner of the Austrians? Have you forgotten that the allied sovereigns have left one hundred and fifty thousand soldiers within a day's march of Paris?"

Sullen murmurs were heard among Lacheneur's followers.

"But all this is nothing," continued the baron. "The chief danger lies in the fact that there are as many traitors as dupes in an undertaking of this sort."

"Whom do you call dupes, Monsieur?"

"All those who take their illusions for realities, as you have done; all those who, because they desire anything very much, really believe that it will come to pass. Do you really suppose that neither the Duc de Sairmeuse nor the Marquis de Courtornieu has been warned of it?"

Lacheneur shrugged his shoulders.

"Who could have warned them?"

But his tranquillity was feigned; the look which he cast upon Jean proved it.

And it was in the coldest possible tone that he added:

"It is probable that at this very hour the duke and the marquis are in the power of our friends."

The *curé* now attempted to join his efforts to those of the baron.

"You will not go, Lacheneur," he said. "You will not remain deaf to the voice of reason. You are an honest man; think of the frightful responsibility you assume! What! upon these frail hopes, you dare to peril the lives of hundreds of brave men? I tell you that you will not succeed; you will be betrayed; I am sure you will be betrayed!"

An expression of horror contracted Lacheneur's features. It was evident to all that he was deeply moved.

It is impossible to say what might have happened had it not been for the intervention of Chanlouineau.

This sturdy peasant came forward, brandishing his gun.

"We are wasting too much time in foolish prat-
tling," he exclaimed with a fierce oath.

Lacheneur started as if he had been struck by a whip.
He rudely freed himself and leaped into the saddle.

"Forward!" he ordered.

But the baron and the priest did not yet despair;
they sprang to the horse's head.

"Lacheneur," cried the priest, "beware! The
blood you are about to spill will fall upon your head,
and upon the heads of your children!"

Appalled by these prophetic words, the little band
paused.

Then someone issued from the ranks, clad in the costume of a peasant.

"Marie-Anne!" exclaimed the *abbé* and the baron
in the same breath.

"Yes, I," responded the young girl, removing the
large hat which had partially concealed her face; "I
wish to share the dangers of those who are dear to me
—share in their victory or their defeat. Your counsel
comes too late, gentlemen. Do you see those lights on
the horizon? They tell us that the people of these
communes are repairing to the cross-roads at the
Croix d'Arcy, the general rendezvous. Before two
o'clock fifteen hundred men will be gathered there
awaiting my father's commands. Would you have
him leave these men, whom he has called from their
peaceful firesides, without a leader? Impossible!"

She evidently shared the madness of her lover and
father, even if she did not share all their hopes.

"No, there must be no more hesitation, no more
parleying," she continued. "Prudence now would be
the height of folly. There is no more danger in a retreat than in an advance. Do not try to detain my

father, gentlemen; each moment of delay may, perhaps, cost a man's life. And now, my friends, forward!"

A loud cheer answered her, and the little band descended the hill.

But M. d'Escorval could not allow his own son, whom he saw in the ranks, to depart thus.

"Maurice!" he cried.

The young man hesitated, but at last approached.

"You will not follow these madmen, Maurice?" said the baron.

"I must follow them, father."

"I forbid it."

"Alas! father, I cannot obey you. I have promised —I have sworn. I am second in command."

His voice was sad, but it was determined.

"My son!" exclaimed M. d'Escorval; "unfortunate child!—it is to certain death that you are marching—to certain death."

"All the more reason that I should not break my word, father."

"And your mother, Maurice, the mother whom you forget!"

A tear glistened in the young man's eye.

"My mother," he replied, "would rather weep for her dead son than keep him near her dishonored, and branded with the names of coward and traitor. Farewell! my father."

M. d'Escorval appreciated the nobility of soul that Maurice displayed in his conduct. He extended his arms, and pressed his beloved son convulsively to his heart, feeling that it might be for the last time.

"Farewell!" he faltered, "farewell!"

Maurice soon rejoined his comrades, whose acclamations were growing fainter and fainter in the distance; but the baron stood motionless, overwhelmed with sorrow.

Suddenly he started from his revery.

" A single hope remains, Abbé ! " he cried.

" Alas ! " murmured the priest.

" Oh—I am not mistaken. Marie-Anne just told us the place of rendezvous. By running to Escorval and harnessing the cabriolet, we might be able to reach the Croix d'Arcy before this party arrive there. Your voice, which touched Lacheneur, will touch the heart of his accomplices. We will persuade these poor, misguided men to return to their homes. Come, Abbé; come quickly ! "

And they departed on the run.

CHAPTER XXII

The clock in the tower of Sairmeuse was striking the hour of eight when Lacheneur and his little band of followers left the Reche.

An hour later, at the Château de Courtornieu, Mlle. Blanche, after finishing her dinner, ordered the carriage to convey her to Montaignac. Since her father had taken up his abode in town they met only on Sunday; on that day either Blanche went to Montaignac, or the marquis paid a visit to the château.

Hence this proposed journey was a deviation from the regular order of things. It was explained, however, by grave circumstances.

It was six days since Martial had presented himself at Courtornieu; and Blanche was half crazed with grief and rage.

What Aunt Medea was forced to endure during this interval, only poor dependents in rich families can understand.

For the first three days Mlle. Blanche succeeded in preserving a semblance of self-control; on the fourth she could endure it no longer, and in spite of the breach of " *les convenances* " which it involved, she sent a messenger to Sairmeuse to inquire for Martial. Was he ill—had he gone away?

The messenger was informed that the marquis was perfectly well, but, as he spent the entire day, from early morn to dewy eve, in hunting, he went to bed every evening as soon as supper was over.

What a horrible insult! Still, she was certain that Martial, on hearing what she had done, would hasten to her to make his excuses. Vain hope! He did not come; he did not even condescend to give one sign of life.

" Ah! doubtless he is with her," she said to Aunt Medea. " He is on his knees before that miserable Marie-Anne—his mistress."

For she had finished by believing—as is not unfrequently the case—the very calumnies which she herself had invented.

In this extremity she decided to make her father her confidant; and she wrote him a note announcing her coming.

She wished her father to compel Lacheneur to leave the country. This would be an easy matter for him, since he was armed with discretionary authority at an epoch when lukewarm devotion afforded an abundant excuse for sending a man into exile.

Fully decided upon this plan, Blanche became calmer on leaving the château; and her hopes overflowed in incoherent phrases, to which poor Aunt Medea listened with her accustomed resignation.

"At last I shall be rid of this shameless creature!" she exclaimed. "We will see if he has the audacity to follow her! Will he follow her? Oh, no; he dare not!"

When the carriage passed through the village of Sairmeuse, Mlle. Blanche noticed an unwonted animation.

There were lights in every house, the saloons seemed full of drinkers, and groups of people were standing upon the public square and upon the doorsteps.

But what did this matter to Mlle. de Courtornieu! It was not until they were a mile or so from Sairmeuse that she was startled from her revery.

"Listen, Aunt Medea," she said, suddenly. "Do you hear anything?"

The poor dependent listened. Both occupants of the carriage heard shouts that became more and more distinct with each revolution of the wheels.

"Let us find out the meaning of this," said Mlle. Blanche.

And lowering one of the carriage-windows, she asked the coachman the cause of the disturbance.

"I see a great crowd of peasants on the hill; they have torches and——"

"Blessed Jesus!" interrupted Aunt Medea, in alarm.

"It must be a wedding," added the coachman, whipping up his horses.

It was not a wedding, but Lacheneur's little band, which had been augmented to the number of about five hundred.

Lacheneur should have been at the Croix d'Arcy

two hours before. But he had shared the fate of most
popular chiefs. When an impetus had been given to
the movement he was no longer master of it.

Baron d'Escorval had made him lose twenty minutes ; he was delayed four times as long in Sairmeuse.
When he reached that village, a little behind time, he
found the peasants scattered through the wine-shops,
drinking to the success of the enterprise.

To tear them from their merry-making was a long
and difficult task.

And to crown all, when they were finally induced to
resume their line of march, it was impossible to persuade them to extinguish the pine knots which they
had lighted to serve as torches.

Prayers and threats were alike unavailing. " They
wished to see their way," they said.

Poor deluded creatures ! They had not the slightest conception of the difficulties and the perils of the
enterprise they had undertaken.

They were going to capture a fortified city, defended
by a numerous garrison, as if they were bound on a
pleasure jaunt.

Gay, thoughtless, and animated by the imperturbable confidence of a child, they were marching along,
arm in arm, singing patriotic songs.

On horseback, in the centre of the band, M. Lacheneur felt his hair turning white with anguish.

Would not this delay ruin everything? What would
the others, who were waiting at the Croix d'Arcy,
think ! What were they doing at this very moment?

" Onward ! onward ! " he repeated.

Maurice, Chanlouineau, Jean, Marie-Anne, and
about twenty of the old soldiers of the Empire, understood and shared Lacheneur's despair. They knew

the terrible danger they were incurring, and they, too, repeated:

"Faster! Let us march faster!"

Vain exhortation! It pleased these people to go slowly.

Suddenly the entire band stopped. Some of the peasants, chancing to look back, had seen the lamps of Mlle. de Courtornieu's carriage gleaming in the darkness.

It came rapidly onward, and soon overtook them. The peasants recognized the coachman's livery, and greeted the vehicle with shouts of derision.

M. de Courtornieu, by his avariciousness, had made even more enemies than the Duc de Sairmeuse; and all the peasants who thought they had more or less reason to complain of his extortions were delighted at this opportunity to frighten him.

For, that they were not thinking of vengeance, is conclusively proved by the sequel.

Hence great was their disappointment when, on opening the carriage-door, they saw within the vehicle only Mlle. Blanche and Aunt Medea, who uttered the most piercing shrieks.

But Mlle. de Courtornieu was a brave woman.

"Who are you?" she demanded, haughtily, "and what do you desire?"

"You will know to-morrow," replied Chanlouineau. "Until then, you are our prisoner."

"I see that you do not know who I am, boy."

"Excuse me. I do know who you are, and, for this very reason, I request you to descend from your carriage. She must leave the carriage, must she not, Monsieur d'Escorval ?"

"Very well! I declare that I will not leave my carriage; tear me from it if you dare!"

They would certainly have dared had it not been for Marie-Anne, who checked some peasants as they were springing toward the carriage.

"Let Mademoiselle de Courtornieu pass without hinderance," said she.

But this permission might produce such serious consequences that Chanlouineau found courage to resist.

"That cannot be, Marie-Anne," said he; "she will warn her father. We must keep her as a hostage; her life may save the life of our friends."

Mlle. Blanche had not recognized her former friend, any more than she had suspected the intentions of this crowd of men.

But Marie-Anne's name, uttered with that of D'Escorval enlightened her at once.

She understood it all, and trembled with rage at the thought that she was at the mercy of her rival. She resolved to place herself under no obligation to Marie-Anne Lacheneur.

"Very well," said she, "we will descend."

Her former friend checked her.

"No," said she, "no! This is not the place for a young girl."

"For an honest young girl, you should say," replied Blanche, with a sneer.

Chanlouineau was standing only a few feet from the speaker with his gun in his hand. If a man had uttered those words he would have been instantly killed. Marie-Anne did not deign to notice them.

"Mademoiselle will turn back," she said, calmly; "and as she can reach Montaignac by the other road, two men will accompany her as far as Courtornieu."

She was obeyed. The carriage turned and rolled away, but not so quickly that Marie-Anne failed to hear Blanche cry:

"Beware, Marie! I will make you pay dearly for your insulting patronage!"

The hours were flying by. This incident had occupied ten minutes more—ten centuries—and the last trace of order had disappeared.

M. Lacheneur could have wept with rage. He called Maurice and Chanlouineau.

"I place you in command," said he; "do all that you can to hurry these idiots onward. I will ride as fast as I can to the Croix d'Arcy."

He started, but he was only a short distance in advance of his followers when he saw two men running toward him at full speed. One was clad in the attire of a well-to-do bourgeois; the other wore the old uniform of captain in the Emperor's guard.

"What has happened ?" Lacheneur cried, in alarm.

"All is discovered!"

"Great God!"

"Major Carini has been arrested."

"By whom? How?"

"Ah ! there was a fatality about it ! Just as we were perfecting our arrangements to capture the Duc de Sairmeuse, the duke surprised us. We fled, but the cursed noble pursued us, overtook Carini, seized him by the collar, and dragged him to the citadel."

Lacheneur was overwhelmed; the *abbé's* gloomy prophecy again resounded in his ears.

"So I warned my friends, and hastened to warn you," continued the officer. "The affair is an utter failure!"

He was only too correct; and Lacheneur knew it even better than he did. But, blinded by hatred and anger, he would not acknowledge that the disaster was irreparable.

He affected a calmness which he did not in the least feel.

" You are easily discouraged, gentlemen," he said, bitterly. " There is, at least, one more chance."

" The devil! Then you have resources of which we are ignorant? "

" Perhaps—that depends. You have just passed the Croix d'Arcy; did you tell any of those people what you have just told me? "

" Not a word."

" How many men are there at the rendezvous? "

" At least two thousand."

" And what is their mood? "

" They are burning to begin the struggle. They are cursing our slowness, and told me to entreat you to make haste."

" In that case our cause is not lost," said Lacheneur, with a threatening gesture. " Wait here until the peasants come up, and say to them that you were sent to tell them to make haste. Bring them on as quickly as possible, and have confidence in me; I will be re-sponsible for the success of the enterprise."

He said this, then putting spurs to his horse, gal-loped away. He had deceived the men. He had no other resources. He did not have the slightest hope of success. It was an abominable falsehood. But, if this edifice, which he had erected with such care and labor, was to totter and fall, he desired to be buried be-neath its ruins. They would be defeated; he was sure of it, but what did that matter? In the conflict he would seek death and find it.

Bitter discontent pervaded the crowd at the Croix d'Arcy; and after the passing of the officers, who had hastened to warn Lacheneur of the disaster at Montaignac, the murmurs of dissatisfaction were changed to curses.

These peasants, nearly two thousand in number, were indignant at not finding their leader awaiting them at the rendezvous.

"Where is he?" they asked. "Who knows but he is afraid at the last moment? Perhaps he is concealing himself while we are risking our lives and the bread of our children here."

And already the epithets of mischief-maker and traitor were flying from lip to lip, and increasing the anger in every breast.

Some were of the opinion that the crowd should disperse; others wished to march against Montaignac without Lacheneur, and that, immediately.

But these deliberations were interrupted by the furious gallop of a horse.

A carriage appeared, and stopped in the centre of the open space.

Two men alighted; Baron d'Escorval and Abbé Midon.

They were in advance of Lacheneur. They thought they had arrived in time.

Alas! here, as on the Reche, all their efforts, all their entreaties, and all their threats were futile.

They had come in the hope of arresting the movement; they only precipitated it.

"We have gone too far to draw back," exclaimed one of the neighboring farmers, who was the recognized leader in Lacheneur's absence. "If death is before us, it is also behind us. To attack and conquer— that is our only hope of salvation. Forward, then, at once. That is the only way of disconcerting our enemies. He who hesitates is a coward! Forward!"

A shout of approval from two thousand throats replied:

"Forward!"

They unfurled the tri-color, that much regretted flag
that reminded them of so much glory, and so many
great misfortunes; the drums began to beat, and with
shouts of: "Vive Napoleon II.!" the whole column
took up its line of march.

Pale, with clothing in disorder, and voices husky
with fatigue and emotion, M. d'Escorval and the *abbé*
followed the rebels, imploring them to listen to reason.

They saw the precipice toward which these misguided creatures were rushing, and they prayed God
for an inspiration to check them.

In fifty minutes the distance separating the Croix
d'Arcy from Montaignac is traversed.

Soon they see the gate of the citadel, which was to
have been opened for them by their friends within the
walls.

It is eleven o'clock, and yet this gate stands open.

Does not this circumstance prove that their friends
are masters of the town, and that they are awaiting
them in force?

They advance, so certain of success that those who
have guns do not even take the trouble to load them.

M. d'Escorval and the *abbé* alone foresee the catastrophe.

The leader of the expedition is near them, they entreat him not to neglect the commonest precautions,
they implore him to send some two men on in advance
to reconnoitre; they, themselves, offer to go, on condition that the peasants will await their return before
proceeding farther.

But their prayers are unheeded.

The peasants pass the outer line of fortifications in safety. The head of the advancing column reaches the drawbridge.

The enthusiasm amounts to delirium; who will be the first to enter is the only thought.

Alas! at that very moment a pistol is fired.

It is a signal, for instantly, and on every side, resounds a terrible fusillade.

Three or four peasants fall, mortally wounded. The rest pause, frozen with terror, thinking only of escape.

The indecision is terrible; but the leader encourages his men, there are a few of Napoleon's old soldiers in the ranks. A struggle begins, all the more frightful by reason of the darkness!

But it is not the cry of " Forward! " that suddenly rends the air.

The voice of a coward sends up the cry of panic:

" We are betrayed! Let him save himself who can! "

This is the end of all order. A wild fear seizes the throng; and these men flee madly, despairingly, scattered as withered leaves are scattered by the power of the tempest.

CHAPTER XXIII

Chupin's stupefying revelations and the thought that Martial, the heir of his name and dukedom, should degrade himself so low as to enter into a conspiracy with vulgar peasants, drove the Duc de Sairmeuse nearly wild.

But the Marquis de Courtornieu's coolness restored the duke's *sang-froid*.

He ran to the barracks, and in less than half an hour

five hundred foot-soldiers and three hundred of the Montaignac chasseurs were under arms.

With these forces at his disposal it would have been easy enough to suppress this movement without the least bloodshed. It was only necessary to close the gates of the city. It was not with fowling-pieces and clubs that these poor peasants could force an entrance into a fortified town.

But such moderation did not suit a man of the duke's violent temperament, a man who was ever longing for struggle and excitement, a man whose ambition prompted him to display his zeal.

He had ordered the gate of the citadel to be left open, and had concealed some of his soldiers behind the parapets of the outer fortifications.

He then stationed himself where he could command a view of the approach to the citadel, and deliberately chose his moment for giving the signal to fire.

Still, a strange thing happened. Of four hundred shots, fired into a dense crowd of fifteen hundred men, only three had hit the mark.

More humane than their chief, nearly all the soldiers had fired in the air.

But the duke had not time to investigate this strange occurrence now. He leaped into the saddle, and placing himself at the head of about five hundred men, cavalry and infantry, he started in pursuit of the fugitives.

The peasants had the advantage of their pursuers by about twenty minutes.

Poor simple creatures!

They might easily have made their escape. They had only to disperse, to scatter; but, unfortunately, the thought never once occurred to the majority of them. A few ran across the fields and gained their homes in safety; the others, frantic and despairing, overcome by the strange vertigo that seizes the bravest in moments of panic, fled like a flock of frightened sheep.

Fear lent them wings, for did they not hear each moment shots fired at the laggards?

But there was one man, who, at each of these detonations, received, as it were, his death-wound—this man was Lacheneur.

He had reached the Croix d'Arcy just as the firing at Montaignac began. He listened and waited. No discharge of musketry replied to the first fusillade. There might have been butchery, but combat, no.

Lacheneur understood it all; and he wished that every ball had pierced his own heart.

He put spurs to his horse and galloped to the crossroads. The place was deserted. At the entrance of one of the roads stood the cabriolet which had brought M. d'Escorval and the *abbé*.

At last M. Lacheneur saw the fugitives approaching in the distance. He dashed forward to meet them, trying by mingled curses and insults to stay their flight.

"Cowards!" he vociferated, "traitors! You flee— and you are ten against one! Where are you going? To your own homes. Fools! you will find the *gendarmes* there only awaiting your coming to conduct you to the scaffold. Is it not better to die with your weapons in your hands? Come—right about. Follow me! We may still conquer. Re-inforcements are at hand; two thousand men are following me!"

He promised them two thousand men; had he promised them ten thousand, twenty thousand—an army and cannon, it would have made no difference.

Not until they reached the wide-open space of the cross-roads, where they had talked so confidently scarcely an hour before, did the most intelligent of the throng regain their senses, while the others fled in every direction.

About a hundred of the bravest and most determined of the conspirators gathered around M. Lacheneur. In the little crowd was the *abbé*, gloomy and despondent. He had been separated from the baron. What had been his fate? Had he been killed or taken prisoner? Was it possible that he had made his escape?

The worthy priest dared not go away. He waited, hoping that his companion might rejoin him, and deemed himself fortunate in finding the carriage still there. He was still waiting when the remnant of the column confided to Maurice and Chanlouineau came up.

Of the five hundred men that composed it on its departure from Sairmeuse, only fifteen remained, including the two retired officers.

Marie-Anne was in the centre of this little party.

M. Lacheneur and his friends were trying to decide what course it was best for them to pursue. Should each man go his way? or should they unite, and by an obstinate resistance, give all their comrades time to reach their homes?

The voice of Chanlouineau put an end to all hesitation.

" I have come to fight," he exclaimed, " and I shall sell my life dearly."

" We will make a stand then !" cried the others.

But Chanlouineau did not follow them to the spot which they had considered best adapted to the prolonged defence; he called Maurice and drew him a little aside.

" You, Monsieur d'Escorval," he said, almost rough-ly, " are going to leave here and at once."

" I—I came here, Chanlouineau, as you did, to do my duty."

" Your duty, Monsieur, is to serve Marie-Anne. Go at once, and take her with you."

" I shall remain," said Maurice, firmly.

He was going to join his comrades when Chanloui-neau stopped him.

" You have no right to sacrifice your life here," he said, quietly. " Your life belongs to the woman who has given herself to you."

" Wretch! how dare you!"

Chanlouineau sadly shook his head.

" What is the use of denying it?" said he.

" It was so great a temptation that only an angel could have resisted it. It was not your fault, nor was it hers. Lacheneur was a bad father. There was a day when I wished either to kill myself or to kill you, I knew not which. Ah! only once again will you be as near death as you were that day. You were scarce-ly five paces from the muzzle of my gun. It was God who stayed my hand by reminding me of her despair. Now that I am to die, as well as Lacheneur, someone must care for Marie-Anne. Swear that you will marry her. You may be involved in some difficulty on ac-count of this affair; but I have here the means of sav-ing you."

A sound of firing interrupted him; the soldiers of the Duc de Sairmeuse were approaching.

" Good God!" exclaimed Chanlouineau, " and Marie-Anne!"

They rushed in pursuit of her, and Maurice was the first to discover her, standing in the centre of the open space clinging to the neck of her father's horse. He took her in his arms, trying to drag her away.

" Come ! " said he, " come ! "

But she refused.

" Leave me, leave me ! " she entreated.

" But all is lost ! "

" Yes, I know that all is lost—even honor. Leave me here. I must remain; I must die, and thus hide my shame. It must, it shall be so ! "

Just then Chanlouineau appeared.

Had he divined the secret of her resistance? Perhaps; but without uttering a word, he lifted her in his strong arms as if she had been a child and bore her to the carriage guarded by Abbé Midon.

" Get in," he said, addressing the priest, " and quick —take Mademoiselle Lacheneur. Now, Maurice, in your turn ! "

But already the duke's soldiers were masters of the field. Seeing a group in the shadow, at a little distance, they rushed to the spot.

The heroic Chanlouineau seized his gun, and brandishing it like a club, held the enemy at bay, giving Maurice time to spring into the carriage, catch the reins and start the horse off at a gallop.

All the cowardice and all the heroism displayed on that terrible night will never be really known.

Two minutes after the departure of Marie-Anne and of Maurice, Chanlouineau was still battling with the foe.

A dozen or more soldiers were in front of him. Twenty shots had been fired, but not a ball had struck him. His enemies always believed him invulnerable.

" Surrender ! " cried the soldiers, amazed by such valor; " surrender ! "

"Never! never!"

He was truly formidable; he brought to the support of his marvellous courage a superhuman strength and agility. No one dared come within reach of those brawny arms, that revolved with the power and velocity of the sails of a wind-mill.

Then it was that a soldier, confiding his musket to the care of a companion, threw himself flat upon his belly, and crawling unobserved around behind this obscure hero, seized him by the legs. He tottered like an oak beneath the blow of the axe, struggled furiously, but taken at such a disadvantage was thrown to the ground, crying, as he fell:

"Help! friends, help!"

But no one responded to this appeal.

At the other end of the open space those upon whom he called had, after a desperate struggle, yielded.

The main body of the duke's infantry was near at hand.

The rebels heard the drums beating the charge; they could see the bayonets gleaming in the sunlight.

Lacheneur, who had remained in the same spot, utterly ignoring the shot that whistled around him, felt that his few remaining comrades were about to be exterminated.

In that supreme moment the whole past was revealed to him as by a flash of lightning. He read and judged his own heart. Hatred had led him to crime. He loathed himself for the humiliation which he had imposed upon his daughter. He cursed himself for the falsehoods by which he had deceived these brave men, for whose death he would be accountable.

Enough blood had flowed; he must save those who remained.

"Cease firing, my friends," he commanded; "re-treat!"

They obeyed—he could see them scatter in every direction.

He too could flee; was he not mounted upon a gallant steed, which would bear him beyond the reach of the enemy?

But he had sworn that he would not survive defeat. Maddened with remorse, despair, sorrow, and impotent rage, he saw no refuge save in death.

He had only to wait for it; it was fast approaching; he preferred to rush to meet it. Gathering up the reins, he dashed the rowels in his steed and, alone, charged upon the enemy.

The shock was rude, the ranks opened, there was a moment of confusion.

But Lacheneur's horse, its chest cut open by the bayonets, reared, beat the air with his hoofs, then fell backward, burying his rider beneath him.

And the soldiers marched on, not suspecting that beneath the body of the horse the brave rider was struggling to free himself.

It was half-past one in the morning—the place was deserted.

Nothing disturbed the silence save the moans of a few wounded men, who called upon their comrades for succor.

But before thinking of the wounded, M. de Sairmeuse must decide upon the course which would be most likely to redound to his advantage and to his political glory.

Now that the insurrection had been suppressed, it was necessary to exaggerate its magnitude as much as possible, in order that his reward should be in proportion to the service supposed to have been rendered.

Some fifteen or twenty rebels had been captured; but that was not a sufficient number to give the victory the *éclat* which he desired. He must find more culprits to drag before the provost-marshal or before a military commission.

He, therefore, divided his troops into several detachments, and sent them in every direction with orders to explore the villages, search all isolated houses, and arrest all suspected persons.

His task here having been completed, he again recommended the most implacable severity, and started on a brisk trot for Montaignac.

He was delighted; certainly he blessed—as had M. de Courtornieu—these honest and artless conspirators; but one fear, which he vainly tried to dismiss, impaired his satisfaction.

His son, the Marquis de Sairmeuse, was he, or was he not, implicated in this conspiracy?

He could not, he would not, believe it; and yet the recollection of Chupin's assurance troubled him.

On the other hand, what could have become of Martial? The servant who had been sent to warn him—had he met him? Was the marquis returning? And by which road? Could it be possible that he had fallen into the hands of the peasants?

The duke's relief was intense when, on returning home, after a conference with M. de Courtornieu, he learned that Martial had arrived about a quarter of an hour before.

" The marquis went at once to his own room on dismounting from his horse," added the servant.

" Very well," replied the duke. " I will seek him there."

Before the servants he said, " Very well;" but se-

cretly, he exclaimed: "Abominable impertinence!
What! I am on horseback at the head of my troops,
my life imperilled, and my son goes quietly to bed
without even assuring himself of my safety!"

He reached his son's room, but found the door
closed and locked on the inside. He rapped.

"Who is there?" demanded Martial.

"It is I; open the door."

Martial drew the bolt; M. de Sairmeuse entered, but
the sight that met his gaze made him tremble.

Upon the table was a basin of blood, and Martial,
with chest bared, was bathing a large wound in his
right breast.

"You have been fighting!" exclaimed the duke, in
a husky voice.

"Yes."

"Ah ! then you were, indeed——"

"I was where? what?"

"At the convocation of these miserable peasants
who, in their parricidal folly, have dared to dream of
the overthrow of the best of princes !"

Martial's face betrayed successively profound surprise, and a more violent desire to laugh.

"I think you must be jesting, Monsieur," he replied.

The young man's words and manner reassured the
duke a little, without entirely dissipating his suspicions.

"Then these vile rascals attacked you ?" he exclaimed.

"Not at all. I have been simply obliged to fight a
duel."

"With whom ? Name the scoundrel who has dared
to insult you!"

A faint flush tinged Martial's cheek; but it was in his usual careless tone that he replied:

"Upon my word, no; I shall not give his name. You would trouble him, perhaps; and I really owe the fellow a debt of gratitude. It happened upon the highway; he might have assassinated me without ceremony, but he offered me open combat. Besides, he was wounded far more severely than I."

All M. de Sairmeuse's doubts had returned.

"And why, instead of summoning a physician, are you attempting to dress this wound yourself?"

"Because it is a mere trifle, and because I wish to keep it a secret."

The duke shook his head.

"All this is scarcely plausible," he remarked, "especially after the assurance of your complicity, which I have received."

"Ah!" said he; "and from whom? From your spy-in-chief, no doubt—that rascal Chupin. It surprises me to see that you can hesitate for a moment between the word of your son and the stories of such a wretch."

"Do not speak ill of Chupin, Marquis; he is a very useful man. Had it not been for him, we should have been taken unawares. It was through him that I learned of this vast conspiracy organized by Lacheneur——"

"What! is it Lacheneur——"

"Who is at the head of the movement? yes, Marquis. Ah! your usual discernment has failed you in this instance. What, you have been a constant visitor at this house, and you have suspected nothing? And you contemplate a diplomatic career! But this is not all. You know now for what purpose the money

which you so lavishly bestowed upon them has been
employed. They have used it to purchase guns, powder, and ammunition."

The duke had become satisfied of the injustice of
his suspicions; but he was now endeavoring to irritate
his son.

It was a fruitless effort. Martial knew very well that
he had been duped, but he did not think of resenting it.

" If Lacheneur has been captured," he thought; " if
he should be condemned to death and if I should save
him, Marie-Anne would refuse me nothing."

CHAPTER XXIV

Having penetrated the mystery that enveloped his
son's frequent absence, the Baron d'Escorval had concealed his fears and his chagrin from his wife.

It was the first time that he had ever had a secret
from the faithful and courageous companion of his
existence.

Without warning her, he went to beg Abbé Midon
to follow him to the Reche, to the house of M. Lacheneur.

The silence, on his part, explains Mme. d'Escorval's
astonishment when, on the arrival of the dinner-hour,
neither her son nor her husband appeared.

Maurice was sometimes late; but the baron, like all
great workers, was punctuality itself. What extraordinary thing could have happened ?

Her surprise became uneasiness when she learned
that her husband had departed in company with Abbé
Midon. They had harnessed the horse themselves, and
instead of driving through the court-yard as usual,

they had driven through the stable-yard into a lane leading to the public road.

What did all this mean ?   Why these strange precautions ?

Mme. d'Escorval waited, oppressed by vague forebodings.

The servants shared her anxiety. The baron was so equable in temper, so kind and just to his inferiors, that his servants adored him, and would have gone through a fiery furnace for him.

So, about ten o'clock, they hastened to lead to their mistress a peasant who was returning from Sairmeuse.

This man, who was slightly intoxicated, told the strangest and most incredible stories.

He said that all the peasantry for ten leagues around were under arms, and that the Baron d'Escorval was the leader of the revolt.

He did not doubt the final success of the movement, declaring that Napoleon II., Marie-Louise, and all the marshals of the Empire were concealed in Montaignac.

Alas ! it must be confessed that Lacheneur had not hesitated to utter the grossest falsehoods in his anxiety to gain followers.

Mme. d'Escorval could not be deceived by these ridiculous stories, but she could believe, and she did believe that the baron was the prime mover in this insurrection.

And this belief, which would have carried consternation to the hearts of so many women, reassured her.

She had entire, absolute, and unlimited faith in her husband. She believed him superior to all other men —infallible, in short. The moment he said: " This is so ! " she believed it implicitly.

Hence, if her husband had organized a movement,

that movement was right. If he had attempted it, it was because he expected to succeed. Therefore, it was sure to succeed.

Impatient, however, to know the result, she sent the gardener to Sairmeuse with orders to obtain information without awakening suspicion, if possible, and to hasten back as soon as he could learn anything of a positive nature.

He returned in about two hours, pale, frightened, and in tears.

The disaster had already become known, and had been related to him with the most terrible exaggerations. He had been told that hundreds of men had been killed, and that a whole army was scouring the country, massacring defenceless peasants and their families.

While he was telling his story, Mme. d'Escorval felt that she was going mad.

She saw—yes, positively, she saw her son and her husband, dead—or still worse, mortally wounded upon the public highway—they were lying with their arms crossed upon their breasts, livid, bloody, their eyes staring wildly—they were begging for water—a drop of water.

" I will find them ! " she exclaimed, in frenzied accents. " I will go to the field of battle, I will seek for them among the dead, until I find them. Light some torches, my friends, and come with me, for you will aid me, will you not ? You loved them ; they were so good ! You would not leave their dead bodies unburied ! oh ! the wretches ! the wretches who have killed them ! "

The servants were hastening to obey when the furious gallop of a horse and the sound of carriage-wheels were heard upon the drive.

" Here they are! " exclaimed the gardener; " here they are ! "

Mme. d'Escorval, followed by the servants, rushed to the door just in time to see a cabriolet enter the court-yard, and the horse, panting, exhausted, and flecked with foam, miss his footing, and fall.

Abbé Midon and Maurice had already leaped to the ground and were lifting out an apparently lifeless body.

Even Marie-Anne's great energy had not been able to resist so many successive shocks; the last trial had overwhelmed her. Once in the carriage, all immediate danger having disappeared, the excitement which had sustained her fled. She became unconscious, and all the efforts of Maurice and of the priest had failed to restore her.

But Mme. d'Escorval did not recognize Mlle. Lacheneur in the masculine habiliments in which she was clothed.

She only saw that it was not her husband whom they had brought with them; and a convulsive shudder shook her from head to foot.

" Your father, Maurice! " she exclaimed, in a stifled voice; " and your father ! "

The effect was terrible. Until that moment, Maurice and the *curé* had comforted themselves with the hope that M. d'Escorval would reach home before them.

Maurice tottered, and almost dropped his precious burden. The *abbé* perceived it, and at a sign from him, two servants gently lifted Marie-Anne, and bore her to the house.

Then the *curé* approached Mme. d'Escorval.

" Monsieur will soon be here, Madame," said he, at hazard; " he fled first——"

"Baron d'Escorval could not have fled," she interrupted. "A general does not desert when face to face
with the enemy. If a panic seizes his soldiers, he
rushes to the front, and either leads them back to combat, or takes his own life."

"Mother!" faltered Maurice; "mother!"

"Oh! do not try to deceive me. My husband was
the organizer of this conspiracy—his confederates
beaten and dispersed must have proved themselves
cowards. God have mercy upon me; my husband is
dead!"

In spite of the *abbé's* quickness of perception, he
could not understand such assertions on the part of the
baroness; he thought that sorrow and terror must have
destroyed her reason.

"Ah! Madame," he exclaimed, "the baron had
nothing to do with this movement; far from it——"

He paused; all this was passing in the court-yard, in
the glare of the torches which had been lighted up by
the servants. Anyone in the public road could hear
and see all. He realized the imprudence of which they
were guilty.

"Come, Madame," said he, leading the baroness
toward the house; "and you, also, Maurice, come !"

It was with the silent and passive submission of
great misery that Mme. d'Escorval obeyed the *curé*.

Her body alone moved in mechanical obedience;
her mind and heart were flying through space to the
man who was her all, and whose mind and heart were
even then, doubtless, calling to her from the dread
abyss into which he had fallen.

But when she had passed the threshold of the drawing-room, she trembled and dropped the priest's arm,
rudely recalled to the present reality.

She recognized Marie-Anne in the lifeless form extended upon the sofa.

"Mademoiselle Lacheneur!" she faltered, "here in this costume—dead!"

One might indeed believe the poor girl dead, to see her lying there rigid, cold, and as white as if the last drop of blood had been drained from her veins. Her beautiful face had the immobility of marble; her half-opened, colorless lips disclosed teeth convulsively clinched, and a large dark-blue circle surrounded her closed eyelids.

Her long black hair, which she had rolled up closely to slip under her peasant's hat, had become unbound, and flowed down in rich masses over her shoulders and trailed upon the floor.

"She is only in a state of syncope; there is no danger," declared the *abbé*, after he had examined Marie-Anne. "It will not be long before she regains consciousness."

And then, rapidly but clearly, he gave the necessary directions to the servants, who were astonished at their mistress.

Mme. d'Escorval looked on with eyes dilated with terror. She seemed to doubt her own sanity, and incessantly passed her hand across her forehead, thickly beaded with cold sweat.

"What a night!" she murmured. "What a night!"

"I must remind you, Madame," said the priest, sympathizingly, but firmly, "that reason and duty alike forbid you thus to yield to despair! Wife, where is your energy? Christian, what has become of your confidence in a just and beneficial God?"

"Oh! I have courage, Monsieur," faltered the wretched woman. "I am brave!"

The *abbé* led her to a large arm-chair, where he forced her to seat herself, and in a gentler tone, he resumed:

" Besides, why should you despair, Madame? Your son, certainly, is with you in safety. Your husband has not compromised himself; he has done nothing which I myself have not done."

And briefly, but with rare precision, he explained the part which he and the baron had played during this unfortunate evening.

But this recital, instead of reassuring the baroness, seemed to increase her anxiety.

" I understand you," she interrupted, " and I believe you. But I also know that all the people in the country round about are convinced that my husband commanded the insurrectionists. They believe it, and they will say it."

" And what of that? "

" If he has been arrested, as you give me to understand, he will be summoned before a court-martial. Was he not the friend of the Emperor? That is a crime, as you very well know. He will be convicted and sentenced to death."

" No, Madame, no! Am I not here? I will appear before the tribunal, and I shall say: 'Here I am!, I have seen and I know all.' "

" But they will arrest you, alas, Monsieur, because you are not a priest according to the hearts of these cruel men. They will throw you in prison, and you will meet him upon the scaffold."

Maurice had been listening, pale and trembling.

But on hearing these last words, he sank upon his knees, hiding his face in his hands:

" Ah! I have killed my father! " he exclaimed.

210 THE HONOR OF THE NAME

"Unhappy child! what do you say?"

The priest motioned him to be silent; but he did not see him, and he pursued:

"My father was ignorant even of the existence of this conspiracy of which Monsieur Lacheneur was the guiding spirit; but I knew it—I wished him to succeed, because on his success depended the happiness of my life. And then—wretch that I was!—when I wished to attract to our ranks some timid or wavering accomplice, I used the loved and respected name of D'Escorval. Ah, I was mad! I was mad!"

Then, with a despairing gesture, he added:

"And yet, even now, I have not the courage to curse my folly! Oh, mother, mother, if you knew——"

His sobs interrupted him. Just then a faint moan was heard.

Marie-Anne was regaining consciousness. Already she had partially risen from the sofa, and sat regarding this terrible scene with an air of profound wonder, as if she did not understand it in the least.

Slowly and gently she put back her hair from her face, and opened and closed her eyes, which seemed dazzled by the light of the candles.

She endeavored to speak, to ask some question, but Abbé Midon commanded silence by a gesture.

Enlightened by the words of Mme. d'Escorval and by the confession of Maurice, the *abbé* understood at once the extent of the frightful danger that menaced the baron and his son.

How was this danger to be averted? What must be done?

He had no time for explanation or reflection; with each moment, a chance of salvation fled. He must decide and act without delay.

The *abbé* was a brave man. He darted to the door,
and called the servants who were standing in the hall
and on the staircase.

When they were gathered around him:

" Listen to me, intently," said he, in that quick and
imperious voice that impresses one with the certainty
of approaching peril, " and remember that your master's life depends, perhaps, upon your discretion. We
can rely upon you, can we not ? "

Every hand was raised as if to call upon God to witness their fidelity.

" In less than an hour," continued the priest, " the
soldiers sent in pursuit of the fugitives will be here.
Not a word must be uttered in regard to what has
passed this evening. Everyone must be led to suppose that I went away with the baron and returned
alone. Not one of you must have seen Mademoiselle
Lacheneur. We are going to find a place of concealment for her. Remember, my friends, if there is the
slightest suspicion of her presence here, all is lost. If
the soldiers question you, endeavor to convince them
that Monsieur Maurice has not left the house this
evening."

He paused, trying to think if he had forgotten any
precaution that human prudence could suggest, then
added :

" One word more ; to see you standing about at this
hour of the night will awaken suspicion at once. But
this is what I desire. We will plead in justification,
the alarm that you feel at the absence of the baron, and
also the indisposition of madame—for madame is going to retire—she will thus escape interrogation. And
you, Maurice, run and change your clothes ; and, above
all, wash your hands, and sprinkle some perfume upon
them."

All present were so impressed with the imminence of the danger, that they were more than willing to obey the priest's orders.

Marie-Anne, as soon as she could be moved, was carried to a tiny room under the roof. Mme. d'Escorval retired to her own apartment, and the servants went back to the office.

Maurice and the *abbé* remained alone in the drawing-room, silent and appalled by horrible forebodings.

The unusually calm face of the priest betrayed his terrible anxiety. He now felt convinced that Baron d'Escorval was a prisoner, and all his efforts were now directed toward removing any suspicion of complicity from Maurice.

" This was," he reflected, " the only way to save the father."

A violent peal of the bell attached to the gate interrupted his meditations.

He heard the footsteps of the gardener as he hastened to open it, heard the gate turn upon its hinges, then the measured tramp of soldiers in the court-yard.

A loud voice commanded:

" Halt ! "

The priest looked at Maurice and saw that he was as pale as death.

" Be calm," he entreated ; " do not be alarmed. Do not lose your self-possession—and do not forget my instructions."

" Let them come," replied Maurice. " I am prepared ! "

The drawing-room door was flung violently open, and a young man, wearing the uniform of a captain of grenadiers, entered. He was scarcely twenty-five years of age, tall, fair-haired, with blue eyes and little

waxed mustache. His whole person betokened an excessive elegance exaggerated to the verge of the ridiculous. His face ordinarily must have indicated extreme self-complacency; but at the present moment it
wore a really ferocious expression.

Behind him, in the passage, were a number of armed
soldiers.

He cast a suspicious glance around the room, then,
in a harsh voice:

" Who is the master of this house? " he demanded.

" The Baron d'Escorval, my father, who is absent,"
replied Maurice.

" Where is he? "

The *abbé*, who, until now, had remained seated, rose.

" On hearing of the unfortunate outbreak of this
evening," he replied, " the baron and myself went to
these peasants, in the hope of inducing them to relinquish their foolish undertaking. They would not listen to us. In the confusion that ensued, I became
separated from the baron; I returned here very anxious, and am now awaiting his return."

The captain twisted his mustache with a sneering
air.

" Not a bad invention! " said he. " Only I do not
believe a word of this fiction."

A light gleamed in the eyes of the priest, his lips
trembled, but he held his peace.

" Who are you? " rudely demanded the officer.

" I am the *curé* of Sairmeuse."

" Honest men ought to be in bed at this hour. And
you are racing about the country after rebellious peasants. Really, I do not know what prevents me from
ordering your arrest."

That which did prevent him was the priestly robe, all

powerful under the Restoration. With Maurice he was more at ease.

" How many are there in this family? "

" Three; my father, my mother—ill at this moment —and myself."

" And how many servants? "

" Seven—four men and three women."

" You have neither received nor concealed anyone this evening? "

" No one."

" It will be necessary to prove this," said the captain.

And turning toward the door:

" Corporal Bavois! " he called.

This man was one of those old soldiers who had followed the Emperor over all Europe. Two small, ferocious gray eyes lighted his tanned, weather-beaten face, and an immense hooked nose surmounted a heavy, bristling mustache.

" Bavois," commanded the officer, " you will take half a dozen men and search this house from top to bottom. You are an old fox that knows a thing or two. If there is any hiding-place here, you will be sure to discover it; if anyone is concealed here, you will bring the person to me. Go, and make haste! "

The corporal departed on his mission; the captain resumed his questions.

" And now," said he, turning to Maurice, " what have you been doing this evening? "

The young man hesitated for an instant; then, with well-feigned indifference, replied:

" I have not put my head outside the door this evening."

" Hum! that must be proved. Let me see your hands."

The soldier's tone was so offensive that Maurice felt the angry blood mount to his forehead.   Fortunately, a warning glance from the *abbé* made him restrain his wrath.

He offered his hands to the inspection of the captain, who examined them carefully, outside and in, and finally smelled them.

" Ah! these hands are too white and smell too sweet to have been dabbling in powder."

He was evidently surprised that this young man should have had so little courage as to remain in the shelter of the fireside while his father was leading the peasants on to battle.

" Another thing," said he, " you must have weapons here."

" Yes, hunting rifles."

" Where are they? "

" In a small room on the ground-floor."

" Take me there."

They conducted him to the room, and on finding that none of the double-barrelled guns had been used for some days, he seemed considerably annoyed.

He appeared furious when the corporal came and told him that he had searched everywhere, but had found nothing of a suspicious character.

" Send for the servants," was his next order.

But all the servants faithfully repeated the lesson which the *abbé* had given them.

The captain saw that he was not likely to discover the mystery, although he was well satisfied that one existed.

Swearing that they should pay dearly for it, if they were deceiving him, he again called Bavois.

" I must continue my search," said he.   " You, with

two men, will remain here, and render a strict account of all that you see and hear. If Monsieur d'Escorval returns, bring him to me at once; do not allow him to escape. Keep your eyes open, and good luck to you!"

He added a few words in a low voice, then left the room as abruptly as he had entered it.

The departing footsteps of the soldiers were soon lost in the stillness of the night, and then the corporal gave vent to his disgust in a frightful oath.

"*Hein!*" said he, to his men, "you have heard that cadet. Listen, watch, arrest, report. So he takes us for spies! Ah! if our old leader knew to what base uses his old soldiers were degraded!"

The two men responded by a sullen growl.

"As for you," pursued the old trooper, addressing Maurice and the *abbé*, "I, Bavois, corporal of grenadiers, declare in my name and in that of my two men, that you are as free as birds, and that we shall arrest no one. More than that, if we can aid you in any way, we are at your service. The little fool that commanded us this evening thought we were fighting. Look at my gun; I have not fired a shot from it; and my comrades fired only blank cartridges."

The man might possibly be sincere, but it was scarcely probable.

"We have nothing to conceal," replied the cautious priest.

The old corporal gave a knowing wink.

"Ah! you distrust me! You are wrong; and I am going to prove it. Because, you see, though it is easy to gull that fool who just left here, it is not so easy to deceive Corporal Bavois. Very well! it was scarcely prudent to leave in the court-yard a gun that certainly had not been charged for firing at swallows."

The *curé* and Maurice exchanged a glance of consternation. Maurice now recollected, for the first time, that when he sprang from the carriage to lift out Marie-Anne, he propped his loaded gun against the wall. It had escaped the notice of the servants.

"Secondly," pursued Bavois, "there is someone concealed in the attic. I have excellent ears. Thirdly, I arranged it so that no one should enter the sick lady's room."

Maurice needed no further proof. He extended his hand to the corporal, and, in a voice trembling with emotion, he said:

"You are a brave man!"

A few moments later, Maurice, the *abbé*, and Mme. d'Escorval were again assembled in the drawing-room, deliberating upon the measures which must be taken, when Marie-Anne appeared.

She was still frightfully pale; but her step was firm, her manner quiet and composed.

"I must leave this house," she said to the baroness. "Had I been conscious, I would never have accepted hospitality which is likely to bring dire misfortune on your family. Alas! your acquaintance with me has cost you too many tears and too much sorrow already. Do you understand now why I wished you to regard us as strangers? A presentiment told me that my family would be fatal to yours!"

"Poor child!" exclaimed Mme. d'Escorval; "where will you go?"

Marie-Anne lifted her beautiful eyes to the heaven in which she placed her trust.

"I do not know, Madame," she replied; "but duty commands me to go. I must learn what has become of my father and my brother, and share their fate."

"What!" exclaimed Maurice; "still this thought of death. You, who no longer——"

He paused; a secret which was not his own had almost escaped his lips. But visited by a sudden inspiration, he threw himself at his mother's feet.

"Oh, my mother! my dearest mother, do not allow her to depart. I may perish in my attempt to save my father. She will be your daughter then—she whom I have loved so much. You will encircle her with your tender and protecting love——"

Marie-Anne remained.

CHAPTER XXV

The secret which approaching death had wrestled from Marie-Anne in the fortification at the Croix d'Arcy, Mme. d'Escorval was ignorant of when she joined her entreaties to those of her son to induce the unfortunate girl to remain.

But the fact occasioned Maurice scarcely an uneasiness.

His faith in his mother was complete, absolute; he was sure that she would forgive when she learned the truth.

Loving and chaste wives and mothers are always most indulgent to those who have been led astray by the voice of passion.

Such noble women can, with impunity, despise and brave the prejudices of hypocrites.

These reflections made Maurice feel more tranquil in regard to Marie-Anne's future, and he now thought only of his father.

Day was breaking; he declared that he would assume some disguise and go to Montaignac at once.

On hearing these words, Mme. d'Escorval turned and hid her face in the sofa-cushions to stifle her sobs.

She was trembling for her husband's life, and now her son must precipitate himself into danger. Perhaps before the sun sank to rest, she would have neither husband nor son.

And yet she did not say " no." She felt that Maurice was only fulfilling a sacred duty. She would have loved him less had she supposed him capable of cowardly hesitation. She would have dried her tears, if necessary, to bid him " go."

Moreover, what was not preferable to the agony of suspense which they had been enduring for hours ?

Maurice had reached the door when the *abbé* stopped him.

" You must go to Montaignac," said he, " but it would be folly to disguise yourself. You would certainly be recognized, and the saying: ' He who conceals himself is guilty,' will assuredly be applied to you. You must go openly, with head erect, and you must even exaggerate the assurance of innocence. Go straight to the Duc de Sairmeuse and the Marquis de Courtornieu. I will accompany you ; we will go in the carriage."

Maurice seemed undecided.

" Obey these counsels, my son," said Mme. d'Escorval ; " the *abbé* knows much better than we do what is best."

" I will obey, mother."

The *curé* had not waited for this assent to go and give an order for harnessing the horses. Mme. d'Escorval left the room to write a few lines to a lady friend, whose husband exerted considerable influence in Montaignac. Maurice and Marie-Anne were left alone.

It was the first moment of freedom and solitude which they had found since Marie-Anne's confession.

They stood for a moment, silent and motionless, then Maurice advanced, and clasping her in his arms, he whispered:

" Marie-Anne, my darling, my beloved, I did not know that one could love more fondly than I loved you yesterday; but now— And you—you wish for death when another precious life depends upon yours."

She shook her head sadly.

" I was terrified," she faltered. " The future of shame that I saw—that I still—alas ! see before me, appalled me. Now I am resigned. I will uncomplainingly endure the punishment for my horrible fault—I will submit to the insults and disgrace that await me ! "

" Insults, to you ! Ah ! woe to who dares ! But will you not now be my wife in the sight of men, as you are in the sight of God ? The failure of your father's scheme sets you free ! "

" No, no, Maurice, I am not free ! Ah ! it is you who are pitiless ! I see only too well that you curse me, that you curse the day when we met for the first time ! Confess it ! Say it ! "

Marie-Anne lifted her streaming eyes to his.

" Ah ! I should lie if I said that. My cowardly heart has not that much courage ! I suffer—I am disgraced and humiliated, but——"

He could not finish ; he drew her to him, and their lips and their tears met in one long kiss.

" You love me," exclaimed Maurice, " you love me in spite of all ! We shall succeed. I will save your father, and mine—I will save your brother ! "

The horses were neighing and stamping in the courtyard. The *abbé* cried: " Come, let us start." Mme.

d'Escorval entered with a letter, which she handed to Maurice.

She clasped in a long and convulsive embrace the son whom she feared she should never see again; then, summoning all her courage, she pushed him away, uttering only the single word:

" Go ! "

He departed; and when the sound of the carriage-wheels had died away in the distance, Mme. d'Escorval and Marie-Anne fell upon their knees, imploring the mercy and aid of a just God.

They could only pray. The *curé* and Maurice could act.

Abbé Midon's plan, which he explained to young d'Escorval, as the horses dashed along, was as simple as the situation was terrible.

" If, by confessing your own guilt, you could save your father, I should tell you to deliver yourself up, and to confess the whole truth. Such would be your duty. But this sacrifice would be not only useless, but dangerous. Your confession of guilt would only implicate your father still more. You would be arrested, but they would not release him, and you would both be tried and convicted. Let us, then, allow—I will not say justice, for that would be blasphemy—but these blood-thirsty men, who call themselves judges, to pursue their course, and attribute all that you have done to your father. When the trial comes, you will prove his innocence, and produce *alibis* so incontestable, that they will be forced to acquit him. And I understand the people of our country so well, that I am sure not one of them will reveal our stratagem."

" And if we should not succeed," asked Maurice. gloomily, " what could I do then ? "

The question was so terrible that the priest dared not respond to it. He and Maurice were silent during the remainder of the drive.

They reached the city at last, and Maurice saw how wise the *abbé* had been in preventing him from assuming a disguise.

Armed with the most absolute power, the Duc de Sairmeuse and the Marquis de Courtornieu had closed all the gates of Montaignac save one.

Through this gate all who desired to leave or enter the city were obliged to pass, and two officers were stationed there to examine all comers and goers, to question them, and to take their name and residence.

At the name " D'Escorval," the two officers evinced such surprise that Maurice noticed it at once.

" Ah ! you know what has become of my father ! " he exclaimed.

" The Baron d'Escorval is a prisoner, Monsieur," replied one of the officers.

Although Maurice had expected this response, he turned pale.

" Is he wounded ? " he asked, eagerly.

" He has not a scratch. But enter, sir, and pass on."

From the anxious looks of these officers one might have supposed that they feared they should compromise themselves by conversing with the son of so great a criminal.

The carriage rolled beneath the gate-way ; but it had not traversed two hundred yards of the Grand Rue before the *abbé* and Maurice had remarked several posters and notices affixed to the walls.

" We must see what this is," they said, in a breath.

They stopped near one of these notices, before which a reader had already stationed himself ; they descended from the carriage, and read the following order :

"ARTICLE I.—The inmates of the house in which the elder Lacheneur shall be found will be handed over to a military commission for trial.

"ARTICLE II.—Whoever shall deliver the body of the elder Lacheneur, dead or alive, will receive a reward of twenty thousand francs."

This was signed Duc de Sairmeuse.

"God be praised!" exclaimed Maurice, "Marie-Anne's father has escaped! He had a good horse, and in two hours——"

A glance and a nudge of the elbow from the *abbé* checked him.

The *abbé* drew his attention to the man standing near them. This man was none other than Chupin.

The old scoundrel had also recognized them, for he took off his hat to the *curé*, and with an expression of intense covetousness in his eyes, he said: "Twenty thousand francs! what a sum! A man could live comfortably all his life on the interest of it."

The *abbé* and Maurice shuddered as they re-entered their carriage.

"Lacheneur is lost if this man discovers his retreat," murmured the priest.

"Fortunately, he must have crossed the frontier before this," replied Maurice. "A hundred to one he is beyond reach."

"And if you should be mistaken. What, if wounded and faint from loss of blood, Lacheneur has had only strength to drag himself to the nearest house and ask the hospitality of its inmates?"

"Oh! even in that case he is safe; I know our peasants. There is not one who is capable of selling the life of a proscribed man."

The noble enthusiasm of youth drew a sad smile from the priest.

" You forget the dangers to be incurred by those who shelter him. Many a man who would not soil his hands with the price of blood might deliver up a fugitive from fear."

They were passing through the principal street, and they were struck with the mournful aspect of the place —the little city which was ordinarily so bustling and gay.

Fear and consternation evidently reigned there. The shops were closed; the shutters of the houses had not been opened. A lugubrious silence pervaded the town. One might have supposed that there was general mourning, and that each family had lost one of its members.

The manner of the few persons seen upon the thoroughfare was anxious and singular. They hurried on, casting suspicious glances on every side.

Two or three who were acquaintances of the Baron d'Escorval averted their heads, on seeing his carriage, to avoid the necessity of bowing.

The *abbé* and Maurice found an explanation of this evident terror on reaching the hotel to which they had ordered the coachman to take them.

They had designated the Hôtel de France, where the baron always stopped when he visited Montaignac, and whose proprietor was none other than Laugeron, that friend of Lacheneur, who had been the first to warn him of the arrival of the Duc de Sairmeuse.

This worthy man, on hearing what guests had arrived, went to the court-yard to meet them, with his white cap in his hand.

On such a day politeness was heroism. Was he connected with the conspiracy ?   It has always been supposed so.

He invited Maurice and the *abbé* to take some refreshments in a way that made them understand he
was anxious to speak with them, and he conducted
them to a retired room where he knew they would be
secure from observation.

Thanks to one of the Duc de Sairmeuse's *valets de
chambre* who frequented the house, the host knew as
much as the authorities; he knew even more, since he
had also received information from the rebels who had
escaped capture.

From him the *abbé* and Maurice received their first
positive information.

In the first place, nothing had been heard of Lacheneur, or of his son Jean; thus far they had escaped the
most rigorous pursuit.

In the second place, there were, at this moment, two
hundred prisoners in the citadel, and among them the
Baron d'Escorval and Chanlouineau.

And lastly, since morning there had been at least
sixty arrests in Montaignac.

It was generally supposed that these arrests were the
work of some traitor, and all the inhabitants were
trembling with fear.

But M. Laugeron knew the real cause. It had been
confided to him under pledge of secrecy by his guest,
the duke's *valet de chambre*.

" It is certainly an incredible story, gentlemen," he
said; " nevertheless, it is true. Two officers belonging
to the Montaignac militia, on returning from their expedition this morning at daybreak, on passing the
Croix d'Arcy, found a man, clad in the uniform of the
Emperor's body-guard, lying dead in the fosse."

Maurice shuddered.

The unfortunate man, he could not doubt, was the brave old soldier who had spoken to Lacheneur.

"Naturally," pursued M. Laugeron, "the two officers examined the body of the dead man. Between his lips they found a paper, which they opened and read. It was a list of all the conspirators in the village. The brave man, knowing he was mortally wounded, endeavored to destroy this fatal list; but the agonies of death prevented him from swallowing it——"

But the *abbé* and Maurice had not time to listen to the commentaries with which the hotel proprietor accompanied his recital.

They despatched a messenger to Mme. d'Escorval and to Marie-Anne, in order to reassure them, and, without losing a moment, and fully determined to brave all, they went to the house occupied by the Duc de Sairmeuse.

A crowd had gathered about the door. At least a hundred persons were standing there; men with anxious faces, women in tears, soliciting, imploring an audience.

They were the friends and relatives of the unfortunate men who had been arrested.

Two footmen, in gorgeous livery and pompous in bearing, had all they could do to keep back the struggling throng.

The *abbé*, hoping that his priestly dress would win him a hearing, approached and gave his name. But he was repulsed like the others.

"Monsieur le Duc is busy, and can receive no one," said the servant. "Monsieur le Duc is preparing his report for His Majesty."

And in support of this assertion, he pointed to the horses, standing saddled in the court-yard, and the couriers who were to bear the despatches.

The priest sadly rejoined his companions.

"We must wait!" said he.

Intentionally or not, the servants were deceiving these poor people. The duke, just then, was not troubling himself about despatches. A violent altercation was going on between the Marquis de Courtornieu and himself.

Each of these noble personages aspired to the leading *rôle*—the one which would be most generously rewarded, undoubtedly. It was a conflict of ambitions and of wills.

It had begun by the exchange of a few recriminations, and it quickly reached stinging words, bitter allusions, and at last, even threats.

The marquis declared it necessary to inflict the most frightful—he said the most *salutary* punishment upon the offender; the duke, on the contrary, was inclined to be indulgent.

The marquis declared that since Lacheneur, the prime mover, and his son, had both eluded pursuit, it was an urgent necessity to arrest Marie-Anne.

The other declared that the arrest and imprisonment of this young girl would be impolitic, that such a course would render the authorities odious, and the rebels more zealous.

As each was firmly wedded to his own opinion, the discussion was heated, but they failed to convince each other.

"These rebels must be put down with a strong hand!" urged M. de Courtornieu.

"I do not wish to exasperate the populace," replied the duke.

"Bah! what does public sentiment matter?"

"It matters a great deal when you cannot depend

upon your soldiers. Do you know what happened last night? There was powder enough burned to win a battle; there were only fifteen peasants wounded. Our men fired in the air. You forget that the Montaignac militia is composed, for the most part, at least of men who formerly fought under Bonaparte, and who are burning to turn their weapons against us."

But neither the one nor the other dared to tell the real cause of his obstinacy.

Mlle. Blanche had been at Montaignac that morning. She had confided her anxiety and her sufferings to her father; and she made him swear that he would profit by this opportunity to rid her of Marie-Anne.

On his side, the duke, persuaded that Marie-Anne was his son's mistress, wished, at any cost, to prevent her appearance before the tribunal. At last the marquis yielded.

The duke had said to him: " Very well ! let us end this dispute," at the same time glancing so meaningly at a pair of pistols that the worthy marquis felt a disagreeable chilliness creep up his spine.

They then went together to examine the prisoners, preceded by a detachment of soldiery who drove back the crowd, which gathered again to await the duke's return. So all day Maurice watched the aërial telegraph established upon the citadel, and whose black arms were moving incessantly.

"What orders are travelling through space ? " he said to the *abbé;* " is it life or is it death? "

CHAPTER XXVI

" Above all, make haste ! " Maurice had said to the messenger charged with bearing a letter to the baroness.

Nevertheless, the man did not reach Escorval until night-fall.

Beset by a thousand fears, he had taken the unfrequented roads and had made long circuits to avoid all the people he saw approaching in the distance.

Mme. d'Escorval tore the letter rather than took it from his hands. She opened it, read it aloud to Marie-Anne, and merely said :

" Let us go—at once."

But this was easier said than done.

They kept but three horses at Escorval. One was nearly dead from its terrible journey of the previous night ; the other two were in Montaignac.

What were the ladies to do ? To trust to the kindness of their neighbors was the only resource open to them.

But these neighbors having heard of the baron's arrest, firmly refused to lend their horses. They believed they would gravely compromise themselves by rendering any service to the wife of a man upon whom the burden of the most terrible of accusations was resting.

Mme. d'Escorval and Marie-Anne were talking of pursuing their journey on foot, when Corporal Bavois, enraged at such cowardice, swore by the sacred name of thunder that this should not be.

" One moment ! " said he. " I will arrange the matter."

He went away, but reappeared about a quarter of an

hour afterward, leading an old plough-horse by the mane. This clumsy and heavy steed he harnessed into the cabriolet as best he could.

But even this did not satisfy the old trooper's complaisance.

His duties at the château were over, as M. d'Escorval had been arrested, and nothing remained for Corporal Bavois but to rejoin his regiment.

He declared that he would not allow these ladies to travel at night, and unattended, on the road where they might be exposed to many disagreeable encounters, and that he, in company with two grenadiers, would escort them to their journey's end.

" And it will go hard with soldier or civilian who ventures to molest them, will it not, comrades ? " he exclaimed.

As usual, the two men assented with an oath.

So, as they pursued their journey, Mme. d'Escorval and Marie-Anne saw the three men preceding or following the carriage, or oftener walking beside it.

Not until they reached the gates of Montaignac did the old soldier forsake his *protégées*, and then, not without bidding them a respectful farewell, in the name of his companions as well as himself; not without telling them, if they had need of him, to call upon Bavois, corporal of grenadiers, company first, stationed at the citadel.

The clocks were striking ten when M. d'Escorval and Marie-Anne alighted at the Hôtel de France.

They found Maurice in despair, and even the *abbé* disheartened. Since Maurice had written to them, events had progressed with fearful rapidity.

They knew now the orders which had been forwarded by signals from the citadel. These orders had been printed and affixed to the walls. The signals had said :

" Montaignac must be regarded as in a state of siege. The military authorities have been granted discretionary power. A military commission will exercise jurisdiction instead of, and in place of, the courts. Let peaceable citizens take courage ; let the evil-disposed tremble ! As for the rabble, the sword of the law is about to strike ! "

Only six lines in all—but each word was a menace.

That which filled the *abbé's* heart with dismay was the substitution of a military commission for a court-martial.

This upset all his plans, made all his precautions useless, and destroyed his hopes of saving his friend.

A court-martial was, of course, hasty and often unjust in its decisions ; but still, it observed some of the forms of procedure practised in judicial tribunals. It still preserved something of the solemnity of legal justice, which desires to be enlightened before it condemns.

A military commission would infallibly neglect all legal forms ; and summarily condemn and punish the accused parties, as in time of war a spy is tried and punished.

" What ! " exclaimed Maurice, " they dare to condemn without investigating, without listening to testimony, without allowing the accused time to prepare any defence ? "

The *abbé* was silent. This exceeded his most sinister apprehensions. Now, he believed anything possible.

Maurice spoke of an investigation. It had commenced that day, and it was still going on by the light of the jailer's lantern.

That is to say, the Duc de Sairmeuse and the Marquis de Courtornieu were passing the prisoners in review.

They numbered three hundred, and the duke and his companion had decided to summon before the commission thirty of the most dangerous conspirators.

How were they to select them ? By what method could they discover the extent of each prisoner's guilt ? It would have been difficult for them to explain.

They went from one to another, asking any question that entered their minds, and after the terrified man replied, according as they thought his countenance good or bad, they said to the jailer who acompanied them : " Keep this one until another time," or, " This one for to-morrow."

By daylight, they had thirty names upon their list : and the names of the Baron d'Escorval and Chanlouineau led all the rest.

Although the unhappy party at the Hôtel de France could not suspect this fact, they suffered an agony of fear and dread through the long night which seemed to them eternal.

As soon as day broke, they heard the beating of the *réveille* at the citadel ; the hour when they might commence their efforts anew had come.

The *abbé* announced that he was going alone to the duke's house, and that he would find a way to force an entrance.

He had bathed his red and swollen eyes in fresh water, and was prepared to start on his expedition, when someone rapped cautiously at the door of the chamber.

Maurice cried : " Come in," and M. Laugeron instantly entered the room.

His face announced some dreadful misfortune ; and the worthy man was really terrified.

He had just learned that the military commission had been organized.

In contempt of all human laws and the commonest rules of justice, the presidency of this tribunal of vengeance and of hatred had been bestowed upon the Duc de Sairmeuse.

And he had accepted it—he who was at the same time to play the part of participant, witness, and judge.

The other members of the commission were military men.

" And when does the commission enter upon its functions ? " inquired the *abbé*.

" To-day," replied the host, hesitatingly; " this morning—in an hour—perhaps sooner ! "

The *abbé* understood what M. Laugeron meant, but dared not say: " The commission is assembling, make haste."

" Come ! " he said to Maurice, " I wish to be present when your father is examined."

Ah ! what would not the baroness have given to follow the priest and her son ? But she could not; she understood this, and submitted.

They set out, and as they stepped into the street they saw a soldier a little way from them, who made a friendly gesture.

They recognized Corporal Bavois, and paused.

But he, passing them with an air of the utmost indifference, and apparently without observing them, hastily dropped these words:

" I have seen Chanlouineau. Be of good cheer; he promises to save Monsieur d'Escorval ! "

CHAPTER XXVII

In the citadel of Montaignac, within the second line of fortifications, stands an old building known as the chapel.

Originally consecrated to worship, the structure had, at the time of which we write, fallen into disuse. It was so damp that it would not even serve as an arsenal for an artillery regiment, for the guns rusted there more quickly than in the open air. A black mould covered the walls to a height of six or seven feet.

This was the place selected by the Duc de Sairmeuse and the Marquis de Courtornieu for the assembling of the military commission.

On first entering it, Maurice and the *abbé* felt a cold chill strike to their very hearts; and an indefinable anxiety paralyzed all their faculties.

But the commission had not yet commenced its *séance;* and they had time to look about them.

The arrangements which had been made in transforming this gloomy hall into a tribunal, attested the precipitancy of the judges and their determination to finish their work promptly and mercilessly.

The arrangements denoted an absence of all form; and one could divine at once the frightful certainty of the result.

Three large tables taken from the mess-room, and covered with horse-blankets instead of tapestry, stood upon the platform. Some unpainted wooden chairs awaited the judges; but in the centre glittered the president's chair, a superbly carved and gilded *fauteuil*, sent by the Duc de Sairmeuse.

Several wooden benches had been provided for the prisoners.

Ropes stretched from one wall to the other divided the chapel into two parts.   It was a precaution against the public.

A superfluous precaution, alas !

The *abbé* and Maurice had expected to find the crowd too great for the hall, large as it was, and they found the chapel almost unoccupied.

There were not twenty persons in the building. Standing back in the shadow of the wall were perhaps a dozen men, pale and gloomy, a sullen fire smouldering in their eyes, their teeth tightly clinched.   They were army officers retired on half pay.   Three men, attired in black, were conversing in low tones near the door. In a corner stood several country-women with their aprons over their faces.   They were weeping bitterly, and their sobs alone broke the silence.   They were the mothers, wives, or daughters of the accused men.

Nine o'clock sounded.   The rolling of the drum made the panes of the only window tremble.   A loud voice outside shouted, " Present arms ! "   The military commission entered, followed by the Marquis de Courtornieu and several civil functionaries.

The duke was in full uniform, his face a little more crimson, and his air a trifle more haughty than usual.

" The session is open ! " pronounced the Duc de Sairmeuse, the president.

Then, in a rough voice, he added :

" Bring in the culprits."

He had not even the grace to say " the accused."

They came in, one by one, to the number of twenty, and took their places on the benches at the foot of the platform.

Chanlouineau held his head proudly erect, and looked composedly about him.

Baron d'Escorval was calm and grave; but not more so than when, in days gone by, he had been called upon to express his opinion in the councils of the Empire.

Both saw Maurice, who was so overcome that he had to lean upon the *abbé* for support. But while the baron greeted his son with a simple bend of the head, Chanlouineau made a gesture that clearly signified:

"Have confidence in me—fear nothing."

The attitude of the other prisoners betrayed surprise rather than fear. Perhaps they were unconscious of the peril they had braved, and the extent of the danger that now threatened them.

When the prisoners had taken their places, the chief counsel for the prosecution rose.

His presentation of the case was characterized by intense violence, but lasted only five minutes. He briefly narrated the facts, exalted the merits of the government, of the Restoration, and concluded by a demand that sentence of death should be pronounced upon the culprits.

When he ceased speaking, the duke, addressing the first prisoner upon the bench, said, rudely:

"Stand up."

The prisoner rose.

"Your name and age?"

"Eugene Michel Chanlouineau, aged twenty-nine, farmer by occupation."

"An owner of national lands, probably?"

"The owner of lands which, having been paid for with good money and made fertile by labor, are rightfully mine."

The duke did not wish to waste time on discussion.

" You have taken part in this rebellion?" he pursued.

" Yes."

" You are right in avowing it, for witnesses will be introduced who will prove this fact conclusively."

Five grenadiers entered; they were the men whom Chanlouineau had held at bay while Maurice, the *abbé*, and Marie-Anne were entering the carriage.

These soldiers declared upon oath that they recognized the accused; and one of them even went so far as to pronounce a glowing eulogium upon him, declaring him to be a solid fellow, of remarkable courage.

Chanlouineau's eyes during this deposition betrayed an agony of anxiety. Would the soldiers allude to this circumstance of the carriage? No; they did not allude to it.

" That is sufficient," interrupted the president.

Then turning to Chanlouineau:

" What were your motives?" he inquired.

" We hoped to free ourselves from a government imposed upon us by foreigners; to free ourselves from the insolence of the nobility, and to retain the lands that were justly ours."

" Enough! You were one of the leaders of the revolt?"

" One of the leaders—yes."

" Who were the others?"

A faint smile flitted over the lips of the young farmer, as he replied:

" The others were Monsieur Lacheneur, his son Jean, and the Marquis de Sairmeuse."

The duke bounded from his gilded arm-chair.

" Wretch!" he exclaimed, " rascal! vile scoundrel!"

He caught up a heavy inkstand that stood upon the table before him: and one would have supposed that he was about to hurl it at the prisoner's head.

Chanlouineau stood perfectly unmoved in the midst of the assembly, which was excited to the highest pitch by his startling declaration.

"You questioned me," he resumed, "and I replied. You may gag me if my responses do not please you. If there were witnesses *for* me as there are against me, I could prove the truth of my words. As it is, all the prisoners here will tell you that I am speaking the truth. Is it not so, you others ? "

With the exception of Baron d'Escorval, there was not one prisoner who was capable of understanding the real bearing of these audacious allegations; but all, nevertheless, nodded their assent.

"The Marquis de Sairmeuse was so truly our leader," exclaimed the daring peasant, "that he was wounded by a sabre-thrust while fighting by my side."

The face of the duke was more purple than that of a man struck with apoplexy; and his fury almost deprived him of the power of speech.

"You lie, scoundrel ! you lie ! " he gasped.

"Send for the marquis," said Chanlouineau, tranquilly, "and see whether or not he is wounded."

A refusal on the part of the duke could not fail to arouse suspicion. But what could he do? Martial had concealed his wound the day before; it was now impossible to confess that he had been wounded.

Fortunately for the duke, one of the judges relieved him of his embarrassment.

"I hope, Monsieur, that you will not give this arrogant rebel the satisfaction he desires. The commission opposes his demand."

Chanlouineau laughed loudly.

"Very naturally," he exclaimed. "To-morrow my head will be off, and you think nothing will then remain to prove what I say. I have another proof, fortunately—material and indestructible proof—which it is beyond your power to destroy, and which will speak when my body is six feet under ground."

"What is the proof?" demanded another judge, upon whom the duke looked askance.

The prisoner shook his head.

"I will give it to you when you offer me my life in exchange for it," he replied. "It is now in the hands of a trusty person, who knows its value. It will go to the King if necessary. We would like to understand the part which the Marquis de Sairmeuse has played in this affair—whether he was truly with us, or whether he was only an instigating agent."

A tribunal regardful of the immutable rules of justice, or even of its own honor, would, by virtue of its discretionary powers, have instantly demanded the presence of the Marquis de Sairmeuse.

But the military commission considered such a course quite beneath its dignity.

These men arrayed in gorgeous uniforms were not judges charged with the vindication of a cruel law, but still a law—they were the instruments, commissioned by the conquerors, to strike the vanquished in the name of that savage code which may be summed up in two words: "*vae victis.*"

The president, the noble Duc de Sairmeuse, would not have consented to summon Martial on any consideration. Nor did his associate judges wish him to do so.

Had Chanlouineau foreseen this? Probably. Yet, why had he ventured so hazardous a blow?

The tribunal, after a short deliberation, decided that it would not admit this testimony which had so excited the audience, and stupefied Maurice and Abbé Midon.

The examination was continued, therefore, with increased bitterness.

"Instead of designating imaginary leaders," resumed the duke, " you would do well to name the real instigator of this revolt—not Lacheneur, but an individual seated upon the other end of the bench, the elder D'Escorval——"

" Monsieur le Baron d'Escorval was entirely ignorant of the conspiracy, I swear it by all that I hold most sacred——"

" Hold your tongue!" interrupted the counsel for the prosecution. " Instead of wearying the patience of the commission by such ridiculous stories, try to merit its indulgence."

Chanlouineau's glance and gesture expressed such disdain that the man who interrupted him was abashed.

" I wish no indulgence," he said. " I have played, I have lost; here is my head. But if you were not more cruel than wild beasts you would take pity on the poor wretches who surround me. I see at least ten among them who were not our accomplices, and who certainly did not take up arms. Even the others did not know what they were doing. No, they did not ! "

Having spoken, he resumed his seat, proud, indifferent, and apparently oblivious to the murmur which ran through the audience, the soldiers of the guard and even to the platform, at the sound of his vibrant voice.

The despair of the poor peasant women had been reawakened, and their sobs and moans filled the immense hall.

The retired officers had grown even more pale and

gloomy; and tears streamed down the wrinkled cheeks of several.

"That one is a man!" they were thinking.

The *abbé* leaned over and whispered in the ear of Maurice:

"Evidently Chanlouineau has some plan. He intends to save your father. How, I cannot understand."

The judges were conversing in low tones with considerable animation.

A difficulty had presented itself.

The prisoners, ignorant of the charges which would be brought against them, and not expecting instant trial, had not thought of procuring a defender.

And this circumstance, bitter mockery! frightened this iniquitous tribunal, which did not fear to trample beneath its feet the most sacred rules of justice.

The judges had decided; their verdict was, as it were, rendered in advance, and yet they wished to hear a voice raised in defence of those who were already doomed.

It chanced that three lawyers, retained by the friends of several of the prisoners, were in the hall.

They were the three men that Maurice, on his entrance, had noticed conversing near the door of the chapel.

The duke was informed of this fact. He turned to them, and motioned them to approach; then, pointing to Chanlouineau:

"Will you undertake this culprit's defence?" he demanded.

For a moment the lawyers made no response. This monstrous *séance* had aroused a storm of indignation

and disgust within their breasts, and they looked questioningly at each other.

"We are all disposed to undertake the prisoner's defence," at last replied the eldest of the three; "but we
see him for the first time; we are ignorant of his
grounds of defence. We must ask a delay; it is indispensable, in order to confer with him."

"The court can grant you no delay," interrupted M.
de Sairmeuse; "will you accept the defence, yes or
no?"

The advocate hesitated, not that he was afraid, for he
was a brave man: but he was endeavoring to find some
argument strong enough to trouble the conscience of
these judges.

"I will speak in his behalf," said the advocate, at
last, "but not without first protesting with all my
strength against these unheard-of modes of procedure."

"Oh! spare us your homilies, and be brief."

After Chanlouineau's examination, it was difficult to
improvise there, on the spur of the moment, a plea in
his behalf. Still, his courageous advocate, in his indignation, presented a score of arguments which would
have made any other tribunal reflect.

But all the while he was speaking the Duc de Sairmeuse fidgeted in his gilded arm-chair with every sign
of angry impatience.

"The plea was very long," he remarked, when the
lawyer had concluded, "terribly long. We shall never
get through with this business if each prisoner takes up
as much time!"

He turned to his colleagues as if to consult them,
but suddenly changing his mind he proposed to the
prosecuting counsel that he should unite all the cases,
try all the culprits in a body, with the exception of the
elder D'Escorval.

" This will shorten our task, for, in case we adopt this course, there will be but two judgments to be pronounced," he said. " This will not, of course, prevent each individual from defending himself."

The lawyers protested against this. A judgment in a lump, like that suggested by the duke, would destroy all hope of saving a single one of these unfortunate men from the guillotine.

" How can we defend them," the lawyers pleaded, " when we know nothing of the situation of each of the prisoners? we do not even know their names. We shall be obliged to designate them by the cut of their coats and by the color of their hair."

They implored the tribunal to grant them a week for preparation, four days, even twenty-four hours. Futile efforts! The president's proposition was adopted.

Consequently, each prisoner was called to the desk according to the place which he occupied upon the benches. Each man gave his name, his age, his abode, and his profession, and received an order to return to his place.

Six or seven prisoners were actually granted time to say that they were absolutely ignorant of the conspiracy, and that they had been arrested while conversing quietly upon the public highway. They begged to be allowed to furnish proof of the truth of their assertions; they invoked the testimony of the soldiers who had arrested them.

M. d'Escorval, whose case had been separated from the others, was not summoned to the desk. He would be interrogated last.

" Now the counsel for the defence will be heard," said the duke; " but make haste; lose no time! It is already twelve o'clock."

Then began a shameful, revolting, and unheard-of
scene. The duke interrupted the lawyers every other
moment, bidding them be silent, questioning them, or
jeering at them.

"It seems incredible," said he, "that anyone can
think of defending such wretches!"

Or again:

"Silence! You should blush with shame for having constituted yourself the defender of such rascals!"

But the lawyers persevered even while they realized
the utter uselessness of their efforts. But what could
they do under such circumstances? The defence of
these twenty-nine prisoners lasted only one hour and a
half.

Before the last word was fairly uttered, the Duc de
Sairmeuse gave a sigh of relief, and in a tone which
betrayed his delight, said:

"Prisoner Escorval, stand up."

Thus called upon, the baron rose, calm and dignified.
Terrible as his sufferings must have been, there was no
trace of it upon his noble face.

He had even repressed the smile of disdain which the
duke's paltry affection in not giving him the title which
belonged to him, brought to his lips.

But Chanlouineau sprang up at the same time, trembling with indignation, his face all aglow with anger.

"Remain seated," ordered the duke, "or you shall
be removed from the court-room."

Chanlouineau, nevertheless, declared that he would
speak; that he had some remarks to add to the plea
made by the defending counsel.

Upon a sign from the duke, two gendarmes approached and placed their hands upon his shoulders.
He allowed them to force him back into his seat,

though he could easily have crushed them with one
pressure of his brawny arm.

An observer would have supposed that he was furious; secretly, he was delighted. The aim he had had
in view was now attained. In the glance he cast upon
the *abbé*, the latter could read:

" Whatever happens, watch over Maurice; restrain
him. Do not allow him to defeat my plans by any
outbreak."

This caution was not unnecessary. Maurice was
terribly agitated; he could not see, he felt that he was
suffocating, that he was losing his reason.

" Where is the self-control you promised me? " murmured the priest.

But no one observed the young man's condition.
The attention was rapt, breathless. So profound
was the silence that the measured tread of the sentinels
without could be distinctly heard.

Each person present felt that the decisive moment
for which the tribunal had reserved all its attention and
efforts had come.

To convict and condemn the poor peasants, of whom
no one would think twice, was a mere trifle. But to
bring low an illustrious man who had been the counsellor and faithful friend of the Emperor! What glory,
and what an opportunity for the ambitious!

The instinct of the audience spoke the truth. If the
tribunal had acted informally in the case of the obscure
conspirators, it had carefully prepared its suit against
the baron.

Thanks to the activity of the Marquis de Courtornieu, the prosecution had found seven charges against
the baron, the least grave of which was punishable by
death.

" Which of you," demanded M. de Sairmeuse, " will consent to defend this great culprit? "

" I! " exclaimed three advocates, in a breath.

" Take care," said the duke, with a malicious smile; " the task is not light."

" Not light! " It would have been better to say dangerous. It would have been better to say that the defender risked his career, his peace, and his liberty; very probably, his life.

" Our profession has its exigencies," nobly replied the oldest of the advocates.

And the three courageously took their places beside the baron, thus avenging the honor of their robe which had just been miserably sullied, in a city where, among more than a hundred thousand souls, two pure and innocent victims of a furious reaction had not—oh, shame!—been able to find a defender.

" Prisoner," resumed M. de Sairmeuse, " state your name and profession."

" Louis Guillaume, Baron d'Escorval, Commander of the Order of the Legion of Honor, formerly Councillor of State under the Empire."

" So you avow these shameful services? You confess——"

" Pardon, Monsieur; I am proud of having had the honor of serving my country, and of being useful to her in proportion to my ability——"

With a furious gesture the duke interrupted him.

" That is excellent! " he exclaimed. " These gentlemen, the commissioners, will appreciate that. It was, undoubtedly, in the hope of regaining your former position that you entered into a conspiracy against a magnanimous prince with these vile wretches! "

" These peasants are not vile wretches, but misguided men, Monsieur. Moreover, you know—yes, you know as well as I do myself—that I have had no hand in this conspiracy."

"You were arrested in the ranks of the conspirators with weapons in your hands!"

"I was unarmed, Monsieur, as you are well aware; and if I was among the peasantry, it was only because I hoped to induce them to relinquish their senseless enterprise."

"You lie!"

The baron paled beneath the insult, but he made no reply.

There was, however, one man in the assemblage who could no longer endure this horrible and abominable injustice, and this man was Abbé Midon, who, only a moment before, had advised Maurice to be calm.

He brusquely quitted his place, and advanced to the foot of the platform.

"The Baron d'Escorval speaks the truth," he cried, in a ringing voice; "the three hundred prisoners in the citadel will swear to it; these prisoners here would say the same if they stood upon the guillotine; and I, who accompanied him, who walked beside him, I, a priest, swear before the God who will judge all men, Monsieur de Sairmeuse, I swear that all which it was in human power to do to arrest this movement we have done!"

The duke listened with an ironical smile.

"They did not deceive me, then, when they told me that this army of rebels had a chaplain! Ah! Monsieur, you should sink to the earth with shame. You, a priest, mingle with such scoundrels as these—with these enemies of our good King and of our holy religion! Do not deny this! Your haggard features, your swollen eyes, your disordered attire soiled with dust and mud betray your guilt. Must I, a soldier, remind you of what is due your sacred calling? Hold your peace, Monsieur, and depart!"

The counsel for the prisoner sprang up.

"We demand," they cried, "that this witness be heard. He must be heard! Military commissions are not above the laws that regulate ordinary tribunals."

"If I do not speak the truth," resumed the *abbé*, "I am a perjured witness, worse yet, an accomplice. It is your duty, in that case, to have me arrested."

The duke's face expressed a hypocritical compassion.

"No, Monsieur le Curé," said he, "I shall not arrest you. I would avert the scandal which you are trying to cause. We will show your priestly garb the respect the wearer does not deserve. Again, and for the last time, retire, or I shall be obliged to employ force."

What would further resistance avail? Nothing. The *abbé*, with a face whiter than the plastered walls, and eyes filled with tears, came back to his place beside Maurice.

The lawyers, meanwhile, were uttering their protests with increasing energy. But the duke, by a prolonged hammering upon the table with his fists, at last succeeded in reducing them to silence.

"Ah! you wish testimony!" he exclaimed. "Very well, you shall have it. Soldiers, bring in the first witness."

A movement among the guards, and almost immediately Chupin appeared. He advanced deliberately, but his countenance betrayed him. A close observer could have read his anxiety and his terror in his eyes, which wandered restlessly about the room.

And there was a very appreciable terror in his voice

when, with hand uplifted, he swore to tell the truth, the whole truth, and nothing but the truth.

"What do you know regarding the prisoner D'Escorval?" demanded the duke.

"I know that he took part in the rebellion on the night of the fourth."

"Are you sure of this?"

"I can furnish proofs."

"Submit them to the consideration of the commission."

The old scoundrel began to gain more confidence.

"First," he replied, "it was to the house of Monsieur d'Escorval that Lacheneur hastened after he had, much against his will, restored to Monsieur le Duc the château of Monsieur le Duc's ancestors. Monsieur Lacheneur met Chanlouineau there, and from that day dates the plot of this insurrection."

"I was Lacheneur's friend," said the baron; "it was perfectly natural that he should come to me for consolation after a great misfortune."

M. de Sairmeuse turned to his colleague.

"You hear that!" said he. "This D'Escorval calls the restitution of a deposit a great misfortune! Go on, witness."

"In the second place," resumed Chupin, "the accused was always prowling about Lacheneur's house."

"That is false," interrupted the baron. "I never visited the house but once, and on that occasion I implored him to renounce."

He paused, comprehending only when it was too late, the terrible significance of his words. But having begun, he would not retract, and he added:

"I implored him to renounce this project of an insurrection."

" Ah! then you knew his wicked intentions? "

" I suspected them."

" Not to reveal a conspiracy makes one an accomplice, and means the guillotine."

Baron d'Escorval had just signed his death-warrant.

Strange caprice of destiny! He was innocent, and yet he was the only one among the accused whom a regular tribunal could have legally condemned.

Maurice and the *abbé* were prostrated with grief; but Chanlouineau, who turned toward them, had still upon his lips a smile of confidence.

How could he hope when all hope seemed absolutely lost?

But the commissioners made no attempt to conceal their satisfaction. M. de Sairmeuse, especially, evinced an indecent joy.

" Ah, well! Messieurs? " he said to the lawyers, in a sneering tone.

The counsel for the defence poorly dissimulated their discouragement; but they nevertheless endeavored to question the validity of such a declaration on the part of their client. He had said that he *suspected* the conspiracy, not that he *knew* it. It was quite a different thing.

" Say at once that you wish still more overwhelming evidence," interrupted the duke. " Very well! You shall have it. Continue your deposition, witness."

" The accused," continued Chupin, " was present at all the conferences held at Lacheneur's house. The proof of this is as clear as daylight. Being obliged to cross the Oiselle to reach the Reche, and fearing the ferryman would notice his frequent nocturnal voyages, the baron had an old boat repaired which he had not used for years."

"Ah! that is a remarkable circumstance, prisoner; do you recollect having your boat repaired?"

"Yes; but not for the purpose which this man mentions."

"For what purpose, then?"

The baron made no response. Was it not in compliance with the request of Maurice that the boat had been put in order?

"And finally," continued Chupin, "when Lacheneur set fire to his house to give the signal for the insurrection, the prisoner was with him."

"That," exclaimed the duke, "is conclusive evidence."

"I was, indeed, at the Reche," interrupted the baron; "but it was, as I have already told you, with the firm determination of preventing this outbreak."

M. de Sairmeuse gave utterance to a little disdainful laugh.

"Ah, gentlemen!" he said, addressing the commissioners, "can you not see that the prisoner's courage does not equal his depravity? But I will confound him. What did you do, prisoner, when the insurgents left the Reche?"

"I returned to my home with all possible haste, took a horse and repaired to the Croix d'Arcy."

"Then you knew that this was the spot appointed for the general rendezvous?"

"Lacheneur had just informed me."

"If I believed your story, I should tell you that it was your duty to have hastened to Montaignac and informed the authorities. But what you say is untrue. You did not leave Lacheneur, you accompanied him."

"No, Monsieur, no!"

"And what if I could prove this fact beyond all question?"

"Impossible, Monsieur, since such was not the case."

By the malicious satisfaction that lighted M. de Sair-meuse's face, the *abbé* knew that this wicked judge had some terrible weapon in his hands, and that Baron d'Escorval was about to be overwhelmed by one of those fatal coincidences which explain, although they do not justify, judicial errors.

At a sign from the counsel for the prosecution, the Marquis de Courtornieu left his seat and came forward to the platform.

"I must request you, Monsieur le Marquis," said the duke, "to have the goodness to read to the commission the deposition written and signed by your daughter."

This scene must have been prepared in advance for the audience. M. de Courtornieu cleaned his glasses, drew from his pocket a paper which he unfolded, and amid a death-like silence, he read:

"I, Blanche de Courtornieu, do declare upon oath that, on the evening of the fourth of February, between ten and eleven o'clock, on the public road leading from Sairmeuse to Montaignac, I was assailed by a crowd of armed brigands. While they were deliberating as to whether they should take possession of my person and pillage my carriage, I overheard one of these men say to another, speaking of me: ' She must get out, must she not, Monsieur d'Escorval?' I believe that the brigand who uttered these words was a peasant named Chanlouineau, but I dare not assert it on oath."

A terrible cry, followed by inarticulate moans, interrupted the marquis.

The suffering which Maurice endured was too great for his strength and his reason. He was about to spring forward and cry:

" It was I who addressed those words to Chanlouineau.   I alone am guilty ; my father is innocent! "

But fortunately the *abbé* had the presence of mind to
hold him back, and place his hand over the poor
youth's lips.

But the priest would not have been able to restrain
Maurice without the aid of the retired army officers,
who were standing beside him.

Divining all, perhaps, they surrounded Maurice,
took him up, and carried him from the room by main
force, in spite of his violent resistance.

All this occupied scarcely ten seconds.

" What is the cause of this disturbance? " inquired
the duke, looking angrily over the audience.

No one uttered a word.

" At the least noise the hall shall be cleared," added
M. de Sairmeuse.   " And you, prisoner, what have
you to say in self-justification, after this crushing accusation by Mademoiselle de Courtornieu? "

" Nothing," murmured the baron.

" So you confess your guilt? "

Once outside, the *abbé* confided Maurice to the care
of three officers, who promised to go with him, to
carry him by main force, if need be, to the hotel, and
keep him there.

Relieved on this score, the priest re-entered the hall
just in time to see the baron seat himself without making any response, thus indicating that he had relinquished all intention of defending his life.

Really, what could he say?   How could he defend
himself without betraying his son?

Until now there had not been one person who did
not believe in the baron's entire innocence.   Could it
be that he was guilty?   His silence must be accepted

as a confession of guilt; at least, some present believed
so.

Baron d'Escorval appeared to be guilty. Was that
not a sufficiently great victory for the Duc de Sairmeuse?

He turned to the lawyers, and with an air of weariness and disdain he said:

" Now speak, since it is absolutely necessary; but no
long phrases! We should have finished here an hour
ago."

The oldest lawyer rose, trembling with indignation,
ready to dare anything for the sake of giving free utterance to his thought, but the baron checked him.

" Do not try to defend me," he said, calmly; " it
would be labor wasted. I have only a word to say to
my judges. Let them remember what the noble and
generous Marshal Moncey wrote to the King: ' The
scaffold does not make friends.' "

This recollection was not of a nature to soften the
hearts of the judges. The marshal, for that saying,
had been deprived of his office, and condemned to three
months' imprisonment.

As the advocates made no further attempt to argue
the case, the commission retired to deliberate. This
gave M. d'Escorval an opportunity to speak with his
defenders. He shook them warmly by the hand, and
thanked them for their devotion and for their courage.

The good man wept.

Then the baron, turning to the oldest among them,
quickly and in a low voice said:

" I have a last favor to ask of you. When the sentence of death shall have been pronounced upon me,
go at once to my son. You will say to him that his
dying father commands him to live; he will understand

you. Tell him it is my last wish; that he live—live for his mother!"

He said no more; the judges were returning.

Of the thirty prisoners, nine were declared not guilty, and released.

The remaining twenty-one, and M. d'Escorval and Chanlouineau were among the number, were condemned to death.

But the smile had not once forsaken Chanlouineau's lips.

CHAPTER XXVIII

The *abbé* had been right in feeling he could trust the officers to whose care he had confided Maurice.

Finding their entreaties would not induce him to leave the citadel, they seized him and literally carried him away. He made the most desperate efforts to escape; each step was a struggle.

"Leave me!" he exclaimed; "let me go where duty calls me. You only dishonor me in pretending to save me."

His agony was terrible. He had thrown himself headlong into this absurd undertaking, and now the responsibility of his acts had fallen upon his father. He, the culprit, would live, and his innocent father would perish on the guillotine. It was to this his love for Marie-Anne had led him, that radiant love which in other days had smiled so joyously.

But our capacity for suffering has its limits.

When they had carried him to the room in the hotel where his mother and Marie-Anne were waiting in agonized surprise, that irresistible torpor which follows suffering too intense for human endurance, crept over him.

"Nothing is decided yet," the officers answered in response to Mme. d'Escorval's questions. "The *curé* will hasten here as soon as the verdict is rendered."

Then, as they had promised not to lose sight of Maurice, they seated themselves in gloomy silence.

The house was silent. One might have supposed the hotel deserted. At last, a little before four o'clock, the *abbé* came in, followed by the lawyer to whom the baron had confided his last wishes.

"My husband!" exclaimed Mme. d'Escorval, springing wildly from her chair.

The priest bowed his head; she understood.

"Death!" she faltered. "They have condemned him!"

And overcome by the terrible blow, she sank back, inert, with hanging arms.

But the weakness did not last long; she again sprang up, her eyes brilliant with heroic resolve.

"We must save him!" she exclaimed. "We must wrest him from the scaffold. Up, Maurice! up, Marie-Anne! No more weak lamentations, we must to work! You, also, gentlemen, will aid me. I can count upon your assistance, Monsieur le Curé. What are we going to do? I do not know! But something must be done. The death of this just man would be too great a crime. God will not permit it."

She suddenly paused, with clasped hands, and eyes uplifted to heaven, as if seeking divine inspiration.

"And the King," she resumed; "will the King consent to such a crime? No. A king can refuse mercy, but he cannot refuse justice. I will go to him. I will tell him all! Why did not this thought come to me sooner? We must start for Paris without losing an instant. Maurice, you will accompany me. One of you gentlemen will go at once and order post-horses."

Thinking they would obey her, she hastened into the next room to make preparations for her journey.

"Poor woman!" the lawyer whispered to the *abbé*, "she does not know that the sentence of a military commission is executed in twenty-four hours."

"Well?"

"It requires four days to make the journey to Paris."

He reflected a moment, then added:

"But, after all, to let her go would be an act of mercy. Did not Ney, on the morning of his execution, implore the King to order the removal of his wife who was sobbing and moaning in his cell?"

The *abbé* shook his head.

"No," said he; "Madame d'Escorval will never forgive us if we prevent her from receiving her husband's last farewell."

She, at that very moment, re-entered the room, and the priest was trying to gather courage to tell her the cruel truth, when someone knocked violently at the door.

One of the officers went to open it, and Bavois, the corporal of grenadiers, entered, his right hand lifted to his cap, as if he were in the presence of his superior officer.

"Is Mademoiselle Lacheneur here?" he demanded.

Marie-Anne came forward.

"I am she, Monsieur," she replied; "what do you desire of me?"

"I am ordered, Mademoiselle, to conduct you to the citadel."

"Ah!" exclaimed Maurice, in a ferocious tone; "so they imprison women also!"

The worthy corporal struck himself a heavy blow upon the forehead.

"I am an old stupid!" he exclaimed, "and express myself badly. I meant to say that I came to seek mademoiselle at the request of one of the condemned, a man named Chanlouineau, who desires to speak with her."

"Impossible, my good man," said one of the officers; "they would not allow this lady to visit one of the condemned without special permission——"

"Well, she has this permission," said the old soldier.

Assuring himself, with a glance, that he had nothing to fear from anyone present, he added, in lower tones:

"This Chanlouineau told me that the *curé* would understand his reasons."

Had the brave peasant really found some means of salvation? The *abbé* almost began to believe it.

"You must go with this worthy man, Marie-Anne," said he.

The poor girl shuddered at the thought of seeing Chanlouineau again, but the idea of refusing never once occurred to her.

"Let us go," she said, quietly.

But the corporal did not stir from his place, and winking, according to his habit when he desired to attract the attention of his hearers:

"In one moment," he said. "This Chanlouineau, who seems to be a shrewd fellow, told me to tell you that all was going well. May I be hung if I can see how! Still such is his opinion. He also told me to tell you not to stir from this place, and not to attempt anything until mademoiselle returns, which will be in less than an hour. He swears to you that he will keep his promise; he only asks you to pledge your word that you will obey him——"

"We will take no action until an hour has passed," said the *abbé*. "I promise that——"

"That is all. Salute company. And now, Mademoiselle, on the double-quick, march! The poor
devil over there must be on coals of fire."

That a condemned prisoner should be allowed to receive a visit from the daughter of the leader of the rebellion—of that Lacheneur who had succeeded in making his escape—was indeed surprising.

But Chanlouineau had been ingenious enough to
discover a means of procuring this special permission.

With this aim in view, when sentence of death was
passed upon him, he pretended to be overcome with
terror, and to weep piteously.

The soldiers could scarcely believe their eyes when
they saw this robust young fellow, who had been so insolent and defiant a few hours before, so overcome that
they were obliged to carry him to his cell.

There, his lamentations were redoubled; and he
begged the guard to go to the Duc de Sairmeuse, or
the Marquis de Courtornieu, and tell them he had revelations of the greatest importance to make.

That potent word "revelations" made M. de Courtornieu hasten to the prisoner's cell.

He found Chanlouineau on his knees, his features
distorted by what was apparently an agony of fear.
The man dragged himself toward him, took his hands
and kissed them, imploring mercy and forgiveness,
swearing that to preserve his life he was ready to do
anything, yes, anything, even to deliver up M. Lacheneur.

To capture Lacheneur! Such a prospect had
powerful attractions for the Marquis de Courtornieu.

"Do you know, then, where this brigand is concealed?" he inquired.

Chanlouineau admitted that he did not know, but

declared that Marie-Anne, Lacheneur's daughter, knew her father's hiding-place. She had, he declared, perfect confidence in him ; and if they would only send for her, and allow him ten minutes' private conversation with her, he was sure he could obtain the secret of her father's place of concealment. So the bargain was quickly concluded.

The prisoner's life was promised him in exchange for the life of Lacheneur.

A soldier, who chanced to be Corporal Bavois, was sent to summon Marie-Anne.

And Chanlouineau waited in terrible anxiety. No one had told him what had taken place at Escorval, but he divined it by the aid of that strange prescience which so often illuminates the mind when death is near at hand.

He was almost certain that Mme. d'Escorval was in Montaignac; he was equally certain that Marie-Anne was with her ; and if she were, he knew that she would come.

And he waited, counting the seconds by the throbbings of his heart.

He waited, understanding the cause of every sound without, distinguishing with the marvellous acuteness of senses excited to the highest pitch by passion, sounds which would have been inaudible to another person.

At last, at the end of the corridor, he heard the rustling of a dress against the wall.

" It is she," he murmured.

Footsteps approached ; the heavy bolts were drawn back, the door opened, and Marie-Anne entered, accompanied by Corporal Bavois.

" Monsieur de Courtornieu promised me that we should be left alone ! " exclaimed Chanlouineau.

" Therefore, I go at once," replied the old soldier. " But I have orders to return for mademoiselle in half an hour."

When the door closed behind the worthy corporal, Chanlouineau took Marie-Anne's hand and drew her to the tiny grated window.

" Thank you for coming," said he, " thank you. I can see you and speak to you once more. Now that my hours are numbered, I may reveal the secret of my soul and of my life. Now, I can venture to tell you how ardently I have loved you—how much I still love you."

Involuntarily Marie-Anne drew away her hand and stepped back.

This outburst of passion, at such a moment, seemed at once unspeakably sad and frightful.

" Have I, then, offended you? " said Chanlouineau, sadly. " Forgive one who is about to die! You cannot refuse to listen to the voice of one, who after to-morrow, will have vanished from earth forever.

" I have loved you for a long time, Marie-Anne, for more than six years. Before I saw you, I loved only my possessions. To raise fine crops, and to amass a fortune, seemed to me, then, the greatest possible happiness here below.

" Why did I meet you? But at that time you were so high, and I, so low, that never in my wildest dreams did I aspire to you. I went to church each Sunday only that I might worship you as peasant women worship the Blessed Virgin; I went home with my eyes and my heart full of you—and that was all.

" Then came the misfortune that brought us nearer to each other; and your father made me as insane, yes, as insane as himself.

" After the insults he received from the Sairmeuse, your father resolved to revenge himself upon these arrogant nobles, and he selected me for his accomplice. He had read my heart. On leaving the house of Baron d'Escorval, on that Sunday evening, which you must remember, the compact that bound me to your father was made.

" ' You love my daughter, my boy,' said he. ' Very well, aid me, and I promise you, in case we succeed, she shall be your wife. Only,' he added, ' I must warn you that you hazard your life.'

" But what was life in comparison with the hope that dazzled me! From that night I gave body, soul, and fortune to the cause. Others were influenced by hatred, or by ambition; but I was actuated by neither of these motives.

" What did the quarrels of the great matter to me—a simple laborer? I knew that the greatest were powerless to give my crops a drop of rain in season of drought, or a ray of sunshine during the rain.

" I took part in this conspiracy because I loved you ——"

" Ah! you are cruel!" exclaimed Marie-Anne, " you are pitiless! "

It seemed to the poor girl that he was reproaching her for the horrible fate which Lacheneur had brought upon him, and for the terrible part which her father had imposed upon her, and which she had not been strong enough to refuse to perform.

But Chanlouineau scarcely heard Marie-Anne's exclamation. All the bitterness of the past had mounted to his brain like fumes of alcohol. He was scarcely conscious of his own words.

" But the day soon came," he continued, " when my

foolish illusions were destroyed. You could not be mine since you belonged to another. I might have broken my compact! I thought of doing so, but had not the courage. To see you, to hear your voice, to dwell beneath the same roof with you, was happiness. I longed to see you happy and honored; I fought for the triumph of another, for him whom you had chosen ——"

A sob that had risen in his throat choked his utterance; he buried his face in his hands to hide his tears, and, for a moment, seemed completely overcome.

But he mastered his weakness after a little and in a firm voice, he said:

" We must not linger over the past. Time flies and the future is ominous."

As he spoke, he went to the door and applied first his eye, then his ear to the opening, to see that there were no spies without.

No one was in the corridor; he could not hear a sound.

He came back to Marie-Anne's side, and tearing the sleeve of his jacket open with his teeth, he drew from it two letters, wrapped carefully in a piece of cloth.

" Here," he said, in a low voice, " is a man's life! "

Marie-Anne knew nothing of Chanlouineau's promises and hopes, and bewildered by her distress, she did not at first understand.

" This," she exclaimed, " is a man's life! "

" Hush, speak lower! " interrupted Chanlouineau.
" Yes, one of these letters might perhaps save the life of one who has been condemned to death."

" Unfortunate man! Why do you not make use of it and save yourself? "

The young man sadly shook his head.

" Is it possible that you could ever love me? " he said, simply. " No, it is not. I have, therefore, no desire to live. Rest beneath the sod is preferable to the misery I am forced to endure. Moreover I was justly condemned. I knew what I was doing when I left the Reche with my gun upon my shoulder, and my sword by my side; I have no right to complain. But those cruel judges have condemned an innocent man ——"

" Baron d'Escorval? "

" Yes—the father of—Maurice! "

His voice changed in uttering the name of this man, for whose happiness he would have given ten lives had they been his to give.

" I wish to save him," he added, " I can do it."

" Oh! if what you said were true? But you undoubtedly deceive yourself."

" I know what I am saying."

Fearing that some spy outside would overhear him, he came close to Marie-Anne and said, rapidly, and in a low voice:

" I never believed in the success of this conspiracy. When I sought for a weapon of defence in case of failure, the Marquis de Sairmeuse furnished it. When it became necessary to send a circular warning our accomplices of the date decided upon for the uprising, I persuaded Monsieur Martial to write a model. He suspected nothing. I told him it was for a wedding; he did what I asked. This letter, which is now in my possession, is the rough draft of the circular; and it was written by the hand of the Marquis de Sairmeuse. It is impossible for him to deny it. There is an erasure on each line. Everyone would regard it as the handiwork of a man who was seeking to convey his real meaning in ambiguous phrases.

Chanlouineau opened the envelope and showed her the famous letter which he had dictated, and in which the space for the date of the insurrection was left blank.

" My dear friend, we are at last agreed, and the marriage is decided, etc."

The light that had sparkled in Marie-Anne's eye was suddenly extinguished.

" And you believe that this letter can be of any service? " she inquired, in evident discouragement.

" I do not *think* it ! "

" But——"

With a gesture, he interrupted her.

" We must not lose time in discussion—listen to me. Of itself, this letter might be unimportant, but I have arranged matters in such a way that it will produce a powerful effect. I declared before the commission that the Marquis de Sairmeuse was one of the leaders of the movement. They laughed; and I read incredulity on the faces of the judges. But calumny is never without its effect. When the Duc de Sairmeuse is about to receive a reward for his services, there will be enemies in plenty to remember and to repeat my words. He knew this so well that he was greatly agitated, ever while his colleagues sneered at my accusation."

" To accuse a man falsely is a great crime," murmured the honest Marie-Anne.

" Yes, but I wish to save my friend, and I cannot choose my means. I was all the more sure of success as I knew that the marquis had been wounded. I declared that he was fighting against the troops by my side; I demanded that he should be summoned before the tribunal; I told them that I had in my possession unquestionable proofs of his complicity."

"Did you say that the Marquis de Sairmeuse had been wounded?" inquired Marie-Anne.

Chanlouineau's face betrayed the most intense astonishment.

"What!" he exclaimed, "you do not know——"

Then after an instant's reflection:

"Fool that I am!" he resumed. "Who could have told you what had happened? You remember that when we were travelling over the Sairmeuse road on our way to the Croix d'Arcy, and after your father had left us to ride on in advance, Maurice placed himself at the head of one division, and you walked beside him, while your brother Jean and myself stayed behind to urge on the laggards. We were performing our duty conscientiously when suddenly we heard the gallop of a horse behind us. 'We must know who is coming,' Jean said to me.

"We paused. The horse soon reached us; we caught the bridle and held him. Can you guess who the rider was? Martial de Sairmeuse.

"To describe your brother's fury on recognizing the marquis would be impossible.

"'At last I find you, wretched noble!' he exclaimed, 'and now we will settle our account! After reducing my father, who has just given you a fortune, to despair and penury, you have tried to degrade my sister. I will have my revenge! Down, we must fight!'"

Marie-Anne could scarcely tell whether she was awake or dreaming.

"My brother," she murmured, "has challenged the marquis! Is it possible?"

"Brave as Monsieur Martial is," pursued Chanlouineau, "he did not seem inclined to accept the invita-

tion. He stammered out something like this: 'You
are mad—you are jesting—have we not always been
friends? What does this mean?'

" Jean ground his teeth in rage. ' This means that
we have endured your insulting familiarity long
enough,' he replied, ' and if you do not dismount and
meet me in open combat, I will blow your brains out!'

" Your brother, as he spoke, manipulated his pistol
in so threatening a manner that the marquis dismounted, and addressing me:

" ' You see, Chanlouineau,' he said, ' I must fight a
duel or submit to assassination. If Jean kills me there
is no more to be said—but if I kill him, what is to be
done?'

" I told him he would be free to depart on condition
he would give me his word not to return to Montaignac
before two o'clock.

" ' Then I accept the challenge,' said he; ' give me a
weapon.'

" I gave him my sword, your brother drew his, and
they took their places in the middle of the highway."

The young farmer paused to take breath, then said,
more slowly:

" Marie-Anne, your father and I have misjudged
your brother. Poor Jean's appearance is terribly
against him. His face indicates a treacherous, cowardly nature, his smile is cunning, and his eyes always
shun yours. We have distrusted him, but we should
ask his pardon. A man who fights as I saw him fight,
is deserving of confidence. For this combat in the
public road, and in the darkness of the night, was terrible. They attacked each other silently but furiously. At last Jean fell."

" Ah! my brother is dead!" exclaimed Marie-Anne.

"No," responded Chanlouineau; "at least we have reason to hope not; and I know he has not lacked any attention. This duel had another witness, a man named Poignot, whom you must remember; he was one of your father's tenants. He took Jean, promising me that he would conceal him and care for him.

"As for the marquis, he showed me that he too was wounded, and then he remounted his horse, saying:

"'What could I do? He would have it so.'"

Marie-Anne understood now.

"Give me the letter," she said to Chanlouineau, "I will go to the duke. I will find some way to reach him, and then God will tell me what course to pursue."

The noble peasant handed the girl the tiny scrap of paper which might have been his own salvation.

"On no account," said he, "must you allow the duke to suppose that you have upon your person the proof with which you threaten him. Who knows of what he might be capable under such circumstances? He will say, at first, that he can do nothing—that he sees no way to save the baron. You will tell him that he must find a means, if he does not wish this letter sent to Paris, to one of his enemies——"

He paused; he heard the grating of the bolt. Corporal Bavois reappeared.

"The half hour expired ten minutes ago," he said, sadly. "I have my orders."

"Coming," said Chanlouineau; "all is ended!"

And handing Marie-Anne the second letter:

"This is for you," he added. "You will read it when I am no more. Pray, pray, do not weep thus! Be brave! You will soon be the wife of Maurice. And when you are happy, think sometimes of the poor peasant who loved you so much."

Marie-Anne could not utter a word, but she lifted her face to his.

" Ah! I dared not ask it! " he exclaimed.

And for the first time he clasped her in his arms and pressed his lips to her pallid cheek.

" Now adieu," he said once more. " Do not lose a moment. Adieu! "

CHAPTER XXIX

The prospect of capturing Lacheneur, the chief conspirator, excited the Marquis de Courtornieu so much that he had not been able to tear himself away from the citadel to return home to his dinner.

Remaining near the entrance of the dark corridor leading to Chanlouineau's cell, he watched Marie-Anne depart; but as he saw her go out into the twilight with a quick, alert step, he felt a sudden doubt of Chanlouineau's sincerity.

" Can it be that this miserable peasant has deceived me? " he thought.

So strong was this suspicion that he hastened after her, determined to question her—to ascertain the truth —to arrest her, if necessary.

But he no longer possessed the agility of youth, and when he reached the gateway the guard told him that Mlle. Lacheneur had already passed out. He rushed out after her, looked about on every side, but could see no trace of her. He re-entered the citadel, furious with himself for his own credulity.

" Still, I can visit Chanlouineau," thought he, " and to-morrow will be time enough to summon this creature and question her."

" This creature " was even then hastening up the long, ill-paved street that led to the Hôtel de France.

Regardless of self, and of the curious gaze of a few passers-by, she ran on, thinking only of shortening the terrible anxiety which her friends at the hotel must be enduring.

" All is not lost ! " she exclaimed, on re-entering the room.

" My God, Thou hast heard my prayers ! " murmured the baroness.

Then, suddenly seized by a horrible dread, she added :

" Do not attempt to deceive me. Are you not trying to elude me with false hopes? That would be cruel ! "

" I am not deceiving you, Madame. Chanlouineau has given me a weapon, which, I hope and believe, places the Duc de Sairmeuse in our power. He is omnipotent in Montaignac; the only man who could oppose him, Monsieur de Courtornieu, is his friend. I believe that Monsieur d'Escorval can be saved."

" Speak ! " cried Maurice ; " what must we do ? "

" Pray and wait, Maurice. I must act alone in this matter, but be assured that I—the cause of all your misfortune—will leave nothing undone which is possible for mortal to do."

Absorbed in the task which she had imposed upon herself, Marie-Anne had failed to remark a stranger who had arrived during her absence—an old white-haired peasant.

The *abbé* called her attention to him.

" Here is a courageous friend," said he, " who since morning, has been searching for you everywhere, in order to give you news of your father."

Marie-Anne was so overcome that she could scarcely falter her gratitude.

" Oh, you need not thank me," answered the brave
peasant. " I said to myself: ' The poor girl must be
terribly anxious. I ought to relieve her of her misery.'
So I came to tell you that Monsieur Lacheneur is safe
and well, except for a wound in the leg, which causes
him considerable suffering, but which will be healed in
two or three weeks. My son-in-law, who was hunting
yesterday in the mountains, met him near the frontier
in company with two of his friends. By this time he
must be in Piedmont, beyond the reach of the *gendarmes.*"

" Let us hope now," said the *abbé*, " that we shall
soon hear what has become of Jean."

" I know, already, Monsieur," responded Marie-
Anne ; " my brother has been badly wounded, and he is
now under the protection of kind friends."

She bowed her head, almost crushed beneath her
burden of sorrow, but soon rallying, she exclaimed:

" What am I doing! What right have I to think of
my friends, when upon my promptness and upon my
courage depends the life of an innocent man compromised by them ? "

Maurice, the *abbé*, and the officers surrounded the
brave young girl. They wished to know what she was
about to attempt, and to dissuade her from incurring
useless danger.

She refused to reply to their pressing questions.
They wished to accompany her, or, at least, to follow
her at a distance, but she declared that she must go
alone.

" I will return in less than two hours, and then we
can decide what must be done," said she, as she hastened away.

To obtain an audience with the Duc de Sairmeuse was certainly a difficult matter; Maurice and the *abbé* had proved that only too well the previous day. Besieged by weeping and heart-broken families, he shut himself up securely, fearing, perhaps, that he might be moved by their entreaties.

Marie-Anne knew this, but it did not alarm her. Chanlouineau had given her a word, the same which he had used; and this word was a key which would unlock the most firmly and obstinately locked doors.

In the vestibule of the house occupied by the Duc de Sairmeuse, three or four valets stood talking.

"I am the daughter of Monsieur Lacheneur," said Marie-Anne, addressing one of them. "I must speak to the duke at once, on matters connected with the revolt."

"The duke is absent."

"I came to make a revelation."

The servant's manner suddenly changed.

"In that case follow me, Mademoiselle."

She followed him up the stairs and through two or three rooms. At last he opened a door, saying, "enter." She went in.

It was not the Duc de Sairmeuse who was in the room, but his son, Martial.

Stretched upon a sofa, he was reading a paper by the light of a large candelabra.

On seeing Marie-Anne he sprang up, as pale and agitated as if the door had given passage to a spectre.

"You!" he stammered.

But he quickly mastered his emotion, and in a second his quick mind revolved all the possibilities that might have produced this visit.

"Lacheneur has been arrested!" he exclaimed,

" and you, wishing to save him from the fate which the military commission will pronounce upon him, have thought of me. Thank you, dearest Marie-Anne, thank you for your confidence. I will not abuse it. Let your heart be reassured. We will save your father, I promise you—I swear it. How, I do not yet know. But what does that matter? It is enough that he shall be saved. I will have it so!"

His voice betrayed the intense passion and joy that was surging in his heart.

"My father has not been arrested," said Marie-Anne, coldly.

"Then," said Martial, with some hesitation, "then it is Jean who is a prisoner."

"My brother is in safety. If he survives his wounds he will escape all attempts at capture."

From white the Marquis de Sairmeuse had turned as red as fire. By Marie-Anne's manner he saw that she knew of the duel. He made no attempt to deny it; but he tried to excuse himself.

"It was Jean who challenged me," said he; "I tried to avoid it. I only defended my own life in fair combat, and with equal weapons——"

Marie-Anne interrupted him.

"I reproach you for nothing, Monsieur le Marquis," she said, quietly.

"Ah! Marie-Anne, I am more severe than you. Jean was right to challenge me. I deserved his anger. He knew the baseness of which I had been guilty; but you—you were ignorant of it. Oh! Marie-Anne, if I wronged you in thought it was because I did not know you. Now I know that you, above all others, are pure and chaste."

He tried to take her hands; she repulsed him

with horror; and broke into a fit of passionate sobbing.

Of all the blows she had received this last was most terrible and overwhelming.

What humiliation and shame! Now, indeed, was her cup of sorrow filled to overflowing. " Chaste and pure!" he had said. Oh, bitter mockery!

But Martial misunderstood the meaning of the poor girl's gesture.

"Oh! I comprehend your indignation," he resumed, with growing eagerness. " But if I have injured you even in thought, I now offer you reparation. I have been a fool—a miserable fool—for I love you; I love, and can love you only. I am the Marquis de Sairmeuse. I am the possessor of millions. I entreat you, I implore you to be my wife."

Marie-Anne listened in utter bewilderment. Vertigo seized her; even reason seemed to totter upon its throne.

But now, it had been Chanlouineau who, in his prison-cell, cried that he died for love of her. Now, it was Martial who avowed his willingness to sacrifice his ambition and his future for her sake.

And the poor peasant condemned to death, and the son of the all-powerful Duc de Sairmeuse, had avowed their passion in almost the very same words.

Martial paused, awaiting some response—a word, a gesture. But Marie-Anne remained mute, motionless, frozen.

"You are silent," he cried, with increased vehemence. " Do you question my sincerity? No, it is impossible! Then why this silence? Do you fear my father's opposition? You need not. I know how to gain his consent. Besides, what does his approbation matter to us? Have we any need of him? Am I not my own master? Am I not rich—immensely rich? I should be a miserable fool, a coward, if I hesitated between his stupid prejudices and the happiness of my life."

He was evidently obliging himself to weigh all the possible objections, in order to answer them and overrule them.

" Is it on account of your family that you hesitate? " he continued. " Your father and brother are pursued, and France is closed against them. Very well, we will leave France, and they shall come and live near you. Jean will no longer dislike me when you are my wife. We will all live in England or in Italy. Now I am grateful for the fortune that will enable me to make life a continual enchantment for you. I love you—and in the happiness and tender love which shall be yours in the future, I will compel you to forget all the bitterness of the past! "

Marie-Anne knew the Marquis de Sairmeuse well enough to understand the intensity of the love revealed by these astounding propositions.

And for that very reason she hesitated to tell him that he had won this triumph over his pride in vain.

She was anxiously wondering to what extremity his wounded vanity would carry him, and if a refusal would not transform him into a bitter enemy.

" Why do you not answer? " asked Martial, with evident anxiety.

She felt that she must reply, that she must speak, say something; but she could not unclose her lips.

" I am only a poor girl, Monsieur le Marquis," she murmured, at last. " If I accepted your offer, you would regret it continually."

" Never ! "

"But you are no longer free. You have already plighted your troth. Mademoiselle Blanche de Cour- tornieu is your promised wife."

"Ah! say one word—only one—and this engage- ment, which I detest, is broken."

She was silent. It was evident that her mind was fully made up, and that she refused his offer.

"Do you hate me, then?" asked Martial, sadly.

If she had allowed herself to tell the whole truth Marie-Anne would have answered "Yes." The Mar- quis de Sairmeuse did inspire her with an almost insur- mountable aversion.

"I no more belong to myself than you belong to yourself, Monsieur," she faltered.

A gleam of hatred, quickly extinguished, shone in Martial's eye.

"Always Maurice!" said he.

"Always."

She expected an angry outburst, but he remained perfectly calm.

"Then," said he, with a forced smile, "I must be- lieve this and other evidence. I must believe that you have forced me to play a most ridiculous part. Until now I doubted it."

The poor girl bowed her head, crimsoning with shame to the roots of her hair; but she made no at- tempt at denial.

"*I* was not my own mistress," she stammered; "my father commanded and threatened, and I—I obeyed him."

"That matters little," he interrupted; "your *rôle* has not been that which a pure young girl should play."

It was the only reproach he had uttered, and still he regretted it, perhaps because he did not wish her to

know how deeply he was wounded, perhaps because—
as he afterward declared—he could not overcome his
love for Marie-Anne.

" Now," he resumed, " I understand your presence
here. You come to ask mercy for Monsieur d'Escorval."

" Not mercy, but justice. The baron is innocent."

Martial approached Marie-Anne, and lowering his
voice :

" If the father is innocent," he whispered, " then it is
the son who is guilty."

She recoiled in terror. He knew the secret which
the judges could not, or would not penetrate.

But seeing her anguish, he had pity.

" Another reason," said he, " for attempting to save
the baron ! His blood shed upon the guillotine would
form an impassable gulf between Maurice and you. I
will join my efforts to yours."

Blushing and embarrassed, Marie-Anne dared not
thank him. How was she about to reward his generosity? By vilely traducing him. Ah ! she would infinitely have preferred to see him angry and revenge-
ful.

Just then a valet opened the door, and the Duc de
Sairmeuse, still in full uniform, entered.

" Upon my word ! " he exclaimed, as he crossed the
threshold, " I must confess that Chupin is an admirable
hunter. Thanks to him——"

He paused abruptly; he had not perceived Marie-
Anne until now.

" The daughter of that scoundrel Lacheneur ! " said
he, with an air of the utmost surprise. " What does
she desire here ? "

The decisive moment had come—the life of the baron

hung upon Marie-Anne's courage and address. The consciousness of the terrible responsibility devolving upon her restored her self-control and calmness as if by magic.

"I have a revelation to sell to you, Monsieur," she said, resolutely.

The duke regarded her with mingled wonder and curiosity; then, laughing heartily, he threw himself upon a sofa, exclaiming:

"Sell it, my pretty one—sell it!"

"I cannot speak until I am alone with you."

At a sign from his father, Martial left the room.

"You can speak now," said the duke.

She did not lose a second.

"You must have read, Monsieur," she began, "the circular convening the conspirators."

"Certainly; I have a dozen copies in my pocket."

"By whom do you suppose it was written?"

"By the elder D'Escorval, or by your father."

"You are mistaken, Monsieur; that letter was the work of the Marquis de Sairmeuse, your son."

The duke sprang up, fire flashing from his eyes, his face purple with anger.

"Zounds! girl! I advise you to bridle your tongue!"

"The proof of what I have asserted exists."

"Silence, you hussy, or——"

"The lady who sends me here, Monsieur, possesses the original of this circular written by the hand of Monsieur Martial, and I am obliged to tell you——"

She did not have an opportunity to complete the sentence. The duke sprang to the door, and, in a voice of thunder, called his son.

As soon as Martial entered the room:

"Repeat," said the duke—"repeat before my son what you have just said to me."

Boldly, with head erect, and clear, firm voice, Marie-Anne repeated her accusation.

She expected, on the part of the marquis, an indignant denial, cruel reproaches, or an angry explanation. Not a word. He listened with a nonchalant air, and she almost believed she could read in his eyes an encouragement to proceed, and a promise of protection.

When she had concluded:

"Well!" demanded the duke, imperiously.

"First," replied Martial, lightly, "I would like to see this famous circular."

The duke handed him a copy.

"Here—read it."

Martial glanced over it, laughed heartily, and exclaimed:

"A clever trick."

"What do you say?"

"I say that this Chanlouineau is a sly rascal. Who the devil would have thought the fellow so cunning to see his honest face? Another lesson to teach one not to trust to appearances."

In all his life the Duc de Sairmeuse had never received so severe a shock.

"Chanlouineau was not lying, then," he said to his son, in a choked, unnatural voice; "you *were* one of the instigators of this rebellion, then?"

Martial's face grew dark, and in a tone of disdainful hauteur, he replied:

"This is the fourth time, sir, that you have addressed that question to me, and for the fourth time I answer: 'No.' That should suffice. If the fancy had seized me for taking part in this movement, I should frankly

confess it.   What possible reason could I have for concealing anything from you?"

"The facts!" interrupted the duke, in a frenzy of
passion; "the facts!"

"Very well," rejoined Martial, in his usual indifferent tone; "the fact is that the model of this circular
does exist, that it was written in my best hand on a
very large sheet of very poor paper.   I recollect that in
trying to find appropriate expressions I erased and re-
wrote several words.   Did I date this writing?   I
think I did, but I could not swear to it."

"How do you reconcile this with your denials?"
exclaimed M. de Sairmeuse.

"I can do this easily.   Did I not tell you just now
that Chanlouineau had made a tool of me?"

The duke no longer knew what to believe; but what
exasperated him more than all else was his son's imperturbable tranquillity.

"Confess, rather, that you have been led into this
filth by your mistress," he retorted, pointing to Marie-
Anne.

But this insult Martial would not tolerate.

"Mademoiselle Lacheneur is not my mistress," he
replied, in a tone so imperious that it was a menace.
"It is true, however, that it rests only with her to decide whether she will be the Marquise de Sairmeuse to-
morrow.   Let us abandon these recriminations, they
do not further the progress of our business."

The faint glimmer of reason which still lighted M.
de Sairmeuse's mind, checked the still more insulting
reply that rose to his lips.   Trembling with suppressed
rage, he made the circuit of the room several times, and
finally paused before Marie-Anne, who remained in the
same place, as motionless as a statue.

"Come, my good girl," said he, " give me the writ-ing."

" It is not in my possession, sir."

" Where is it?"

" In the hands of a person who will give it to you only under certain conditions."

" Who is this person?"

" I am not at liberty to tell you."

There was both admiration and jealousy in the look that Martial fixed upon Marie-Anne.

He was amazed by her coolness and presence of mind. Ah! how powerful must be the passion that imparted such a ringing clearness to her voice, such brilliancy to her eyes, such precision to her responses.

" And if I should not accept the—the conditions which are imposed, what then?" asked M. de Sair-meuse.

" In that case the writing will be utilized."

" What do you mean by that?"

" I mean, sir, that early to-morrow morning a trusty messenger will start for Paris, charged with the task of submitting this document to the eyes of certain persons who are not exactly friends of yours. He will show it to Monsieur Laine, for example—or to the Duc de Richelieu; and he will, of course, explain to them its significance and its value. Will this writing prove the complicity of the Marquis de Sairmeuse? Yes, or no? Have you, or have you not, dared to try and to condemn to death the unfortunate men who were only the tools of your son?"

" Ah, wretch! hussy! viper!" interrupted the duke. He was beside himself. A foam gathered upon his lips, his eyes seemed starting from their sockets; he was no longer conscious of what he was saying.

"This," he exclaimed, with wild gestures, "is enough to appall me! Yes, I have bitter enemies, envious rivals who would give their right hand for his execrable letter. Ah! if they obtain it they will demand an investigation, and then farewell to the rewards due to my services.

"It will be shouted from the house-tops that Chanlouineau, in the presence of the tribunal, declared you, Marquis, his leader and his accomplice. You will be obliged to submit to the scrutiny of physicians, who, seeing a freshly healed wound, will require you to tell where you received it, and why you concealed it.

"Of what shall I *not* be accused? They will say that I expedited matters in order to silence the voice that had been raised against my son. Perhaps they will even say that I secretly favored the insurrection; I shall be vilified in the journals.

"And who has thus ruined the fortunes of our house, that promised so brilliantly? You, you alone, Marquis.

"You believe in nothing, you doubt everything— you are cold, sceptical, disdainful, *blasé*. But a pretty woman makes her appearance on the scene. You go wild like a school-boy and are ready to commit any act of folly. It is you who I am addressing, Marquis. Do you hear me? Speak! what have you to say?"

Martial had listened to this tirade with unconcealed scorn, and without even attempting to interrupt it.

Now he responded, slowly:

"I think, sir, if Mademoiselle Lacheneur *had* any doubts of the value of the document she possesses, she has them no longer."

This response fell upon the duke's wrath like a bucket of ice-water. He instantly comprehended his folly; and frightened by his own words, he stood stupefied with astonishment.

Without deigning to add another word, the marquis turned to Marie-Anne.

" Will you be so kind as to explain what is required of my father in exchange for this letter? "

" The life and liberty of Monsieur d'Escorval."

The duke started as if he had received an electric shock.

" Ah! " he exclaimed. " I knew they would ask something that was impossible! "

He sank back in his arm-chair. A profound despair succeeded his frenzy. He buried his face in his hands, evidently seeking some expedient.

" Why did you not come to me before judgment was pronounced? " he murmured. " Then I could have done anything—now, my hands are bound. The commission has spoken; the judgment must be executed ——"

He rose, and in the tone of a man who is resigned to anything, he said:

" Decidedly. I should risk more in attempting to save the baron "—in his anxiety he gave M. d'Escorval his title—" a thousand times more than I have to fear from my enemies. So, Mademoiselle "—he no longer said, " my good girl "—" you can utilize your document."

The duke was about leaving the room, but Martial detained him by a gesture.

" Think again before you decide. Our situation is not without a precedent. A few months ago the Count de Lavalette was condemned to death. The King wished to pardon him, but his ministers and friends opposed it. Though the King was master, what did he do? He seemed to be deaf to all the supplications made in the prisoner's behalf. The scaffold was erected, and yet Lavalette was saved! And no one was compromised—yes, a jailer lost his position; he is living on his income now."

Marie-Anne caught eagerly at the idea so cleverly presented by Martial.

"Yes," she exclaimed, "the Count de Lavalette, protected by royal connivance, succeeded in making his escape."

The simplicity of the expedient—the authority of the example—seemed to make a vivid impression upon the duke. He was silent for a moment, and Marie-Anne fancied she saw an expression of relief steal over his face.

"Such an attempt would be very hazardous," he murmured; "yet, with care, and if one were sure that the secret would be kept——"

"Oh! the secret will be religiously preserved, Monsieur," interrupted Marie-Anne.

With a glance Martial recommended silence; then turning to his father, he said:

"One can always consider an expedient, and calculate the consequences—that does not bind one. When is this sentence to be carried into execution?"

"To-morrow," responded the duke.

But even this terrible response did not cause Marie-Anne any alarm. The duke's anxiety and terror had taught her how much reason she had to hope; and she saw that Martial had openly espoused her cause.

"We have, then, only the night before us," resumed the marquis. "Fortunately, it is only half-past seven, and until ten o'clock my father can visit the citadel without exciting the slightest suspicion."

He paused suddenly.   His eyes, in which had shone
almost absolute confidence, became gloomy.   He had
just discovered an unexpected and, as it seemed to him,
almost insurmountable difficulty.

"Have we any intelligent men in the citadel?" he
murmured.   "The assistance of a jailer or of a soldier
is indispensable."

He turned to his father, and brusquely asked:

"Have you any man in whom you can confide?"

"I have three or four spies—they can be bought
——"

"No! the wretch who betrays his comrade for a few
sous, will betray you for a few louis.   We must have
an honest man who sympathizes with the opinions of
Baron d'Escorval—an old soldier who fought under
Napoleon, if possible."

A sudden inspiration visited Marie-Anne's mind.

"I know the man that you require!" she cried.

"You?"

"Yes, I.   At the citadel."

"Take care!   Remember that he must risk much.
If this should be discovered, those who take part in it
will be sacrificed."

"He of whom I speak is the man you need.   I will
be responsible for him."

"And he is a soldier?"

"He is only an humble corporal; but the nobility
of his nature entitles him to the highest rank.   Believe
me, we can safely confide in him."

If she spoke thus, she who would willingly have
given her life for the baron's salvation, she must be absolutely certain.

So thought Martial.

"I will confer with this man," said he.   "What is
his name?"

" He is called Bavois, and he is a corporal in the first company of grenadiers."

" Bavois," repeated Martial, as if to fix the name in his memory; " Bavois. My father will find some pretext for desiring him summoned."

" It is easy to find a pretext. He was the brave soldier left on guard at Escorval after the troops left the house."

" This promises well," said Martial. He had risen and gone to the fireplace in order to be nearer his father.

" I suppose," he continued, " the baron has been separated from the other prisoners ? "

" Yes, he is alone, in a large and very comfortable room."

" Where is it ? "

" On the second story of the corner tower."

But Martial, who was not so well acquainted with the citadel as his father, was obliged to reflect a moment.

" The corner tower ! " said he; " is not that the tall tower which one sees from a distance, and which is built on a spot where the rock is almost perpendicular ? "

" Precisely."

By the promptness M. de Sairmeuse displayed in replying, it was easy to see that he was ready to risk a good deal to effect the prisoner's deliverance.

" What kind of a window is that in the baron's room ? " inquired Martial.

" It is quite large and furnished with a double row of iron bars, securely fastened into the stone walls."

" It is easy enough to cut these bars. On which side does this window look ? "

" On the country."

" That is to say, it overlooks the precipice. The devil ! That is a serious difficulty, and yet, in one respect, it is an advantage, for they station no sentinels there, do they ? "

" Never. Between the citadel wall and the edge of the precipice there is barely standing-room. The soldiers do not venture there even in the daytime."

" There is one more important question. What is the distance from Monsieur d'Escorval's window to the ground? "

" It is about forty feet from the base of the tower."

" Good ! And from the base of the tower to the foot of the precipice—how far is that ? "

" Really, I scarcely know. Sixty feet, at least, I should think."

" Ah, that is high, terrible high. The baron fortunately is still agile and vigorous."

The duke began to be impatient.

" Now," said he to his son, " will you be so kind as to explain your plan ? "

Martial had gradually resumed the careless tone which always exasperated his father.

" He is sure of success," thought Marie-Anne.

" My plan is simplicity itself," replied Martial. " Sixty and forty are one hundred. It is necessary to procure one hundred feet of strong rope. It will make a very large bundle; but no matter. I will twist it around me, envelop myself in a large cloak, and accompany you to the citadel. You will send for Corporal Bavois; you will leave me alone with him in a quiet place; I will explain our wishes."

M. de Sairmeuse shrugged his shoulders.

" And how will you procure a hundred feet of rope

at this hour in Montaignac ? Will you go about from shop to shop? You might as well trumpet your project at once."

" I shall attempt nothing of the kind. What I cannot do the friends of the Escorval family will do."

The duke was about to offer some new objection when his son interrupted him.

" Pray do not forget the danger that threatens us," he said, earnestly, " nor the little time that is left us. I have committed a fault, leave me to repair it."

And turning to Marie-Anne:

" You may consider the baron saved," he pursued; " but it is necessary for me to confer with one of his friends. Return at once to the Hôtel de France and tell the *curé* to meet me on the Place d'Armes, where I go to await him."

CHAPTER XXX

Though among the first to be arrested at the time of the panic before Montaignac, the Baron d'Escorval had not for an instant deluded himself with false hopes.

" I am a lost man," he thought. And confronting death calmly, he now thought only of the danger that threatened his son.

His mistake before the judges was the result of his preoccupation.

He did not breathe freely until he saw Maurice led from the hall by Abbé Midon and the friendly officers, for he knew that his son would try to confess connection with the affair.

Then, calm and composed, with head erect, and steadfast eye, he listened to the death-sentence.

In the confusion that ensued in removing the prisoners from the hall, the baron found himself beside
Chanlouineau, who had begun his noisy lamentations.

"Courage, my boy," he said, indignant at such apparent cowardice.

"Ah! it is easy to talk," whined the young farmer.

Then seeing that no one was observing them, he
leaned toward the baron, and whispered:

"It is for you I am working. Save all your strength
for to-night."

Chanlouineau's words and burning glance surprised
M. d'Escorval, but he attributed both to fear. When
the guards took him back to his cell, he threw himself
upon his pallet, and before him rose that vision of the
last hour, which is at once the hope and despair of those
who are about to die.

He knew the terrible laws that govern a court-martial. The next day—in a few hours—at dawn, perhaps,
they would take him from his cell, place him in front
of a squad of soldiers, an officer would lift his sword,
and all would be over.

Then what was to become of his wife and his son?

His agony on thinking of these dear ones was terrible. He was alone; he wept.

But suddenly he started up, ashamed of his weakness. He must not allow these thoughts to unnerve
him. He was determined to meet death unflinchingly.
Resolved to shake off the profound melancholy that
was creeping over him, he walked about his cell, forcing his mind to occupy itself with material objects.

The room which had been allotted to him was very
large. It had once communicated with the apartment
adjoining; but the door had been walled up for a long
time. The cement which held the large blocks of stone

together had crumbled away, leaving crevices through which one might look from one room into the other.

M. d'Escorval mechanically applied his eye to one of these interstices. Perhaps he had a friend for a neighbor, some wretched man who was to share his fate. He saw no one. He called, first in a whisper, then louder. No voice responded to his.

" If I could only tear down this thin partition," he thought.

He trembled, then shrugged his shoulders. And if he did, what then? He would only find himself in another apartment similar to his own, and opening like his upon a corridor full of guards, whose monotonous tramp he could plainly hear as they passed to and fro.

What folly to think of escape! He knew that every possible precaution must have been taken to guard against it.

Yes, he knew this, and yet he could not refrain from examining his window. Two rows of iron bars protected it. These were placed in such a way that it was impossible for him to put out his head and see how far he was above the ground. The height, however, must be considerable, judging from the extent of the view.

The sun was setting; and through the violet haze the baron could discern an undulating line of hills, whose culminating point must be the land of the Reche.

The dark masses of foliage that he saw on the right were probably the forests of Sairmeuse. On the left, he divined rather than saw, nestling between the hills, the valley of the Oiselle and Escorval.

Escorval, that lovely retreat where he had known such happiness, where he had hoped to die the calm and serene death of the just.

And remembering his past felicity, and thinking of

his vanished dreams, his eyes once more filled with tears. But he quickly dried them on hearing the door of his cell open.

Two soldiers appeared.

One of the men bore a torch, the other, one of those long baskets divided into compartments which are used in carrying meals to the officers on guard.

These men were evidently deeply moved, and yet, obeying a sentiment of instinctive delicacy, they affected a sort of gayety.

" Here is your dinner, Monsieur," said one soldier; " it ought to be very good, for it comes from the cuisine of the commander of the citadel."

M. d'Escorval smiled sadly. Some attentions on the part of one's jailer have a sinister significance. Still, when he seated himself before the little table which they prepared for him, he found that he was really hungry.

He ate with a relish, and chatted quite cheerfully with the soldiers.

" Always hope for the best, sir," said one of these worthy fellows. " Who knows? Stranger things have happened! "

When the baron finished his repast, he asked for pen, ink, and paper. They brought what he desired.

He found himself again alone; but his conversation with the soldiers had been of service to him. His weakness had passed; his *sang-froid* had returned; he would now reflect.

He was surprised that he had heard nothing from Mme. d'Escorval and from Maurice.

Could it be that they had been refused access to the prison? No, they could not be; he could not imagine that there existed men sufficiently cruel to prevent a doomed man from pressing to his heart, in a last embrace, his wife and his son.

Yet, how was it that neither the baroness nor Maurice had made an attempt to see him! Something must have prevented them from doing so. What could it be?

He imagined the worst misfortunes. He saw his wife writhing in agony, perhaps dead. He pictured Maurice, wild with grief, upon his knees at the bedside of his mother.

But they might come yet. He consulted his watch. It marked the hour of seven.

But he waited in vain. No one came.

He took up his pen, and was about to write, when he heard a bustle in the corridor outside. The clink of spurs resounded on the flags; he heard the sharp clink of the rifle as the guard presented arms.

Trembling, the baron sprang up, saying:

" They have come at last! "

He was mistaken; the footsteps died away in the distance.

" A round of inspection! " he murmured.

But at the same moment, two objects thrown through the tiny opening in the door of his cell fell on the floor in the middle of the room.

M. d'Escorval caught them up. Someone had thrown him two files.

His first feeling was one of distrust. He knew that there were jailers who left no means untried to dishonor their prisoners before delivering them to the executioner.

Was it a friend, or an enemy, that had given him these instruments of deliverance and of liberty.

Chanlouineau's words and the look that accompanied them recurred to his mind, perplexing him still more.

He was standing with knitted brows, turning and returning the fine and well-tempered files in his hands, when he suddenly perceived upon the floor a tiny scrap of paper which had, at first, escaped his notice.

He snatched it up, unfolded it, and read:

"Your friends are at work. Everything is prepared for your escape. Make haste and saw the bars of your window. Maurice and his mother embrace you. Hope, courage!"

Beneath these few lines was the letter M.

But the baron did not need this initial to be reassured. He had recognized Abbé Midon's handwriting.

"Ah! he is a true friend," he murmured.

Then the recollection of his doubts and despair arose in his mind.

"This explains why neither my wife nor son came to visit me," he thought. "And I doubted their energy —and I was complaining of their neglect!"

Intense joy filled his breast; he raised the letter that promised him life and liberty to his lips, and enthusiastically exclaimed:

"To work! to work!"

He had chosen the finest of the two files, and was about to attack the ponderous bars, when he fancied he heard someone open the door of the next room.

Someone had opened it, certainly. The person closed it again, but did not lock it.

Then the baron heard someone moving cautiously about. What did all this mean? Were they incarcerating some new prisoner, or were they stationing a spy there?

Listening breathlessly, the baron heard a singular sound, whose cause it was absolutely impossible to explain.

Noiselessly he advanced to the former communicating door, knelt, and peered through one of the interstices.

The sight that met his eyes amazed him.

A man was standing in a corner of the room. The baron could see the lower part of the man's body by the light of a large lantern which he had deposited on the floor at his feet. He was turning around and around very quickly, by this movement unwinding a long rope which had been twined around his body as thread is wound about a bobbin.

M. d'Escorval rubbed his eyes as if to assure himself that he was not dreaming. Evidently this rope was intended for him. It was to be attached to the broken bars.

But how had this man succeeded in gaining admission to this room? Who could it be that enjoyed such liberty in the prison? He was not a soldier—or, at least, he did not wear a uniform.

Unfortunately, the highest crevice was in such a place that the visual ray did not strike the upper part of the man's body; and, despite the baron's efforts, he was unable to see the face of this friend—he judged him to be such—whose boldness verged on folly.

Unable to resist his intense curiosity, M. d'Escorval was on the point of rapping on the wall to question him, when the door of the room occupied by this man, whom the baron already called his saviour, was impetuously thrown open.

Another man entered, whose face was also outside the baron's range of vision; and the new-comer, in a tone of astonishment, exclaimed:

"Good heavens! what are you doing?"

The baron drew back in despair.

"All is discovered!" he thought.

The man whom M. d'Escorval believed to be his friend did not pause in his labor of unwinding the rope, and it was in the most tranquil voice that he responded:

"As you see, I am freeing myself from this burden of rope, which I find extremely uncomfortable. There are at least sixty yards of it, I should think—and what a bundle it makes! I feared they would discover it under my cloak."

"And what are you going to do with all this rope?" inquired the new-comer.

"I am going to hand it to Baron d'Escorval, to whom I have already given a file. He must make his escape to-night."

So improbable was this scene that the baron could not believe his own ears.

"I cannot be awake; I must be dreaming," he thought.

The new-comer uttered a terrible oath, and, in an almost threatening tone, he said:

"We will see about that! If you have gone mad, I, thank God! still possess my reason! I will not permit——"

"Pardon!" interrupted the other, coldly, "you will permit it. This is merely the result of your own—credulity. When Chanlouineau asked you to allow him to receive a visit from Mademoiselle Lacheneur, that was the time you should have said: 'I will not permit it.' Do you know what the fellow desired? Simply to give Mademoiselle Lacheneur a letter of mine, so compromising in its nature, that if it ever reaches the hands of a certain person of my acquaintance, my father and I will be obliged to reside in London in future. Then farewell to the projects for an alliance between our two families!"

The new-comer heaved a mighty sigh, accompanied by a half-angry, half-sorrowful exclamation; but the other, without giving him any opportunity to reply, resumed:

"You, yourself, Marquis, would doubtless be compromised. Were you not a chamberlain during the reign of Bonaparte? Ah, Marquis! how could a man of your experience, a man so subtle, and penetrating, and acute, allow himself to be duped by a low, ignorant peasant?"

Now M. d'Escorval understood. He was not dreaming; it was the Marquis de Courtornieu and Martial de Sairmeuse who were talking on the other side of the wall.

This poor M. de Courtornieu had been so entirely crushed by Martial's revelation that he no longer made any effort to oppose him.

"And this terrible letter?" he groaned.

"Marie-Anne Lacheneur gave it to Abbé Midon, who came to me and said: 'Either the baron will escape, or this letter will be taken to the Duc de Richelieu.' I voted for the baron's escape, I assure you. The *abbé* procured all that was necessary; he met me at a rendezvous which I appointed in a quiet spot; he coiled all his rope about my body, and here I am."

"Then you think if the baron escapes they will give you back your letter?"

"Most assuredly."

"Deluded man! As soon as the baron is safe, they will demand the life of another prisoner, with the same menaces."

" By no means."

" You will see."

" I shall see nothing of the kind, for a very simple reason. I have the letter now in my pocket. The *abbé* gave it to me in exchange for my word of honor."

M. de Courtornieu's exclamation proved that he considered the *abbé* an egregious fool.

" What ! " he exclaimed. " You hold the proof, and— But this is madness ! Burn this accursed letter by the flames of this lantern, and let the baron go where his slumbers will be undisturbed."

Martial's silence betrayed something like stupor.

" What ! you would do this—you ? " he demanded, at last.

" Certainly—and without the slightest hesitation."

" Ah, well ! I cannot say that I congratulate you."

The sneer was so apparent that M. de Courtornieu was sorely tempted to make an angry response. But he was not a man to yield to his first impulse—this former chamberlain under the Emperor, now become a *grand prévôt* under the Restoration.

He reflected. Should he, on account of a sharp word, quarrel with Martial—with the only suitor who had pleased his daughter? A rupture—then he would be left without any prospect of a son-in-law ! When would Heaven send him such another ? And how furious Mlle. Blanche would be !

He concluded to swallow the bitter pill; and it was with a paternal indulgence of manner that he said :

" You are young, my dear Martial."

The baron was still kneeling by the partition, his ear glued to the crevices, holding his breath in an agony of suspense.

" You are only twenty, my dear Martial," pursued the Marquis de Courtornieu; "you possess the ardent enthusiasm and generosity of youth. Complete your undertaking; I shall interpose no obstacle; but remember that all may be discovered—and then——"

"Have no fears, sir," interrupted the young marquis; "I have taken every precaution. Did you see a single soldier in the corridor, just now? No. That is because my father has, at my solicitation, assembled all the officers and guards under pretext of ordering exceptional precautions. He is talking to them now. This gave me an opportunity to come here unobserved. No one will see me when I go out. Who, then, will dare suspect me of having any hand in the baron's escape?"

"If the baron escapes, justice will demand to know who aided him."

Martial laughed.

"If justice seeks to know, she will find a culprit of my providing. Go now; I have told you all. I had but one person to fear: that was yourself. A trusty messenger requested you to join me here. You came; you know all, you have agreed to remain neutral. I am tranquil. The baron will be safe in Piedmont when the sun rises."

He picked up his lantern, and added, gayly:

"But let us go—my father cannot harangue those soldiers forever."

"But," insisted M. de Courtornieu, "you have not told me——"

"I will tell you all, but not here. Come, come!"

They went out, locking the door behind them; and then the baron rose from his knees.

All sorts of contradictory ideas, doubts, and conjectures filled his mind.

What could this letter have contained? Why had not Chanlouineau used it to procure his own salvation? Who would have believed that Martial would be so faithful to a promise wrested from him by threats?

But this was a time for action, not for reflection. The bars were heavy, and there were two rows of them.

M. d'Escorval set to work.

He had supposed that the task would be difficult. It was a thousand times more so than he had expected; he discovered this almost immediately.

It was the first time that he had ever worked with a file, and he did not know how to use it. His progress was despairingly slow.

Nor was that all. Though he worked as cautiously as possible, each movement of the instrument across the iron produced a harsh, grating sound that froze his blood with terror. What if someone should overhear this noise? And it seemed to him impossible for it to escape notice, since he could plainly distinguish the measured tread of the guards, who had resumed their watch in the corridor.

So slight was the result of his labors, that at the end of twenty minutes he experienced a feeling of profound discouragement.

At this rate, it would be impossible for him to sever the first bar before daybreak. What, then, was the use of spending his time in fruitless labor? Why mar the dignity of death by the disgrace of an unsuccessful effort to escape?

He was hesitating when footsteps approached his cell. He hastened to seat himself at the table.

The door opened and a soldier entered, to whom an officer who did not cross the threshold remarked:

" You have your instructions, Corporal, keep a close watch. If the prisoner needs anything, call."

M. de Escorval's heart throbbed almost to bursting. What was coming now?

Had M. de Courtornieu's counsels carried the day, or had Martial sent someone to aid him?

"We must not be dawdling here," said the corporal, as soon as the door was closed.

M. d'Escorval bounded from his chair. This man was a friend. Here was aid and life.

"I am Bavois," continued the corporal. "Some one said to me just now: 'A friend of the Emperor is in danger; are you willing to lend him a helping hand?' I replied: 'Present,' and here I am!"

This certainly was a brave soul. The baron extended his hand, and in a voice trembling with emotion:

"Thanks," said he; "thanks to you who, without knowing me, expose yourself to the greatest danger for my sake."

Bavois shrugged his shoulders disdainfully.

"Positively, my old hide is no more precious than yours. If we do not succeed, they will chop off our heads with the same axe. But we shall succeed. Now, let us cease talking and proceed to business."

As he spoke he drew from beneath his long overcoat a strong iron crowbar and a small vial of brandy, and deposited them upon the bed.

He then took the candle and passed it back and forth before the window five or six times.

"What are you doing?" inquired the baron, in suspense.

"I am signalling to your friends that everything is progressing favorably. They are down there waiting for us; and see, now they are answering."

The baron looked, and three times they saw a little

flash of flame like that produced by the burning of a pinch of gunpowder.

"Now," said the corporal, "we are all right. Let us see what progress you have made with the bars."

"I have scarcely begun," murmured M. d'Escorval.

The corporal inspected the work.

"You may indeed say that you have made no progress," said he; "but, never mind, I have been a locksmith, and I know how to handle a file."

Having drawn the cork from the vial of brandy which he had brought, he fastened the stopper to the end of one of the files, and swathed the handle of the instrument with a piece of damp linen.

"That is what they call putting a *stop* on the instrument," he remarked, by way of explanation.

Then he made an energetic attack on the bars. It at once became evident that he had not exaggerated his knowledge of the subject, nor the efficacy of his precautions for deadening the sound. The harsh grating that had so alarmed the baron was no longer heard, and Bavois, finding he had nothing more to dread from the keenest ears, now made preparations to shelter himself from observation.

To cover the opening in the door would arouse suspicion at once—so the corporal adopted another expedient.

Moving the little table to another part of the room, he placed the light upon it, in such a position that the window remained entirely in shadow.

Then he ordered the baron to sit down, and handing him a paper, said:

"Now read aloud, without stopping for an instant, until you see me cease work."

By this method they might reasonably hope to deceive the guards outside in the corridor. Some of them, indeed, did come to the door and look in, then went away to say to their companions:

"We have just taken a look at the prisoner. He is very pale, and his eyes are glittering feverishly. He is reading aloud to divert his mind. Corporal Bavois is looking out of the window. It must be dull music for him."

The baron's voice would also be of advantage in overpowering any suspicious sound, should there be one.

And while Bavois worked, M. d'Escorval read, read, read.

He had completed the perusal of the entire paper, and was about to begin it again, when the old soldier, leaving the window, motioned him to stop.

"Half the task is completed," he said, in a whisper. "The lower bars are cut."

"Ah! how can I ever repay you for your devotion!" murmured the baron.

"Hush! not a word!" interrupted Bavois. "If I escape with you, I can never return here; and I shall not know where to go, for the regiment, you see, is my only family. Ah, well! if you will give me a home with you, I shall be content."

Whereupon he swallowed a big draught of brandy, and set to work with renewed ardor.

The corporal had cut one of the second row of bars, when he was interrupted by M. d'Escorval, who, without discontinuing his reading, had approached and pulled Bavois's long coat to attract his attention.

He turned quickly.

"What is it?"

"I heard a singular noise."

" Where? "

" In the adjoining room where the ropes are."

Honest Bavois muttered a terrible oath.

" Do they intend to betray us? I risked my life, and they promised me fair play."

He placed his ear against an opening in the partition, and listened for a long time. Nothing, not the slightest sound.

" It must have been some rat that you heard," he said, at last. " Resume your reading."

And he began his work again. This was the only interruption, and a little before four o'clock everything was ready. The bars were cut, and the ropes, which had been drawn through an opening in the wall, were coiled under the window.

The decisive moment had come. Bavois took the counterpane from the bed, fastened it over the opening in the door, and filled up the key-hole.

" Now," said he, in the same measured tone which he would have used in instructing his recruits, " attention, sir, and obey the word of command."

Then he calmly explained that the escape would consist of two distinct operations ; the first in gaining the narrow platform at the base of the tower ; the second, in descending to the foot of the precipitous rock.

The *abbé*, who understood this, had brought Martial two ropes ; the one to be used in the descent of the precipice being considerably longer than the other.

" I will fasten the shortest rope under your arms, Monsieur, and I will let you down to the base of the tower. When you have reached it, I will pass you the longer rope and the crowbar. Do not miss them. If we find ourselves without them, on that narrow ledge of rock, we shall either be compelled to deliver ourselves up, or throw ourselves down the precipice. I shall not be long in joining you. Are you ready? "

M. d'Escorval lifted his arms, the rope was fastened securely about him, and he crawled through the window.

From there the height seemed immense. Below, in the barren fields that surrounded the citadel, eight persons were waiting, silent, anxious, breathless.

They were Mme. d'Escorval and Maurice, Marie-Anne, Abbé Midon, and the four retired army officers.

There was no moon; but the night was very clear, and they could see the tower quite plainly.

Soon after four o'clock sounded they saw a dark object glide slowly down the side of the tower—it was the baron. After a little, another form followed very rapidly—it was Bavois.

Half of the perilous journey was accomplished.

From below, they could see the two figures moving about on the narrow platform. The corporal and the baron were exerting all their strength to fix the crowbar securely in a crevice of the rock.

In a moment or two one of the figures stepped from the projecting rock and glided gently down the side of the precipice.

It could be none other than M. d'Escorval. Transported with happiness, his wife sprang forward with open arms to receive him.

Wretched woman! A terrific cry rent the still night air.

M. d'Escorval was falling from a height of fifty feet; he was hurled down to the foot of the rocky precipice. The rope had parted.

Had it broken naturally?

Maurice, who examined the end of it, exclaimed with

horrible imprecations of hatred and vengeance that they had been betrayed—that their enemy had arranged to deliver only a dead body into their hands—that the rope, in short, had been foully tampered with—cut!

CHAPTER XXXI

Chupin had not taken time to sleep, nor scarcely time to drink, since that unfortunate morning when the Duc de Sairmeuse ordered affixed to the walls of Montaignac, that decree in which he promised twenty thousand francs to the person who should deliver up Lacheneur, dead or alive.

"Twenty thousand francs," Chupin muttered gloomily; "twenty sacks with a hundred pistoles in each! Ah! if I could discover Lacheneur; even if he were dead and buried a hundred feet under ground, I should gain the reward."

The appellation of traitor, which he would receive; the shame and condemnation that would fall upon him and his, did not make him hesitate for a moment.

He saw but one thing—the reward—the blood-money.

Unfortunately, he had nothing whatever to guide him in his researches; no clew, however vague.

All that was known in Montaignac was that M. Lacheneur's horse was killed at the Croix d'Arcy.

But no one knew whether Lacheneur himself had been wounded. or whether he had escaped from the fray uninjured. Had he reached the frontier? or had he found an asylum in the house of one of his friends?

Chupin was thus hungering for the price of blood, when, on the day of the trial, as he was returning from the citadel, after making his deposition, he entered a drinking saloon. While there he heard the name of Lacheneur uttered in low tones near him.

Two peasants were emptying a bottle of wine, and one of them, an old man, was telling the other that he had come to Montaignac to give Mlle. Lacheneur news of her father.

He said that his son-in-law had met the chief conspirator in the mountains which separate the *arrondissement* of Montaignac from Savoy. He even mentioned the exact place of meeting, which was near Saint Pavin-des-Gottes, a tiny village of only a few houses.

Certainly the worthy man did not think he was committing a dangerous indiscretion. In his opinion, Lacheneur had, ere this, crossed the frontier, and was out of danger.

In this he was mistaken.

The frontier bordering on Savoy was guarded by soldiers, who had received orders to allow none of the conspirators to pass.

The passage of the frontier, then, presented many great difficulties, and even if a man succeeded in effecting it, he might be arrested and imprisoned on the other side, until the formalities of extradition had been complied with.

Chupin saw his advantage, and instantly decided on his course.

He knew that he had not a moment to lose. He threw a coin down upon the counter, and without waiting for his change, rushed back to the citadel, and asked the sergeant at the gate for pen and paper.

The old rascal generally wrote slowly and painfully; to-day it took him but a moment to trace these lines:

" I know Lacheneur's retreat, and beg monseigneur
to order some mounted soldiers to accompany me, in
order to capture him.   CHUPIN."

This note was given to one of the guards, with a request to take it to the Duc de Sairmeuse, who was
presiding over the military commission.

Five minutes later, the soldier reappeared with the
same note.

Upon the margin the duke had written an order,
placing at Chupin's disposal a lieutenant and eight
men chosen from the Montaignac chasseurs, who
could be relied upon, and who were not suspected (as
were the other troops) of sympathizing with the rebels.

Chupin also requested a horse for his own use, and
this was accorded him. The duke had just received
this note when, with a triumphant air, he abruptly entered the room where Marie-Anne and his son were ne-
gotiating for the release of Baron d'Escorval.

It was because he believed in the truth of the rather
hazardous assertion made by his spy that he exclaimed,
upon the threshold:

" Upon my word! it must be confessed that this
Chupin is an incomparable huntsman! Thanks to
him——"

Then he saw Mlle. Lacheneur, and suddenly checked
himself.

Unfortunately, neither Martial nor Marie-Anne
were in a state of mind to notice this remark and its
interruption.

Had he been questioned, the duke would probably
have allowed the truth to escape him, and M. Lacheneur might have been saved.

But Lacheneur was one of those unfortunate beings

who seem to be pursued by an evil destiny which they can never escape.

Buried beneath his horse, M. Lacheneur had lost consciousness.

When he regained his senses, restored by the fresh morning air, the place was silent and deserted. Not far from him, he saw two dead bodies which had not yet been removed.

It was a terrible moment, and in the depth of his soul he cursed death, which had refused to heed his entreaties. Had he been armed, doubtless, he would have ended by suicide; the most cruel mental torture which man was ever forced to endure—but he had no weapon.

He was obliged to accept the chastisement of life.

Perhaps, too, the voice of honor whispered that it was cowardice to strive to escape the responsibility of one's acts by death.

At last, he endeavored to draw himself out from beneath the body of his horse.

This proved to be no easy matter, as his foot was still in the stirrup, and his limbs were so badly cramped that he could scarcely move them. He finally succeeded in freeing himself, however, and, on examination, discovered that he, who it would seem ought to have been killed ten times over, had only one hurt—a bayonet-wound in the leg, extending from the ankle almost to the knee.

Such a wound, of course, caused him not a little suffering, and he was trying to bandage it with his handkerchief, when he heard the sound of approaching footsteps.

He had no time for reflection; he sprang into the forest that lies to the left of the Croix d'Arcy.

The troops were returning to Montaignac after pursuing the rebels for more than three miles. There were about two hundred soldiers, and they were bringing back, as prisoners, about twenty peasants.

Hidden by a great oak scarcely fifteen paces from the road, Lacheneur recognized several of the prisoners in the gray light of dawn. It was only by the merest chance that he escaped discovery; and he fully realized how difficult it would be for him to gain the frontier without falling into the hands of the detachment of soldiery, who were doubtless scouring the country in every direction.

Still he did not despair.

The mountains lay only two leagues away; and he firmly believed that he could successfully elude his pursuers as soon as he gained the shelter of the hills.

He began his journey courageously.

Alas! he had not realized how exhausted he had become from the excessive labor and excitement of the past few days, and by the loss of blood from his wound, which he could not stanch.

He tore up a pole in one of the vineyards to serve as a staff, and dragged himself along, keeping in the shelter of the woods as much as possible, and creeping along beside the hedges and in the ditches when he was obliged to traverse an open space.

To the great physical suffering, and the most cruel mental anguish, was now added an agony that momentarily increased—hunger.

He had eaten nothing for thirty hours, and he felt terribly weak from lack of nourishment. This torture soon became so intolerable that he was willing to brave anything to appease it.

At last he perceived the roofs of a tiny hamlet. He

decided to enter it and ask for food. He was on the outskirts of the village, when he heard the rolling of a drum. Instinctively he hid behind a wall. But it was only a town-crier beating his drum to call the people together.

And soon a voice rose so clear and penetrating that each word it uttered fell distinctly on Lacheneur's ears.

It said:

" This is to inform you that the authorities of Montaignac promise to give a reward of twenty thousand francs—two thousand pistoles, you understand—to him who will deliver up the man known as Lacheneur, dead or alive. Dead or alive, you understand. If he is dead, the compensation will be the same; twenty thousand francs! It will be paid in gold."

With a bound, Lacheneur had risen, wild with despair and horror. Though he had believed himself utterly exhausted, he found superhuman strength to flee.

A price had been set upon his head. This frightful thought awakened in his breast the frenzy that renders a hunted wild beast so dangerous.

In all the villages around him he fancied he could hear the rolling of drums, and the voice of the crier proclaiming this infamous edict.

Go where he would now, he was a tempting bait offered to treason and cupidity. In what human creature could he confide? Under what roof could he ask shelter?

And even if he were dead, he would still be worth a fortune.

Though he died from lack of nourishment and exhaustion under a bush by the wayside, his emaciated body would still be worth twenty thousand francs.

And the man who found his corpse would not give it burial. He would place it on his cart and bear it to Montaignac. He would go to the authorities and say: " Here is Lacheneur's body—give me the reward ! "

How long and by what paths he pursued his flight, he could not tell.

But several hours after, as he traversed the wooded hills of Charves, he saw two men, who sprang up and fled at his approach. In a terrible voice, he called after them:

" Eh ! you men ! do each of you desire a thousand pistoles? I am Lacheneur."

They paused when they recognized him, and Lacheneur saw that they were two of his followers. They were well-to-do farmers, and it had been very difficult to induce them to take part in the revolt.

These men had part of a loaf of bread and a little brandy. They gave both to the famished man.

They sat down beside him on the grass, and while he was eating they related their misfortunes. Their connection with the conspiracy had been discovered ; their houses were full of soldiers, who were hunting for them, but they hoped to reach Italy by the aid of a guide who was waiting for them at an appointed place.

Lacheneur extended his hand to them.

" Then I am saved," said he. " Weak and wounded as I am, I should perish if I were left alone."

But the two farmers did not accept the hand he offered.

" We should leave you," said the younger man, gloomily, " for you are the cause of our misfortunes. You deceived us, Monsieur Lacheneur."

He dared not protest, so just was the reproach.

" Nonsense ! let him come all the same," said the other, with a peculiar glance at his companion.

So they walked on, and that same evening, after nine hours of travelling on the mountains, they crossed the frontier.

But this long journey was not made without bitter reproaches, and even more bitter recriminations.

Closely questioned by his companions, Lacheneur, exhausted both in mind and body, finally admitted the insincerity of the promises with which he had inflamed the zeal of his followers. He acknowledged that he had spread the report that Marie-Louise and the young King of Rome were concealed in Montaignac, and that this report was a gross falsehood. He confessed that he had given the signal for the revolt without any chance of success, and without means of action, leaving everything to chance. In short, he confessed that nothing was real save his hatred, his implacable hatred of the Sairmeuse family.

A dozen times, at least, during this terrible avowal, the peasants who accompanied him were on the point of hurling him down the precipices upon whose verge they were walking.

" So it was to gratify his own spite," they thought, quivering with rage, " that he sets everybody to fighting and killing one another—that he ruins us, and drives us into exile. We will see."

The fugitives went to the nearest house after crossing the frontier.

It was a lonely inn, about a league from the little village of Saint-Jean-de-Coche, and was kept by a man named Balstain.

They rapped, in spite of the lateness of the hour— it was past midnight. They were admitted, and they ordered supper.

But Lacheneur, weak from loss of blood, and ex-

hausted by his long tramp, declared that he would eat
no supper.

He threw himself upon a bed in an adjoining room,
and was soon asleep.

This was the first time since their meeting with
Lacheneur that his companions had found an opportunity to talk together in private.

The same idea had occurred to both of them.

They believed that by delivering up Lacheneur to the
authorities, they might obtain pardon for themselves.

Neither of these men would have consented to receive a single sou of the money promised to the betrayer; but to exchange their life and liberty for the
life and liberty of Lacheneur did not seem to them a
culpable act, under the circumstances.

"For did he not deceive us?" they said to themselves.

They decided, at last, that as soon as they had finished their supper, they would go to Saint-Jean-de-
Coche and inform the Piedmontese guards.

But they reckoned without their host.

They had spoken loud enough to be overheard by
Balstain, the innkeeper, who had learned, during the
day, of the magnificent reward which had been promised to Lacheneur's captor.

When he heard the name of the guest who was sleeping quietly under his roof, a thirst for gold seized him.
He whispered a word to his wife, then escaped through
the window to run and summon the *gendarmes*.

He had been gone half an hour before the peasants
left the house; for to muster up courage for the act
they were about to commit they had been obliged to
drink heavily.

They closed the door so violently on going out that

Lacheneur was awakened by the noise. He sprang up, and came out into the adjoining room.

The wife of the innkeeper was there alone.

" Where are my friends? " he asked, anxiously. " Where is your husband? "

Moved by sympathy, the woman tried to falter some excuse, but finding none, she threw herself at his feet, crying:

" Fly, Monsieur, save yourself—you are betrayed! "

Lacheneur rushed back into the other room, seeking a weapon with which he could defend himself, an issue through which he could flee!

He had thought that they might abandon him, but betray him—no, never!

" Who has sold me? " he asked, in a strained, unnatural voice.

" Your friends—the two men who supped there at that table."

" Impossible, Madame, impossible! "

He did not suspect the designs and hopes of his former comrades; and he could not, he would not believe them capable of ignobly betraying him for gold.

" But," pleaded the innkeeper's wife, still on her knees before him, " they have just started for Saint-Jean-de-Coche, where they will denounce you. I heard them say that your life would purchase theirs. They have certainly gone to summon the *gendarmes!* Is this not enough, or am I obliged to endure the shame of confessing that my own husband, too, has gone to betray you."

Lacheneur understood it all now! And this supreme misfortune, after all the misery he had endured, broke him down completely.

Great tears gushed from his eyes, and sinking down into a chair, he murmured:

"Let them come; I am ready for them. No, I will not stir from here. My miserable life is not worth such a struggle."

But the wife of the traitor rose, and grasping the unfortunate man's clothing, she shook him, she dragged him to the door—she would have carried him had she possessed sufficient strength.

"You shall not remain here," said she, with extraordinary vehemence. "Fly, save yourself. You shall not be taken here; it will bring misfortune upon our house!"

Bewildered by these violent adjurations, and urged on by the instinct of self-preservation, so powerful in every human heart, Lacheneur stepped out upon the threshold.

The night was very dark, and a chilling fog intensified the gloom.

"See, Madame," said the poor fugitive gently, "how can I find my way through these mountains, which I do not know, and where there are no roads—where the foot-paths are scarcely discernible."

With a quick movement Balstain's wife pushed Lacheneur out, and turning him as one does a blind man to set him on the right track:

"Walk straight before you," said she, "always against the wind. God will protect you. Farewell!"

He turned to ask further directions, but she had re-entered the house and closed the door.

Upheld by a feverish excitement, he walked for long hours. He soon lost his way, and wandered on through the mountains, benumbed with cold, stumbling over rocks, sometimes falling.

Why he was not precipitated to the depths of some chasm it is difficult to explain.

He lost all idea of his whereabouts, and the sun was high in the heavens when he at last met a human being of whom he could inquire his way.

It was a little shepherd-boy, in pursuit of some stray goats, whom he encountered; but the lad, frightened by the wild and haggard appearance of the stranger, at first refused to approach.

The offer of a piece of money induced him to come a little nearer.

"You are on the summit of the mountain, Monsieur," said he; "and exactly on the boundary line. Here is France; there is Savoy."

"And what is the nearest village?"

"On the Savoyard side, Saint-Jean-de-Coche; on the French side, Saint-Pavin."

So after all his terrible exertions, Lacheneur was not a league from the inn.

Appalled by this discovery, he remained for a moment undecided which course to pursue.

What did it matter? Why should the doomed hesitate? Do not all roads lead to the abyss into which they must sink?

He remembered the *gendarmes!* that the innkeeper's wife had warned him against, and slowly and with great difficulty descended the steep mountain-side leading down to France.

He was near Saint-Pavin, when, before an isolated cottage, he saw a pretty peasant woman spinning in the sunshine.

He dragged himself toward her, and in weak tones begged her hospitality.

On seeing this man, whose face was ghastly pale, and whose clothing was torn and soiled with dust and blood, the woman rose, evidently more surprised than alarmed.

She looked at him closely, and saw that his age, his stature, and his features corresponded with the descriptions of Lacheneur, which had been scattered thickly about the frontier.

" You are the conspirator they are hunting for, and for whom they promise a reward of twenty thousand francs," she said.

Lacheneur trembled.

" Yes, I am Lacheneur," he replied, after a moment's hesitation; " I am Lacheneur. Betray me, if you will, but in charity's name give me a morsel of bread, and allow me to rest a little."

At the words " betray me," the young woman made a gesture of horror and disgust.

" We betray you, sir! " said she. " Ah! you do not know the Antoines! Enter our house, and lie down upon the bed while I prepare some refreshments for you. When my husband comes home, we will see what can be done."

It was nearly sunset when the master of the house, a robust mountaineer, with a frank face, returned.

On beholding the stranger seated at his fireside he turned frightfully pale.

" Unfortunate woman! " he whispered to his wife, " do you not know that any man who shelters this fugitive will be shot, and his house levelled to the ground? "

Lacheneur rose with a shudder.

He had not known this. He knew the infamous reward which had been promised to his betrayer; but he had not known the danger his presence brought upon these worthy people.

" I will go at once, sir," said he, gently.

But the peasant placed his large hand kindly upon his guest's shoulder, and forced him to resume his seat.

"It was not to drive you away that I said what I did," he remarked. "You are at home, and you shall remain here until I can find some means of insuring your safety."

The pretty peasant woman flung her arms about her husband's neck, and in tones of the most ardent affection exclaimed: "Ah! you are a noble man, Antoine."

He smiled, embraced her tenderly, then, pointing to the open door:

"Watch!" he said. "I feel it my duty to tell you, sir, that it will not be easy to save you," resumed the honest peasant. "The promises of reward have set all evil-minded people on the alert. They know that you are in the neighborhood. A rascally innkeeper has crossed the frontier for the express purpose of betraying your whereabouts to the French *gendarmes*."

"Balstain?"

"Yes, Balstain; and he is hunting for you now. That is not all. As I passed through Saint-Pavin, on my return, I saw eight mounted soldiers, guided by a peasant, also on horseback. They declared that they knew you were concealed in the village, and they were going to search every house."

These soldiers were none other than the Montaignac chasseurs, placed at Chupin's disposal by the Duc de Sairmeuse.

It was indeed as Antoine had said.

The task was certainly not at all to their taste, but they were closely watched by the lieutenant in command, who hoped to receive some substantial reward if the expedition was crowned with success. Antoine, meanwhile, continued his exposition of his hopes and fears.

"Wounded and exhausted as you are," he was saying to Lacheneur, "you will be in no condition to make
a long march in less than a fortnight. Until then you
must conceal yourself. Fortunately, I know a safe retreat in the mountain, not far from here. I will take
you there to-night, with provisions enough to last you
for a week."

A stifled cry from his wife interrupted him.

He turned, and saw her fall almost fainting against
the door, her face whiter than her coif, her finger pointing to the path that led from Saint-Pavin to their cottage.

"The soldiers—they are coming!" she gasped.

Quicker than thought, Lacheneur and the peasant
sprang to the door to see for themselves.

The young woman had spoken the truth.

The Montaignac chasseurs were climbing the steep
foot-path slowly, but surely.

Chupin walked in advance, urging them on with
voice, gesture and example.

An imprudent word from the little shepherd-boy,
whom M. Lacheneur had questioned, had decided the
fugitive's fate.

On returning to Saint-Pavin, and hearing that the
soldiers were searching for the chief conspirator, the
lad chanced to say:

"I met a man just now on the mountain who asked
me where he was; and I saw him go down the foot-
path leading to Antoine's cottage."

And in proof of his words, he proudly displayed the
piece of silver which Lacheneur had given him.

"One more bold stroke and we have our man!" exclaimed Chupin. "Come, comrades!"

And now the party were not more than two hundred

feet from the house in which the proscribed man had found an asylum.

Antoine and his wife looked at each other with anguish in their eyes.

They saw that their visitor was lost.

" We must save him! we must save him!" cried the woman.

" Yes, we must save him!" repeated the husband, gloomily. " They shall kill me before I betray a man in my own house."

" If he would hide in the stable behind the bundles of straw——"

" They would find him! These soldiers are worse than tigers, and the wretch who leads them on must have the keen scent of a blood-hound."

He turned quickly to Lacheneur.

" Come, sir," said he, " let us leap from the back window and flee to the mountains. They will see us, but no matter! These horsemen are always clumsy runners. If you cannot run, I will carry you. They will probably fire at us, but they will miss us."

" And your wife?" asked Lacheneur.

The honest mountaineer shuddered ; but he said :

" She will join us."

Lacheneur took his friend's hand and pressed it tenderly.

" Ah! you are noble people," he exclaimed, " and God will reward you for your kindness to a poor fugitive. But you have done too much already. I should be the basest of men if I consented to uselessly expose you to danger. I can bear this life no longer; I have no wish to escape."

He drew the sobbing woman to him and kissed her upon the forehead.

" I have a daughter, young and beautiful like yourself, as generous and proud. Poor Marie-Anne! And
I have pitilessly sacrificed her to my hatred! I should
not complain; come what may, I have deserved it."

The sound of approaching footsteps became more
and more distinct. Lacheneur straightened himself
up, and seemed to be gathering all his energy for the
decisive moment.

" Remain inside," he said, imperiously, to Antoine
and his wife. " I am going out; they must not arrest
me in your house."

As he spoke, he stepped outside the door, with a firm
tread, a dauntless brow, a calm and assured mien.

The soldiers were but a few feet from him.

" Halt!" he exclaimed, in a strong, ringing voice.
" It is Lacheneur you are seeking, is it not? I am he!
I surrender myself."

An unbroken stillness reigned. Not a sound, not a
word replied.

The spectre of death that hovered above his head imparted such an imposing majesty to his person that the
soldiers paused, silent and awed.

But there was one man who was terrified by this res-
onant voice, and that was Chupin.

Remorse filled his cowardly heart, and pale and
trembling, he tried to hide behind the soldiers.

Lacheneur walked straight to him.

" So it is you who have sold my life, Chupin?" he
said, scornfully. " You have not forgotten, I see
plainly, how often Marie-Anne has filled your empty
larder—and now you take your revenge."

The miserable wretch seemed crushed. Now that he
had done this foul deed, he knew what treason really
was.

"So be it," said M. Lacheneur. "You will receive the price of my blood; but it will not bring you good fortune—traitor!"

But Chupin, indignant with himself for his weakness, was already trying to shake off the fear that mastered him.

"You have conspired against the King," he stammered. "I have done only my duty in denouncing you."

And turning to the soldiers, he said:

"As for you, comrades, you may rest assured that the Duc de Sairmeuse will testify his gratitude for your services."

They had bound Lacheneur's hands, and the party were about to descend the mountain, when a man appeared, bareheaded, covered with perspiration, and panting for breath.

Twilight was falling, but M. Lacheneur recognized Balstain.

"Ah! you have him!" he exclaimed, as soon as he was within hearing distance, and pointing to the prisoner. "The reward belongs to me—I denounced him first on the other side of the frontier. The *gendarmes* at Saint-Jean-de-Coche will testify to that. He would have been captured last night in my house, but he ran away in my absence; and I have been following the bandit for sixteen hours."

He spoke with extraordinary vehemence and volubility, beside himself with fear lest he was about to lose his reward, and lest his treason would bring him nothing save disgrace and obloquy.

"If you have any right to the reward, you must prove it before the proper authorities," said the officer in command.

"If I have any right!" interrupted Balstain; "who contests my right, then?"

He looked threateningly around, and his eyes fell on Chupin.

"Is it you?" he demanded. "Do you dare to assert that you discovered the brigand?"

"Yes, it was I who discovered his hiding-place."

"You lie, impostor!" vociferated the innkeeper; "you lie!"

The soldiers did not move. This scene repaid them for the disgust they had experienced during the afternoon.

"But," continued Balstain, "what else could one expect from a vile knave like Chupin? Everyone knows that he has been obliged to flee from France a dozen times on account of his crimes. Where did you take refuge when you crossed the frontier, Chupin? In my house, in the inn kept by honest Balstain. You were fed and protected there. How many times have I saved you from the *gendarmes* and from the galleys? More times than I can count. And to reward me, you steal my property; you steal this man who was mine——"

"He is insane!" said the terrified Chupin, "he is mad!"

Then the innkeeper changed his tactics.

"At least you will be reasonable," he exclaimed. "Let us see, Chupin, what you will do for an old friend? Divide, will you not? No, you say no? What will you give me, comrade? A third? Is that too much? A quarter, then——"

Chupin felt that all the soldiers were enjoying his terrible humiliation. They were sneering at him, and only an instant before they had avoided coming in contact with him with evident horror.

Transported with anger, he pushed Balstain violently aside, crying to the soldiers:

" Come—are we going to spend the night here? "

An implacable hatred gleamed in the eye of the
Piedmontese.

He drew his knife from his pocket, and making the
sign of the cross in the air:

" Saint-Jean-de-Coche," he exclaimed, in a ringing
voice, " and you, Holy Virgin, hear my vow. May
my soul burn in hell if I ever use a knife at my repasts
until I have plunged this, which I now hold, into the
heart of the scoundrel who has defrauded me! "

Having said this, he disappeared in the woods, and
the soldiers took up their line of march.

But Chupin was no longer the same. All his accustomed impudence had fled. He walked on with bowed
head, a prey to the most sinister presentiments.

He felt assured that an oath like that of Balstain's,
and uttered by such a man, was equivolent to a death-
warrant, or at least to a speedy prospect of assassination.

This thought tormented him so much that he would
not allow the detachment to spend the night at Saint-
Pavin, as had been agreed upon. He was impatient
to leave the neighborhood.

After supper Chupin sent for a cart; the prisoner,
securely bound, was placed in it, and the party started
for Montaignac.

The great bell was striking two when Lacheneur
was brought into the citadel.

At that very moment M. d'Escorval and Corporal
Bavois were making their preparations for escape.

CHAPTER XXXII

Alone in his cell, Chanlouineau, after Marie-Anne's departure, abandoned himself to the most frightful despair.

He had just given more than life to the woman he loved so fervently.

For had he not, in the hope of obtaining an interview with her, perilled his honor by simulating the most ignoble fear? While doing so, he thought only of the success of his ruse. But now he knew only too well what those who had witnessed his apparent weakness would say of him.

"This Chanlouineau is only a miserable coward after all," he fancied he could hear them saying among themselves. "We have seen him on his knees, begging for mercy, and promising to betray his accomplices."

The thought that his memory would be tarnished with charges of cowardice and treason drove him nearly mad.

He actually longed for death, since it would give him an opportunity to retrieve his honor.

"They shall see, then," he cried, wrathfully, "if I turn pale and tremble before the soldiers."

He was in this state of mind when the door opened to admit the Marquis de Courtornieu, who, after seeing Mlle. Lacheneur leave the prison, came to Chanlouineau to ascertain the result of her visit.

"Well, my good fellow—" began the marquis, in his most condescending manner.

"Leave?" cried Chanlouineau, in a fury of passion. "Leave, or——"

Without waiting to hear the end of the sentence the marquis made his escape, greatly surprised and not a little dismayed by this sudden change.

"What a dangerous and blood-thirsty rascal!" he remarked to the guard. "It would, perhaps, be advisable to put him in a strait-jacket!"

Ah! there was no necessity for that. The heroic peasant had thrown himself upon his straw pallet, oppressed with feverish anxiety.

Would Marie-Anne know how to make the best use of the weapon which he had placed in her hands?

If he hoped so, it was because she would have as her counsellor and guide a man in whose judgment he had the most implicit confidence—Abbé Midon.

"Martial will be afraid of the letter," he said to himself, again and again; "certainly he will be afraid."

In this Chanlouineau was entirely mistaken. His discernment and intelligence were certainly above his station, but he was not sufficiently acute to read a character like that of the young Marquis de Sairmeuse.

The document which he had written in a moment of *abandon* and blindness, was almost without influence in determining his course.

He pretended to be greatly alarmed, in order to frighten his father; but in reality he considered the threat puerile.

Marie-Anne would have obtained the same assistance from him if she had not possessed this letter.

Other influences had decided him: the difficulties and dangers of the undertaking, the risks to be incurred, the prejudices to be braved.

To save the life of Baron d'Escorval—an enemy— to wrest him from the execution on the very steps of the scaffold, as it were, seemed to him a delightful en-

terprise. And to assure the happiness of the woman
he adored by saving the life of an enemy, even after
his suit had been refused, seemed a chivalrous act
worthy of him.

Besides, what an opportunity it afforded for the exercise of his *sang-froid*, his diplomatic talent, and the
finesse upon which he prided himself!

It was necessary to make his father his dupe. That
was an easy task.

It was necessary to impose upon the credulity of the
Marquis de Courtornieu. This was a difficult task,
yet he succeeded.

But poor Chanlouineau could not conceive of such
contradictions, and he was consumed with anxiety.

Willingly would he have consented to be put to the
torture before receiving his death-blow, if he might
have been allowed to follow Marie-Anne in her undertakings.

What was she doing? How could he ascertain?

A dozen times during the evening he called his
guards, under every possible pretext, and tried to compel them to talk with him. He knew very well that
these men could be no better informed on the subject
than he was himself, that he could place no confidence
in their reports—but that made no difference.

The drums beat for the evening roll-call, then for the
extinguishment of lights—after that, silence.

Standing at the window of his cell, Chanlouineau
concentrated all his faculties in a superhuman effort of
attention.

It seemed to him, if the baron regained his liberty,
he would be warned of it by some sign. Those whom
he had saved owed him, he thought, this slight token
of gratitude.

A little after two o'clock he heard sounds that made him tremble. There was a great bustle in the corridors; guards running to and fro, and calling each other, a rattling of keys, and the opening and shutting of doors.

The passage was suddenly illuminated; he looked out, and by the uncertain light of the lanterns, he thought he saw Lacheneur, as pale as a ghost, pass the cell, led by some soldiers.

Lacheneur! Could this be possible? He doubted his own eyesight. He thought it must be a vision born of the fever burning in his brain.

Later, he heard a despairing cry. But was it surprising that one should hear such a sound in a prison, where twenty men condemned to death were suffering the agony of that terrible night which precedes the day of execution.

At last, the gray light of early dawn came creeping in through the prison-bars. Chanlouineau was in despair.

" The letter was useless ! " he murmured.

Poor generous peasant! His heart would have leaped for joy could he have cast a glance on the courtyard of the citadel.

More than an hour had passed after the sounding of the *reveille*, when two countrywomen, who were carrying their butter and eggs to market, presented themselves at the gate of the fortress.

They declared that while passing through the fields at the base of the precipitous cliff upon which the citadel was built, they had discovered a rope dangling from the side of the rock. A rope! Then one of the condemned prisoners must have escaped. The guards hastened to Baron d'Escorval's room—it was empty.

The baron had fled, taking with him the man who had been left to guard him—Corporal Bavois, of the grenadiers.

The amazement was as intense as the indignation, but the fright was still greater.

There was not a single officer who did not tremble on thinking of his responsibility; not one who did not see his hopes of advancement blighted forever.

What should they say to the formidable Duc de Sairmeuse and to the Marquis de Courtornieu, who, in spite of his calm and polished manners, was almost as much to be feared. It was necessary to warn them, however, and a sergeant was despatched with the news.

Soon they made their appearance, accompanied by Martial; all frightfully angry.

M. de Sairmeuse especially seemed beside himself.

He swore at everybody, accused everybody, threatened everybody.

He began by consigning all the keepers and guards to prison; he even talked of demanding the dismissal of all the officers.

"As for that miserable Bavois," he exclaimed, "as for that cowardly deserter, he shall be shot as soon as we capture him, and we will capture him, you may depend upon it!"

They had hoped to appease the duke's wrath a little, by informing him of Lacheneur's arrest; but he knew this already, for Chupin had ventured to awake him in the middle of the night to tell him the great news.

The baron's escape afforded the duke an opportunity to exalt Chupin's merits.

"The man who has discovered Lacheneur will know how to find this traitor D'Escorval," he remarked.

M. de Courtornieu, who was more calm, "took

measures for the restoration of a great culprit to the hand of justice," as he said.

He sent couriers in every direction, ordering them to make close inquiries throughout the neighborhood.

His commands were brief, but to the point; they were to watch the frontier, to submit all travellers to a rigorous examination, to search the house, and to sow the description of D'Escorval broadcast through the land.

But first of all he ordered the arrest both of Abbé Midon—the Curé of Sairmeuse, and of the son of Baron d'Escorval.

Among the officers present there was one, an old lieutenant, medalled and decorated, who had been deeply wounded by imputations uttered by the Duc de Sairmeuse.

He stepped forward with a gloomy air, and said that these measures were doubtless all very well, but the most pressing and urgent duty was to institute an investigation at once, which, while acquainting them with the method of escape, would probably reveal the accomplices.

On hearing the word "investigation," neither the Duc de Sairmeuse nor the Marquis de Courtornieu could repress a slight shudder.

They could not ignore the fact that their reputations were at stake, and that the merest trifle might disclose the truth. A precaution neglected, the most insignificant detail, a word, a gesture might ruin their ambitious hopes forever.

They trembled to think that this officer might be a man of unusual shrewdness, who had suspected their simplicity, and was impatient to verify his presumptions.

No, the old lieutenant had not the slightest suspicion. He had spoken on the impulse of the moment, merely to give vent to his displeasure. He was not even keen enough to remark the rapid glance interchanged between the marquis and the duke.

Martial noticed this look, however, and with a politeness too studied not to be ridicule, he addressed the lieutenant:

" Yes, we must institute an investigation; that suggestion is as shrewd as it is opportune," he remarked.

The old officer turned away with a muttered oath.

" That coxcomb is poking fun at me," he thought; " and he and his father and that prig deserve—but what is one to do? "

In spite of his bold remark, Martial felt that he must not incur the slightest risk.

To whom must the charge of this investigation be intrusted? To the duke and to the marquis, of course, since they were the only persons who would know just how much to conceal, and just how much to disclose.

They began their task immediately, with an *empressement* which could not fail to silence all doubts, in case any existed in the minds of their subordinates.

But who could be suspicious? The success of the plot had been all the more certain from the fact that the baron's escape seemed likely to injure the interests of the very parties who had favored it.

Martial thought he knew the details of the escape as exactly as the fugitives themselves. He had been the author, even if they had been the actors, of the drama of the preceding night.

He was soon obliged to admit that he was mistaken in this opinion.

The investigation revealed facts which seemed incomprehensible to him.

It was evident that the Baron d'Escorval and Corporal Bavois had been compelled to accomplish two successive descents.

To do this the prisoners had realized (since they had succeeded) the necessity of having two ropes. Martial had provided them; the prisoners must have used them. And yet only one rope could be found—the one which the peasant woman had perceived hanging from the rocky platform, where it was made fast to an iron crowbar.

From the window to the platform, there was no rope.

"This is most extraordinary!" murmured Martial, thoughtfully.

"Very strange!" approved M. de Courtornieu.

"How the devil could they have reached the base of the tower?"

"That is what I cannot understand."

But Martial found another cause for surprise.

On examining the rope that remained—the one which had been used in making the second descent—he discovered that it was not a single piece. Two pieces had been knotted together. The longest piece had evidently been too short.

How did this happen? Could the duke have made a mistake in the height of the cliff? or had the *abbé* measured the rope incorrectly?

But Martial had also measured it with his eye, and it had seemed to him that the rope was much longer, fully a third longer, than it now appeared.

"There must have been some accident," he remarked to his father and to the marquis; "but what?"

"Well, what does it matter?" replied the marquis, "you have the compromising letter, have you not?"

But Martial's was one of those minds that never rest when confronted by an unsolved problem.

He insisted on going to inspect the rocks at the foot of the precipice.

There they discovered large spots of blood.

" One of the fugitives must have fallen," said Martial, quickly, " and was dangerously wounded ! "

" Upon my word ! " exclaimed the Duc de Sairmeuse, " if Baron d'Escorval has broken his neck, I shall be delighted ! "

Martial's face turned crimson, and he looked searchingly at his father.

" I suppose, Monsieur, that you do not mean one word of what you are saying," Martial said, coldly. " We pledged ourselves, upon the honor of our name, to save Baron d'Escorval. If he has been killed it will be a great misfortune to us, Monsieur, a great misfortune."

When his son addressed him in his haughty and freezing tone the duke never knew how to reply. He was indignant, but his son's was the stronger nature.

" Nonsense ! " exclaimed M. de Courtornieu ; " if the rascal had merely been wounded we should have known it."

Such was the opinion of Chupin, who had been sent for by the duke, and who had just made his appearance.

But the old scoundrel, who was usually so loquacious and so officious, replied briefly ; and, strange to say, did not offer his services.

Of his imperturbable assurance, of his wonted impudence, of his obsequious and cunning smile, absolutely nothing remained.

His restless eyes, the contraction of his features, his gloomy manner, and the occasional shudder which he could not repress, all betrayed his secret perturbation.

So marked was the change that even the Duc de Sairmeuse observed it.

" What calamity has happened to you, Master Chupin ? " he inquired.

" This has happened," he responded, sullenly: " when I was coming here the children of the town threw mud and stones at me, and ran after me, shouting : ' Traitor ! traitor ! ' "

He clinched his fists ; he seemed to be meditating vengeance, and he added :

" The people of Montaignac are pleased. They know that the baron has escaped, and they are rejoicing."

Alas ! this joy was destined to be of short duration, for this was the day appointed for the execution of the conspirators.

It was Wednesday.

At noon the gates of the citadel were closed, and the gloom was profound and universal, when the heavy rolling of drums announced the preparations for the frightful holocaust.

Consternation and fear spread through the town ; the silence of death made itself felt on every side ; the streets were deserted, and the doors and shutters of every house were closed.

At last, as three o'clock sounded, the gates of the fortress were opened to give passage to fourteen doomed men, each accompanied by a priest.

Fourteen ! for seized by remorse or fright at the last moment, M de Courtornieu and the Duc de Sairmeuse had granted a reprieve to six of the prisoners, and at that very hour a courier was hastening toward Paris with six petitions for pardons, signed by the Military Commission.

Chanlouineau was not among those for whom royal clemency had been solicited.

When he left his cell, without knowing whether or not his letter had availed, he counted the condemned with poignant anxiety.

His eyes betrayed such an agony of anguish that the priest who accompanied him leaned toward him and whispered:

" For whom are you looking, my son? "

" For Baron d'Escorval."

" He escaped last night."

" Ah! now I shall die content!" exclaimed the heroic peasant.

He died as he had sworn he would die, without even changing color—calm and proud, the name of Marie-Anne upon his lips.

CHAPTER XXXIII

Ah, well, there was one woman, a fair young girl, whose heart had not been touched by the sorrowful scenes of which Montaignac had been the theatre.

Mlle. Blanche de Courtornieu smiled as brightly as ever in the midst of a stricken people; and surrounded by mourners, her lovely eyes remained dry.

The daughter of a man who, for a week, exercised the power of a dictator, she did not lift her finger to save a single one of the condemned prisoners from the executioner.

They had stopped her carriage on the public road. This was a crime which Mlle. de Courtornieu could never forget.

She also knew that she owed it to Marie-Anne's intercession that she had not been held prisoner. This she could never forgive.

So it was with the bitterest resentment that, on the morning following her arrival in Montaignac, she recounted what she styled her "humiliations" to her father, i.e., the inconceivable arrogance of that Lacheneur girl, and the frightful brutality of which the peasants had been guilty.

And when the Marquis de Courtornieu asked if she would consent to testify against Baron d'Escorval, she coldly replied:

"I think that such is my duty, and I shall fulfil it, however painful it may be."

She knew perfectly well that her deposition would be the baron's death-warrant; but she persisted in her resolve, veiling her hatred and her insensibility under the name of virtue.

But we must do her the justice to admit that her testimony was sincere.

She really believed that it was Baron d'Escorval who was with the rebels, and whose opinion Chanlouineau had asked.

This error on the part of Mlle. Blanche rose from the custom of designating Maurice by his Christian name, which prevailed in the neighborhood.

In speaking of him everyone said "Monsieur Maurice." When they said "Monsieur d'Escorval," they referred to the baron.

After the crushing evidence against the accused had been written and signed in her fine and aristocratic hand-writing, Mlle. de Courtornieu bore herself with partly real and partly affected indifference. She would not, on any account, have had people suppose that anything relating to these plebeians—these low peasants—could possibly disturb her proud serenity. She would not so much as ask a single question on the subject.

But this superb indifference was, in great measure, assumed. In her inmost soul she was blessing this conspiracy which had caused so many tears and so much blood to flow. Had it not removed her rival from her path?

" Now," she thought, " the marquis will return to me, and I will make him forget the bold creature who has bewitched him! "

Chimeras! The charm had vanished which had once caused the love of Martial de Sairmeuse to oscillate between Mlle. de Courtornieu and the daughter of Lacheneur.

Captivated at first by the charms of Mlle. Blanche, he soon discovered the calculating ambition and the utter worldliness concealed beneath such seeming simplicity and candor. Nor was he long in discerning her intense vanity, her lack of principle, and her unbounded selfishness; and, comparing her with the noble and generous Marie-Anne, his admiration was changed into indifference, or rather repugnance.

He did return to her, however, or at least he seemed to return to her, actuated, perhaps, by that inexplicable sentiment that impels us sometimes to do that which is most distasteful to us, and by a feeling of discouragement and despair, knowing that Marie-Anne was now lost to him forever.

He also said to himself that a pledge had been interchanged between the duke and the Marquis de Courtornieu; that he, too, had given his word, and that Mlle. Blanche was his betrothed.

Was it worth while to break this engagement? Would he not be compelled to marry some day? Why not fulfil the pledge that had been made? He was as willing to marry Mlle. de Courtornieu as anyone else,

since he was sure that the only woman whom he had
ever truly loved—the only woman whom he ever could
love—was never to be his.

Master of himself when near her, and sure that he
would ever remain the same, it was easy to play the
part of lover with that perfection and that charm which
—sad as it is to say it—the real passion seldom or never
attains. He was assisted by his self-love, and also by
that instinct of duplicity which leads a man to contra-
dict his thoughts by his acts.

But while he seemed to be occupied only with
thoughts of his approaching marriage, his mind was
full of intense anxiety concerning Baron d'Escorval.

What had become of the baron and of Bavois after
their escape? What had become of those who were
awaiting them on the rocks—for Martial knew all their
plans—Mme. d'Escorval and Marie-Anne, the *abbé*
and Maurice, and the four officers?

There were, then, ten persons in all who had disappeared. And Martial asked himself again and again,
how it could be possible for so many individuals to
mysteriously disappear, leaving no trace behind them.

" It unquestionably denotes a superior ability,"
thought Martial, " I recognize the hand of the priest."

It was, indeed, remarkable, since the search ordered
by the Duc de Sairmeuse and the marquis had been
pursued with feverish activity, greatly to the terror of
those who had instituted it. Still what could they do?
They had imprudently excited the zeal of their subordinates, and now they were unable to moderate it. But
fortunately all efforts to discover the fugitives had
proved unavailing.

One witness testified, however, that on the morning
of the escape, he met, just before daybreak, a party of

about a dozen persons, men and women, who seemed to be carrying a dead body.

This circumstance, taken in connection with the broken rope and the blood-stains, made Martial tremble.

He had also been strongly impressed by another circumstance, which was revealed as the investigation progressed.

All the soldiers who were on guard that eventful night were interrogated. One of them testified as follows:

" I was on guard in the corridor communicating with the prisoner's apartment in the tower, when at about half-past two o'clock, after Lacheneur had been placed in his cell, I saw an officer approaching me. I challenged him; he gave me the countersign, and, naturally, I allowed him to pass. He went down the corridor, and entered the room adjoining that in which Monsieur d'Escorval was confined. He remained there about five minutes."

" Did you recognize this officer? " Martial eagerly inquired.

And the soldier answered: " No. He wore a large cloak, the collar of which was turned up so high that it covered his face to the very eyes."

Who could this mysterious officer have been? What was he doing in the room where the ropes had been deposited?

Martial racked his brain to discover an answer to these questions.

The Marquis de Courtornieu himself seemed much disturbed.

" How could you be ignorant that there were many sympathizers with this movement in the garrison? "

he said, angrily. "You might have known that this visitor, who concealed his face so carefully, was an accomplice who had been warned by Bavois, and who came to see if he needed a helping hand."

This was a plausible explanation, still it did not satisfy Martial.

"It is very strange," he thought, "that Monsieur d'Escorval has not even deigned to let me know he is in safety. The service which I have rendered him deserves that acknowledgment, at least."

Such was his disquietude that he resolved to apply to Chupin, even though this traitor inspired him with extreme repugnance.

But it was no longer easy to obtain the services of the old spy. Since he had received the price of Lacheneur's blood—the twenty thousand francs which had so fascinated him—Chupin had deserted the house of the Duc de Sairmeuse.

He had taken up his quarters in a small inn on the outskirts of the town; and he spent his days alone in a large room on the second floor.

At night he barricaded the doors, and drank, drank, drank; and until daybreak they could hear him cursing and singing or struggling against imaginary enemies.

Still he dared not disobey the order brought by a soldier, summoning him to the Hôtel de Sairmeuse at once.

"I wish to discover what has become of Baron d'Escorval," said Martial.

Chupin trembled, he who had formerly been bronze, and a fleeting color dyed his cheeks.

"The Montaignac police are at your disposal," he answered sulkily. "They, perhaps, can satisfy the curiosity of Monsieur le Marquis. I do not belong to the police."

Was he in earnest, or was he endeavoring to augment the value of his services by refusing them? Martial inclined to the latter opinion.

"You shall have no reason to complain of my generosity," said he. "I will pay you well."

But on hearing the word "pay," which would have made his eyes gleam with delight a week before, Chupin flew into a furious passion.

"So it was to tempt me again that you summoned me here!" he exclaimed. "You would do better to leave me quietly at my inn."

"What do you mean, fool?"

But Chupin did not even hear this interruption, and, with increasing fury, he continued:

"They told me that, by betraying Lacheneur, I should be doing my duty and serving the King. I betrayed him, and now I am treated as if I had committed the worst of crimes. Formerly, when I lived by stealing and poaching, they despised me, perhaps; but they did not shun me as they did the pestilence. They called me rascal, robber, and the like; but they would drink with me all the same. To-day I have twenty thousand francs, and I am treated as if I were a venomous beast. If I approach a man, he draws back; if I enter a room, those who are there leave it."

The recollection of the insults he had received made him more and more frantic with rage.

"Was the act I committed so ignoble and abominable?" he pursued. "Then why did your father propose it? The shame should fall on him. He should not have tempted a poor man with wealth like that. If, on the contrary, I have done well, let them make laws to protect me."

Martial comprehended the necessity of reassuring his troubled mind.

" Chupin, my boy," said he, " I do not ask you to discover Monsieur d'Escorval in order to denounce him; far from it—I only desire you to ascertain if any-one at Saint-Pavin, or at Saint-Jean-de-Coche, knows of his having crossed the frontier."

On hearing the name Saint-Jean-de-Coche, Chupin's face blanched.

" Do you wish me to be murdered? " he exclaimed, remembering Balstain and his vow. " I would have you know that I value my life, now that I am rich."

And seized with a sort of panic he fled precipitately. Martial was stupefied with astonishment.

" One might really suppose that the wretch was sorry for what he had done," he thought.

If that was really the case, Chupin was not alone.

M. de Courtornieu and the Duc de Sairmeuse were secretly blaming themselves for the exaggerations in their first reports, and the manner in which they had magnified the proportions of the rebellion. They accused each other of undue haste, of neglect of the proper forms of procedure, and the injustice of the verdict rendered.

Each endeavored to make the other responsible for the blood which had been spilled; one tried to cast the public odium upon the other.

Meanwhile they were both doing their best to obtain a pardon for the six prisoners who had been reprieved.

They did not succeed.

One night a courier arrived at Montaignac, bearing the following laconic despatch :

" The twenty-one convicted prisoners must be executed."

That is to say, the Duc de Richelieu, and the council of ministers, headed by M. Decazes, the minister of police, had decided that the petitions for clemency must be refused.

This despatch was a terrible blow to the Duc de Sairmeuse and M. de Courtornieu. They knew, better than anyone else, how little these poor men, whose lives they had tried, too late, to save, deserved death. They knew it would soon be publicly proven that two of the six men had taken no part whatever in the conspiracy.

What was to be done?

Martial desired his father to resign his authority; but the duke had not courage to do it.

M. de Courtornieu encouraged him. He admitted that all this was very unfortunate, but declared, since the wine had been drawn, that it was necessary to drink it, and that one could not draw back now without causing a terrible scandal.

The next day the dismal rolling of drums was again heard, and the six doomed men, two of whom were known to be innocent, were led outside the walls of the citadel and shot, on the same spot where, only a week before, fourteen of their comrades had fallen.

And the prime mover in the conspiracy had not yet been tried.

Confined in the cell next to that which Chanlouineau had occupied, Lacheneur had fallen into a state of gloomy despondency, which lasted during his whole term of imprisonment. He was terribly broken, both in body and in mind.

Once only did the blood mount to his pallid cheek, and that was on the morning when the Duc de Sairmeuse entered the cell to interrogate him.

" It was you who drove me to do what I did," he said.
" God sees us, and judges us ! "

Unhappy man! his faults had been great; his chastisement was terrible.

He had sacrificed his children on the altar of his wounded pride; he had not even the consolation of pressing them to his heart and of asking their forgiveness before he died.

Alone in his cell he could not distract his mind from thoughts of his son and of his daughter; but such was the terrible situation in which he had placed himself that he dared not ask what had become of them.

Through a compassionate keeper, he learned that nothing had been heard of Jean, and that it was supposed Marie-Anne had gone to some foreign country with the D'Escorval family.

When summoned before the court for trial, Lacheneur was calm and dignified in manner. He attempted no defence, but responded with perfect frankness. He took all the blame upon himself, and would not give the name of one of his accomplices.

Condemned to be beheaded, he was executed on the following day. In spite of the rain, he desired to walk to the place of execution. When he reached the scaffold, he ascended the steps with a firm tread, and, of his own accord, placed his head upon the block.

A few seconds later, the rebellion of the 4th of March counted its twenty-first victim.

And that same evening the people everywhere were talking of the magnificent rewards which were to be bestowed upon the Duc de Sairmeuse and the Marquis de Courtornieu; and it was also asserted that the nuptials of the children of these great houses were to take place before the close of the week.

CHAPTER XXXIV

That Martial de Sairmeuse was to marry Mlle. Blanche de Courtornieu did not surprise the inhabitants of Montaignac in the least.

But spreading such a report, with Lacheneur's execution fresh in the minds of everyone, could not fail to bring odium upon these men who had held absolute power, and who had exercised it so mercilessly.

Heaven knows that M. de Courtornieu and the Duc de Sairmeuse were now doing their best to make the people of Montaignac forget the atrocious cruelty of which they had been guilty during their dictatorship.

Of the hundred or more who were confined in the citadel, only eighteen or twenty were tried, and they received only some very slight punishment; the others were released.

Major Carini, the leader of the conspirators in Montaignac, who had expected to lose his head, heard himself, with astonishment, sentenced to two years' imprisonment.

But there are crimes which nothing can efface or extenuate. Public opinion attributed this sudden clemency on the part of the duke and the marquis to fear.

People execrated them for their cruelty, and despised them for their apparent cowardice.

They were ignorant of this, however, and hastened forward the preparations for the nuptials of their children, without suspecting that the marriage was considered a shameless defiance of public sentiment on their part.

The 17th of April was the day which had been appointed for the bridal, and the wedding-feast was to be held at the Château de Sairmeuse, which, at a great expense, had been transformed into a fairy palace for the occasion.

It was in the church of the little village of Sairmeuse, on the loveliest of spring days, that this marriage cere-mony was performed by the *curé* who had taken the place of poor Abbé Midon.

At the close of the address to the newly wedded pair, the priest uttered these words, which he believed pro-phetic:

" You will be, you *must* be happy ! "

Who would not have believed as he did? Where could two young people be found more richly dowered with all the attributes likely to produce happiness, *i.e.*, youth, rank, health, and riches.

But though an intense joy sparkled in the eyes of the new Marquis de Sairmeuse, there were those among the guests who observed the bridegroom's preoccupation. One might have supposed that he was making an effort to drive away some gloomy thought.

At the moment when his young wife hung upon his arm, proud and radiant, a vision of Marie-Anne rose before him, more life-like, more potent than ever.

What had become of her that she had not been seen at the time of her father's execution? Courageous as he knew her to be, if she had made no attempt to see her father, it must have been because she was ignorant of his approaching doom.

" Ah! if she had but loved him," Martial thought, " what happiness would have been his. But, now he was bound for life to a woman whom he did not love."

At dinner, however, he succeeded in shaking off the sadness that oppressed him, and when the guests rose to repair to the drawing-rooms, he had almost forgot-ten his dark forebodings.

He was rising in his turn, when a servant approached him with a mysterious air.

"Someone desires to see the marquis," whispered the valet.

"Who?"

"A young peasant who will not give his name."

"On one's wedding-day, one must grant an audience to everybody," said Martial.

And gay and smiling he descended the staircase.

In the vestibule, lined with rare and fragrant plants, stood a young man. He was very pale, and his eyes glittered with feverish brilliancy.

On recognizing him Martial could not restrain an exclamation of surprise.

"Jean Lacheneur!" he exclaimed; "imprudent man!"

The young man stepped forward.

"You believed that you were rid of me," he said, bitterly. "Instead, I return from afar. You can have your people arrest me if you choose."

Martial's face crimsoned at the insult; but he retained his composure.

"What do you desire?" he asked, coldly.

Jean drew from his pocket a folded letter.

"I am to give you this on behalf of Maurice d'Escorval."

With an eager hand, Martial broke the seal. He glanced over the letter, turned as pale as death, staggered and said only one word.

"Infamous!"

"What must I say to Maurice?" insisted Jean. "What do you intend to do?"

With a terrible effort Martial had conquered his weakness. He seemed to deliberate for ten seconds,

then seizing Jean's arm, he dragged him up the staircase, saying:

" Come—you shall see."

Martial's countenance had changed so much during
the three minutes he had been absent that there was an
exclamation of terror when he reappeared, holding
an open letter in one hand and leading with the other
a young peasant whom no one recognized.

" Where is my father? " he demanded, in a husky
voice; " where is the Marquis de Courtornieu? "

The duke and the marquis were with Mme. Blanche
in the little *salon* at the end of the main hall.

Martial hastened there, followed by a crowd of wondering guests, who, foreseeing a stormy scene, were
determined not to lose a syllable.

He walked directly to M. de Courtornieu, who was
standing by the fireplace, and handing him the letter:

" Read! " said he, in a terrible voice.

M. de Courtornieu obeyed. He became livid; the
paper trembled in his hands; his eyes fell, and he was
obliged to lean against the marble mantel for support.

" I do not understand," he stammered: " no, I do
not understand."

The duke and Mme. Blanche both sprang forward.

" What is it? " they asked in a breath; " what has
happened? "

With a rapid movement, Martial tore the paper from
the hands of the Marquis de Courtornieu, and addressing his father:

" Listen to this letter," he said, imperiously.

Three hundred people were assembled there, but the
silence was so profound that the voice of the young
marquis penetrated to the farthest extremity of the
hall as he read:

" MONSIEUR LE MARQUIS—In exchange for a dozen
lines that threatened you with ruin, you promised us,
upon the honor of your name, the life of Baron
d'Escorval.

" You did, indeed, bring the ropes by which he was
to make his escape, but they had been previously cut,
and my father was precipitated to the rocks below.

" You have forfeited your honor, Monsieur. You
have soiled your name with ineffaceable opprobrium.
While so much as a drop of blood remains in my veins,
I will leave no means untried to punish you for your
cowardice and vile treason.

" By killing me you would, it is true, escape the chastisement I am reserving for you. Consent to fight
with me. Shall I await you to-morrow on the Reche?
At what hour? With what weapons?

" If you are the vilest of men, you can appoint a
rendezvous, and then send your *gendarmes* to arrest
me. That would be an act worthy of you.

" MAURICE D'ESCORVAL."

The duke was in despair. He saw the secret of the
baron's flight made public—his political prospects
ruined.

" Hush!" he said, hurriedly, and in a low voice;
" hush, wretched man, you will ruin us!"

But Martial seemed not even to hear him. When
he had finished his reading:

" Now, what do you think?" he demanded, looking
the Marquis de Courtornieu full in the face.

" I am still unable to comprehend," said the old
nobleman, coldly.

Martial lifted his hand; everyone believed that he
was about to strike the man who had been his father-
in-law only a few hours.

"Very well! *I* comprehend!" he exclaimed. "I know now who that officer was who entered the room in which I had deposited the ropes—and I know what took him there."

He crumbled the letter between his hands and threw it in M. de Courtornieu's face, saying:

"Here is your reward—coward!"

Overwhelmed by this *dénouement* the marquis sank into an arm-chair, and Martial, still holding Jean Lacheneur by the arm, was leaving the room, when his young wife, wild with despair, tried to detain him.

"You shall not go!" she exclaimed, intensely exasperated; "you shall not! Where are you going? To rejoin the sister of the man, whom I now recognize?"

Beside himself, Martial pushed his wife roughly aside.

"Wretch!" said he, "how dare you insult the noblest and purest of women? Ah, well—yes—I am going to find Marie-Anne. Farewell!"

And he passed on.

CHAPTER XXXV

The ledge of rock upon which Baron d'Escorval and Corporal Bavois rested in their descent from the tower was very narrow.

In the widest place it did not measure more than a yard and a half, and its surface was uneven, cut by innumerable fissures and crevices, and sloped suddenly at the edge. To stand there in the daytime, with the wall of the tower behind one, and the precipice at one's feet, would have been considered very imprudent.

Of course, the task of lowering a man from this ledge, at dead of night, was perilous in the extreme.

Before allowing the baron to descend, honest Bavois took every possible precaution to save himself from being dragged over the verge of the precipice by the weight he would be obliged to sustain.

He placed his crowbar firmly in a crevice of the rock, then bracing his feet against the bar, he seated himself firmly, throwing his shoulders well back, and it was only when he was sure of his position that he said to the baron:

" I am here and firmly fixed, comrade; now let yourself down."

The sudden parting of the rope hurled the brave corporal rudely against the tower wall, then he was thrown forward by the rebound.

His unalterable *sang-froid* was all that saved him.

For more than a minute he hung suspended over the abyss into which the baron had just fallen, and his hands clutched at the empty air.

A hasty movement, and he would have fallen.

But he possessed a marvellous power of will, which prevented him from attempting any violent effort. Prudently, but with determined energy, he screwed his feet and his knees into the crevices of the rock, feeling with his hands for some point of support, and gradually sinking to one side, he finally succeeded in dragging himself from the verge of the precipice.

It was time, for a cramp seized him with such violence that he was obliged to sit down and rest for a moment.

That the baron had been killed by his fall, Bavois did not doubt for an instant. But this catastrophe did not produce much effect upon the old soldier, who had seen so many comrades fall by his side on the field of battle.

What did amaze him was the breaking of the rope—

a rope so large that one would have supposed it capable of sustaining the weight of ten men like the baron.

As he could not, by reason of the darkness, see the ruptured place, Bavois felt it with his finger; and, to his inexpressible astonishment, he found it smooth. No filaments, no rough bits of hemp, as usual after a break; the surface was perfectly even.

The corporal comprehended what Maurice had com· prehended below.

" The scoundrels have cut the rope!" he exclaimed, with a frightful oath.

And a recollection of what had happened three or four hours previous arose in his mind.

" This," he thought, " explains the noise which the poor baron heard in the next room! And I said to him: ' Nonsense! it is a rat!' "

Then he thought of a very simple method of verifying his conjectures. He passed the cord about the crowbar and pulled it with all his strength. It parted in three places.

This discovery appalled him.

A part of the rope had fallen with the unfortunate baron, and it was evident that the remaining fragments tied together would not be long enough to reach to the base of the rock.

From this isolated ledge it was impossible to reach the ground upon which the citadel was built.

" You are in a fine fix, Corporal," he growled.

Honest Bavois looked the situation full in the face, and saw that it was desperate.

" Well, Corporal, your jig is up!" he murmured. "At daybreak they will find that the baron's cell is empty. They will poke their heads out of the window, and they will see you here, like a stone saint upon his

pedestal. Naturally, you will be captured, tried, condemned: and you will be led out to take your turn in
the ditches. Ready! Aim! Fire! And that will be
the end of your story."

He stopped short. A vague idea had entered his
mind, which he felt might possibly be his salvation.

It came to him in touching the rope which he had
used in his descent from the prison to the ledge, and
which, firmly attached to the bars, hung down the side
of the tower.

"If you had that rope which hangs there useless,
Corporal, you could add it to these fragments, and then
it would be long enough to carry you to the foot of the
rock. But how shall I obtain it? It is certainly impossible to go back after it! and how can I pull it down
when it is so securely fastened to the bars?"

He sought a way, found it, and pursued it, talking to
himself all the while as if there were two corporals;
one prompt to conceive, the other, a trifle stupid, to
whom it was necessary to explain everything in detail.

"Attention, Corporal," said he. "You are going to
knot these five pieces of rope together and attach them
to your waist; then you are going to climb up to that
window, hand over hand. Not an easy matter! A
carpeted staircase is preferable to that rope dangling
there. But no matter, you are not finical, Corporal!
So you climb it, and here you are in the cell again.
What are you going to do? A mere nothing. You
are unfastening the cord attached to the bars; you will
tie it to this, and that will give you eighty feet of good
strong rope. Then you will pass the rope about one
of the bars that remain intact; the rope will thus be
doubled; then you let yourself down again, and when
you are here, you have only to untie one of the knots,

and the rope is at your service. Do you understand, Corporal?"

The corporal did understand so well that in less than twenty minutes he was back again upon the narrow shelf of rock, the difficult and dangerous operation which he had planned accomplished.

Not without a terrible effort; not without torn and bleeding hands and knees.

But he had succeeded in obtaining the rope, and now he was certain that he could make his escape from his dangerous position. He laughed gleefully, or rather with that chuckle which was habitual to him.

Anxiety, then joy, had made him forget M. d'Escorval. At the thought of him, he was smitten with remorse.

"Poor man!" he murmured. "I shall succeed in saving my miserable life, for which no one cares, but I was unable to save him. Undoubtedly, by this time his friends have carried him away."

As he uttered these words he was leaning over the abyss. He doubted the evidence of his own senses when he saw a faint light moving here and there in the depths below.

What had happened? For something very extraordinary must have happened to induce intelligent men like the baron's friends to display this light, which, if observed from the citadel, would betray their presence and ruin them.

But Corporal Bavois's moments were too precious to be wasted in idle conjectures.

"Better go down on the double-quick," he said aloud, as if to spur on his courage. "Come, my friend, spit on your hands and be off!"

As he spoke the old soldier threw himself flat on his

belly and crawled slowly backward to the verge of the precipice. The spirit was strong, but the flesh shuddered. To march upon a battery had always been a mere pastime to the worthy corporal; but to face an unknown peril, to suspend one's life upon a cord, was a different matter.

Great drops of perspiration, caused by the horror of his situation, stood out upon his brow when he felt that half his body had passed the edge of the precipice, and that the slightest movement would now launch him into space.

He made this movement, murmuring:

"If there is a God who watches over honest people let Him open His eyes this instant!"

The God of the just was watching.

Bavois arrived at the end of his dangerous journey with torn and bleeding hands, but safe.

He fell like a mass of rock; and the rudeness of the shock drew from him a groan resembling the roar of an infuriated beast.

For more than a minute he lay there upon the ground stunned and dizzy.

When he rose two men seized him roughly.

"Ah, no foolishness," he said quickly. "It is I, Bavois."

This did not cause them to relax their hold.

"How does it happen," demanded one, in a threatening tone, "that Baron d'Escorval falls and you succeed in making the descent in safety a few moments later?"

The old soldier was too shrewd not to understand the whole import of this insulting question.

The sorrow and indignation aroused within him gave him strength to free himself from the hands of his captors.

" *Mille tonnerres!* " he exclaimed, " so I pass for a traitor, do I ! No, it is impossible—listen to me."

Then rapidly, but with surprising clearness, he related all the details of his escape, his despair, his perilous situation, and the almost insurmountable obstacles which he had overcome. To hear was to believe.

The men—they were, of course, the retired army officers who had been waiting for the baron—offered the honest corporal their hands, sincerely sorry that they had wounded the feelings of a man who was so worthy of their respect and gratitude.

" You will forgive us, Corporal," they said, sadly. " Misery renders men suspicious and unjust, and we are very unhappy."

" No offence," he growled. " If I had trusted poor Monsieur d'Escorval, he would be alive now."

" The baron still breathes," said one of the officers.

This was such astounding news that Bavois was utterly confounded for a moment.

" Ah ! I will give my right hand, if necessary, to save him ! " he exclaimed, at last.

" If it is possible to save him, he will be saved, my friend. That worthy priest whom you see there, is an excellent physician. He is examining Monsieur d'Escorval's wounds now. It was by his order that we procured and lighted this candle, which may bring our enemies upon us at any moment; but this is not a time for hesitation."

Bavois looked with all his eyes, but from where he was standing he could discover only a confused group of moving figures.

" I would like to see the poor man," he said, sadly.

" Come nearer, my good fellow; fear nothing ! "

He stepped forward, and by the flickering light of

the candle which Marie-Anne held, he saw a spectacle
which moved him more than the horrors of the bloodiest battle-field.

The baron was lying upon the ground, his head supported on Mme. d'Escorval's knee.

His face was not disfigured; but he was pale as
death itself, and his eyes were closed.

At intervals a convulsive shudder shook his frame,
and a stream of blood gushed from his mouth.

His clothing was hacked—literally hacked in pieces;
and it was easy to see that his body had sustained many
frightful wounds.

Kneeling beside the unconscious man, Abbé Midon,
with admirable dexterity, was stanching the blood
and applying bandages which had been torn from the
linen of those present.

Maurice and one of the officers were assisting him.

"Ah! if I had my hands on the scoundrel who cut
the rope," cried the corporal, in a passion of indignation; "but patience. I shall have him yet."

"Do you know who it was?"

"Only too well!"

He said no more. The *abbé* had done all it was possible to do, and he now lifted the wounded man a little
higher on Mme. d'Escorval's knee.

This change of position elicited a moan that betrayed
the unfortunate baron's intense sufferings. He opened
his eyes and faltered a few words—they were the first
he had uttered.

"Firmin!" he murmured, "Firmin!"

It was the name of the baron's former secretary, a
man who had been absolutely devoted to his master,
but who had been dead for several years.

It was evident that the baron's mind was wandering. Still he had some vague idea of his terrible situation, for in a stifled, almost inaudible voice, he added:

"Oh! how I suffer! Firmin, I will not fall into the hands of the Marquis de Courtornieu alive. You shall kill me rather—do you hear me? I command it."

This was all; then his eyes closed again, and his head fell back a dead weight. One would have supposed that he had yielded up his last sigh.

Such was the opinion of the officers; and it was with poignant anxiety they drew the *abbé* a little aside.

"Is it all over?" they asked. "Is there any hope?"

The priest sadly shook his head, and pointing to heaven:

"My hope is in God!" he said, reverently.

The hour, the place, the terrible catastrophe, the present danger, the threatening future, all combined to lend a deep solemnity to the words of the priest.

So profound was the impression that, for more than a minute, these men, familiar with peril and scenes of horror, stood in awed silence.

Maurice, who approached, followed by Corporal Bavois, brought them back to the exigencies of the present.

"Ought we not to make haste and carry away my father?" he asked. "Must we not be in Piedmont before evening?"

"Yes!" exclaimed the officers, "let us start at once."

But the priest did not move, and in a despondent voice, he said:

"To make any attempt to carry Monsieur d'Escorval across the frontier in his present condition would cost him his life."

This seemed so inevitably a death-warrant for them all, that they shuddered.

"My God! what shall we do?" faltered Maurice. "What course shall we pursue?"

Not a voice replied. It was clear that they hoped for salvation through the priest alone.

He was lost in thought, and it was some time before he spoke.

"About an hour's walk from here," he said, at last, "beyond the Croix d'Arcy, is the hut of a peasant upon whom I can rely. His name is Poignot; and he was formerly in Monsieur Lacheneur's employ. With the assistance of his three sons, he now tills quite a large farm. We must procure a litter and carry Monsieur d'Escorval to the house of this honest peasant."

"What, Monsieur," interrupted one of the officers, "you wish us to procure a litter at this hour of the night, and in this neighborhood?"

"It must be done."

"But, will it not awaken suspicion?"

"Most assuredly."

"The Montaignac police will follow us."

"I am certain of it."

"The baron will be recaptured?"

"No."

The *abbé* spoke in the tone of a man who, by virtue of assuming all the responsibility, feels that he has a right to be obeyed.

"When the baron has been conveyed to Poignot's house," he continued, "one of you gentlemen will take the wounded man's place upon the litter; the others will carry him, and the party will remain together until it has reached Piedmontese territory. Then you will separate and pretend to conceal yourselves, but do it in such a way that you are seen everywhere."

All present comprehended the priest's simple plan.

They were to throw the emissaries sent by the Duc de Sairmeuse and the Marquis de Courtornieu off the track; and at the very moment it was apparently proven that the baron was in the mountains, he would be safe in Poignot's house.

"One word more," added the priest. "It will be necessary to make the *cortége* which accompanies the pretended baron resemble as much as possible the little party that would be likely to attend Monsieur d'Escorval. Mademoiselle Lacheneur will accompany you; Maurice also. People know that I would not leave the baron, who is my friend; my priestly robe would attract attention; one of you must assume it. God will forgive this deception on account of its worthy motive.

It was now necessary to procure the litter; and the officers were trying to decide where they should go to obtain it, when Corporal Bavois interrupted them.

"Give yourselves no uneasiness," he remarked; " I know an inn not far from here where I can procure one."

He departed on the run, and five minutes later reappeared with a small litter, a thin mattress, and a coverlid. He had thought of everything.

The wounded man was lifted carefully and placed upon the mattress.

A long and difficult operation which, in spite of extreme caution, drew many terrible groans from the baron.

When all was ready, each officer took an end of the litter, and the little procession, headed by the *abbé*, started on its way. They were obliged to proceed slowly on account of the suffering which the least

jolting inflicted upon the baron. Still they made some
progress, and by daybreak they were about half way to
Poignot's house.

It was then that they met some peasants going to
their daily toil. Both men and women paused to look
at them, and when the little *cortége* had passed they still
stood gazing curiously after these people who were apparently carrying a dead body.

The priest did not seem to trouble himself in regard
to these encounters; at least, he made no attempt to
avoid them.

But he did seem anxious and cautious when, after a
three hours' march, they came in sight of Poignot's
cottage.

Fortunately there was a little grove not far from the
house. The *abbé* made the party enter it, recommending the strictest prudence, while he went on in advance to confer with this man, upon whose decision the
safety of the whole party depended.

As the priest approached the house, a small, thin
man, with gray hair and a sunburned face emerged
from the stable.

It was Father Poignot.

"What! is this you, Monsieur le Curé!" he exclaimed, delightedly. "Heavens! how pleased my
wife will be. We have a great favor to ask of you——"

And then, without giving the *abbé* an opportunity to
open his lips, he began to tell him his perplexities. The
night of the revolt he had given shelter to a poor man
who had received an ugly sword-thrust. Neither his
wife nor himself knew how to dress the wound, and he
dared not call in a physician.

"And this wounded man," he added, "is Jean Lacheneur, the son of my former employer."

A terrible anxiety seized the priest's heart.

Would this man, who had already given an asylum to one wounded conspirator, consent to receive another?

The *abbé's* voice trembled as he made known his petition.

The farmer turned very pale and shook his head gravely, while the priest was speaking.   When the *abbé* had finished:

" Do you know, sir," he asked, coldly, " that I incur a great risk by converting my house into a hospital for these rebels? "

The *abbé* dared not answer.

" They told me," Father Poignot continued, " that I was a coward, because I would not take part in the revolt.   Such was not my opinion.   Now I choose to shelter these wounded men—I shelter them.   In my opinion, it requires quite as much courage as it does to go and fight."

" Ah! you are a brave man! " cried the *abbé*.

" I know that very well!   Bring Monsieur d'Escorval.   There is no one here but my wife and boys— no one will betray him! "

A half hour later the baron was lying in a small loft, where Jean Lacheneur was already installed.

From the window, Abbé Midon and Mme. d'Escorval watched the little *cortége*, organized for the purpose of deceiving the Duc de Sairmeuse's spies, as it moved rapidly away.

Corporal Bavois, with his head bound up with blood-stained linen, had taken the baron's place upon the litter.

This was one of the troubled epochs in history that try men's souls.   There is no chance for hypocrisy; each man stands revealed in his grandeur, or in his pettiness of soul.

Certainly much cowardice was displayed during the early days of the second Restoration; but many deeds of sublime courage and devotion were performed.

These officers who befriended Mme. d'Escorval and Maurice—who lent their aid to the *abbé*—knew the baron only by name and reputation.

It was sufficient for them to know that he was the friend of their former ruler—the man whom they had made their idol, and they rejoiced with all their hearts when they saw M. d'Escorval reposing under Father Poignot's roof in comparative security.

After this, their task, which consisted in misleading the government emissaries, seemed to them mere child's play.

But all these precautions were unnecessary. Public sentiment had declared itself in an unmistakable manner, and it was evident that Lacheneur's hopes had not been without some foundation.

The police discovered nothing, not so much as a single detail of the escape. They did not even hear of the little party that had travelled nearly three leagues in the full light of day, bearing a wounded man upon a litter.

Among the two thousand peasants who believed that this wounded man was Baron d'Escorval, there was not one who turned informer or let drop an indiscreet word.

But on approaching the frontier, which they knew to be strictly guarded, the fugitives became even more cautious.

They waited until nightfall before presenting themselves at a lonely inn, where they hoped to procure a guide to lead them through the defiles of the mountains.

Frightful news awaited them there. The innkeeper informed them of the bloody massacre at Montaignac.

With tears rolling down his cheeks, he related the details of the execution, which he had heard from an eye-witness.

Fortunately, or unfortunately, he knew nothing of M. d'Escorval's flight or of M. Lacheneur's arrest.

But he was well acquainted with Chanlouineau, and he was inconsolable over the death of that "handsome young fellow, the best farmer in the country."

The officers, who had left the litter a short distance from the inn, decided that they could confide at least a part of their secret to this man.

"We are carrying one of our wounded comrades," they said to him. "Can you guide us across the frontier to-night?"

The innkeeper replied that he would do so very willingly, that he would promise to take them safely past the military posts; but that he would not think of going upon the mountain before the moon rose.

By midnight the fugitives were *en route;* by daybreak they set foot on Piedmont territory.

They had dismissed their guide some time before. They now proceeded to break the litter in pieces; and handful by handful they cast the wool of the mattress to the wind.

"Our task is accomplished," the officer said to Maurice. "We will now return to France. May God protect you! Farewell!"

It was with tears in his eyes that Maurice saw these brave men, who had just saved his father's life, depart. Now he was the sole protector of Marie-Anne, who, pale and overcome with fatigue and emotion, trembled on his arm.

But no—Corporal Bavois still lingered by his side.

"And you, my friend," he asked, sadly, "what are you going to do?"

"Follow you," replied the old soldier. "I have a right to a home with you; that was agreed between your father and myself! So do not hurry, the young lady does not seem well, and I see the village only a short distance away."

CHAPTER XXXVI

Essentially a woman in grace and beauty, as well as in devotion and tenderness, Marie-Anne was capable of a virile bravery. Her energy and her coolness during those trying days had been the admiration and the astonishment of all around her.

But human endurance has its limits. Always after excessive efforts comes a moment when the shrinking flesh fails the firmest will.

When Marie-Anne tried to begin her journey anew, she found that her strength was exhausted; her swollen feet would no longer sustain her, her limbs sank under her, her head whirled, and an intense freezing coldness crept over her heart.

Maurice and the old soldier were obliged to support her, almost carry her. Fortunately they were not far from the village, whose church-tower they had discerned through the gray mists of morning.

Soon the fugitives could distinguish the houses on the outskirts of the town. The corporal suddenly stopped short with an oath.

"*Mille tonnerres!*" he exclaimed; "and my uniform! To enter the village in this rig would excite suspicion at once; before we had a chance to sit down, the Piedmontese *gendarmes* would arrest us."

He reflected for a moment, twirling his mustache furiously; then, in a tone that would have made a passer-by tremble, he said:

" All things are fair in love and war. The next peasant who passes——"

" But I have money," interrupted Maurice, unbuckling a belt filled with gold, which he had put on under his clothing on the night of the revolt.

" Eh! we are fortunate!" cried Bavois. " Give me some, and I will soon find some shop in the suburbs where I can purchase a change of clothing."

He departed; but it was not long before he reappeared, transformed by a peasant's costume, which fitted him perfectly. His small, thin face was almost hidden beneath an immense broad-brimmed hat.

" Now, steady, forward, march!" he said to Maurice and Marie-Anne, who scarcely recognized him in this disguise.

The town, which they soon reached, was called Saliente. They read the name upon a guide-post.

The fourth house after entering the place was a hostelry, the Traveller's Rest. They entered it, and ordered the hostess to take the young lady to a room and to assist her in disrobing.

The order was obeyed, and Maurice and the corporal went into the dining-room and ordered something to eat.

The desired refreshments were served, but the glances cast upon the guests were by no means friendly. It was evident that they were regarded with suspicion.

A large man, who was apparently the proprietor of the house, hovered around them, and at last embraced a favorable opportunity to ask their names.

" My name is Dubois," replied Maurice, without the slightest hesitation. " I am travelling on business, and this man here is my farmer."

These replies seemed to reassure the host a little.

" And what is your business? " he inquired.

" I came into this land of inquisitive people to buy mules," laughed Maurice, striking his belt of money.

On hearing the jingle of the coin the man lifted his cap deferentially. Raising mules was the chief industry of the country. This bourgeois was very young, but he had a well-filled purse, and that was enough.

" You will excuse me," resumed the host, in quite a different tone. " You see, we are obliged to be very careful. There has been some trouble in Montaignac."

The imminence of the peril and the responsibility devolving upon him, gave Maurice an assurance unusual to him; and it was in the most careless, off-hand manner possible that he concocted a quite plausible story to explain his early arrival on foot accompanied by a sick wife. He congratulated himself upon his address, but the old corporal was far from satisfied.

" We are too near the frontier to bivouac here," he grumbled. " As soon as the young lady is on her feet again we must hurry on."

He believed, and Maurice hoped, that twenty-four hours of rest would restore Marie-Anne.

They were mistaken. The very springs of life in her existence seemed to have been drained dry. She did not appear to suffer, but she remained in a death-like torpor, from which nothing could arouse her. They spoke to her but she made no response. Did she hear? did she comprehend? It was extremely doubtful.

By rare good fortune the mother of the proprietor proved to be a good, kind-hearted old woman, who would not leave the bedside of Marie-Anne—of Mme. Dubois, as she was called at the Traveller's Rest.

It was not until the evening of the third day that they heard Marie-Anne utter a word.

" Poor girl ! " she sighed ; " poor, wretched girl ! "

It was of herself that she spoke.

By a phenomenon not very unusual after a crisis in which reason has been temporarily obscured, it seemed to her that it was someone else who had been the victim of all the misfortunes, whose recollections gradually returned to her like the memory of a painful dream.

What strange and terrible events had taken place since that August Sabbath, when, on leaving the church with her father, she heard of the arrival of the Duc de Sairmeuse.

And that was only eight months ago.

What a difference between those days when she lived happy and envied in that beautiful Château de Sairmeuse, of which she believed herself the mistress, and at the present time, when she found herself lying in the comfortless room of a miserable country inn, attended by an old woman whom she did not know, and with no other protection than that of an old soldier—a deserter, whose life was in constant danger—and that of her proscribed lover.

From this total wreck of her cherished ambitions, of her hopes, of her fortune, of her happiness, and of her future, she had not even saved her honor.

But was she alone responsible? Who had imposed upon her the odious *rôle* which she had played with Maurice, Martial, and Chanlouineau?

As this last name darted through her mind, the scene in the prison-cell rose suddenly and vividly before her.

Chanlouineau had given her a letter, saying as he did so:

" You will read this when I am no more."

She might read it now that he had fallen beneath the bullets of the soldiery. But what had become of it? From the moment that he gave it to her until now she had not once thought of it.

She raised herself in bed, and in an imperious voice:

" My dress," she said to the old nurse, seated beside her ; " give me my dress."

The woman obeyed ; with an eager hand Marie-Anne examined the pocket.

She uttered an exclamation of joy on finding the letter there.

She opened it, read it slowly twice, then, sinking back on her pillows, she burst into tears.

Maurice anxiously approached her.

" What is the matter? " he inquired anxiously.

She handed him the letter, saying : " Read."

Chanlouineau was only a poor peasant. His entire education had been derived from an old country pedagogue, whose school he attended for three winters, and who troubled himself much less about the progress of his students than about the size of the books which they carried to and from the school.

This letter, which was written upon the commonest kind of paper, was sealed with a huge wafer, as large as a two-sou piece, which he had purchased from a grocer in Sairmeuse.

The chirography was labored, heavy and trembling ; it betrayed the stiff hand of a man more accustomed to guiding the plough than the pen.

The lines zigzagged toward the top or toward the

bottom of the page, and faults of orthography were everywhere apparent.

But if the writing was that of a vulgar peasant, the thoughts it expressed were worthy of the noblest, the proudest in the land.

This was the letter which Chanlouineau had written, probably on the eve of the insurrection:

" MARIE-ANNE—The outbreak is at hand. Whether it succeeds, or whether it fails, I shall die. That was decided on the day when I learned that you could marry none other than Maurice d'Escorval.

" But the conspiracy will not succeed; and I understand your father well enough to know that he will not survive its defeat. And if Maurice and your brother should both be killed, what would become of you? Oh, my God, would you not be reduced to beggary?

" The thought has haunted me continually. I have reflected, and this is my last will:

" I give and bequeath to you all my property, all that I possess:

" My house, the Borderie, with the gardens and vineyards pertaining thereto, the woodland and the pastures of Berarde, and five lots of land at Valrollier.

" You will find an inventory of this property, and of my other possessions which I devise to you, deposited with the lawyer at Sairmeuse.

" You can accept this bequest without fear; for, having no parents, my control over my property is absolute.

" If you do not wish to remain in France, this property will sell for at least forty thousand francs.

" But it would, it seems to me, be better for you to remain in your own country. The house on the Borderie is comfortable and convenient, since I have had it divided into three rooms and thoroughly repaired.

" Upstairs is a room that has been fitted up by the best upholsterer in Montaignac. I intended it for you. Beneath the hearth-stone in this room you will find a box containing three hundred and twenty-seven louis d'or and one hundred and forty-six livres.

" If you refuse this gift, it will be because you scorn me even after I am dead. Accept it, if not for your own sake, for the sake of—I dare not write it; but you will understand my meaning only too well.

" If Maurice is not killed, and I shall try my best to stand between him and danger, he will marry you. Then you will, perhaps, be obliged to ask his consent in order to accept my gift. I hope that he will not refuse it. One is not jealous of the dead!

" Besides, he knows well that you have scarcely vouchsafed a glance to the poor peasant who has loved you so much.

" Do not be offended at anything I have said, I am in such agony that I cannot weigh my words.

"Adieu, adieu, Marie-Anne.

"CHANLOUINEAU."

Maurice also read twice, before handing it back, this letter whose every word palpitated with sublime passion.

He was silent for a moment, then, in a husky voice, he said:

" You cannot refuse; it would be wrong."

His emotion was so great that he could not conceal it, and he left the room.

He was overwhelmed by the grandeur of soul exhibited by this peasant, who, after saving the life of his successful rival at the Croix d'Arcy, had wrested Baron d'Escorval from the hands of his executioners, and who had never allowed a complaint nor a reproach to escape his lips, and whose protection over the woman he adored extended even from beyond the grave.

In comparison with this obscure hero, Maurice felt himself insignificant, mediocre, unworthy.

Good God! what if this comparison should arise in Marie-Anne's mind as well? How could he compete with the memory of such nobility of soul and heroic self-sacrifice?

Chanlouineau was mistaken; one may, perhaps, be jealous of the dead!

But Maurice took good care to conceal this poignant anxiety and these sorrowful thoughts, and during the days that followed, he presented himself in Marie-Anne's room with a calm, even cheerful face.

For she, unfortunately, was not restored to health. She had recovered the full possession of her mental faculties, but her strength had not yet returned. She was still unable to sit up; and Maurice was forced to relinquish all thought of quitting Saliente, though he felt the earth burn beneath his feet.

This persistent weakness began to astonish the old nurse. Her faith in herbs, gathered by the light of the moon, was considerably shaken.

Honest Bavois was the first to suggest the idea of consulting a physician whom he had found in this land of savages.

Yes; he had found a really skilful physician in the neighborhood, a man of superior ability. Attached at one time to the beautiful court of Prince Eugene, he had been obliged to flee from Milan, and had taken refuge in this secluded spot.

This physician was summoned, and promptly made his appearance. He was one of those men whose age it is impossible to determine. His past, whatever it might have been, had wrought deep furrows on his brow, and his glance was as keen and piercing as his lancet.

After visiting the sick-room, he drew Maurice aside.

" Is this young lady really your wife, Monsieur— Dubois ? "

He hesitated so strangely over this name, Dubois, that Maurice felt his face crimson to the roots of his hair.

" I do not understand your question," he retorted, angrily.

" I beg your pardon, of course, but you seem very young for a married man, and your hands are too soft to belong to a farmer. And when I spoke to this young lady of her husband, she blushed scarlet. The man who accompanies you has terrible mustaches for a farmer. Besides, you must remember that there have been troubles across the frontier at Montaignac."

From crimson Maurice had turned white. He felt that he was discovered—that he was in this man's power.

What should he do?

What good would denial do?

He reflected that confession is sometimes the height of prudence, and that extreme confidence often meets with sympathy and protection ; so, in a voice trembling with anxiety, he said:

" You are not mistaken, Monsieur. My friend and myself both are fugitives, undoubtedly condemned to death in France at this moment."

And without giving the doctor time to respond, he narrated the terrible events that had happened at Sairmeuse, and the history of his unfortunate love-affair.

He omitted nothing. He neither concealed his own name nor that of Marie-Anne.

When his recital was completed, the physician pressed his hand.

"It is just as I supposed," said he. "Believe me, Monsieur—Dubois, you must not tarry here. What I have discovered others will discover. And above all, do not warn the hotel-keeper of your departure. He has not been deceived by your explanation. Self-interest alone has kept his mouth closed. He has seen your money, and so long as you spend it at his house he will hold his tongue; but if he discovers that you are going away, he will probably betray you."

"Ah! sir, but how is it possible for us to leave this place?"

"In two days the young lady will be on her feet again," interrupted the physician. "And take my advice. At the next village, stop and give your name to Mademoiselle Lacheneur."

"Ah! sir," Maurice exclaimed; "have you considered the advice you offer me? How can I, a proscribed man —a man condemned to death perhaps—how can I obtain the necessary papers?"

The physician shook his head.

"Excuse me, you are no longer in France, Monsieur d'Escorval, you are in Piedmont."

"Another difficulty!"

"No, because in this country, people marry, or at least they can marry, without all the formalities that cause you so much anxiety."

"Is it possible?" Maurice exclaimed.

"Yes, if you can find a priest who will consent to your union, inscribe your name upon his parish register and give you a certificate, you will be so indissolubly united, Mademoiselle Lacheneur and you, that the court of Rome would never grant you a divorce."

To suspect the truth of these affirmations was difficult, and yet Maurice doubted still.

" So, sir," he said, hesitatingly, " in case I was able to find a priest——"

The physician was silent. One might have supposed he was blaming himself for meddling with matters that did not concern him.

Then, almost brusquely, he said:

" Listen to me attentively, Monsieur d'Escorval. I am about to take my leave, but before I go, I shall take occasion to recommend a good deal of exercise for the sick lady—I will do this before your host. Consequently, day after to-morrow, Wednesday, you will hire mules, and you, Mademoiselle Lacheneur and your old friend, the soldier, will leave the hotel as if going on a pleasure excursion. You will push on to Vigano, three leagues from here, where I live. I will take you to a priest, one of my friends; and he, upon my recommendation, will perform the marriage ceremony. Now reflect, shall I expect you on Wednesday? "

" Oh, yes, yes, Monsieur. How can I ever thank you? "

" By not thanking me at all. See, here is the inn-keeper; you are Monsieur Dubois, again."

Maurice was intoxicated with joy. He understood the irregularity of such a marriage, but he knew it would reassure Marie-Anne's troubled conscience. Poor girl! she was suffering an agony of remorse. It was that which was killing her.

He did not speak to her on the subject, however, fearing something might occur to interfere with the project.

But the old physician had not given his word lightly, and everything took place as he had promised.

The priest at Vigano blessed the marriage of Maurice d'Escorval and of Marie-Anne Lacheneur, and after inscribing their names upon the church register, he gave them a certificate, upon which the physician and Corporal Bavois figured as witnesses.

That same evening the mules were sent back to Saliente, and the fugitives resumed their journey.

Abbé Midon had counselled them to reach Turin as quickly as possible.

" It is a large city," he said; " you will be lost in the crowd. I have more than one friend there, whose name and address are upon this paper. Go to them, and in that way I will try to send you news of your father."

So it was toward Turin that Maurice, Marie-Anne, and Corporal Bavois directed their steps.

But their progress was very slow, for they were obliged to avoid frequented roads, and renounce the ordinary modes of transportation.

The fatigue of travel, instead of exhausting Marie-Anne, seemed to revive her. After five or six days the color came back to her cheek and her strength returned.

" Fate seems to have relaxed her rigor," said Maurice, one day. " Who knows what compensations the future may have in store for us! "

No, fate had not taken pity upon them; it was only a short respite granted by destiny. One lovely April morning the fugitives stopped for breakfast at an inn on the outskirts of a large city.

Maurice having finished his repast was just leaving the table to settle with the hostess, when a despairing cry arrested him.

Marie-Anne, deadly pale, and with eyes staring wildly at a paper which she held in her hand, exclaimed in frenzied tones:

" Here! Maurice! Look! "

It was a French journal about a fortnight old, which had probably been left there by some traveller.

Maurice seized it and read:

" Yesterday, Lacheneur, the leader of the revolt in Montaignac, was executed. The miserable mischief-maker exhibited upon the scaffold the audacity for which he has always been famous."

" My father has been put to death!" cried Marie-Anne, " and I—his daughter—was not there to receive his last farewell!"

She rose, and in an imperious voice:

" I will go no farther," she said; " we must turn back now without losing an instant. I wish to return to France."

To return to France was to expose themselves to frightful peril. What good would it do? Was not the misfortune irreparable?

So Corporal Bavois suggested, very timidly. The old soldier trembled at the thought that they might suspect him of being afraid.

But Maurice would not listen.

He shuddered. It seemed to him that Baron d'Escorval must have been discovered and arrested at the same time that Lacheneur was captured.

" Yes, let us start at once on our return!" he exclaimed.

They immediately procured a carriage to convey them to the frontier. One important question, however, remained to be decided. Should Maurice and Marie-Anne make their marriage public? She wished to do so, but Maurice entreated her, with tears in his eyes, to conceal it.

" Our marriage certificate will not silence the evil disposed," said he. " Let us keep our secret for the present. We shall doubtless remain in France only a few days."

Unfortunately, Marie-Anne yielded.

" Since you wish it," said she, " I will obey you. No one shall know it."

The next day, which was the 17th of April, the fugitives at nightfall reached Father Poignot's house.

Maurice and Corporal Bavois were disguised as peasants.

The old soldier had made one sacrifice that drew tears from his eyes ; he had shaved off his mustache.

CHAPTER XXXVII

When Abbé Midon and Martial de Sairmeuse held their conference, to discuss and to decide upon the arrangements for the Baron d'Escorval's escape, a difficulty presented itself which threatened to break off the negotiation.

" Return my letter," said Martial, " and I will save the baron."

" Save the baron," replied the *abbé*, " and your letter shall be returned."

But Martial's was one of those natures which become exasperated by the least shadow of suspicion.

The idea that anyone should suppose him influenced by threats, when in reality, he had yielded only to Marie-Anne's tears, angered him beyond endurance.

" These are my last words, Monsieur," he said, emphatically. " Restore to me, now, this instant, the letter which was obtained from me by Chanlouineau's ruse, and I swear to you, by the honor of my name, that all which it is possible for any human being to do to save the baron, I will do. If you distrust my word, good-evening."

The situation was desperate, the danger imminent, the time limited; Martial's tone betrayed an inflexible determination.

The *abbé* could not hesitate. He drew the letter from his pocket and handing it to Martial:

" Here it is, Monsieur," he said, solemnly, " remember that you have pledged the honor of your name."

" I will remember it, Monsieur le Curé. Go and obtain the ropes."

The *abbé's* sorrow and amazement were intense, when, after the baron's terrible fall, Maurice announced that the cord had been cut. And yet he could not make up his mind that Martial was guilty of the execrable act. It betrayed a depth of duplicity and hypocrisy which is rarely found in men under twenty-five years of age. But no one suspected his secret thoughts. It was with the most unalterable *sang-froid* that he dressed the baron's wounds and made arrangements for the flight. Not until he saw M. d'Escorval installed in Poignot's house did he breathe freely.

The fact that the baron had been able to endure the journey, proved that in this poor maimed body remained a power of vitality for which the priest had not dared to hope.

Some way must now be discovered to procure the surgical instruments and the remedies which the condition of the wounded man demanded.

But where and how could he procure them?

The police kept a close watch over the physicians and druggists in Montaignac, in the hope of discovering the wounded conspirators through them.

But the *curé,* who had been for ten years physician and surgeon for the poor of his parish, had an almost complete set of surgical instruments and a well-filled medicine-chest.

"This evening," said he, "I will obtain what is needful."

When night came, he put on a long blue blouse, shaded his face by an immense slouch hat, and directed his steps toward Sairmeuse.

Not a light was visible through the windows of the presbytery; Bibiane, the old housekeeper, must have gone out to gossip with some of the neighbors.

The priest effected an entrance into the house, which had once been his, by forcing the lock of the door opening on the garden; he found the requisite articles, and retired without having been discovered.

That night the *abbé* hazarded a cruel but indispensable operation. His heart trembled, but not the hand that held the knife, although he had never before attempted so difficult a task.

"It is not upon my weak powers that I rely: I have placed my trust in One who is on High."

His faith was rewarded. Three days later the wounded man, after quite a comfortable night, seemed to regain consciousness.

His first glance was for his devoted wife, who was seated by his bedside; his first word was for his son.

"Maurice?" he asked.

"Is in safety," replied the *abbé*. "He must be on the way to Turin."

M. d'Escorval's lips moved as if he were murmuring a prayer; then, in a feeble voice:

"We owe you a debt of gratitude which we can never pay," he murmured, "for I think I shall pull through."

He did "pull through," but not without terrible suffering, not without difficulties that made those around him tremble with anxiety. Jean Lacheneur, more fortunate, was on his feet by the end of the week.

Forty days had passed, when one evening—it was the 17th of April—while the *abbé* was reading a newspaper to the baron, the door gently opened and one of the Poignot boys put in his head, then quickly withdrew it.

The priest finished the paragraph, laid down the paper, and quietly went out.

" What is it? " he inquired of the young man.

" Ah! Monsieur, Monsieur Maurice, Mademoiselle Lacheneur and the old corporal have just arrived; they wish to come up."

In three bounds the *abbé* descended the narrow staircase.

" Unfortunate creatures! " he exclaimed, addressing the three imprudent travellers, " what has induced you to return here? "

Then turning to Maurice:

" Is it not enough that *for* you, and *through* you, your father has nearly died? Are you afraid he will not be recaptured, that you return here to set the enemies upon his track? Depart! "

The poor boy, quite overwhelmed, faltered his excuse. Uncertainty seemed to him worse than death; he had heard of M. Lacheneur's execution; he had not reflected, he would go at once; he asked only to see his father and to embrace his mother.

The priest was inflexible.

" The slightest emotion might kill your father," he declared; " and to tell your mother of your return, and of the dangers to which you have foolishly exposed yourself, would cause her untold tortures. Go at once. Cross the frontier again this very night."

Jean Lacheneur, who had witnessed this scene, now approached.

" It is time for me to depart," said he, " and I entreat you to care for my sister, the place for her is here, not upon the highways."

The *abbé* deliberated for a moment, then he said, brusquely:

" So be it; but go at once; your name is not upon the proscribed list. You will not be pursued."

Thus, suddenly separated from his wife, Maurice wished to confer with her, to give her some parting advice; but the *abbé* did not allow him an opportunity.

" Go, go at once," he insisted. " Farewell! "

The good *abbé* was too hasty.

Just when Maurice stood sorely in need of wise counsel, he was thus delivered over to the influence of Jean Lacheneur's furious hatred. As soon as they were outside:

" This," exclaimed Jean, " is the work of the Sairmeuse and the Marquis de Courtornieu! I do not even know where they have thrown the body of my murdered parent; you cannot even embrace the father who has been traitorously assassinated by them! "

He laughed a harsh, discordant, terrible laugh, and continued:

" And yet, if we ascended that hill, we could see the Château de Sairmeuse in the distance, brightly illuminated. They are celebrating the marriage of Martial de Sairmeuse and Blanche de Courtornieu. *We* are homeless wanderers without friends, and without a shelter for our heads: *they* are feasting and making merry."

Less than this would have sufficed to rekindle the wrath of Maurice. He forgot everything in saying to himself that to disturb this *fête* by his appearance would be a vengeance worthy of him.

" I will go and challenge Martial now, on the instant, in the presence of the revellers," he exclaimed.

But Jean interrupted him.

"No, not that! They are cowards; they would arrest you. Write; I will be the bearer of the letter."

Corporal Bavois heard them; but he did not oppose their folly. He thought it all perfectly natural, under the circumstances, and esteemed them the more for their rashness.

Forgetful of prudence they entered the first shop, and the challenge was written and confided to Jean Lacheneur.

CHAPTER XXXVIII

To disturb the merrymaking at the Château de Sairmeuse; to change the joy of the bridal-day into sadness; to cast a gloom over the nuptials of Martial and Mlle. Blanche de Courtornieu.

This, in truth, was all that Jean Lacheneur hoped to do.

As for believing that Martial, triumphant and happy, would accept the challenge of Maurice, a miserable outlaw, he did not believe it.

While awaiting Martial in the vestibule of the château, he armed himself against the scorn and sneers which he would probably receive from this haughty nobleman whom he had come to insult.

But Martial's kindly greeting had disconcerted him a little.

But he was reassured when he saw the terrible effect produced upon the marquis by the insulting letter.

"We have cut him to the quick," he thought.

When Martial seized him by the arm and led him upstairs, he made no resistance.

While they traversed the brightly lighted drawing-

rooms and passed through the crowd of astonished
guests, Jean thought neither of his heavy shoes nor of
his peasant dress.

Breathless with anxiety, he wondered what was to
come.

He soon knew.

Leaning against the gilded door-post, he witnessed
the terrible scene in the little *salon.*

He saw Martial de Sairmeuse, frantic with passion,
cast into the face of his father-in-law Maurice d'Escorval's letter.

One might have supposed that all this did not affect
him in the least, he stood so cold and unmoved, with
compressed lips and downcast eyes; but appearances
were deceitful. His heart throbbed with wild exultation; and if he cast down his eyes, it was only to conceal
the joy that sparkled there.

He had not hoped for so prompt and so terrible a revenge.

Nor was this all.

After brutally repulsing Blanche, his newly wedded
wife, who attempted to detain him, Martial again seized
Jean Lacheneur's arm.

" Now," said he, " follow me ! "

Jean followed him still without a word.

They again crossed the grand hall, but instead of
going to the vestibule Martial took a candle that was
burning upon a side table, and opened a little door leading to the private staircase.

" Where are you taking me? " inquired Jean Lacheneur.

Martial, who had already ascended two or three
steps, turned.

" Are you afraid? " he asked.

The other shrugged his shoulders, and coldly replied:

"If you put it in that way, let us go on."

They entered the room which Martial had occupied since taking possession of the château. It was the same room that had once belonged to Jean Lacheneur; and nothing had been changed. He recognized the brightly flowered curtains, the figures on the carpet, and even an old arm-chair where he had read many a novel in secret.

Martial hastened to a small writing-desk, and took from it a paper which he slipped into his pocket.

"Now," said he, "let us go. We must avoid another scene. My father and—my wife will be seeking me. I will explain when we are outside."

They hastily descended the staircase, passed through the gardens, and soon reached the long avenue.

Then Jean Lacheneur suddenly paused.

"To come so far for a simple yes or no is, I think, unnecessary," said he. "Have you decided? What answer am I to give Maurice d'Escorval?"

"Nothing! You will take me to him. I must see him and speak with him in order to justify myself. Let us proceed!"

But Jean Lacheneur did not move.

"What you ask is impossible!" he replied.

"Why?"

"Because Maurice is pursued. If he is captured, he will be tried and undoubtedly condemned to death. He is now in a safe retreat, and I have no right to disclose it."

Maurice's safe retreat was, in fact, only a neighboring wood, where in company with the corporal, he was awaiting Jean's return.

But Jean could not resist the temptation to make this

response, which was far more insulting than if he had simply said:

"We fear informers!"

Strange as it may appear to one who knew Martial's proud and violent nature, he did not resent the insult.

"So you distrust me!" he said, sadly.

Jean Lacheneur was silent—another insult.

"But," insisted Martial, "after what you have just seen and heard you can no longer suspect me of having cut the ropes which I carried to the baron."

"No! I am convinced that you are innocent of that atrocious act."

"You saw how I punished the man who dared to compromise the honor of the name of Sairmeuse. And this man is the father of the young girl whom I wedded to-day."

"I have seen all this; but I must still reply: 'Impossible.'"

Jean was amazed at the patience, we should rather say, the humble resignation displayed by Martial de Sairmeuse.

Instead of rebelling against this manifest injustice, Martial drew from his pocket the paper which he had just taken from his desk, and handing it to Jean:

"Those who have brought upon me the shame of having my word doubted shall be punished for it," he said grimly. "You do not believe in my sincerity, Jean. Here is a proof, which I expect you to give to Maurice, and which cannot fail to convince even you."

"What is this proof?"

"The letter written by my hand, in exchange for which my father assisted in the baron's escape. An inexplicable presentiment prevented me from burning this compromising letter. To-day, I rejoice that such was the case. Take it, and use it as you will."

Anyone save Jean Lacheneur would have been touched by the generosity of soul. But Jean was implacable. His was a nature which nothing can disarm, which nothing can mollify; hatred in his heart was a passion which, instead of growing weaker with time, increased and became more terrible.

He would have sacrificed anything at that moment for the ineffable joy of seeing this proud and detested marquis at his feet.

" Very well, I will give it to Maurice," he responded, coldly.

" It should be a bond of alliance, it seems to me," said Martial, gently.

Jean Lacheneur made a gesture terrible in its irony and menace.

" A bond of alliance! " he exclaimed. " You are too fast, Monsieur le Marquis! Have you forgotten all the blood that flows between us? You did not cut the ropes; but who condemned the innocent Baron d'Escorval to death? Was it not the Duc de Sairmeuse? An alliance! You have forgotten that you and yours sent my father to the scaffold! How have you rewarded the man whose heroic honesty gave you back a fortune? By murdering him, and by ruining the reputation of his daughter."

" I offered my name and my fortune to your sister."

" I would have killed her with my own hand had she accepted your offer. Let this prove to you that I do not forget. If any great disgrace ever tarnishes the proud name of Sairmeuse, think of Jean Lacheneur. My hand will be in it."

He was so frantic with passion that he forgot his usual caution. By a violent effort he recovered his self-possession, and in calmer tones he added:

" And if you are so desirous of seeing Maurice, be at the Reche to-morrow at mid-day. He will be there."

Having said this, he turned abruptly aside, sprang over the fence skirting the avenue, and disappeared in the darkness.

" Jean," cried Martial, in almost supplicating tones; " Jean, come back—listen to me ! "

No response.

A sort of bewilderment had seized the young marquis, and he stood motionless and dazed in the middle of the road.

A horse and rider on their way to Montaignac, that nearly ran over him, aroused him from his stupor, and the consciousness of his acts, which he had lost while reading the letter from Maurice, came back to him.

Now he could judge of his conduct calmly.

Was it indeed he, Martial, the phlegmatic sceptic, the man who boasted of his indifference and his insensibility, who had thus forgotten all self-control?

Alas, yes. And when Blanche de Courtornieu, now and henceforth the Marquise de Sairmeuse, accused Marie-Anne of being the cause of his frenzy, she had not been entirely wrong.

Martial, who regarded the opinion of the entire world with disdain, was rendered frantic by the thought that Marie-Anne despised him, and considered him a traitor and a coward.

It was for her sake, that in his outburst of rage, he resolved upon such a startling justification. And if he besought Jean to lead him to Maurice d'Escorval, it was because he hoped to find Marie-Anne not far off, and to say to her:

" Appearances were against me, but I am innocent; and I have proved it by unmasking the real culprit."

It was to Marie-Anne that he wished this famous letter to be given, thinking that she, at least, could not fail
to be surprised at his generosity.

His expectations had been disappointed; and now he
realized what a terrible scandal he had created.

" It will be the devil to arrange! " he explained; " but
nonsense! it will be forgotten in a month.   The best way
will be to face those gossips at once: I will return immediately."

He said: " I will return," in the most deliberate manner; but in proportion as he neared the château, his
courage failed him.

The guests must have departed ere this, and Martial
concluded that he would probably find himself alone
with his young wife, his father, and the Marquis de
Courtornieu.   What   reproaches, tears, anger and
threats he would be obliged to encounter.

" No," he muttered.   " I am not such a fool!   Let
them have a night to calm themselves.   I will not appear
until to-morrow."

But where should he pass the night?   He was in evening dress and bareheaded; he began to feel cold.   The
house belonging to the duke in Montaignac would afford him a refuge.

" I shall find a bed, some servants, a fire, and a
change of clothing there—and to-morrow, a horse to
return."

It was quite a distance to walk; but in his present
mood this did not displease him.

The servant who came to open the door when he
rapped, was speechless with astonishment on recognizing him.

" You, Monsieur! " he exclaimed.

" Yes, it is I.   Light a good fire in the drawing-room
for me, and bring me a change of clothing."

The valet obeyed, and soon Martial found himself alone, stretched upon a sofa before the cheerful blaze.

" It would be a good thing to sleep and forget my troubles," he said to himself.

He tried; but it was not until early morning that he fell into a feverish slumber.

He awoke about nine o'clock, ordered breakfast, concluded to return to Sairmeuse, and he was eating with a good appetite, when suddenly:

" Have a horse saddled instantly ! " he exclaimed.

He had just remembered the rendezvous with Maurice. Why should he not go there?

He set out at once, and thanks to a spirited horse, he reached the Reche at half-past eleven o'clock.

The others had not yet arrived; he fastened his horse to a tree near by, and leisurely climbed to the summit of the hill.

This spot had been the site of Lacheneur's house. The four walls remained standing, blackened by fire.

Martial was contemplating the ruins, nor without deep emotion, when he heard a sharp crackling in the underbrush.

He turned; Maurice, Jean, and Corporal Bavois were approaching.

The old soldier carried under his arm a long and narrow package, enveloped in a piece of green serge. It contained the swords which Jean Lacheneur had gone to Montaignac during the night to procure from a retired officer.

" We are sorry to have kept you waiting," began Maurice, " but you will observe that it is not yet midday. Since we scarcely expected to see you——"

" I was too anxious to justify myself not to be here early," interrupted Martial.

Maurice shrugged his shoulders disdainfully.

" It is not a question of self-justification, but of fighting," he said, in a tone rude even to insolence.

Insulting as were the words and the gesture that accompanied them, Martial never so much as winced.

" Sorrow has rendered you unjust," said he, gently,
" or Monsieur Lacheneur here has told you nothing."

" Jean has told me all."

" Well, then ? "

Martial's coolness drove Maurice frantic.

" Well," he replied, with extreme violence, " my
hatred is unabated even if my scorn is diminished. You
have owed me an opportunity to avenge myself, Monsieur, ever since the day we met on the square at Sairmeuse in the presence of Mademoiselle Lacheneur. You
said to me on that occasion: ' We shall meet again.'
Here we stand now face to face. What insults must I
heap upon you to decide you to fight ? "

A flood of crimson dyed Martial's face. He seized
one of the swords which Bavois offered him, and assumed an attitude of defence.

" You will have it so," said he in a husky voice. " The
thought of Marie-Anne can no longer save you."

But the blades had scarcely crossed before a cry from
Jean and from Corporal Bavois arrested the combat.

" The soldiers ! " they exclaimed ; " let us fly ! "

A dozen soldiers were indeed approaching at the top
of their speed.

" Ah ! I spoke the truth ! " exclaimed Maurice. " The
coward came, but the *gendarmes* accompanied him."

He bounded back, and breaking his sword over his
knee, he hurled the fragments in Martial's face, saying :

" Here, miserable wretch ! "

" Wretch ! " repeated Jean and Corporal Bavois,
" traitor ! coward ! "

And they fled, leaving Martial thunderstruck.

He struggled hard to regain his composure. The soldiers were very near; he ran to meet them, and addressing the officer in command, he said, imperiously:

" Do you know who I am? "

" Yes," replied the sergeant, respectfully, " you are the son of the Duc de Sairmeuse."

" Very well! I forbid you to follow those men."

The sergeant hesitated at first; then, in a decided tone, he replied:

" I cannot obey you, sir. I have my orders."

And addressing his men:

" Forward! " he exclaimed. He was about to set the example, when Martial seized him by the arm.

" At least you will not refuse to tell me who sent you here? "

" Who sent us? The colonel, of course, in obedience to orders from the *grand prévôt*, Monsieur de Courtornieu. He sent the order last night. We have been hidden in that grove since daybreak. But release me —*tonnerre!* would you have my expedition fail entirely? "

He hurried away, and Martial, staggering like a drunken man, descended the slope, and remounted his horse.

But he did not repair to the Château de Sairmeuse; he returned to Montaignac, and passed the remainder of the afternoon in the solitude of his own room.

That evening he sent two letters to Sairmeuse. One to his father. the other to his wife.

CHAPTER XXXIX

Terrible as Martial imagined the scandal to be which he had created, his conception of it by no means equalled the reality.

Had a thunder-bolt burst beneath that roof, the guests at Sairmeuse could not have been more amazed and horrified.

A shudder passed over the assembly when Martial, terrible in his passion, flung the crumbled letter full in the face of the Marquis de Courtornieu.

And when the marquis sank half-fainting into an arm-chair some young ladies of extreme sensibility could not repress a cry of fear.

For twenty seconds after Martial disappeared with Jean Lacheneur, the guests stood as motionless as statues, pale, mute, stupefied.

It was Blanche who broke the spell.

While the Marquis de Courtornieu was panting for breath—while the Duc de Sairmeuse was trembling and speechless with suppressed anger, the young marquise made an heroic attempt to come to the rescue.

With her hand still aching from Martial's brutal clasp, a heart swelling with rage and hatred, and a face whiter than her bridal veil, she had strength to restrain her tears and to compel her lips to smile.

" Really this is placing too much importance on a trifling misunderstanding which will be explained to-morrow," she said, almost gayly, to those nearest her.

And stepping into the middle of the hall she made a sign to the musicians to play a country-dance.

But when the first measures floated through the air,

the company, as if by unanimous consent, hastened toward the door.

One might have supposed the château on fire—the guests did not withdraw, they actually fled.

An hour before, the Marquis de Courtornieu and the Duc de Sairmeuse had been overwhelmed with the most obsequious homage and adulation.

But now there was not one in that assembly daring enough to take them openly by the hand.

Just when they believed themselves all-powerful they were rudely precipitated from their lordly eminence. Disgrace and perhaps punishment were to be their portion.

Heroic to the last, the bride endeavored to stay the tide of retreating guests.

Stationing herself near the door, with her most bewitching smile upon her lips, Madame Blanche spared neither flattering words nor entreaties in her efforts to reassure the deserters.

Vain attempt! Useless sacrifice! Many ladies were not sorry of an opportunity to repay the young Marquise de Sairmeuse for the disdain and the caustic words of Blanche de Courtornieu.

Soon all the guests, who had so eagerly presented themselves that morning, had disappeared, and there remained only one old gentleman who, on account of his gout, had deemed it prudent not to mingle with the crowd.

He bowed in passing before the young marquise, and blushing at this insult to a woman, he departed as the others had done.

Blanche was now alone. There was no longer any necessity for constraint. There were no more curious witnesses to enjoy her sufferings and to make comment upon them. With a furious gesture she tore her bridal veil and the wreath of orange flowers from her head, and trampled them under foot.

A servant was passing through the hall; she stopped him.

"Extinguish the lights everywhere!" she ordered, with an angry stamp of her foot as if she had been in her own father's house, and not at Sairmeuse.

He obeyed her, and then, with flashing eyes and dishevelled hair, she hastened to the little *salon* in which the *dénouement* had taken place.

A crowd of servants surrounded the marquis, who was lying like one stricken with apoplexy.

"All the blood in his body has flown to his head," remarked the duke, with a shrug of his shoulders.

For the duke was furious with his former friends.

He scarcely knew with whom he was most angry, Martial or the Marquis de Courtornieu.

Martial, by this public confession, had certainly imperilled, if he had not ruined, their political future.

But, on the other hand, had not the Marquis de Courtornieu represented a Sairmeuse as being guilty of an act of treason revolting to any honorable heart?

Buried in a large arm-chair, he sat watching, with contracted brows, the movements of the servants, when his daughter-in-law entered the room.

She paused before him, and with arms folded tightly across her breast, she said, angrily:

"Why did you remain here while I was left alone to endure such humiliation? Ah! had I been a man! All our guests have fled, Monsieur—all!"

M. de Sairmeuse sprang up.

"Ah, well! what if they have? Let them go to the devil!"

Of the guests that had just left his house there was not one whom the duke really regretted—not one whom he regarded as an equal. In giving a marriage-feast for his son, he had bidden all the gentry of the neighborhood. They had come—very well! They had fled—*bon voyage!*

If the duke cared at all for their desertion, it was only because it presaged with terrible eloquence the disgrace that was to come.

Still he tried to deceive himself.

" They will return, Madame; you will see them return, humble and repentant! But where can Martial be? "

The lady's eyes flashed, but she made no reply.

" Did he go away with the son of that rascal, Lacheneur? "

" I believe so."

" It will not be long before he returns——"

" Who can say? "

M. de Sairmeuse struck the marble mantel heavily with his clinched fist.

" My God! " he exclaimed; " this is an overwhelming misfortune."

The young wife believed that he was anxious and angry on her account. But she was mistaken. He was thinking only of his disappointed ambition.

Whatever he might pretend, the duke secretly confessed his son's superiority and his genius for intrigue, and he was now extremely anxious to consult him.

" He has wrought this evil; it is for him to repair it! And he is capable of it if he chooses," he murmured.

Then, aloud, he resumed:

" Martial must be found—he must be found——"

With an angry gesture, Blanche interrupted him.

" You must seek Marie-Anne if you wish to find—
my husband."

The duke was of the same opinion, but he dared not
avow it.

" Anger leads you astray, Marquise," said he.

" I know what I know."

" Martial will soon make his appearance, believe me.
If he went away, he will soon return. They shall go
for him at once, or I will go for him myself——"

He left the room with a muttered oath, and Blanche
approached her father, who still seemed to be unconscious.

She seized his arm and shook it roughly, saying, in
the most peremptory tone:

" Father! father! "

This voice, which had so often made the Marquis de
Courtornieu tremble, was far more efficacious than
eau de cologne. He opened one eye the least bit in
the world, then quickly closed it; but not so quickly
that his daughter failed to discover it.

" I wish to speak with you," she said; " get up."

He dared not disobey, and slowly and with difficulty,
he raised himself.

" Ah! how I suffer! " he groaned; " how I suffer! "

His daughter glanced at him scornfully; then, in a
tone of bitter irony, she remarked:

" Do you think I am in Paradise? "

" Speak," sighed the marquis. " What do you wish
to say? "

The bride turned haughtily to the servants.

" Leave the room! " she said, imperiously.

They obeyed, and, after she had locked the door:

" Let us speak of Martial," she began.

At the sound of this name, the marquis bounded
from his chair with clinched fists.

" Ah, the wretch ! " he exclaimed.

" Martial is my husband, father."

" And you !—after what he has done—you dare to defend him ? "

" I do not defend him ; but I do not wish him to be murdered."

At that moment the news of Martial's death would have given the Marquis de Courtornieu infinite satisfaction.

" You heard, father," continued Blanche, " the rendezvous appointed to-morrow, at mid-day, on the Reche. I know Martial ; he has been insulted, and he will go there. Will he encounter a loyal adversary? No. He will find a crowd of assassins. You alone can prevent him from being assassinated."

" I ! and how ? "

" By sending some soldiers to the Reche, with orders to conceal themselves in the grove—with orders to arrest these murderers at the proper moment."

The marquis gravely shook his head.

" If I do that," said he, " Martial is quite capable——"

" Of anything ! yes, I know it. But what does it matter to you, since I am willing to assume the responsibility ? "

M. de Courtornieu vainly tried to penetrate the bride's real motive.

" The order to Montaignac must be sent at once," she insisted.

Had she been less excited she would have discerned the gleam of malice in her father's eye. He was thinking that this would afford him an ample revenge, since he could bring dishonor upon Martial, who had shown so little regard for the honor of others.

" Very well; since you will have it so," he said, with
feigned reluctance.

His daughter made haste to bring him ink and pens,
and with trembling hands he prepared a series of minute instructions for the commander at Montaignac.

Blanche herself gave the letter to a servant, with directions to depart at once; and it was not until she had
seen him set off on a gallop that she went to her own
apartments—the apartments in which Martial had
gathered together all that was most beautiful and luxurious.

But this splendor only aggravated the misery of the
deserted wife, for that she was deserted she did not
doubt for a moment. She was sure that her husband
would not return; she did not expect him.

The Duc de Sairmeuse was searching the neighborhood with a party of servants, but she knew that it was
labor lost; that they would not encounter Martial.

Where could he be? Near Marie-Anne most assuredly—and at the thought a wild desire to wreak
her vengeance on her rival took possession of her
heart.

Martial, at Montaignac, had ended by going to sleep.

Blanche, when daylight came, exchanged the snowy
bridal robes for a black dress, and wandered about the
garden like a restless spirit.

She spent most of the day shut up in her room, refusing to allow the duke, or even her father, to enter.

In the evening, about eight o'clock, they received
tidings from Martial.

A servant brought two letters; one, sent by Martial
to his father, the other, to his wife.

For a moment or more Blanche hesitated to open
the one intended for her. It would determine her destiny; she was afraid.

At last she broke the seal and read:

" MADAME LA MARQUISE—Between you and me all is
ended; reconciliation is impossible.

" From this moment you are free. I esteem you
enough to hope that you will respect the name of Sairmeuse, from which I cannot relieve you.

" You will agree with me, I am sure, in thinking a
quiet separation preferable to the scandal of a divorce
suit.

" My lawyer will pay you an allowance befitting the
wife of a man whose income amounts to three hundred
thousand francs.

" MARTIAL DE SAIRMEUSE."

Blanche staggered beneath this terrible blow. She
was indeed deserted, and deserted, as she supposed, for
another.

" Ah ! " she exclaimed, " that creature ! that creature ! I will kill her ! "

CHAPTER XL

The twenty-four hours which Blanche had spent in
measuring the extent of her terrible misfortune, the
duke had spent in raving and swearing.

He had not even thought of going to bed.

After his fruitless search for his son he returned to
the château, and began a continuous tramp to and fro
in the great hall.

He was almost sinking from weariness when his
son's letter was handed him.

It was very brief.

Martial did not vouchsafe any explanation; he did

not even mention the rupture between his wife and himself.

"I cannot return to Sairmeuse," he wrote, "and yet it is of the utmost importance that I should see you.

"You will, I trust, approve my determinations when I explain the reasons that have guided me in making them.

"Come to Montaignac, then, the sooner the better. I am waiting for you."

Had he listened to the prompting of his impatience, the duke would have started at once. But how could he thus abandon the Marquis de Courtornieu, who had accepted his hospitality, and especially Blanche, his son's wife?

He must, at least, see them, speak to them, and warn them of his intended departure.

He attempted this in vain. Mme. Blanche had shut herself up in her own apartments, and remained deaf to all entreaties for admittance. Her father had been put to bed, and the physician who had been summoned to attend him, declared the marquis to be at death's door.

The duke was therefore obliged to resign himself to the prospect of another night of suspense, which was almost intolerable to a character like his.

"To-morrow, after breakfast, I will find some pretext to escape, without telling them I am going to see Martial," he thought.

He was spared this trouble. The next morning, at about nine o'clock, while he was dressing, a servant came to inform him that M. de Courtornieu and his daughter were awaiting him in the drawing-room.

Much surprised, he hastened down.

When he entered the room, the marquis, who was

seated in an arm-chair, rose, leaning heavily upon the shoulder of Aunt Medea.

Mme. Blanche came rapidly forward to meet the duke, as pale as if every drop of blood had been drawn from her veins.

" We are going, Monsieur le Duc," she said, coldly, " and we wish to make our adieux."

" What! you are going? Will you not——"

The young bride interrupted him by a sad gesture, and drawing Martial's letter from her bosom, she handed it to M. de Sairmeuse, saying.

" Will you do me the favor to peruse this, Monsieur? "

The duke glanced over the short epistle, and his astonishment was so intense that he could not even find an oath.

" Incomprehensible! " he faltered; " incomprehensible! "

" Incomprehensible, indeed," repeated the young wife, sadly, but without bitterness. " I was married yesterday; to-day I am deserted. It would have been generous to have reflected the evening before and not the next day. Tell Martial, however, that I forgive him for having destroyed my life, for having made me the most miserable of creatures. I also forgive him for the supreme insult of speaking to me of his fortune. I trust he may be happy. Adieu, Monsieur le Duc, we shall never meet again. Adieu! "

She took her father's arm, and they were about to retire, when M. de Sairmeuse hastily threw himself between them and the door.

" You shall not depart thus! " he exclaimed. " I will not suffer it. Wait, at least, until I have seen Martial. Perhaps he is not as culpable as you suppose——"

" Enough! " interrupted the marquis; " enough!
This is one of those outrages which can never be repaired. May your conscience forgive you, as I, myself, forgive you. Farewell! "

This was said so perfectly, with such entire harmony
of intonation and gesture, that M. de Sairmeuse was
bewildered.

With an absolutely wonderstruck air he watched the
marquis and his daughter depart, and they had been
gone some moments before he recovered himself sufficiently to exclaim:

" Old hypocrite! does he believe me his dupe? "

His dupe! M. de Sairmeuse was so far from being
his dupe, that his next thought was:

" What is to follow this farce? He says that he
pardons us—that means that he has some crushing
blow in store for us."

This conviction filled him with disquietude. He
really felt unable to cope successfully with the perfidious marquis.

" But Martial is a match for him! " he exclaimed.
" Yes, I must see Martial at once."

So great was his anxiety that he lent a helping hand
in harnessing the horses he had ordered, and when the
carriage was ready, he announced his determination to
drive himself.

As he urged the horses furiously on he tried to reflect, but the most contradictory ideas seethed in his
brain, and he lost all power to consider the situation
calmly.

He burst into Martial's room like a tornado.

" I think you must certainly have gone mad, Marquis," he exclaimed. " That is the only valid excuse
you can offer."

But Martial, who had been expecting this visit, had prepared himself for it.

" Never, on the contrary, have I felt more calm and composed in mind," he replied. " Allow me to ask you one question. Was it you who sent the soldiers to the rendezvous which Maurice d'Escorval had appointed? "

" Marquis ! "

" Very well ! Then it was another act of infamy on the part of the Marquis de Courtornieu."

The duke made no reply. In spite of his faults and his vices, this haughty man possessed the characteristic of the old French nobility—fidelity to his word and undoubted valor.

He thought it perfectly natural, even necessary, that Martial should fight with Maurice ; and he thought it a contemptible act to send armed soldiers to seize an honest and confiding opponent.

" This is the second time," pursued Martial, " that this scoundrel has attempted to bring dishonor upon our name ; and if I desire to convince people of the truth of this assertion, I must break off all connection with him and his daughter. I have done this. I do not regret it, since I married her only out of deference to your wishes, and because it seemed necessary for me to marry, and because all women, save one who can never be mine, are alike to me."

Such utterances were not at all calculated to reassure the duke.

" This sentiment is very noble, no doubt," said he ; " but it has none the less ruined the political prospects of our house."

An almost imperceptible smile curved Martial's lips.

" I believe, on the contrary, that I have saved them," he replied.

" It is useless for us to attempt to deceive ourselves ; this whole affair of the insurrection has been abominable, and you have good reason to bless the opportunity of freeing yourself from the responsibility of it which this quarrel gives you. With a little address, you can throw all the odium upon the Marquis de Courtornieu, and keep for yourself only the prestige of valuable service rendered."

The duke's face brightened.

" Zounds, Marquis ! " he exclaimed ; " that is a good idea ! In the future I shall be infinitely less afraid of Courtornieu."

Martial remained thoughtful.

" It is not the Marquis de Courtornieu whom I fear," he murmured, " but his daughter—my wife."

CHAPTER XLI

One must have lived in the country to know with what inconceivable rapidity news flies from mouth to mouth.

Strange as it may seem, the news of the scene at the château reached Father Poignot's farm-house that same evening.

It had not been three hours since Maurice, Jean Lacheneur and Bavois left the house, promising to re-cross the frontier that same night.

Abbé Midon had decided to say nothing to M. d'Escorval of his son's return, and to conceal Marie-Anne's presence in the house. The baron's condition was so critical that the merest trifle might turn the scale.

About ten o'clock the baron fell asleep, and the *abbé* and Mme. d'Escorval went downstairs to talk with

Marie-Anne. As they were sitting there Poignot's eldest son entered in a state of great excitement.

After supper he had gone with some of his acquaintances to admire the splendors of the *fête*, and he now came rushing back to relate the strange events of the evening to his father's guests.

" It is inconceivable ! " murmured the *abbé*.

He knew but too well, and the others comprehended it likewise, that these strange events rendered their situation more perilous than ever.

" I cannot understand how Maurice could commit such an act of folly after what I had just said to him. The baron's most cruel enemy has been his own son. We must wait until to-morrow before deciding upon anything."

The next day they heard of the meeting at the Reche. A peasant who, from a distance, had witnessed the preliminaries of the duel which had not been fought, was able to give them the fullest details.

He had seen the two adversaries take their places, then the soldiers run to the spot, and afterward pursue Maurice, Jean and Bavois.

But he was sure that the soldiers had not overtaken them. He had met them five hours afterward, harassed and furious ; and the officer in charge of the expedition declared their failure to be the fault of the Marquis de Sairmeuse, who had detained them.

That same day Father Poignot informed the *abbé* that the Duc de Sairmeuse and the Marquis de Courtornieu were at variance. It was the talk of the country. The marquis had returned to his château, accompanied by his daughter, and the duke had gone to Montaignac.

The *abbé's* anxiety on receiving this intelligence was

so poignant that he could not conceal it from Baron d'Escorval.

"You have heard something, my friend," said the baron.

"Nothing, absolutely nothing."

"Some new danger threatens us."

"None, I swear it."

The priest's protestations did not convince the baron.

"Oh, do not deny it!" he exclaimed. "Night before last, when you entered my room after I awoke, you were paler than death, and my wife had certainly been crying. What does all this mean?"

Usually, when the *curé* did not wish to reply to the sick man's questions, it was sufficient to tell him that conversation and excitement would retard his recovery; but this time the baron was not so docile.

"It will be very easy for you to restore my tranquillity," he said. "Confess now, that you are trembling lest they discover my retreat. This fear is torturing me also. Very well, swear to me that you will not allow them to take me alive, and then my mind will be at rest."

"I cannot take such an oath as that," said the *curé,* turning pale.

"And why?" insisted M. d'Escorval. "If I am recaptured, what will happen? They will nurse me, and then, as soon as I can stand upon my feet, they will shoot me down. Would it be a crime to save me from such suffering? You are my best friend; swear to render me this supreme service. Would you have me curse you for saving my life?"

The *abbé* made no response; but his eye, voluntarily or involuntarily, turned with a peculiar expression to the box of medicine standing upon the table near by.

Did he wish to be understood as saying:

"I will do nothing; but you will find a poison there."

M. d'Escorval understood it in this way, for it was with an accent of gratitude that he murmured:

"Thanks!"

Now that he felt that he was master of his life he breathed more freely. From that moment his condition, so long desperate, began to improve.

"I can defy all my enemies from this hour," he said, with a gayety which certainly was not feigned.

Day after day passed and the *abbé's* sinister apprehensions were not realized; he, too, began to regain confidence.

Instead of causing an increase of severity, Maurice's and Jean Lacheneur's frightful imprudence had been, as it were, the point of departure for a universal indulgence.

One might reasonably have supposed that the authorities of Montaignac had forgotten, and desired to have forgotten, if that were possible, Lacheneur's conspiracy, and the abominable slaughter for which it had been made the pretext.

They soon heard at the farm that Maurice and the brave corporal had succeeded in reaching Piedmont.

No allusion was made to Jean Lacheneur, so it was supposed that he had not left the country; but they had no reason to fear for his safety, since he was not upon the proscribed list.

Later, it was rumored that the Marquis de Courtornieu was ill, and that Mme. Blanche did not leave his bedside.

Soon afterward, Father Poignot, on returning from Montaignac, reported that the duke had just passed a week in Paris, and that he was now on his way home with one more decoration—another proof of royal favor—and that he had succeeded in obtaining an order for the release of all the conspirators, who were now in prison.

It was impossible to doubt this intelligence, for the Montaignac papers mentioned this fact, with all the circumstances on the following day.

The *abbé* attributed this sudden and happy change entirely to the rupture between the duke and the marquis, and this was the universal opinion in the neighborhood. Even the retired officers remarked:

" The duke is decidedly better than he is supposed to be, and if he has been severe, it is only because he was influenced by that odious Marquis de Courtornieu."

Marie-Anne alone suspected the truth. A secret presentiment told her that it was Martial de Sairmeuse who had shaken off his wonted apathy, and was working these changes and using and abusing his ascendancy over the mind of his father.

" And it is for your sake," whispered an inward voice, " that Martial is thus working. What does this careless egotist care for these obscure peasants, whose names he does not even know? If he protects them, it is only that he may have a right to protect you, and those whom you love! "

With these thoughts in her mind, she could not but feel her aversion to Martial diminish.

Was not such conduct truly heroic in a man whose dazzling offers she had refused? Was there not real moral grandeur in the feeling that induced Martial to reveal a secret which might ruin the political fortunes of his house, rather than be suspected of an unworthy action? And still the thought of this *grande passion* which she had inspired in so truly great a man never once made her heart quicken its throbbing.

Alas! nothing was capable of touching her heart now; nothing seemed to reach her through the gloomy sadness that enveloped her.

She was but the ghost of the formerly beautiful and radiant Marie-Anne. Her quick, alert tread had become slow and dragging, often she sat for whole days motionless in her chair, her eyes fixed upon vacancy, her lips contracted as if by a spasm, while great tears rolled silently down her cheeks.

Abbé Midon, who was greatly disquieted on her account, often attempted to question her.

"You are suffering, my child," he said, kindly. "What is the matter?"

"I am not ill, Monsieur."

"Why do you not confide in me? Am I not your friend? What do you fear?"

She shook her head sadly and replied:

"I have nothing to confide."

She said this, and yet she was dying of sorrow and anguish.

Faithful to the promise she had made Maurice, she had said nothing of her condition, or of the marriage solemnized in the little church at Vigano. And she saw with inexpressible terror, the approach of the moment when she could no longer keep her secret. Her agony was frightful; but what could she do!

Fly? but where should she go? And by going, would she not lose all chance of hearing from Maurice, which was the only hope that sustained her in this trying hour?

She had almost determined on flight when circumstances—providentially, it seemed to her—came to her aid.

Money was needed at the farm. The guests were unable to obtain any without betraying their whereabouts, and Father Poignot's little store was almost exhausted.

Abbé Midon was wondering what they were to do, when Marie-Anne told him of the will which Chanlouineau had made in her favor, and of the money concealed beneath the hearth-stone in the best chamber.

"I might go to the Borderie at night," suggested Marie-Anne, "enter the house, which is unoccupied, obtain the money and bring it here. I have a right to do so, have I not?"

But the priest did not approve this step.

"You might be seen," said he, "and who knows—perhaps arrested. If you were questioned, what plausible explanation could you give?"

"What shall I do, then?"

"Act openly; you are not compromised. Make your appearance in Sairmeuse to-morrow as if you had just returned from Piedmont; go to the notary, take possession of your property, and install yourself at the Borderie."

Marie-Anne shuddered.

"Live in Chanlouineau's house," she faltered. "I alone!"

"Heaven will protect you, my dear child. I can see only advantages in your installation at the Borderie. It will be easy to communicate with you; and with ordinary precautions there can be no danger. Before your departure we will decide upon a place of rendezvous, and two or three times a week you can meet Father Poignot there. And, in the course of two or three months you can be still more useful to us. When people have become accustomed to your residence at

the Borderie, we will take the baron there. His convalescence will be much more rapid there, than here in
this cramped and narrow loft, where we are obliged to
conceal him now, and where he is really suffering for
light and air."

So it was decided that Father Poignot should accompany Marie-Anne to the frontier that very night;
there she would take the diligence that ran between
Piedmont and Montaignac, passing through the village of Sairmeuse.

It was with the greatest care that the *abbé* dictated to
Marie-Anne the story she was to tell of her sojourn in
foreign lands. All that she said, and all her answers
to questions must tend to prove that Baron d'Escorval
was concealed near Turin.

The plan was carried out in every particular; and
the next day, about eight o'clock, the people of Sairmeuse were greatly astonished to see Marie-Anne
alight from the diligence.

"Monsieur Lacheneur's daughter has returned!"

The words flew from lip to lip with marvellous rapidity, and soon all the inhabitants of the village were
gathered at the doors and windows.

They saw the poor girl pay the driver, and enter the
inn, followed by a boy bearing a small trunk.

In the city, curiosity has some shame; it hides itself
while it spies into the affairs of its neighbors; but in
the country it has no such scruples.

When Marie-Anne emerged from the inn, she found
a crowd awaiting her with open mouths and staring
eyes.

And more than twenty people making all sorts of
comments, followed her to the door of the notary.

He was a man of importance, this notary, and he

welcomed Marie-Anne with all the deference due an heiress of an unencumbered property, worth from forty to fifty thousand francs.

But jealous of his renown for perspicuity, he gave her clearly to understand that he, being a man of experience, had divined that love alone had dictated Chanlouineau's last will and testament.

Marie-Anne's composure and resignation made him really angry.

" You forget what brings me here," she said; " you do not tell me what I have to do! "

The notary, thus interrupted, made no further attempts at consolation.

" *Peste!* " he thought, " she is in a hurry to get possession of her property—the avaricious creature! "

Then aloud:

" The business can be terminated at once, for the justice of the peace is at liberty to-day, and he can go with us to break the seals this afternoon."

So, before evening, all the legal requirements were complied with, and Marie-Anne was formally installed at the Borderie.

She was alone in Chanlouineau's house—alone! Night came on and a great terror seized her heart. It seemed to her that the doors were about to open, that this man who had loved her so much would appear before her, and that she would hear his voice as she heard it for the last time in his grim prison-cell.

She fought against these foolish fears, lit a lamp, and went through this house—now hers—in which everything spoke so forcibly of its former owner.

Slowly she examined the different rooms on the lower floor, noting the recent repairs which had been made and the conveniences which had been added, and at last she ascended to that room above which Chan-louineau had made the tabernacle of his passion.

Here, everything was magnificent, far more so than his words had led her to suppose. The poor peasant who made his breakfast off a crust and a bit of onion had lavished a small fortune on the decorations of this apartment, designed as a sanctuary for his idol.

"How he loved me!" murmured Marie-Anne, moved by that emotion, the bare thought of which had awakened the jealousy of Maurice.

But she had neither the time nor the right to yield to her feelings. Father Poignot was doubtless, even then, awaiting her at the rendezvous.

She lifted the hearth-stone, and found the sum of money which Chanlouineau had named.

The next morning, when he awoke, the *abbé* received the money.

Now, Marie-Anne could breathe freely; and this peace, after so many trials and agitations, seemed to her almost happiness.

Faithful to the *abbé's* instructions, she lived alone; but, by frequent visits, she accustomed the people of the neighborhood to her presence.

Yes, she would have been almost happy, could she have had news of Maurice. What had become of him? Why did he give no sign of life? What would she not have given in exchange for some word of counsel and of love from him?

The time was fast approaching when she would require a confidant; and there was no one in whom she could confide.

In this hour of extremity, when she really felt that her reason was failing her, she remembered the old physician at Vigano, who had been one of the witnesses to her marriage.

"He would help me if I called upon him for aid," she thought.

She had no time to temporize or to reflect; she wrote to him immediately, giving the letter in charge of a youth in the neighborhood.

"The gentleman says you may rely upon him," said the messenger on his return.

That very evening Marie-Anne heard someone rap at her door.   It was the kind-hearted old man who had come to her relief.

He remained at the Borderie nearly a fortnight.

When he departed one morning, before daybreak, he took away with him under his large cloak an infant —a boy—whom he had sworn to cherish as his own child.

CHAPTER XLII

To quit Sairmeuse without any display of violence had cost Blanche an almost superhuman effort.

The wildest anger convulsed her soul at the very moment, when, with an assumption of melancholy dignity, she murmured those words of forgiveness.

Ah! had she obeyed the dictates of her resentment!

But her indomitable vanity aroused within her the heroism of a gladiator dying on the arena, with a smile upon his lips.

Falling, she intended to fall gracefully.

"No one shall see me weep; no one shall hear me complain," she said to her despondent father; "try to imitate me."

And on her return to the Château de Courtornieu, she was a stoic.

Her face, although pale, was as immobile as marble, beneath the curious gaze of the servants.

" I am to be called mademoiselle as in the past," she said, imperiously. " Anyone forgetting this order will be dismissed."

A maid forgot that very day, and uttered the prohibited word, " madame." The poor girl was instantly dismissed, in spite of her tears and protestations.

All the servants were indignant.

" Does she hope to make us forget that she is married and that her husband has deserted her?" they queried.

Alas! she wished to forget it herself. She wished to annihilate all recollection of that fatal day whose sun had seen her a maiden, a wife, and a widow.

For was she not really a widow?

Only it was not death which had deprived her of her husband, but an odious rival—an infamous and perfidious creature lost to all sense of shame.

And yet, though she had been disdained, abandoned, and repulsed, she was no longer free.

She belonged to the man whose name she bore like a badge of servitude—to the man who hated her, who fled from her.

She was not yet twenty; and this was the end of her youth, of her life, of her hopes, and even of her dreams.

Society condemned her to solitude, while Martial was free to rove wheresoever fancy might lead him.

Now she saw the disadvantage of isolating one's self. She had not been without friends in her school-girl days; but after leaving the convent she had alienated them by her haughtiness, on finding them not as high in rank, nor as rich as herself. She was now reduced to the irritating consolations of Aunt Medea, who was a worthy person, undoubtedly, but her tears flowed quite as freely for the loss of a cat, as for the death of a relative.

But Blanche bravely resolved that she would conceal her grief and despair in the recesses of her own
heart.

She drove about the country; she wore the prettiest
dresses in her *trousseau;* she forced herself to appear
gay and indifferent.

But on going to attend high mass in Sairmeuse the
following Sunday, she realized the futility of her efforts.

People did not look at her haughtily, or even curiously; but they turned away their heads to laugh, and
she overheard remarks upon the maiden widow which
pierced her very soul.

They mocked her; they ridiculed her!

"Oh! I will have my revenge!" she muttered.

But she had not waited for these insults before thinking of vengeance; and she had found her father quite
ready to assist her in her plans.

For the first time the father and the daughter were
in accord.

"The Duc de Sairmeuse shall learn what it costs to
aid in the escape of a prisoner and to insult a man like
me. Fortune, favor, position—he shall lose all! I
hope to see him ruined and dishonored at my feet.
You shall see that day! you shall see that day!" said
the marquis, vehemently.

But, unfortunately for him and his plans, he was extremely ill for three days, after the scene at Sairmeuse;
then he wasted three days more in composing a report,
which was intended to crush his former ally.

This delay ruined him, since it gave Martial time to
perfect his plans and to send the Duc de Sairmeuse to
Paris skilfully indoctrinated.

And what did the duke say to the King, who accorded him such a gracious reception?

He undoubtedly pronounced the first reports false, reduced the Montaignac revolution to its proper proportions, represented Lacheneur as a fool, and his followers as inoffensive idiots.

Perhaps he led the King to suppose that the Marquis de Courtornieu might have provoked the outbreak by undue severity. He had served under Napoleon, and possibly had thought it necessary to make a display of his zeal. There have been such cases.

So far as he himself was concerned, he deeply deplored the mistakes into which he had been led by the ambitious marquis, upon whom he cast most of the responsibility for the blood which had been shed.

The result of all this was, that when the Marquis de Courtornieu's report reached Paris, it was answered by a decree depriving him of the office of *grand prévôt*.

This unexpected blow crushed him.

To think that a man as shrewd, as subtle-minded, as quick-witted, and adroit as himself—a man who had passed through so many troubled epochs, who had served with the same obsequious countenance all the masters who would accept his services—to think that such a man should have been thus duped and betrayed!

" It must be that old imbecile, the Duc de Sairmeuse, who has manœuvred so skilfully, and with so much address," he said. " But who advised him? I cannot imagine who it could have been."

Who it was Mme. Blanche knew only too well.

She recognized Martial's hand in all this, as Marie-Anne had done.

" Ah! I was not deceived in him," she thought; " he

is the great diplomatist I believed him to be. At his age to outwit my father, an old politician of such experience and acknowledged astuteness! And he does all this to please Marie-Anne," she continued, frantic with rage. " It is the first step toward obtaining pardon for the friends of that vile creature. She has unbounded influence over him, and so long as she lives there is no hope for me. But, patience."

She was patient, realizing that he who wishes to surely attain his revenge must wait, dissimulate, *prepare* an opportunity, but not force it.

What her revenge should be she had not yet decided ; but she already had her eye upon a man whom she believed would be a willing instrument in her hands, and capable of doing anything for money.

But how had such a man chanced to cross the path of Mme. Blanche? How did it happen that she was cognizant of the existence of such a person?

It was the result of one of those simple combinations of circumstances which go by the name of chance.

Burdened with remorse, despised and jeered at, and stoned whenever he showed himself upon the street, and horror-stricken whenever he thought of the terrible threats of Balstain, the Piedmontese innkeeper, Chupin left Montaignac and came to beg an asylum at the Château de Sairmeuse.

In his ignorance, he thought that the *grand seigneur* who had employed him, and who had profited by his treason, owed him, over and above the promised reward, aid and protection.

But the servants shunned him. They would not allow him a seat at the kitchen-table, nor would the grooms allow him to sleep in the stables. They threw him a bone, as they would have thrown it to a dog; and he slept where he could.

He bore all this uncomplainingly, deeming himself fortunate in being able to purchase comparative safety at such a price.

But when the duke returned from Paris with a policy of forgetfulness and conciliation in his pocket, he would no longer tolerate the presence of this man, who was the object of universal execration.

He ordered the dismissal of Chupin.

The latter resisted, swearing that he would not leave Sairmeuse unless he was forcibly expelled, or unless he received the order from the lips of the duke himself.

This obstinate resistance was reported to the duke. It made him hesitate; but the necessity of the moment, and a word from Martial, decided him.

He sent for Chupin and told him that he must not visit Sairmeuse again under any pretext whatever, softening the harshness of expulsion, however, by the offer of a small sum of money.

But Chupin sullenly refused the money, gathered his belongings together, and departed, shaking his clinched fist at the château, and vowing vengeance on the Sairmeuse family. Then he went to his old home, where his wife and his two boys still lived.

He seldom left the house, and then only to satisfy his passion for hunting. At such times, instead of hiding and surrounding himself with every precaution, as he had done, before shooting a squirrel or a few partridges, in former times, he went boldly to the Sairmeuse or the Courtornieu forests, shot his game, and brought it home openly, almost defiantly.

The rest of the time he spent in a state of semi-intoxication, for he drank constantly and more and more immoderately. When he had taken more than usual,

his wife and his sons generally attempted to obtain
money from him, and if persuasions failed they re-
sorted to blows.

For he had never given them the reward of his treason. What had he done with the twenty thousand
francs in gold which had been paid him? No one
knew. His sons believed he had buried it somewhere;
but they tried in vain to wrest his secret from him.

All the people in the neighborhood were aware of
this state of affairs, and regarded it as a just punishment for the traitor. Mme. Blanche overheard one
of the gardeners telling the story to two of his assist-
ants:

" Ah, the man is an old scoundrel!" he said, his face
crimson with indignation. "He should be in the galleys, and not at large among respectable people."

" He is a man who would serve your purpose," the
voice of hatred whispered in Blanche's ear.

" But how can I find an opportunity to confer with
him?" she wondered. Mme. Blanche was too prudent to think of hazarding a visit to his house, but she
remembered that he hunted occasionally in the Courtornieu woods, and that it might be possible for her to
meet him there.

" It will only require a little perseverance and a few
long walks," she said to herself.

But it cost poor Aunt Medea, the inevitable chap-
eron, two long weeks of almost continued walking.

"Another freak!" groaned the poor relative, overcome with fatigue; " my niece is certainly crazy!"

But one lovely afternoon in May Blanche discovered
what she sought.

It was in a sequestered spot near the lake. Chupin
was tramping sullenly along with his gun in his hand.

glancing suspiciously on every side! Not that he feared the game-keeper or a verbal process, but wherever he went, he fancied he saw Balstain walking in his shadow, with that terrible knife in his hand.

Seeing Mme. Blanche he tried to hide himself in the forest, but she prevented it by calling:

" Father Chupin!"

He hesitated for a moment, then he paused, dropped his gun, and waited.

Aunt Medea was pale with fright.

" Blessed Jesus!" she murmured, pressing her niece's arm; " why do you call that terrible man?"

" I wish to speak with him."

" What, Blanche, do you dare——"

" I must!"

" No, I cannot allow it. I must not——"

" There, that is enough," said Blanche, with one of those imperious glances that deprive a dependent of all strength and courage; " quite enough."

Then, in gentler tones:

" I must talk with this man," she added.

" You, Aunt Medea, will remain at a little distance. Keep a close watch on every side, and if you see anyone approaching, call me, whoever it may be."

Aunt Medea, submissive as she was ever wont to be, obeyed; and Mme. Blanche advanced toward the old poacher, who stood as motionless as the trunks of the giant trees around him.

" Well, my good Father Chupin, what sort of sport have you had to-day?" she began, when she was a few steps from him.

" What do you want with me?" growled Chupin; " for you do want something, or you would not trouble yourself about such as I."

It required all Blanche's determination to repress a gesture of fright and of disgust; but, in a resolute tone, she replied:

"Yes, it is true that I have a favor to ask you."

"Ah, ha! I supposed so."

"A mere trifle which will cost you no trouble and for which you shall be well paid."

She said this so carelessly that one would really have supposed the service was unimportant; but cleverly as she played her part, Chupin was not deceived.

"No one asks trifling services of a man like me," he said coarsely.

"Since I have served the good cause, at the peril of my life, people seem to suppose that they have a right to come to me with their money in their hands, when they desire any dirty work done. It is true that I was well paid for that other job; but I would like to melt all the gold and pour it down the throats of those who gave it to me.

"Ah! I know what it costs the humble to listen to the words of the great! Go your way; and if you have any wickedness in your head, do it yourself!"

He shouldered his gun and was moving away, when Mme. Blanche said, coldly:

"It was because I knew your wrongs that I stopped you; I thought you would be glad to serve me, because I hate the Sairmeuse."

These words excited the interest of the old poacher, and he paused.

"I know very well that you hate the Sairmeuse now —but——"

"But what!"

"In less than a month you will be reconciled. And you will pay the expenses of the war and of the reconciliation? That old wretch, Chupin——"

" We shall never be reconciled."

" Hum!" he growled, after deliberating awhile.
" And if I should aid you, what compensation will you
give me?"

" I will give you whatever you desire—money, land,
a house——"

" Many thanks. I desire something quite different."

" What? Name your conditions."

Chupin reflected a moment, then he replied:

" This is what I desire. I have enemies—I do not
even feel safe in my own house. My sons abuse me
when I have been drinking; my wife is quite
capable of poisoning my wine; I tremble for my
life and for my money. I cannot endure this existence
much longer. Promise me an asylum in the Château
de Courtornieu, and I am yours. In your house I
shall be safe. But let it be understood, I will not be
ill-treated by the servants as I was at Sairmeuse."

" It shall be as you desire."

" Swear it by your hope of heaven."

" I swear."

There was such an evident sincerity in her accent
that Chupin was reassured. He leaned toward her,
and said, in a low voice:

" Now tell me your business."

His small gray eyes glittered with a demoniac light;
his thin lips were tightly drawn over his sharp teeth;
he was evidently expecting some proposition to murder, and he was ready.

His attitude showed this so plainly that Blanche
shuddered.

" Really, what I ask of you is almost nothing," she
replied. " I only wish you to watch the Marquis de
Sairmeuse."

" Your husband? "

" Yes ; my husband. I wish to know what he does, where he goes, and what persons he sees. I wish to know how each moment of his time is spent."

" What ! seriously, frankly, is this all that you desire of me ? " Chupin asked.

" For the present, yes. My plans are not yet decided. It depends upon circumstances what action I shall take."

" You can rely upon me," he responded ; " but I must have a little time."

" Yes, I understand. To-day is Saturday ; will you be ready to report on Thursday ? "

" In five days ? Yes, probably."

" In that case, meet me here on Thursday, at this same hour."

A cry from Aunt Medea interrupted them.

" Someone is coming ! " Mme. Blanche exclaimed. " Quick ! we must not be seen together. Conceal yourself."

With a bound the old poacher disappeared in the forest.

A servant had approached Aunt Medea, and was speaking to her with great animation.

Blanche hastened toward them.

" Ah ! Mademoiselle," exclaimed the servant, " we have been seeking you everywhere for three hours. Your father, monsieur le marquis—*mon Dieu!* what a misfortune ! A physician has been summoned."

" Is my father dead ? "

" No, Mademoiselle, no ; but—how can I tell you ? When the marquis went out this morning his actions were very strange, and—and—when he returned——"

As he spoke the servant tapped his forehead with the end of his forefinger.

"You understand me, Mademoiselle—when he returned, reason had fled!"

Without waiting for her terrified aunt, Blanche darted in the direction of the château.

"How is the marquis?" she inquired of the first servant whom she met.

"He is in his room on the bed; he is more quiet now."

She had already reached his room. He was seated upon the bed, and two servants were watching his every movement. His face was livid, and a white foam had gathered upon his lips. Still, he recognized his daughter.

"Here you are," said he. "I was waiting for you."

She remained upon the threshold, quite overcome, although she was neither tender-hearted nor impressionable.

"My father!" she faltered. "Good heavens! what has happened?" He uttered a discordant laugh.

"Ah, ha!" he exclaimed, "I met him. Do you doubt me? I tell you that I saw the wretch. I know him well; have I not seen his cursed face before my eyes for more than a month—for it never leaves me. I saw him. It was in the forest near the Sanguille rocks. You know the place; it is always dark there, on account of the trees. I was returning slowly, thinking of him, when suddenly he sprang up before me, extending his arms as if to bar my passage.

"'Come,' said he, 'you must come and join me.' He was armed with a gun; he fired——"

The marquis paused, and Blanche summoned sufficient courage to approach him. For more than a minute she fastened upon him that cold and persistent look that is said to exercise such power over those who have lost their reason; then, shaking him energetically by the arm, she said, almost roughly:

"Control yourself, father. You are the victim of an hallucination. It is impossible that you have seen the man of whom you speak."

Who it was that M. de Courtornieu supposed he had seen, Blanche knew only too well; but she dared not, could not, utter the name.

But the marquis had resumed his incoherent narrative.

"Was I dreaming?" he continued. "No, it was certainly Lacheneur who confronted me. I am sure of it, and the proof is, that he reminded me of a circumstance which occurred in my youth, and which was known only to him and me. It happened during the Reign of Terror. He was all-powerful in Montaignac; and I was accused of being in correspondence with the *émigrés*. My property had been confiscated; and every moment I was expecting to feel the hand of the executioner upon my shoulder, when Lacheneur took me into his house. He concealed me; he furnished me with a passport; he saved my money, and he saved my head—I sentenced him to death. That is the reason why I have seen him again. I must rejoin him; he told me so—I am a dying man!"

He fell back upon his pillows, pulled the sheet up over his face, and, lying there, rigid and motionless, one might readily have supposed it was a corpse, whose outlines could be vaguely discerned through the bed-coverings.

Mute with horror, the servants exchanged frightened glances.

Such baseness and ingratitude amazed them. It seemed incomprehensible to them, under such circumstances, that the marquis had not pardoned Lacheneur.

Mme. Blanche alone retained her presence of mind. Turning to her father's valet, she said:

" It is not possible that anyone has attempted to injure my father? "

" I beg your pardon, Mademoiselle, a little more and he would have been killed."

" How do you know this? "

" In undressing the marquis I noticed that he had received a wound in the head. I also examined his hat, and in it I found three holes, which could only have been made by bullets."

The worthy *valet de chambre* was certainly more agitated than the daughter.

" Then someone must have attempted to assassinate my father," she murmured, " and this attack of delirium has been brought on by fright. How can we find out who the would-be murderer was? "

The servant shook his head.

" I suspect that old poacher, who is always prowling around, is the guilty man—Chupin."

" No, it could not have been he."

" Ah! I am almost sure of it. There is no one else in the neighborhood capable of such an evil deed."

Mme. Blanche could not give her reasons for declaring Chupin innocent. Nothing in the world would have induced her to admit that she had met him, talked with him for more than half an hour, and just parted from him.

She was silent. In a few moments the physician arrived.

He removed the covering from M. de Courtornieu's face—he was almost compelled to use force to do it—

examined the patient with evident anxiety, then ordered mustard plasters, applications of ice to the head, leeches, and a potion, for which a servant was to gallop to Montaignac at once. All was bustle and confusion.

When the physician left the sick-room, Mme. Blanche followed him.

" Well, Doctor," she said, with a questioning look.

With considerable hesitation, he replied:

" People sometimes recover from such attacks."

It really mattered little to Blanche whether her father recovered or died, but she felt that an opportunity to recover her lost *prestige* was now afforded her. If she desired to turn public opinion against Martial, she must improvise for herself an entirely different reputation. If she could erect a pedestal upon which she could pose as a patient victim, her satisfaction would be intense. Such an occasion now offered itself, and she seized it at once.

Never did a devoted daughter lavish more touching and delicate attentions upon a sick father. It was impossible to induce her to leave his bedside for a moment. It was only with great difficulty that they could persuade her to sleep for a couple of hours, in an arm-chair in the sick-room.

But while she was playing the *rôle* of Sister of Charity, which she had imposed upon herself, her thoughts followed Chupin. What was he doing in Montaignac? Was he watching Martial as he had promised? How slow the day appointed for the meeting was in coming!

It came at last, however, and after intrusting her father to the care of Aunt Medea, Blanche made her escape.

The old poacher was awaiting her at the appointed place.

" Speak ! " said Mme. Blanche.

" I would do so willingly, only I have nothing to tell you."

" What ! you have not watched the marquis ? "

" Your husband ? Excuse me, I have followed him like his own shadow. But what would you have me say to you ; since the duke left for Paris, your husband has charge of everything. Ah! you would not recognize him! He is always busy now. He is up at cock-crow ; and he goes to bed with the chickens. He writes letters all the morning. In the afternoon he receives all who call upon him. The retired officers are hand and glove with him. He has reinstated five or six of them, and he has granted pensions to two others. He seldom goes out, and never in the evening."

He paused and for more than a minute Blanche was silent. She was confused and agitated by the question that rose to her lips. What humiliation! But she conquered her embarrassment, and turning away her head to hide her crimson face, she said:

" But he certainly has a mistress ! "

Chupin burst into a noisy laugh.

" Well, we have come to it at last," he said, with an audacious familiarity that made Blanche shudder. " You mean that scoundrel Lacheneur's daughter, do you not? that stuck-up minx, Marie-Anne ? "

Blanche felt that denial was useless.

" Yes," she answered; " it is Marie-Anne that I mean."

" Ah, well! she has been neither seen nor heard from. She must have fled with another of her lovers, Maurice d'Escorval."

"You are mistaken."

"Oh, not at all! Of all the Lacheneurs only Jean remains, and he lives like the vagabond that he is, by
poaching and stealing. Day and night he rambles
through the woods with his gun on his shoulder. He
is frightful to look upon, a perfect skeleton, and his
eyes glitter like live coals. If he ever meets me, my
account will be settled then and there."

Blanche turned pale. It was Jean Lacheneur who
had fired at the marquis then. She did not doubt it in
the least.

"Very well!" said she, "I, myself, am sure that
Marie-Anne is in the neighborhood, concealed in Montaignac, probably. I must know. Endeavor to discover her retreat before Monday, when I will meet you
here again."

"I will try," Chupin answered.

He did indeed try; he exerted all his energy and cunning, but in vain. He was fettered by the precautions
which he took against Balstain and against Jean Lacheneur. On the other hand, no one in the neighborhood would have consented to give him the least information.

"Still no news!" he said to Mme. Blanche at
each interview.

But she would not yield. Jealousy will not yield
even to evidence.

Blanche had declared that Marie-Anne had taken her
husband from her, that Martial and Marie-Anne loved
each other, hence it must be so, all proofs to the contrary notwithstanding.

But one morning she found her spy jubilant.

"Good news!" he cried, as soon as he saw her;
"we have caught the minx at last."

CHAPTER XLIII

It was the second day after Marie-Anne's installation at the Borderie.

That event was the general topic of conversation; and Chanlouineau's will was the subject of countless comments.

"Here is Monsieur Lacheneur's daughter with an income of more than two thousand francs, without counting the house," said the old people, gravely.

"An honest girl would have had no such luck as that!" muttered the unattractive maidens who had not been fortunate enough to secure husbands.

This was the great news which Chupin brought to Mme. Blanche.

She listened to it, trembling with anger, her hands so convulsively clinched that the nails penetrated the flesh.

"What audacity!" she exclaimed. "What impudence!"

The old poacher seemed to be of the same opinion.

"If each of her lovers gives her as much she will be richer than a queen. She will have enough to buy both Sairmeuse and Courtornieu, if she choose," he remarked, maliciously.

If he had desired to augment the rage of Mme. Blanche, he had good reason to be satisfied.

"And this is the woman who has alienated Martial's heart from me!" she exclaimed. "It is for this miserable wretch that he abandons me!"

The unworthiness of the unfortunate girl whom she regarded as her rival, incensed her to such a degree that she entirely forgot Chupin's presence. She made no attempt to restrain herself or to hide the secret of her sufferings.

" Are you sure that what you tell me is true? " she asked.

" As sure as that you stand there."

" Who told you all this? "

" No one—I have eyes. I went to the Borderie yes-terday to see for myself, and all the shutters were open. Marie-Anne was leaning out of a window. She does not even wear mourning, the heartless hussy! "

Poor Marie-Anne, indeed, had no dress but the one which Mme. d'Escorval had given her on the night of the insurrection, when she laid aside her masculine habiliments.

Chupin wished to irritate Mme. Blanche still more by other malicious remarks, but she checked him by a gesture.

" So you know the way to the Borderie? " she in-quired.

" Perfectly."

" Where is it? "

" Opposite the mills of the Oiselle, near the river, about a league and a half from here."

" That is true. I remember now. Were you ever in the house? "

" More than a hundred times while Chanlouineau was living."

" Explain the topography of the dwelling! "

Chupin's eyes dilated to their widest extent.

" What do you wish? " he asked, not understanding in the least what was required of him.

" I mean, explain how the house is constructed."

" Ah! now I understand. The house is built upon an open space a little distance from the road. Before it is a small garden, and behind it an orchard enclosed by a hedge. Back of the orchard, to the right, are the vineyards; but on the left side is a small grove that shades a spring.

He paused suddenly, and with a knowing wink, inquired:

" But what use do you expect to make of all this information? "

" What does that matter to you? How is the interior arranged? "

" There are three large square rooms on the ground floor, besides the kitchen and a small dark room."

" Now, what is on the floor above? "

" I have never been up there."

" How are the rooms furnished which you have visited? "

" Like those in any peasant's house."

Certainly no one was aware of the existence of the luxurious apartment which Chanlouineau had intended for Marie-Anne. He had never spoken of it, and had even taken the greatest precautions to prevent anyone from seeing him transport the furniture.

" How many doors are there? " inquired Blanche.

" Three; one opening into the garden, another into the orchard, another communicating with the stables. The staircase leading to the floor above is in the middle room."

" And is Marie-Anne alone at the Borderie? "

" Entirely alone at present; but I suppose it will not be long before her brigand of a brother joins her."

Mme. Blanche fell into a revery so deep and so prolonged that Chupin at last became impatient.

He ventured to touch her upon the arm, and, in a wily voice, he said:

" Well, what shall we decide? "

Blanche shuddered like a wounded man on hearing the terrible click of the surgeon's instruments.

" My mind is not yet made up," she replied. " I must reflect—I will see."

And remarking the old poacher's discontented face, she said, vehemently:

" I will do nothing lightly. Do not lose sight of Martial. If he goes to the Borderie, and he will go there, I must be informed of it. If he writes, and he will write, try to procure one of his letters. I must see you every other day. Do not rest! Strive to deserve the good place I am reserving for you at Courtornieu. Go! "

He departed without a word, but also without attempting to conceal his disappointment and chagrin.

" It serves you right for listening to a silly, affected woman," he growled. " She fills the air with her ravings; she wishes to kill everybody, to burn and destroy everything. She only asks for an opportunity. The occasion presents itself, and her heart fails her. She draws back—she is afraid! "

Chupin did Mme. Blanche great injustice. The movement of horror which he had observed was the instinctive revolt of the flesh, and not a faltering of her inflexible will.

Her reflections were not of a nature to appease her rancor.

Whatever Chupin and all Sairmeuse might say to the contrary, Blanche regarded this story of Marie-Anne's travels as a ridiculous fable. In her opinion, Marie-Anne had simply emerged from the retreat where Martial had deemed it prudent to conceal her.

But why this sudden reappearance? The vindictive

woman was ready to swear that it was out of mere bra-
vado, and intended only as an insult to her.

"And I will have my revenge," she thought. "I
would tear my heart out if it were capable of cowardly
weakness under such provocation!"

The voice of conscience was unheard in this tumult
of passion. Her sufferings, and Jean Lacheneur's attempt upon her father's life seemed to justify the most
extreme measures.

She had plenty of time now to brood over her
wrongs, and to concoct schemes of vengeance. Her
father no longer required her care. He had passed
from the frenzied ravings of insanity and delirium to
the stupor of idiocy.

The physician declared his patient cured.

Cured! The body was cured, perhaps, but reason
had succumbed. All traces of intelligence had disappeared from this once mobile face, so ready to assume
any expression which the most consummate hypocrisy
required.

There was no longer a sparkle in the eye which had
formerly gleamed with cunning, and the lower lip hung
with a terrible expression of stupidity.

And there was no hope of any improvement.

A single passion, the table, took the place of all the
passions which had formerly swayed the life of this
ambitious man.

The marquis, who had always been temperate in his
habits, now ate and drank with the most disgusting
voracity, and he was becoming immensely corpulent.
A soulless body, he wandered about the château and its
surroundings without projects, without aim. Self-
consciousness, all thought of dignity, knowledge of
good and evil, memory—he had lost all these. Even

the instinct of self-preservation, the last which dies within us, had departed, and he had to be watched like a child.

Often, as the marquis roamed about the large gardens, his daughter regarded him from her window with a strange terror in her heart.

But this warning of Providence only increased her desire for revenge.

"Who would not prefer death to such a misfortune?" she murmured. "Ah! Jean Lacheneur's revenge is far more terrible than it would have been had his bullet pierced my father's heart. It is a revenge like this that I desire. It is due me; I will have it!"

She saw Chupin every two or three days; sometimes going to the place of meeting alone, sometimes accompanied by Aunt Medea.

The old poacher came punctually, although he was beginning to tire of his task.

"I am risking a great deal," he growled. "I supposed that Jean Lacheneur would go and live at the Borderie with his sister. Then, I should be safe. But no; the brigand continues to prowl around with his gun under his arm, and to sleep in the woods at night. What game is he hunting? Father Chupin, of course. On the other hand, I know that my rascally innkeeper over there has abandoned his inn and mysteriously disappeared. Where is he? Hidden behind one of these trees, perhaps, deciding in which portion of my body he shall plunge his knife."

What irritated the old poacher most of all was, that after two months of surveillance, he had arrived at the conclusion that, whatever might have been the relations existing between Martial and Marie-Anne in the past, all was now over between them.

But Blanche would not admit this.

"Say that they are more cunning than you, Father Chupin."

"Cunning—and how? Since I have been watching the marquis, he has not once passed outside the fortifications. On the other hand, the postman at Sairmeuse, who has been adroitly questioned by my wife, declares that he has not taken a single letter to the Borderie."

Had it not been for the hope of a safe and pleasant retreat at Courtornieu, Chupin would have abandoned his task; and, in spite of the tempting rewards that were promised him, he had relaxed his surveillance.

If he still came to the rendezvous, it was only because he had fallen into the habit of claiming some money for his expenses each time.

And when Mme. Blanche demanded an account of everything that Martial had done, he told her anything that came into his head.

Mme. Blanche soon discovered this. One day, early in September, she interrupted him as he began the same old story, and, looking him steadfastly in the eye, she said:

"Either you are betraying me, or you are a fool. Yesterday Martial and Marie-Anne spent a quarter of an hour together at the Croix d'Arcy."

CHAPTER XLIV

The old physician at Vigano, who had come to Marie-Anne's aid, was an honorable man. His intellect was of a superior order, and his heart was equal to his intelligence. He knew life; he had loved and suf-

fered, and he possessed two sublime virtues—forbear-
ance and charity.

It was easy for such a man to read Marie-Anne's
character; and while he was at the Borderie he endeavored in every possible way to reassure her, and to
restore the self-respect of the unfortunate girl who had
confided in him.

Had he succeeded? He certainly hoped so.

But when he departed and Marie-Anne was again
left in solitude, she could not overcome the feeling of
despondency that stole over her.

Many, in her situation, would have regained their
serenity of mind, and even rejoiced. Had she not succeeded in concealing her fault? Who suspected it, except, perhaps, the *abbé*.

Hence, Marie-Anne had nothing to fear, and everything to hope.

But this conviction did not appease her sorrow.
Hers was one of those pure and proud natures that are
more sensitive to the whisperings of conscience than
to the clamors of the world.

She had been accused of having three lovers—Chanlouineau, Martial, and Maurice. The calumny had
not moved her. What tortured her was what these
people did not know—the truth.

Nor was this all. The sublime instinct of maternity
had been awakened within her. When she saw the
physician depart, bearing her child, she felt as if soul
and body were being rent asunder. When could she
hope to see again this little son who was doubly dear
to her by reason of the very sorrow and anguish he had
cost her? The tears gushed to her eyes when she
thought that his first smile would not be for her.

Ah! had it not been for her promise to Maurice, she

would unhesitatingly have braved public opinion, and kept her precious child.

Her brave and honest nature could have endured any humiliation far better than the continual lie she was forced to live.

But she had promised; Maurice was her husband, and reason told her that for his sake she must preserve not her honor, alas! but the semblance of honor.

And when she thought of her brother, her blood froze in her veins.

Having learned that Jean was roving about the country, she sent for him; but it was not without much persuasion that he consented to come to the Borderie.

It was easy to explain Chupin's terror when one saw Jean Lacheneur. His clothing was literally in tatters, his face wore an expression of ferocious despair, and a fierce unextinguishable hatred burned in his eyes.

When he entered the cottage, Marie-Anne recoiled in horror. She did not recognize him until he spoke.

" It is I, sister," he said, gloomily.

" You—my poor Jean! you! "

He surveyed himself from head to foot, and said, with a sneering laugh:

" Really, I should not like to meet myself at dusk in the forest."

Marie-Anne shuddered. She fancied that a threat lurked beneath these ironical words, beneath this mockery of himself.

" What a life yours must be, my poor brother! Why did you not come sooner? Now, I have you here, I shall not let you go. You will not desert me. I need protection and love so much. You will remain with me? "

" It is impossible, Marie-Anne."

"And why?"

A fleeting crimson suffused Jean Lacheneur's cheek; he hesitated for a moment, then:

"Because I have a right to dispose of my own life, but not of yours," he replied. "We can no longer be anything to each other. I deny you to-day, that you may be able to deny me to-morrow. Yes, I renounce you, who are my all—the only person on earth whom I love. Your most cruel enemies have not calumniated you more foully than I——"

He paused an instant, then he added:

"I have said openly, before numerous witnesses, that I would never set foot in a house that had been given you by Chanlouineau."

"Jean! you, my brother! said that?"

"I said it. It must be supposed that there is a deadly feud between us. This must be, in order that neither you nor Maurice d'Escorval can be accused of complicity in any deed of mine."

Marie-Anne stood as if petrified.

"He is mad!" she murmured.

"Do I really have that appearance?"

She shook off the stupor that paralyzed her, and seizing her brother's hands:

"What do you intend to do?" she exclaimed. "What do you intend to do? Tell me; I will know."

"Nothing! let me alone."

"Jean!"

"Let me alone," he said, roughly, disengaging himself.

A horrible presentiment crossed Marie-Anne's mind.

She stepped back, and solemnly, entreatingly, she said:

"Take care, take care, my brother. It is not well

to tamper with these matters. Leave to God's justice
the task of punishing those who have wronged us."

But nothing could move Jean Lacheneur, or divert
him from his purpose. He uttered a hoarse, discordant laugh, then striking his gun heavily with his hand,
he exclaimed:

"Here is justice!"

Appalled and distressed beyond measure, Marie-
Anne sank into a chair. She discerned in her
brother's mind the same fixed, fatal idea which had
lured her father on to destruction—the idea for which
he had sacrificed all—family, friends, fortune, the present and the future—even his daughter's honor—the
idea which had caused so much blood to flow, which
had cost the life of so many innocent men, and which
had finally conducted him to the scaffold.

"Jean," she murmured, "remember our father."

The young man's face became livid; his hands
clinched involuntarily, but he controlled his anger.

Advancing toward his sister, in a cold, quiet tone
that added a frightful violence to his threats, he said:

"It is because I remember my father that justice
shall be done. Ah! these miserable nobles would not
display such audacity if all sons had my resolution. A
scoundrel would hesitate before attacking a good man
if he was obliged to say to himself: ' I cannot strike this
honest man, for though he die, his children will surely
call me to account. Their fury will fall on me and
mine; they will pursue us sleeping and waking, pursue
us without ceasing, everywhere, and pitilessly. Their
hatred always on the alert, will accompany us and surround us. It will be an implacable, merciless warfare.
I shall never venture forth without fearing a bullet; I
shall never lift food to my lips without dread of poi-

son. And until we have succumbed, they will prowl about our house, trying to slip in through tiniest opening, death, dishonor, ruin, infamy, and misery!'"

He paused with a nervous laugh, and then, still more slowly, he added:

"That is what the Sairmeuse and Courtornieu have to expect from me."

It was impossible to mistake the meaning of Jean Lacheneur's words. His threats were not the wild ravings of anger. His quiet manner, his icy tones, his automatic gestures betrayed one of those cold rages which endure so long as the man lives.

He took good care to make himself understood, for between his teeth he added:

"Undoubtedly, these people are very high, and I am very low; but when a tiny worm fastens itself to the roots of a giant oak, that tree is doomed."

Marie-Anne knew all too well the uselessness of prayers and entreaties.

And yet she could not, she must not allow her brother to depart in this mood.

She fell upon her knees, and with clasped hands and supplicating voice:

"Jean," said she, "I implore you to renounce these projects. In the name of our mother, return to your better self. These are crimes which you are meditating!"

With a glance of scorn and a shrug of the shoulders, he replied:

"Have done with this. I was wrong to confide my hopes to you. Do not make me regret that I came here."

Then the sister tried another plan. She rose, forced her lips to smile, and as if nothing unpleasant had passed between them, she begged Jean to remain with her that evening, at least, and share her frugal supper.

"Remain," she entreated; "that is not much to do—and it will make me so happy. And since it will be the last time we shall see each other for years, grant me a few hours. It is so long since we have met. I have suffered so much. I have so many things to tell you! Jean, my dear brother, can it be that you love me no longer?"

One must have been bronze to remain insensible to such prayers. Jean Lacheneur's heart swelled almost to bursting; his stern features relaxed, and a tear trembled in his eye.

Marie-Anne saw that tear. She thought she had conquered, and clapping her hands in delight, she exclaimed:

"Ah! you will remain! you will remain!"

No. Jean had already mastered his momentary weakness, though not without a terrible effort; and in a harsh voice:

"Impossible! impossible!" he repeated.

Then, as his sister clung to him imploringly, he took her in his arms and pressed her to his heart.

"Poor sister—poor Marie-Anne—you will never know what it costs me to refuse you, to separate myself from you. But this must be. In even coming here I have been guilty of an imprudent act. You do not understand to what perils you will be exposed if people suspect any bond between us. I trust you and Maurice may lead a calm and happy life. It would be a crime for me to mix you up with my wild schemes. Think of me sometimes, but do not try to see me, or even to learn what has become of me. A man like me struggles, triumphs, or perishes alone."

He kissed Marie-Anne passionately, then lifted her, placed her in a chair, and freed himself from her detaining hands.

"Adieu!" he cried; "when you see me again, our father will be avenged!"

She sprang up to rush after him and to call him back —too late!

He had fled.

"It is over," murmured the wretched girl; "my brother is lost. Nothing will restrain him now."

A vague, inexplicable, but horrible fear, contracted her heart. She felt that she was being slowly but surely drawn into a whirlpool of passion, rancor, vengeance, and crime, and a voice whispered that she would be crushed.

But other thoughts soon replaced these gloomy presentiments.

One evening, while she was preparing her little table, she heard a rustling sound at the door. She turned and looked; someone had slipped a letter under the door.

Courageously, and without an instant's hesitation, she sprang to the door and opened it. No one was there!

The night was dark, and she could distinguish nothing in the gloom without. She listened; not a sound broke the stillness.

Agitated and trembling she picked up the letter, approached the light, and looked at the address.

"The Marquis de Sairmeuse!" she exclaimed, in amazement.

She recognized Martial's handwriting. So he had written to her! He had dared to write to her!

Her first impulse was to burn the letter; she held it

to the flame, then the thought of her friends concealed at Father Poignot's farm made her withdraw it.

"For their sake," she thought, "I must read it."

She broke the seal with the arms of the De Sairmeuse family inscribed upon it, and read:

"MY DEAR MARIE-ANNE—Perhaps you have suspected who it is that has given an entirely new, and certainly surprising, direction to events.

"Perhaps you have also understood the motives that guided him. In that case I am amply repaid for my efforts, for you cannot refuse me your friendship and your esteem.

"But my work of reparation is not yet accomplished. I have prepared everything for a revision of the judgment that condemned Baron d'Escorval to death, or for procuring a pardon.

"You must know where the baron is concealed. Acquaint him with my plans and ascertain whether he prefers a revision of judgment, or a simple pardon.

"If he desires a new trial, I will give him a letter of license from the King.

"I await your reply before acting.

"MARTIAL DE SAIRMEUSE."

Marie-Anne's head whirled.

This was the second time that Martial had astonished her by the grandeur of his passion.

How noble the two men who had loved her and whom she had rejected, had proved themselves to be.

One, Chanlouineau, after dying for her sake, protected her still.

Martial de Sairmeuse had sacrificed the convictions of his life and the prejudice of his race for her sake;

and, with a noble recklessness, hazarded for her the political fortunes of his house.

And yet the man whom she had chosen, the father of her child, Maurice d'Escorval, had not given a sign of life since he quitted her, five months before.

But suddenly, and without reason, Marie-Anne passed from the most profound admiration to the deep-est distrust.

" What if Martial's offer is only a trap? " This was the suspicion that darted through her mind.

" Ah ! " she thought, " the Marquis de Sairmeuse would be a hero if he were sincere ! "

And she did not wish him to be a hero.

The result of these suspicions was that she hesitated five days before repairing to the rendezvous where Father Poignot usually awaited her.

When she did go, she found, not the worthy farmer, but Abbé Midon, who had been greatly alarmed by her long absence.

It was night, but Marie-Anne, fortunately, knew Martial's letter by heart.

The *abbé* made her repeat it twice, the second time very slowly, and when she had concluded:

" This young man," said the priest, " has the voice and the prejudices of his rank and of his education ; but his heart is noble and generous."

And when Marie-Anne disclosed her suspicions :

" You are wrong, my child," said he : " the Marquis is certainly sincere. It would be wrong not to take ad-vantage of his generosity. Such, at least, is my opin-ion. Intrust this letter to me. I will consult the baron, and to-morrow I will tell you our decision."

The *abbé* was awaiting her with feverish impatience

on the same spot, when she rejoined him twenty-four hours later.

"Monsieur d'Escorval agrees with me that we must trust ourselves to the Marquis de Sairmeuse. Only the baron, being innocent, cannot, will not, accept a pardon. He demands a revision of the iniquitous judgment which condemned him."

Although she must have foreseen this determination, Marie-Anne seemed stupefied.

"What!" said she. "Monsieur d'Escorval will give himself up to his enemies? Does not the Marquis de Sairmeuse promise him a letter of license, a safe-conduct from the King?"

"Yes."

She could find no objection, so in a submissive tone, she said:

"In this case, Monsieur, I must ask you for a rough draft of the letter I am to write to the marquis."

The priest did not reply for a moment. It was evident that he felt some misgivings. At last, summoning all his courage, he said:

"It would be better not to write."

"But——"

"It is not that I distrust the marquis, not by any means, but a letter is dangerous; it does not always reach the person to whom it is addressed. You must see Monsieur de Sairmeuse."

Marie-Anne recoiled in horror.

"Never! never!" she exclaimed.

The *abbé* did not seem surprised.

"I understand your repugnance, my child," he said, gently; "your reputation has suffered greatly through the attentions of the marquis."

"Oh! sir, I entreat you."

" But one should not hesitate, my child, when duty speaks. You owe this sacrifice to an innocent man who has been ruined through your father."

He explained to her all that she must say, and did not leave her until she had promised to see the marquis in person. But the cause of her repugnance was not what the *abbé* supposed. Her reputation! Alas! she knew that was lost forever. No, it was not that.

A fortnight before she would not have been disquieted by the prospect of this interview. Then, though she no longer hated Martial, he was perfectly indifferent to her, while now——

Perhaps in choosing the Croix d'Arcy for the place of meeting, she hoped that this spot, haunted by so many cruel memories, would restore her former aversion.

On pursuing the path leading to the place of rendezvous, she said to herself that Martial would undoubtedly wound her by the tone of careless gallantry which was habitual to him.

But in this she was mistaken. Martial was greatly agitated, but he did not utter a word that was not connected with the baron.

It was only when the conference was ended, and he had consented to all the conditions, that he said, sadly:

" We are friends, are we not? "

In an almost inaudible voice she answered:

" Yes."

And that was all. He remounted his horse which had been held by a servant, and departed in the direction of Montaignac.

Breathless, with cheeks on fire, Marie-Anne watched him as he disappeared; and then her inmost heart was revealed as by a lightning flash.

"*Mon Dieu!* wretch that I am!" she exclaimed. "Do I not love? is it possible that I could ever love any other than Maurice, my husband, the father of my child?"

Her voice was still trembling with emotion when she recounted the details of the interview to the *abbé*. But he did not perceive it. He was thinking only of the baron.

"I was sure that Martial would say 'amen,' to everything; I was so certain of it that I have made all the arrangements for the baron to leave the farm. He will await, at your house, a safe-conduct from His Majesty.

"The close air and the heat of the loft are retarding the baron's recovery," the *abbé* pursued, "so be prepared for his coming to-morrow evening. One of the Poignot boys will bring over all our baggage. About eleven o'clock we will put Monsieur d'Escorval in a carriage; and we will all sup together at the Borderie."

"Heaven comes to my aid!" thought Marie-Anne as she walked homeward.

She thought that she would no longer be alone, that Mme. d'Escorval would be with her to talk to her of Maurice, and that all the friends who would surround her would aid her in driving away the thoughts of Martial, which haunted her.

So the next day she was more cheerful than she had been for months, and once, while putting her little house in order, she was surprised to find herself singing at her work.

Eight o'clock was sounding when she heard a peculiar whistle.

It was the signal of the younger Poignot, who came bringing an arm-chair for the sick man, the *abbé's* box of medicine, and a bag of books.

These articles Marie-Anne deposited in the room which Chanlouineau had adorned for her, and which she intended for the baron. After arranging them to her satisfaction she went out to meet young Poignot, who had told her that he would soon return with other articles.

The night was very dark, and Marie-Anne, as she hastened on, did not notice two motionless figures in the shadow of a clump of lilacs in her little garden.

CHAPTER XLV

Detected by Mme. Blanche in a palpable falsehood, Chupin was quite crestfallen for a moment.

He saw the pleasing vision of a retreat at Courtornieu vanish; he saw himself suddenly deprived of frequent gifts which permitted him to spare his hoarded treasure, and even to increase it.

But he soon regained his assurance, and with an affectation of frankness he said:

"I may be stupid, but I could not deceive an infant. Someone must have told you falsely."

Mme. Blanche shrugged her shoulders.

"I obtained my information from two persons, who were ignorant of the interest it would possess for me."

"As truly as the sun is in the heavens I swear——"

"Do not swear; simply confess that you have been wanting in zeal."

The young lady's manner betrayed such positive certainty that Chupin ceased his denials and changed his tactics.

With the most abject humility, he admitted that the evening before he had relaxed his surveillance; he had been very busy; one of his boys had injured his foot; then he had encountered some friends who persuaded him to enter a drinking-saloon, where he had taken more than usual, so that——

He told this story in a whining tone, and every moment he interrupted himself to affirm his repentance and to cover himself with reproaches.

"Old drunkard!" he said, "this will teach you——"

But these protestations, far from reassuring Mme. Blanche, made her still more suspicious.

"All this is very well, Father Chupin," she said, dryly, "but what are you going to do now to repair your negligence?"

"What do I intend to do?" he exclaimed, feigning the most violent anger. "Oh! you will see. I will prove that no one can deceive me with impunity. Near the Borderie is a small grove. I shall station myself there; and may the devil seize me if a cat enters that house unbeknown to me."

Mme. Blanche drew her purse from her pocket, and taking out three louis, she gave them to Chupin, saying:

"Take these, and be more careful in future. Another blunder like this, and I shall be compelled to ask the aid of some other person."

The old poacher went away, whistling quite reassured; but he was wrong. The lady's generosity was only intended to allay his suspicions.

And why should she not suppose he had betrayed her—this miserable wretch, who made it his business to betray others? What reason had she for placing any confidence in his reports? She paid him! Others, by paying him more, would certainly have the preference!

But how could she ascertain what she wished to know? Ah! she saw but one way—a very disagreeable, but a sure way. She, herself, would play the spy.

This idea took such possession of her mind that, after dinner was concluded, and twilight had enveloped the earth in a mantle of gray, she summoned Aunt Medea.

" Get your cloak, quickly, aunt," she commanded. " I am going for a walk, and you must accompany me."

Aunt Medea extended her hand to the bell-rope, but her niece stopped her.

" You will dispense with the services of your maid," said she. " I do not wish anyone in the château to know that we have gone out."

" Are we going alone? "

" Alone."

" Alone, and on foot, at night——"

" I am in a hurry, aunt," interrupted Blanche, " and I am waiting for you."

In the twinkling of an eye Aunt Medea was ready.

The marquis had just been put to bed, the servants were at dinner, and Blanche and Aunt Medea reached the little gate leading from the garden into the open fields without being observed.

" Good heavens! Where are we going? " groaned Aunt Medea.

" What is that to you? Come! "

Mme. Blanche was going to the Borderie.

She could have followed the banks of the Oiselle, but she preferred to cut across the fields, thinking she would be less likely to meet someone.

The night was still, but very dark, and the progress of the two women was often retarded by hedges and ditches. Twice Blanche lost her way. Again and again, Aunt Medea stumbled over the rough ground, and bruised herself against the stones; she groaned, she almost wept, but her terrible niece was pitiless.

" Come! " she said, " or I will leave you to find your way as best you can."

And the poor dependent struggled on.

At last, after a tramp of more than an hour, Blanche ventured to breathe. She recognized Chanlouineau's house, and she paused in the little grove of which Chupin had spoken.

" Are we at our journey's end? " inquired Aunt Medea, timidly.

" Yes, but be quiet. Remain where you are, I wish to look about a little."

" What! you are leaving me alone? Blanche, I entreat you! What are you going to do? *Mon Dieu!* you frighten me. I am afraid, Blanche! "

But her niece had gone. She was exploring the grove, seeking Chupin. She did not find him.

" I knew the wretch was deceiving me," she muttered through her set teeth. " Who knows but Martial and Marie-Anne are there in that house now, mocking me, and laughing at my credulity? "

She rejoined Aunt Medea, whom she found half dead with fright, and both advanced to the edge of the woods, which commanded a view of the front of the house.

A flickering, crimson light gleamed through two windows in the second story. Evidently there was a fire in the room.

" That is right," murmured Blanche, bitterly; " Martial is such a chilly person! "

She was about to approach the house, when a peculiar whistle rooted her to the spot.

She looked about her, and, in spite of the darkness, she discerned in the footpath leading to the Borderie, a man laden with articles which she could not distinguish.

Almost immediately a woman, certainly Marie-Anne, left the house and advanced to meet him.

They exchanged a few words and then walked together to the house. Soon after the man emerged without his burden and went away.

" What does this mean? " murmured Mme. Blanche.

She waited patiently for more than half an hour, and as nothing stirred:

" Let us go nearer," she said to Aunt Medea, " I wish to look through the windows."

They were approaching the house when, just as they reached the little garden, the door of the cottage opened so suddenly that they had scarcely time to conceal themselves in a clump of lilac-bushes.

Marie-Anne came out, imprudently leaving the key in the door, passed down the narrow path, gained the road, and disappeared.

Blanche pressed Aunt Medea's arm with a violence that made her cry out.

" Wait for me here," she said, in a strained, unnatural voice, " and whatever happens, whatever you hear, if you wish to finish your days at Courtornieu, not a word! Do not stir from this spot; I will return."

And she entered the cottage.

Marie-Anne, on going out, had left a candle burning on the table in the front room.

Blanche seized it and boldly began an exploration of the dwelling.

She had gone over the arrangement of the Borderie so often in her own mind that the rooms seemed familiar to her, she seemed to recognize them.

In spite of Chupin's description the poverty of this humble abode astonished her. There was no floor save the ground; the walls were poorly whitewashed; all kinds of grain and bunches of herbs hung suspended from the ceiling; a few heavy tables, wooden benches, and clumsy chairs constituted the entire furniture.

Marie-Anne evidently occupied the back room. It was the only apartment that contained a bed. This was one of those immense country affairs, very high and broad, with tall fluted posts, draped with green serge curtains, sliding back and forth on iron rings.

At the head of the bed, fastened to the wall, hung a receptacle for holy-water. Blanche dipped her finger in the bowl; it was full to the brim.

Beside the window was a wooden shelf supported by a hook, and on the shelf stood a basin and bowl of the commonest earthenware.

" It must be confessed that my husband does not provide a very sumptuous abode for his idol," said Mme. Blanche, with a sneer.

She was almost on the point of asking herself if jealousy had not led her astray.

She remembered Martial's fastidious tastes, and she did not know how to reconcile them with these meagre surroundings. Then, there was the holy-water !

But her suspicions became stronger when she entered the kitchen. Some savory compound was bubbling in a pot over the fire, and several saucepans, in which fragrant stews were simmering, stood among the warm ashes.

" All this cannot be for her," murmured Blanche.

Then she remembered the two windows in the story above which she had seen illuminated by the trembling glow of the fire-light.

"I must examine the rooms above," she thought.

The staircase led up from the middle of the room; she knew this. She quickly ascended the stairs, pushed open a door, and could not repress a cry of surprise and rage.

She found herself in the sumptuously appointed room which Chanlouineau had made the sanctuary of his great love, and upon which he had lavished, with the fanaticism of passion, all that was costly and luxurious.

"Then it is true!" exclaimed Blanche. "And I thought just now that all was too meagre and too poor! Miserable dupe that I am! Below, all is arranged for the eyes of comers and goers. Here, everything is intended exclusively for themselves. Now, I recognize Martial's astonishing talent for dissimulation. He loves this vile creature so much that he is anxious in regard to her reputation; he keeps his visits to her a secret, and this is the hidden paradise of their love. Here they laugh at me, the poor forsaken wife, whose marriage was but a mockery."

She had desired to know the truth; certainty was less terrible to endure than this constant suspicion. And, as if she found a little enjoyment in proving the extent of Martial's love for a hated rival, she took an inventory, as it were, of the magnificent appointments of the chamber, feeling the heavy brocaded silk stuff that formed the curtains, and testing the thickness of the rich carpet with her foot.

Everything indicated that Marie-Anne was expecting someone; the bright fire, the large arm-chair placed before the hearth, the embroidered slippers lying beside the chair.

And whom could she expect save Martial? The

person who had been there a few moments before probably came to announce the arrival of her lover, and she
had gone out to meet him,

For a trifling circumstance would seem to indicate
that this messenger had not been expected.

Upon the mantel stood a bowl of still smoking
bouillon.

It was evident that Marie-Anne was on the point
of drinking this when she heard the signal.

Mme. Blanche was wondering how she could profit
by her discovery, when her eyes fell upon a large oaken
box standing open upon a table near the glass door
leading into the dressing-room, and filled with tiny
boxes and vials.

Mechanically she approached it, and among the bottles she saw two of blue glass, upon which the word
" poison " was inscribed.

" Poison ! " Blanche could not turn her eyes from
this word, which seemed to exert a kind of fascination
over her.

A diabolical inspiration associated the contents of
these vials with the bowl standing upon the mantel.

" And why not ? " she murmured.   " I could escape
afterward."

A terrible thought made her pause.   Martial would
return with Marie-Anne ; who could say that it would
not be he who would drink the contents of the bowl.

" God shall decide ! " she murmured.   " It is better
one's husband should be dead than belong to another ! "

And with a firm hand, she took up one of the vials.

Since her entrance into the cottage Blanche had
scarcely been conscious of her acts.   Hatred and despair had clouded her brain like fumes of alcohol.

But when her hand came in contact with the glass containing the deadly drug, the terrible shock dissipated her bewilderment; she regained the full possession of her faculties; the power of calm deliberation returned.

This is proved by the fact that her first thought was this:

" I am ignorant even of the name of the poison which I hold. What dose must I administer, much or little? "

She opened the vial, not without considerable difficulty, and poured a few grains of its contents into the palm of her hand. It was a fine, white powder, glistening like pulverized glass, and looking not unlike sugar.

" Can it really be sugar? " she thought.

Resolved to ascertain, she moistened the tip of her finger, and collected upon it a few atoms of the powder which she placed upon her tongue.

The taste was like that of an extremely acid apple.

Without hesitation, without remorse, without even turning pale, she poured into the bowl the entire contents of the vial.

Her self-possession was so perfect, she even recollected that the powder might be slow in dissolving, and she stirred it gently for a moment or more.

Having done this—she seemed to think of everything—she tasted the *bouillon*. She noticed a slightly bitter taste, but it was not sufficiently perceptible to awaken distrust.

Now Mme. Blanche breathed freely. If she could succeed in making her escape she was avenged.

She was going toward the door when a sound on the stairs startled her.

Two persons were ascending the staircase.

Where should she go? where could she conceal herself?

She was now so sure she would be detected that she almost decided to throw the bowl into the fire, and then boldly face the intruders.

But no—a chance remained—she darted into the dressing-room. She dared not close the door; the least click of the latch would have betrayed her.

Marie-Anne entered the chamber, followed by a peasant, bearing a large bundle.

"Ah! here is my candle!" she exclaimed, as she crossed the threshold. "Joy must be making me lose my wits! I could have sworn that I left it on the table downstairs."

Blanche shuddered. She had not thought of this circumstance.

"Where shall I put this clothing?" asked the young peasant.

"Lay it down here. I will arrange the articles by and by," replied Marie Anne.

The boy dropped his heavy burden with a sigh of relief.

"This is the last," he exclaimed. "Now, our gentleman can come."

"At what hour will he start?" inquired Marie-Anne.

"At eleven o'clock. It will be nearly midnight when he gets here."

Marie-Anne glanced at the magnificent clock on the mantel.

"I have still three hours before me," said she; "more time than I shall need. Supper is ready; I am going to set the table here, by the fire. Tell him to bring a good appetite."

"I will tell him, and many thanks, Mademoiselle,

for having come to meet me and aid me with my second load. It was not so very heavy, but it was clumsy to handle."

" Will you not accept a glass of wine? "

" No, thank you. I must hasten back. *Au revoir,* Mademoiselle Lacheneur."

" *Au revoir,* Poignot."

This name Poignot had no significance in the ears of Blanche.

Ah! had she heard Monsieur d'Escorval's or the *abbé's* name mentioned, she might have felt some doubt of Marie-Anne's guilt; her resolution might have wavered, and—who knows?

But no. Young Poignot, in referring to the baron had said: " our gentleman," Marie-Anne said: " he."

Is not " he " always the person who is uppermost in our minds, the husband whom one hates or the lover whom one adores?

" Our gentleman ! "   " he ! "   Blanche translated Martial.

Yes, it was the Marquis de Sairmeuse who was to arrive at midnight. She was sure of it. It was he who had been preceded by a messenger bearing clothing. This could only mean that he was about to establish himself at the Borderie. Perhaps he would cast aside all secrecy and live there openly, regardless of his rank, of his dignity, and of his duties; forgetful even of his prejudices.

These conjectures inflamed her fury still more.

Why should she hesitate or tremble after that?

Her only dread now, was lest she should be discovered.

Aunt Medea was, it is true, in the garden; but after the orders she had received the poor woman would remain motionless as stone behind the clump of lilacs, the entire night if necessary.

For two hours and a half Marie-Anne would be alone at the Borderie. Blanche reflected that this would give her ample time to watch the effects of the poison upon her hated rival.

When the crime was discovered she would be far away. No one knew she had been absent from Court-ornieu; no one had seen her leave the château; Aunt Medea would be as silent as the grave. And besides, who would dare to accuse her, Marquise de Sairmeuse *née* Blanche de Courtornieu, of being the murderer?

"But she does not drink it!" Blanche thought.

Marie-Anne had, in fact, forgotten the *bouillon* en-tirely. She had opened the bundle of clothing, and was busily arranging the articles in a wardrobe near the bed.

Who talks of presentiments! She was as gay and vivacious as in her days of happiness; and as she worked, she hummed an air that Maurice had often sung.

She felt that her troubles were nearly over; her friends would soon be around her.

When her task of putting away the clothing was completed and the wardrobe closed, she drew a small table up before the fire.

Not until then did she notice the bowl standing upon the mantel.

"Stupid!" she said, with a laugh; and taking the bowl she raised it to her lips.

From her hiding-place Blanche had heard Marie-Anne's exclamation; she saw the movement, and yet not the slightest remorse struck her soul.

Marie-Anne drank but one mouthful, then, in evi-dent disgust, sat the bowl down.

A horrible dread made the watcher's heart stand still.

"Does she notice a peculiar taste in the *bouillon?*" she thought.

No; but it had grown cold, and a slight coating of grease had formed over the top. Marie-Anne took the spoon, skimmed the *bouillon*, and then stirred it up for some time, to divide the greasy particles.

After she had done this she drank the liquid, put the bowl back upon the mantel, and resumed her work.

It was done. The *dénouement* no longer depended upon Blanche de Courtornieu's will. Come what would, she was a murderess.

But though she was conscious of her crime, the excess of her hatred prevented her from realizing its enormity. She said to herself that it was only an act of justice which she had accomplished; that the vengeance she had taken was not proportionate to the offence, and that nothing could atone for the torture she had endured.

But in a few moments a sinister apprehension took possession of her mind.

Her knowledge of the effects of poison was extremely limited. She had expected to see Marie-Anne fall dead before her, as if stricken down by a thunder-bolt.

But no. The moments slipped by, and Marie-Anne continued her preparations for supper as if nothing had occurred.

She spread a white cloth over the table, smoothed it with her hands, and placed a dish upon it.

"What if she should come in here!" thought Blanche.

The fear of punishment which precedes remorse, made her heart beat with such violence that she could not understand why its throbbings were not heard in the adjoining room. Her terror increased when she saw Marie-Anne take the light and go downstairs. Blanche was left alone. The thought of making her escape occurred to her; but how, and by what way could she leave the house without being seen?

"It must be that poison does not work!" she said, in a rage.

Alas! no. She knew better when Marie-Anne reappeared.

In the few moments she had spent below, her features had become frightfully changed. Her face was livid and mottled with purple spots, her eyes were distended and glittered with a strange brilliancy. She let the plates which she held fall upon the table with a crash.

"The poison! it begins!" thought Blanche.

Marie-Anne stood on the hearth, gazing wildly around her, as if seeking the cause of her incomprehensible suffering. She passed and re-passed her hand across her forehead, which was bathed in a cold perspiration; she gasped for breath. Then suddenly, overcome with nausea, she staggered, pressed her hands convulsively upon her breast, and sank into the armchair, crying:

"Oh, God! how I suffer!"

CHAPTER XLVI

Kneeling by the half-open door, Blanche eagerly watched the workings of the poison which she had administered.

She was so near her victim that she could distinguish the throbbing of her temples, and sometimes she fancied she could feel upon her cheek her rival's breath, which scorched like flame.

An utter prostration followed Marie-Anne's paroxysm of agony. One would have supposed her dead had it not been for the convulsive workings of the jaws and her labored breathing.

But soon the nausea returned, and she was seized with vomiting. Each effort to relieve seemed to wrench her whole body; and gradually a ghastly tint crept over her face, the spots upon her cheeks became more pronounced in tint, her eyes appeared ready to burst from their sockets, and great drops of perspiration rolled down her cheeks.

Her sufferings must have been intolerable. She moaned feebly at times, and occasionally rendered heart-rending shrieks. Then she faltered fragmentary sentences; she begged piteously for water or entreated God to shorten her torture.

"Ah, it is horrible! I suffer too much! Death! My God! grant me death!"

She invoked all the friends she had ever known, calling for aid in a despairing voice.

She called Mme. d'Escorval, the *abbé*, Maurice, her brother, Chanlouineau, Martial!

Martial, this name was more than sufficient to extinguish all pity in the heart of Mme. Blanche.

"Go on! call your lover, call!" she said to herself, bitterly. "He will come too late."

And as Marie-Anne repeated the name in a tone of agonized entreaty:

"Suffer!" continued Mme. Blanche, "suffer, you who have inspired Martial with the odious courage to forsake me, his wife, as a drunken lackey would abandon the lowest of degraded creatures! Die, and my husband will return to me repentant."

No, she had no pity. She felt a difficulty in breathing, but that resulted simply from the instinctive horror which the sufferings of others inspire—an entirely
different physical impression, which is adorned with
the fine name of sensibility, but which is, in reality, the
grossest selfishness.

And yet, Marie-Anne was perceptibly sinking. Soon
she had not strength even to moan; her eyes closed,
and after a spasm which brought a bloody foam to her
lips, her head sank back, and she lay motionless.

" It is over," murmured Blanche.

She rose, but her limbs trembled so that she could
scarcely stand.

Her heart remained firm and implacable; but the
flesh failed.

Never had she imagined a scene like that which she
had just witnessed. She knew that poison caused
death; she had not suspected the agony of that death.

She no longer thought of augmenting Marie-Anne's
sufferings by upbraiding her. Her only desire now
was to leave this house, whose very floor seemed to
scorch her feet.

A strange, inexplicable sensation crept over her; it
was not yet fright, it was the stupor that follows the
commission of a terrible crime—the stupor of the murderer.

Still, she compelled herself to wait a few moments
longer; then seeing that Marie-Anne still remained
motionless and with closed eyes, she ventured to softly
open the door and to enter the room in which her victim was lying.

But she had not advanced three steps before Marie-
Anne suddenly, and as if she had been galvanized by
an electric battery, rose and extended her arms to bar
her enemy's passage.

This movement was so unexpected and so frightful that Mme. Blanche recoiled.

"The Marquise de Sairmeuse," faltered Marie-Anne. "You, Blanche—here!"

And her suffering, explained by the presence of this young girl who once had been her friend, but who was now her bitterest enemy, she exclaimed:

"You are my murderer!"

Blanche de Courtornieu's was one of those iron natures that break, but never bend.

Since she had been discovered, nothing in the world would induce her to deny her guilt.

She advanced resolutely, and in a firm voice:

"Yes," she said, "I have taken my revenge. Do you think I did not suffer that evening when you sent your brother to take away my newly wedded husband, upon whose face I have not gazed since?"

"Your husband! I sent to take him away! I do not understand you."

"Do you then dare to deny that you are not Martial's mistress!"

"The Marquis de Sairmeuse! I saw him yesterday for the first time since Baron d'Escorval's escape."

The effort which she had made to rise and to speak had exhausted her strength. She fell back in the arm-chair.

But Blanche was pitiless.

"You have not seen Martial! Tell me, then, who gave you this costly furniture, these silken hangings, all the luxury that surrounds you?"

"Chanlouineau."

Blanche shrugged her shoulders.

"So be it," she said, with an ironical smile, "but is it Chanlouineau for whom you are waiting this evening?

Is it for Chanlouineau you have warmed these slippers and laid this table? Was it Chanlouineau who sent his clothing by a peasant named Poignot? You see that I know all——"

But her victim was silent.

"For whom are you waiting?" she insisted. "Answer!"

"I cannot!"

"You know that it is your lover! wretched woman —my husband, Martial!"

Marie-Anne was considering the situation as well as her intolerable sufferings and troubled mind would permit.

Could she tell what guests she was expecting?

To name Baron d'Escorval to Blanche, would it not ruin and betray him? They hoped for a safe-conduct, a revision of judgment, but he was none the less under sentence of death, executory in twenty-four hours.

"So you refuse to tell me whom you expect here in an hour—at midnight."

"I refuse."

But a sudden impulse took possession of the sufferer's mind.

Though the slightest movement caused her intolerable agony, she tore open her dress and drew from her bosom a folded paper.

"I am not the mistress of the Marquis de Sairmeuse," she said, in an almost inaudible voice; "I am the wife of Maurice d'Escorval. Here is the proof— read."

No sooner had Blanche glanced at the paper, than she became as pale as her victim. Her sight failed her; there was a strange ringing in her ears, a cold sweat started from every pore.

This paper was the marriage-certificate of Maurice and Marie-Anne, drawn up by the *curé* of Vigano, witnessed by the old physician and Bavois, and sealed with the seal of the parish.

The proof was indisputable. She had committed a useless crime; she had murdered an innocent woman.

The first good impulse of her life made her heart beat more quickly. She did not stop to consider; she forgot the danger to which she exposed herself, and in a ringing voice she cried:

" Help ! help ! "

Eleven o'clock was sounding; the whole country was asleep. The farm-house nearest the Borderie was half a league distant.

The voice of Blanche was lost in the deep stillness of the night.

In the garden below Aunt Medea heard it, perhaps; but she would have allowed herself to be chopped in pieces rather than stir from her place.

And yet, there was one who heard that cry of distress. Had Blanche and her victim been less overwhelmed with despair, they would have heard a noise upon the staircase, which creaked beneath the tread of a man who was cautiously ascending it. But it was not a saviour, for he did not answer the appeal. But even though there had been aid near at hand, it would have come too late.

Marie-Anne felt that there was no longer any hope for her, and that it was the chill of death which was creeping up to her heart. She felt that her life was fast ebbing away.

So, when Blanche seemed about to rush out in search of assistance, she detained her by a gesture, and gently said:

" Blanche."

The murderess paused.

" Do not summon anyone; it would do no good. Remain; be calm, that I may at least die in peace. It will not be long, now."

" Hush! do not speak so. You must not, you shall not die! If you should die—great God! what would my life be afterward? "

Marie-Anne made no reply. The poison was pursuing its work of dissolution. Her breath made a whistling sound as it forced its way through her inflamed throat; her tongue, when she moved it, produced in her mouth the terrible sensation of a piece of red-hot iron; her lips were parched and swollen; her hands, inert and paralyzed, would no longer obey her will.

But the horror of the situation restored Blanche's calmness.

" All is not yet lost," she exclaimed. " It was in that great box there upon the table, where I found "—she dared not utter the word poison—" the white powder which I poured into the bowl. You know this powder; you must know the antidote."

Marie-Anne sadly shook her head.

" Nothing can save me now," she murmured, in an almost inaudible voice; " but I do not complain. Who knows the misery from which death may preserve me? I do not crave life, I have suffered so much during the past year; I have endured such humiliation; I have wept so much! A curse was upon me! "

She was suddenly endowed with that clearness of mental vision so often granted to the dying. She saw how she had wrought her own undoing by consenting to accept the perfidious *rôle* imposed upon her by her father, and how she, herself, had paved the way for the falsehoods, slander, crimes and misfortunes of which she had been the victim.

Her voice grew fainter and fainter. Worn out by suffering, a sensation of drowsiness stole over her. She was falling asleep in the arms of death.

Suddenly such a terrible thought pierced the stupor which enveloped her that she uttered a heart-breaking cry:

" My child! "

Collecting, by a superhuman effort, all the will, energy, and strength that the poison had left her, she straightened herself in her arm-chair, her features contracted by mortal anguish.

" Blanche! " she said, with an energy of which one would have supposed her incapable. " Blanche, listen to me. It is the secret of my life which I am about to disclose; no one suspects it. I have a son by Maurice. Alas! many months have elapsed since my husband disappeared. If he is dead, what will become of my child? Blanche, you, who have killed me, must swear to me that you will be a mother to my child! "

Blanche was utterly overcome.

" I swear! " she sobbed, " I swear! "

" On that condition, but on that condition alone, I pardon you. But take care! Do not forget your oath! Blanche, God sometimes permits the dead to avenge themselves! You have sworn, remember.

" My spirit will allow you no rest if you do not fulfil your vow."

" I will remember," sobbed Blanche; " I will remember. But the child——"

" Ah! I was afraid—cowardly creature that I was! I dreaded the shame—then Maurice insisted—I sent my child away—your jealousy and my death are my punishment. Poor child! I abandoned him to strangers. Wretched woman that I am! Ah! this suffering is too horrible. Blanche, remember——"

She spoke again, but her words were indistinct, inaudible.

Blanche frantically seized the dying woman's arm, and endeavored to arouse her.

"To whom have you confided your child?" she repeated; "to whom? Marie-Anne—a word more—a single word—a name, Marie-Anne!"

The unfortunate woman's lips moved, but the death-rattle sounded in her throat; a terrible convulsion shook her form; she slid down from the chair, and fell full length upon the floor.

Marie-Anne was dead—dead, and she had not disclosed the name of the old physician at Vigano to whom she had intrusted her child. She was dead, and the terrified murderess stood in the middle of the room, as rigid and motionless as a statue. It seemed to her that madness—a madness like that which had stricken her father—was developing itself in her brain.

She forgot everything; she forgot that a guest was expected at midnight; that time was flying, and that she would surely be discovered if she did not flee.

But the man who had entered when she cried for aid was watching over her. When he saw that Marie-Anne had breathed her last, he made a slight noise at the door, and thrust his leering face into the room.

"Chupin!" faltered Mme. Blanche.

"In the flesh," he responded. "This was a grand chance for you. Ah, ha! The business riled your stomach a little, but nonsense! that will soon pass off. But we must not dawdle here; someone may come in. Let us make haste."

Mechanically the murderess advanced; but Marie-Anne's dead body lay between her and the door, barring the passage. To leave the room it was necessary to step over the lifeless form of her victim. She had not courage to do this, and recoiled with a shudder.

But Chupin was troubled by no such scruples. He sprang across the body, lifted Blanche as if she had been a child and carried her out of the house.

He was drunk with joy. Fears for the future no longer disquieted him, now that Mme. Blanche was bound to him by the strongest of chains—complicity in crime.

He saw himself on the threshold of a life of ease and continual feasting. Remorse for Lacheneur's betrayal had ceased to trouble him. He saw himself sumptuously fed, lodged and clothed; above all, effectually guarded by an army of servants.

Blanche, who had experienced a feeling of deadly faintness, was revived by the cool night-air.

" I wish to walk," said she.

Chupin placed her on the ground about twenty paces from the house.

" And Aunt Medea!" she exclaimed.

Her relative was beside her; like one of those dogs who are left at the door when their master enters a house, she had instinctively followed her niece on seeing her borne from the cottage by the old poacher.

" We must not stop to talk," said Chupin. " Come, I will lead the way."

And taking Blanche by the arm, he hastened toward the grove.

" Ah! so Marie-Anne had a child," he said, as they hurried on. " She was pretended to be such a saint! But where the devil has she put it?"

" I shall find it."

" Hum! That is easier said than done."

A shrill laugh resounding in the darkness, interrupted him. He released his hold on the arm of Blanche and assumed an attitude of defence.

Vain precaution! A man concealed behind a tree bounded upon him, and, plunging his knife four times into the old poacher's writhing body, cried:

" Holy Virgin! now is my vow fulfilled! I shall no longer be obliged to eat with my fingers!"

" The innkeeper!" groaned the wounded man, sinking to the earth.

For once in her life, Aunt Medea manifested some energy.

" Come!" she shrieked, wild with fear, dragging her niece away. " Come—he is dead!"

Not quite. The traitor had strength to crawl home and knock at the door.

His wife and youngest son were sleeping soundly. His eldest son, who had just returned home, opened the door.

Seeing his father prostrate on the ground, he thought he was intoxicated, and tried to lift him and carry him into the house, but the old poacher begged him to desist.

" Do not touch me," said he. " It is all over with me; but listen; Lacheneur's daughter has just been poisoned by Madame Blanche. It was to tell you this that I dragged myself here. This knowledge is worth a fortune, my boy, if you are not a fool!"

And he died, without being able to tell his family where he had concealed the price of Lacheneur's blood.

CHAPTER XLVII

Of all the persons who witnessed Baron d'Escorval's terrible fall, the *abbé* was the only one who did not despair.

What a learned doctor would not have dared to do, he did.

He was a priest; he had faith. He remembered the sublime saying of Ambroise Paré: " I dress the wound: God heals it."

After a six months' sojourn in Father Poignot's secluded farm-house, M. d'Escorval was able to sit up and to walk about a little, with the aid of crutches.

Then he began to be seriously inconvenienced by his cramped quarters in the loft, where prudence compelled him to remain; and it was with transports of joy that he welcomed the idea of taking up his abode at the Borderie with Marie-Anne.

When the day of departure had been decided upon, he counted the minutes as impatiently as a school-boy pining for vacation.

" I am suffocating here," he said to his wife. " I am suffocating. Time drags so slowly. When will the happy day come?"

It came at last. During the morning all the articles which they had succeeded in procuring during their stay at the farm-house were collected and packed; and when night came, Poignot's son began the moving.

" Everything is at the Borderie," said the honest fellow, on returning from his last trip, " and Mademoiselle Lacheneur bids the baron bring a good appetite."

" I shall have one, never fear! " responded the baron, gayly. " We shall all have one."

Father Poignot himself was busily engaged in harnessing his best horse to the cart which was to convey M. d'Escorval to his new home.

The worthy man's heart grew sad at the thought of the departure of these guests, for whose sake he had incurred such danger. He felt that he should miss them, that the house would seem gloomy and deserted after they left it.

He would allow no one else to perform the task of arranging the mattress comfortably in the cart. When this had been done to his satisfaction, he heaved a deep sigh, and exclaimed:

" It is time to start ! "

Slowly he ascended the narrow staircase leading to the loft.

M. d'Escorval had not thought of the moment of parting.

At the sight of the honest farmer, who came toward him, his face crimsoned with emotion to bid him farewell, he forgot all the comforts that awaited him at the Borderie, in the remembrance of the loyal and courageous hospitality he had received in the house he was about to leave. The tears sprang to his eyes.

" You have rendered me a service which nothing can repay, Father Poignot," he said, with intense feeling. " You have saved my life."

" Oh ! we will not talk of that, Baron. In my place, you would have done the same—neither more nor less."

" I shall not attempt to express my thanks, but I hope to live long enough to prove that I am not ungrateful."

The staircase was so narrow that they had considerable difficulty in carrying the baron down ; but finally they had him comfortably extended upon his mattress and threw over him a few handsful of straw, which concealed him entirely.

"Farewell, then!" said the old farmer, when the last hand-shake had been exchanged, "or rather *au revoir*, Monsieur le Baron, Madame, and you, my good *curé.*"

"All ready?" inquired young Poignot.

"Yes," replied the invalid.

The cart, driven with the utmost caution by the young peasant, started slowly on its way.

Mme. d'Escorval, leaning upon the *abbé's* arm, walked about twenty paces in the rear.

It was very dark, but had it been as light as day the former *curé* of Sairmeuse might have encountered any of his old parishioners without the least danger of detection.

His hair and his beard had been allowed to grow; his tonsure had entirely disappeared, and his sedentary life had caused him to become much stouter. He was clad like all the well-to-do peasants of the neighborhood, and his face was hidden by a large slouch hat.

He had not felt so tranquil in mind for months. Obstacles which had appeared almost insurmountable had vanished. In the near future he saw the baron declared innocent by impartial judges; he saw himself reinstalled in the presbytery of Sairmeuse.

The recollection of Maurice was the only thing that marred his happiness. Why did he not give some sign of life?

"But if he had met with any misfortune we should have heard of it," thought the priest. "He has with him a brave man—an old soldier who would risk anything to come and tell us."

He was so absorbed in these thoughts that he did not

observe that Mme. d'Escorval was leaning more and more heavily upon his arm.

"I am ashamed to confess it," she said at last, "but I can go no farther. It has been so long since I was out of doors that I have almost forgotten how to walk."

"Fortunately, we are almost there," replied the priest.

A moment after young Poignot stopped his cart in the road, at the entrance of the little footpath leading to the Borderie.

"Our journey is ended!" he remarked to the baron. Then he uttered a low whistle, like that which he had given a few hours before, to warn Marie-Anne of his arrival.

No one appeared; he whistled again, louder this time; then with all his might—still no response.

Mme. d'Escorval and the *abbé* had now overtaken the cart.

"It is very strange that Marie-Anne does not hear me," remarked young Poignot, turning to them. "We cannot take the baron to the house until we have seen her. She knows that very well. Shall I run up and warn her?"

"She is asleep, perhaps," replied the *abbé*; "you stay with your horse, my boy, and I will go and wake her."

Certainly he did not feel the slightest disquietude. All was calm and still; a bright light was shining through the windows of the second story.

Still, when he saw the open door, a vague presentiment of evil stirred his heart.

"What can this mean?" he thought.

There was no light in the lower rooms, and the *abbé* was obliged to feel for the staircase with his hands.

At last he found it and went up. But upon the threshold of the chamber he paused, petrified with horror by the spectacle before him.

Poor Marie-Anne was lying on the floor. Her eyes, which were wide open, were covered with a white film; her black and swollen tongue was hanging from her mouth.

"Dead!" faltered the priest, "dead!"

But this could not be. The *abbé* conquered his weakness, and approaching the poor girl, he took her hand.

It was icy cold; the arm was rigid as iron.

"Poisoned!" he murmured; "poisoned with arsenic."

He rose to his feet, and cast a bewildered glance around the room. His eyes fell upon his medicine-chest, open upon the table.

He rushed to it and unhesitatingly took out a vial, uncorked it, and inverted it on the palm of his hand— it was empty.

"I was not mistaken!" he exclaimed.

But he had no time to lose in conjectures.

The first thing to be done was to induce the baron to return to the farm-house without telling him the terrible misfortune which had occurred.

To find a pretext was easy enough.

The priest hastened back to the wagon, and with well-affected calmness told the baron that it would be impossible for him to take up his abode at the Borderie at present, that several suspicious-looking characters had been seen prowling about, and that they must be more prudent than ever, now they could rely upon the kindly intervention of Martial de Sairmeuse.

At last, but not without considerable reluctance, the baron yielded.

"You desire it, *curé*," he sighed, "so I obey. Come, Poignot, my boy, take me back to your father's house."

Mme. d'Escorval took a seat in the cart beside her husband; the priest watched them as they drove away, and not until the sound of their carriage-wheels had died away in the distance did he venture to go back to the Borderie.

He was ascending the stairs when he heard moans that seemed to issue from the chamber of death. The sound sent all his blood wildly rushing to his heart. He darted up the staircase.

A man was kneeling beside Marie-Anne, weeping bitterly. The expression of his face, his attitude, his sobs betrayed the wildest despair. He was so lost in grief that he did not observe the *abbé's* entrance.

Who was this mourner who had found his way to the house of death?

After a moment, the priest divined who the intruder was, though he did not recognize him.

"Jean!" he cried, "Jean Lacheneur!"

With a bound the young man was on his feet, pale and menacing; a flame of anger drying the tears in his eyes.

"Who are you?" he demanded, in a terrible voice. "What are you doing here? What do you wish with me?"

By his peasant dress and by his long beard, the former *curé* of Sairmeuse was so effectually disguised that he was obliged to tell who he really was.

As soon as he uttered his name, Jean uttered a cry of joy.

"God has sent you here!" he exclaimed. "Marie-Anne cannot be dead! You, who have saved so many others, will save her."

As the priest sadly pointed to heaven, Jean paused, his face more ghastly than before. He understood now that there was no hope.

"Ah!" he murmured, with an accent of frightful despondency, "fate shows us no mercy. I have been watching over Marie-Anne, though from a distance; and this very evening I was coming to say to her: 'Beware, sister—be cautious!'"

"What! you knew——"

"I knew she was in great danger; yes, Monsieur. An hour ago, while I was eating my supper in a restaurant at Sairmeuse, Grollet's son entered. 'Is this you, Jean?' said he. 'I just saw Chupin hiding near your sister's house; when he observed me he slunk away.' I ran here like one crazed. But when fate is against a man, what can he do? I came too late!"

The *abbé* reflected for a moment.

"Then you suppose that it was Chupin?"

"I do not suppose, sir; I *swear* that it was he—the miserable traitor!—who committed this foul deed."

"Still, what motive could he have had?"

Jean burst into one of those discordant laughs that are, perhaps, the most frightful signs of despair.

"You may rest assured that the blood of the daughter will yield him a richer reward than did the father's. Chupin has been the vile instrument; but it was not he who conceived the crime. You will have to seek higher for the culprit, much higher, in the finest château of the country, in the midst of an army of valets at Sairmeuse, in short!"

"Wretched man, what do you mean?"

"What I say."

And coldly, he added:

"Martial de Sairmeuse is the assassin."

The priest recoiled, really appalled by the looks and manner of the grief-stricken man.

"You are mad!" he said, severely.

But Jean gravely shook his head.

"If I seem so to you, sir," he replied, "it is only because you are ignorant of Martial's wild passion for Marie-Anne. He wished to make her his mistress. She had the audacity to refuse this honor; that was a crime for which she must be punished. When the Marquis de Sairmeuse became convinced that Lacheneur's daughter would never be his, he poisoned her that she might not belong to another.

Any attempt to convince Jean of the folly of his accusation would have been vain at that moment. No proofs would have convinced him. He would have closed his eyes to all evidence.

"To-morrow, when he is more calm, I will reason with him," thought the *abbé;* then, turning to Jean, he said:

"We cannot allow the body of the poor girl to remain here upon the floor. Assist me, and we will place it upon the bed."

Jean trembled from head to foot, and his hesitation was apparent.

"Very well!" he said, at last, after a severe struggle.

No one had ever slept upon this bed which poor Chanlouineau had destined for Marie-Anne.

"It shall be for her," he said to himself, "or for no one."

And it was Marie-Anne who rested there first—dead.

When this sad task was accomplished, he threw himself into the same arm-chair in which Marie-Anne had breathed her last, and with his face buried in his hands, and his elbows supported upon his knees, he sat there as silent and motionless as the statues of sorrow placed above the last resting-places of the dead.

The *abbé* knelt at the head of the bed and began the recital of the prayers for the dead, entreating God to grant peace and happiness in heaven to her who had suffered so much upon earth.

But he prayed only with his lips. In spite of his efforts, his mind would persist in wandering.

He was striving to solve the mystery that enshrouded Marie-Anne's death. Had she been murdered? Could it be that she had committed suicide?

This explanation recurred to him, but he could not believe it.

But, on the other hand, how could her death possibly be the result of a crime?

He had carefully examined the room, and he had discovered nothing that betrayed the presence of a stranger.

All that he could prove was, that his vial of arsenic was empty, and that Marie-Anne had been poisoned by the *bouillon*, a few drops of which were left in the bowl that was standing upon the mantel.

"When daylight comes," thought the *abbé*, "I will look outside."

When morning broke, he went into the garden, and made a careful examination of the premises.

At first he saw nothing that gave him the least clew, and was about to abandon the investigations, when, upon entering the little grove, he saw in the distance a large dark stain upon the grass. He went nearer— it was blood!

Much excited, he summoned Jean, to inform him of the discovery.

" Someone has been assassinated here," said Lacheneur; "and it happened last night, for the blood has
not had time to dry."

" The victim lost a great deal of blood," the priest
remarked; " it might be possible to discover who he
was by following up these stains."

" I am going to try," responded Jean. " Go back
to the house, sir; I will soon return."

A child might have followed the track of the wounded man, the blood-stains left in his passage were so
frequent and so distinct.

These tell-tale marks stopped at Chupin's house.
The door was closed; Jean rapped without the slightest hesitation.

The old poacher's eldest son opened the door, and
Jean saw a strange spectacle.

The traitor's body had been thrown on the ground,
in a corner of the room, the bed was overturned and
broken, all the straw had been torn from the mattress,
and the wife and sons of the dead man, armed with
pickaxes and spades, were wildly overturning the
beaten soil that formed the floor of the hovel. They
were seeking the hidden treasures.

" What do you want? " demanded the widow, rudely.

" Father Chupin."

" You can see very plainly that he has been murdered," replied one of the sons.

And brandishing his pick a few inches from Jean's
head, he exclaimed:

" And you, perhaps, are the assassin. But that is
for justice to determine. Now, decamp; if you do
not——"

Had he listened to the promptings of anger, Jean
Lacheneur would certainly have attempted to make
the Chupins repent their menaces.

But a conflict was scarcely permissible under the circumstances.

He departed without a word, and hastened back to the Borderie.

The death of Chupin overturned all his plans, and greatly irritated him.

" I had sworn that the vile wretch who betrayed my father should perish by my hand," he murmured; " and now my vengeance has escaped me. Someone has robbed me of it."

Then he asked himself who the murderer could be.

" Is it possible that Martial assassinated Chupin after he murdered Marie-Anne? To kill an accomplice is an effectual way of assuring one's self of his silence."

He had reached the Borderie, and was about going upstairs, when he thought he heard the sound of voices in the back room.

" That is strange," he said to himself. " Who can it be? "

And impelled by curiosity, he went and tapped upon the communicating door.

The *abbé* instantly made his appearance, hurriedly closing the door behind him. He was very pale, and visibly agitated.

" Who is it? " inquired Jean, eagerly.

" It is—it is. Guess who it is."

" How can I guess? "

" Maurice d'Escorval and Corporal Bavois."

" My God! "

" And it is a miracle that he has not been upstairs."

" But whence does he come? Why have we received no news of him? "

" I do not know. He has been here only five minutes. Poor boy! after I told him that his father was

safe, his first words were: ' And Marie-Anne? ' He
loves her more devotedly than ever. He comes with
his heart full of her, confident and hopeful; and I
tremble—I fear to tell him the truth."

" Oh, terrible! terrible! "

" I have warned you; be prudent—and now, come
in."

They entered the room together; and Maurice and
the old soldier greeted Jean with the most ardent expressions of friendship.

They had not seen each other since the duel on the
Reche, which had been interrupted by the arrival of the
soldiers; and when they parted that day they scarcely
expected to meet again.

" And now we are together once more," said Maurice, gayly, " and we have nothing to fear."

Never had the unfortunate man seemed so cheerful;
and it was with the most jubilant air that he explained
the reason of his long silence.

" Three days after we crossed the frontier," said he,
" Corporal Bavois and I reached Turin. It was time,
for we were tired out. We went to a small inn, and
they gave us a room with two beds.

" That evening, while we were undressing, the corporal said to me: ' I am capable of sleeping two whole
days without waking.' I, too, promised myself a rest
of at least twelve hours. We reckoned without our
host, as you will see.

" It was scarcely daybreak when we were awakened
by a great tumult. A dozen rough-looking men entered our room, and ordered us, in Italian, to dress ourselves. They were too strong for us, so we obeyed;
and an hour later we were in prison, confined in the
same cell. Our reflections, I confess, were not *couleur
de rose.*

" I well remember how the corporal said again and again, in that cool way of his: ' It will require four days to obtain our extradition, three days to take us back to Montaignac—that is seven days; it will take one day more to try me; so I have in all eight days to live."

" Upon my word! that was exactly what I thought," said the old soldier, approvingly.

" For five months," continued Maurice, " instead of saying ' good-night ' to each other, we said: ' To-morrow they will come for us.' But they did not come.

" We were kindly treated. They did not take away my money; and they willingly sold us little luxuries; they also granted us two hours of exercise each day in the court-yard, and even loaned us books to read. In short, I should not have had any particular cause to complain, if I had been allowed to receive or to forward letters, or if I had been able to communicate with my father or with Marie-Anne. But we were in the secret cells, and were not allowed to have any intercourse with the other prisoners.

" At length our detention seemed so strange and became so insupportable to us, that we resolved to obtain some explanation of it, cost what it might.

" We changed our tactics. Up to that time we had been quite submissive; we suddenly became violent and intractable. We made the prison resound with our cries and protestations; we were continually sending for the superintendent; we claimed the intervention of the French ambassador. We were not obliged to wait long for the result.

" One fine afternoon, the superintendent released us, not without expressing much regret at being deprived of the society of such amiable and charming guests.

" Our first act, as you may suppose, was to run to the ambassador. We did not see that dignitary, but his secretary received us. He knit his brows when I told my story, and became excessively grave. I remember each word of his reply.

" ' Monsieur,' said he, ' I can swear that the persecution of which you have been the object in France had nothing whatever to do with your detention here.'

" And as I expressed my astonishment:

" ' One moment,' he added. ' I shall express my opinion very frankly. One of your enemies—I leave you to discover which one—must exert a very powerful influence in Turin. You were in his way, perhaps: he had you imprisoned by the Piedmontese police. ' "

With a heavy blow of his clinched fist, Jean Lacheneur made the table beside him reel.

" Ah! the secretary was right! " he exclaimed. " Maurice, it was Martial de Sairmeuse who caused your arrest——"

" Or the Marquis de Courtornieu," interrupted the abbé, with a warning glance at Jean.

A wrathful light gleamed for an instant in the eyes of Maurice; but it vanished almost immediately, and he shrugged his shoulders carelessly.

" Nonsense," said he, " I do not wish to trouble myself any more about the past. My father is well again, that is the main thing. We can easily find some way of getting him safely across the frontier. Marie-Anne and I, by our devotion, will strive to make him forget that my rashness almost cost him his life. He is so good, so indulgent to the faults of others. We will take up our residence in Italy or in Switzerland. You will accompany us, Monsieur l'Abbé, and you also, Jean. As for you, corporal, it is decided that you belong to our family."

Nothing could be more horrible than to see this man, upon whose life such a terrible blight was about to fall, so bright and full of hope and confidence.

The impression produced upon Jean and the *abbé* was so terrible, that, in spite of their efforts, it showed itself in their faces; and Maurice remarked their agitation.

" What is the matter? " he inquired, in evident surprise.

They trembled, hung their heads, but did not say a word.

The unfortunate man's astonishment changed to a vague, inexpressible fear.

He enumerated all the misfortunes which could possibly have befallen him.

" What has happened? " he asked, in a stifled voice. " My father is safe, is he not? You said that my mother would desire nothing, if I were with her again. Is it Marie-Anne——"

He hesitated.

" Courage, Maurice," murmured the *abbé*. " Courage! "

The stricken man tottered as if about to fall; his face grew whiter than the plastered wall against which he leaned for support.

" Marie-Anne is dead! " he exclaimed.

Jean and the *abbé* were silent.

" Dead! " Maurice repeated—" and no secret voice warned me! Dead! when? "

" She died only last night," replied Jean.

Maurice rose.

" Last night? " said he. " In that case, then, she is still here. Where? upstairs? "

And without waiting for any response, he darted

toward the staircase so quickly that neither Jean nor the *abbé* had time to intercept him.

With three bounds he reached the chamber; he walked straight to the bed, and with a firm hand turned back the sheet that hid the face of the dead.

He recoiled with a heart-broken cry.

Was this indeed the beautiful, the radiant Marie-Anne, whom he had loved to his own undoing! He did not recognize her.

He could not recognize these distorted features, this face swollen and discolored by poison, these eyes which were almost concealed by the purple swelling around them.

When Jean and the priest entered the room they found him standing with head thrown back, eyes dilated with terror, and rigid arm extended toward the corpse.

" Maurice," said the priest, gently, " be calm. Courage! "

He turned with an expression of complete bewilderment upon his features.

" Yes," he faltered, " that is what I need—courage! "

He staggered; they were obliged to support him to an arm-chair.

" Be a man," continued the priest; " where is your energy? To live, is to suffer."

He listened, but did not seem to comprehend.

" Live! " he murmured, " why should I desire to live since she is dead? "

The dread light of insanity glittered in his dry eyes. The *abbé* was alarmed.

" If he does not weep, he will lose his reason! " he thought.

And in an imperious voice, he said:

"You have no right to despair thus; you owe a sacred duty to your child."

The recollection which had given Marie-Anne strength to hold death at bay for a moment, saved Maurice from the dangerous torpor into which he was sinking. He trembled as if he had received an electric shock, and springing from his chair:

"That is true," he cried. "Take me to my child."

"Not just now, Maurice; wait a little."

"Where is it? Tell me where it is."

"I cannot; I do not know."

An expression of unspeakable anguish stole over the face of Maurice, and in a husky voice he said:

"What! you do not know! Did she not confide in you?"

"No. I suspected her secret. I alone——"

"You, alone! Then the child is dead, perhaps. Even if it is living, who can tell me where it is?"

"We shall undoubtedly find something that will give us a clew."

"You are right," faltered the wretched man. "When Marie-Anne knew that her life was in danger, she would not have forgotten her child. Those who cared for her in her last moments must have received some message for me. I wish to see those who watched over her. Who were they?"

The priest averted his face.

"I asked you who was with her when she died," repeated Maurice, in a sort of frenzy.

And, as the *abbé* remained silent, a terrible light dawned on the mind of the stricken man. He understood the cause of Marie-Anne's distorted features now.

"She perished the victim of a crime!" he exclaimed.

" Some monster has killed her. If she died such a death, our child is lost forever! And it was I who recommended, who commanded the greatest precautions! Ah! it is a curse upon me!"

He sank back in his chair, overwhelmed with sorrow and remorse, and silent tears rolled slowly down his cheeks.

" He is saved!" thought the *abbé,* whose heart bled at the sight of such despair. Suddenly someone plucked him by the sleeve.

It was Jean Lacheneur, and he drew the priest into the embrasure of a window.

" What is this about a child?" he asked, harshly.

A flood of crimson suffused the brow of the priest.

" You have heard," he responded, laconically.

" Am I to understand that Marie-Anne was the mistress of Maurice, and that she had a child by him? Is this true? I will not—I cannot believe it! She, whom I revered as a saint! Did her pure forehead and her chaste looks lie? And he—Maurice—he whom I loved as a brother! So, his friendship was only a mask assumed to enable him to steal our honor!"

He hissed these words through his set teeth in such low tones that Maurice, absorbed in his agony of grief, did not overhear him.

" But how did she conceal her shame?" he continued. " No one suspected it—absolutely no one. And what has she done with her child? Appalled by a dread of disgrace, did she commit the crime committed by so many other ruined and forsaken women? Did she murder her own child?"

A hideous smile curved his thin lips.

" If the child is alive," he added, " I will find it, and Maurice shall be punished for his perfidy as he deserves."

He paused; the sound of horses' hoofs upon the road attracted his attention, and that of Abbé Midon.

They glanced out of the window and saw a horseman stop before the little footpath, alight from his horse, throw the reins to his groom, and advance toward the Borderie.

At the sight of the visitor, Jean Lacheneur uttered the frightful howl of an infuriated wild beast.

" The Marquis de Sairmeuse here ! " he exclaimed.

He sprang to Maurice, and shaking him violently, he cried:

" Up ! here is Martial, Marie-Anne's murderer ! Up ! he is coming ! he is at our mercy ! "

Maurice sprang up in a fury of passion, but the *abbé* darted to the door and intercepted the infuriated men as they were about to leave the room.

" Not a word, young men, not a threat ! " he said, imperiously. " I forbid it. At least respect the dead who is lying here ! "

There was such an irresistible authority in his words and glance, that Jean and Maurice stood as if turned to stone.

Before the priest had time to say more, Martial was there.

He did not cross the threshold. With a glance he took in the whole scene; he turned very pale, but not a gesture, not a word escaped his lips.

Wonderful as was his accustomed control over himself, he could not articulate a syllable; and it was only by pointing to the bed upon which Marie-Anne's lifeless form was reposing, that he asked an explanation.

" She was infamously poisoned last evening," replied the *abbé*, sadly.

Maurice, forgetting the priest's commands, stepped forward.

" She was alone and defenceless. I have been at liberty only two days. But I know the name of the man who had me arrested at Turin, and thrown into prison. They told me the coward's name ! "

Instinctively Martial recoiled.

" It was you, infamous wretch ! " exclaimed Maurice. " You confess your guilt, scoundrel ? "

Once again the *abbé* interposed ; he threw himself between the rivals, persuaded that Martial was about to attack Maurice.

But no ; the Marquis de Sairmeuse had resumed the haughty and indifferent manner which was habitual to him. He took from his pocket a bulky envelope, and throwing it upon the table :

" Here," he said coldly, " is what I was bringing to Mademoiselle Lacheneur. It contains first a safe-conduct from His Majesty for Monsieur d'Escorval. From this moment, he is at liberty to leave Poignot's farm-house and return to Escorval. He is free, he is saved, he is granted a new trial, and there can be no doubt of his acquittal. Here is also a decree of his non-complicity rendered in favor of Abbé Midon, and an order from the bishop which reinstates him as Cure of Sairmeuse ; and lastly, a discharge, drawn up in due form, and an acknowledged right to a pension in the name of Corporal Bavois."

He paused, and as his astonished hearers stood rooted to their places with wonder, he turned and approached Marie-Anne's bedside.

With hand uplifted to heaven over the lifeless form of her whom he had loved, and in a voice that would have made the murderess tremble in her innermost soul, he said, solemnly :

" To you, Marie-Anne, I swear that I will avenge you ! "

For a few seconds he stood motionless, then suddenly he stopped, pressed a kiss upon the dead girl's brow, and left the room.

" And you think that man can be guilty ! " exclaimed the *abbé*.   " You see, Jean, that you are mad ! "

" And this last insult to my dead sister is an honor, I suppose," said Jean, with a furious gesture.

"And the wretch binds my hands by saving my father ! " exclaimed Maurice.

From his place by the window, the *abbé* saw Martial remount his horse.

But the marquis did not take the road to Montaignac. It was toward the Château de Courtornieu that he hastened.

CHAPTER XLVIII

The reason of Mme. Blanche had sustained a frightful shock, when Chupin was obliged to lift her and carry her from Marie-Anne's chamber.

But she lost consciousness entirely when she saw the old poacher stricken down by her side.

On and after that night Aunt Medea took her revenge for all the slights she had received.

Scarcely tolerated until then, at Courtornieu, she henceforth made herself respected, and even feared.

She, who usually swooned if a kitten hurt itself, did not utter a cry.   Her extreme fear gave her the courage that not unfrequently animates cowards when they are in some dire extremity.

She seized the arm of her bewildered niece, and, by dint of dragging and pushing, had her back at the château in much less time than it had taken them to go to the Borderie.

It was half-past one o'clock when they reached the little garden-gate, by which they had left the grounds.

No one in the château was aware of their long absence.

This was due to several different circumstances. First, to the precautions taken by Blanche, who had given orders, before going out, that no one should come to her room, on any pretext whatever, unless she rang.

It also chanced to be the birthday of the marquis's *valet de chambre*. The servants had dined more sumptuously than usual. They had toasts and songs over their dessert; and at the conclusion of the repast, they amused themselves by an extempore ball.

They were still dancing at half-past one; all the doors were open, and the two ladies succeeded in gaining the chamber of Blanche without being observed.

When the doors of the apartment had been securely closed, and when there was no longer any fear of listeners, Aunt Medea attacked her niece.

" Now will you explain what happened at the Borderie; and what you were doing there? " she inquired.

Blanche shuddered.

" Why do you wish to know? " she asked.

" Because I suffered agony during the three hours that I spent in waiting for you. What was the meaning of those despairing cries that I heard? Why did you call for aid? I heard a death-rattle that made my hair stand on end with terror. Why was it necessary for Chupin to bring you out in his arms? "

Aunt Medea would have packed her trunks, perhaps, that very evening, had she seen the glance which her niece bestowed upon her.

Blanche longed for power to annihilate this relative

—this witness who might ruin her by a word, but whom she would ever have beside her, a living reproach for her crime.

"You do not answer me," insisted Aunt Medea.

Blanche was trying to decide whether it would be better for her to reveal the truth, horrible as it was, or to invent some plausible explanation.

To confess all! It would be intolerable. She would place herself, body and soul, in Aunt Medea's power.

But, on the other hand, if she deceived her, was it not more than probable that her aunt would betray her by some involuntary exclamation when she heard of the crime which had been committed at the Borderie?

"For she is so stupid!" thought Blanche.

She felt that it would be the wisest plan, under such circumstances, to be perfectly frank, to teach her relative her lesson, and to imbue her with some of her own firmness.

Having come to this conclusion, she disdained all concealment.

"Ah, well!" she said, "I was jealous of Marie-Anne. I thought she was Martial's mistress. I was half crazed, and I killed her."

She expected despairing cries, or a fainting fit; nothing of the kind. Stupid though Aunt Medea was, she had divined the truth before she interrogated her niece. Besides, the insults she had received for years had extinguished every generous sentiment, dried up the springs of emotion, and destroyed every particle of moral sensibility she had ever possessed.

"Ah!" she exclaimed, "it is terrible! What if it should be discovered!"

Then she shed a few tears, but not more than she had often wept for some trifle.

Blanche breathed more freely. Surely she could count upon the silence and absolute submission of her dependent relative. Convinced of this, she began to recount all the details of the frightful drama which had been enacted at the Borderie.

She yielded to a desire which was stronger than her own will; to the wild longing that sometimes unbinds the tongue of the worst criminals, and forces them— irresistibly impels them—to talk of their crimes, even when they distrust their confidant.

But when she came to the proofs which had convinced her of her lamentable mistake, she suddenly paused in dismay.

That certificate of marriage signed by the Curé of Vigano: what had she done with it? where was it? She remembered holding it in her hands.

She sprang up, examined the pocket of her dress and uttered a cry of joy. She had it safe. She threw it into a drawer, and turned the key.

Aunt Medea wished to retire to her own room, but Blanche entreated her to remain. She was unwilling to be left alone—she dared not—she was afraid.

And as if she desired to silence the inward voice that tormented her, she talked with extreme volubility, repeating again and again that she was ready to do anything in expiation of her crime, and that she would brave impossibilities to recover Marie-Anne's child.

And certainly, the task was both difficult and dangerous.

If she sought the child openly, it would be equivalent to a confession of guilt. She would be compelled to act secretly, and with great caution.

"But I shall succeed," she said. "I will spare no expense."

And remembering her vow, and the threats of her dying victim, she added:

" I must succeed. I have sworn—and I was forgiven under those conditions."

Astonishment dried the ever-ready tears of Aunt Medea.

That her niece, with her dreadful crime still fresh in her mind, could coolly reason, deliberate, and make plans for the future, seemed to her incomprehensible.

" What an iron will ! " she thought.

But in her bewilderment she quite overlooked something that would have enlightened any ordinary observer.

Blanche was seated upon her bed, her hair was unbound, her eyes were glittering with delirium, and her incoherent words and her excited gestures betrayed the frightful anxiety that was torturing her.

And she talked and talked, exclaiming, questioning Aunt Medea, and forcing her to reply, only that she might escape from her own thoughts.

Morning had dawned some time before, and the servants were heard bustling about the château, and Blanche, oblivious to all around her, was still explaining how she could, in less than a year, restore Marie-Anne's child to Maurice d'Escorval.

She paused abruptly in the middle of a sentence.

Instinct had suddenly warned her of the danger she incurred in making the slightest change in her habits.

She sent Aunt Medea away, then, at the usual hour, rang for her maid.

It was nearly eleven o'clock, and she was just completing her toilet, when the ringing of the bell announced a visitor.

Almost immediately a maid appeared, evidently in a state of great excitement.

"What is it?" inquired Blanche, eagerly. "Who has come?"

"Ah, Madame—that is, Mademoiselle, if you only knew——"

"*Will* you speak?"

"The Marquis de Sairmeuse is below, in the blue drawing-room; and he begs Mademoiselle to grant him a few moments' conversation."

Had a thunder-bolt riven the earth at the feet of the murderess, she could not have been more terrified.

"All must have been discovered!" this was her first thought. That alone would have brought Martial there.

She almost decided to reply that she was not at home, or that she was extremely ill; but reason told her that she was alarming herself needlessly, perhaps, and that, in any case, the worst was preferable to suspense.

"Tell the marquis that I will be there in a moment," she replied.

She desired a few minutes of solitude to compose her features, to regain her self-possession, if possible, and to conquer the nervous trembling that made her shake like a leaf.

But just as she was most disquieted by the thought of her peril, a sudden inspiration brought a malicious smile to her lip.

"Ah!" she thought, "my agitation will seem perfectly natural. It may even be made of service."

As she descended the grand staircase, she could not help saying to herself:

"Martial's presence here is incomprehensible."

It was certainly very extraordinary; and it had not been without much hesitation that he resolved upon this painful step.

But it was the only means of procuring several important documents which were indispensable in the revision of M. d'Escorval's case.

These documents, after the baron's condemnation, had been left in the hands of the Marquis de Courtornieu. Now that he had lost his reason, it was impossible to ask him for them; and Martial was obliged to apply to the daughter for permission to search for them among her father's papers.

This was why Martial said to himself that morning: " I will carry the baron's safe-conduct to Marie-Anne, and then I will push on to Courtornieu."

He arrived at the Borderie gay and confident, his heart full of hope. Alas! Marie-Anne was dead.

No one would ever know what a terrible blow it had been to Martial; and his conscience told him that he was not free from blame; that he had, at least, rendered the execution of the crime an easy matter.

For it was indeed he who, by abusing his influence, had caused the arrest of Maurice at Turin.

But though he was capable of the basest perfidy when his love was at stake, he was incapable of virulent animosity.

Marie-Anne was dead; he had it in his power to revoke the benefits he had conferred, but the thought of doing so never once occurred to him. And when Jean and Maurice insulted him, he revenged himself only by overwhelming them by his magnanimity. When he left the Borderie, pale as a ghost, his lips still cold from the kiss pressed on the brow of the dead, he said to himself:

" For her sake, I will go to Courtornieu. In memory of her, the baron must be saved."

By the expression on the faces of the valets when

he dismounted in the court-yard of the château and asked to see Mme. Blanche, the marquis was again reminded of the profound sensation which this unexpected visit would produce. But, what did it matter to him? He was passing through one of those crises in which the mind can conceive of no further misfortune, and is therefore indifferent to everything.

Still he trembled when they ushered him into the blue drawing-room. He remembered the room well. It was here that Blanche had been wont to receive him in days gone by, when his fancy was vacillating between her and Marie-Anne.

How many pleasant hours they had passed together here! He seemed to see Blanche again, as she was then, radiant with youth, gay and laughing. Her naïveté was affected, perhaps, but was it any the less charming on that account?

At this very moment Blanche entered the room. She looked so careworn and sad that he scarcely knew her. His heart was touched by the look of patient sorrow imprinted upon her features.

" How much you must have suffered, Blanche," he murmured, scarcely knowing what he said.

It cost her an effort to repress her secret joy. She saw that he knew nothing of her crime. She noticed his emotion, and saw the profit she could derive from it.

" I can never cease to regret having displeased you," she replied, humbly and sadly. " I shall never be consoled."

She had touched the vulnerable spot in every man's heart.

For there is no man so sceptical, so cold, or so *blasé* that his vanity is not pleased with the thought that a woman is dying for his sake.

There is no man who is not moved by this most delicious flattery, and who is not ready and willing to give, at least, a tender pity in exchange for such devotion.

" Is it possible that you could forgive me? " stammered Martial.

The wily enchantress averted her face as if to prevent him from reading in her eyes a weakness of which she was ashamed. It was the most eloquent of replies.

But Martial said no more on this subject. He made known his petition, which was granted, then fearing, perhaps, to promise too much, he said:

" Since you do not forbid it, Blanche, I will return— to-morrow—another day."

As he rode back to Montaignac, Martial's thoughts were busy.

" She really loves me," he thought; " that pallor, that weakness could not be feigned. Poor girl! she is my wife, after all. The reasons that influenced me in my rupture with her father exist no longer, and the Marquis de Courtornieu may be regarded as dead."

All the inhabitants of Sairmeuse were congregated on the public square when Martial passed through the village. They had just heard of the murder at the Borderie, and the *abbé* was now closeted with the justice of the peace, relating the circumstances of the poisoning.

After a prolonged inquest the following verdict was rendered: " That a man known as Chupin, a notoriously bad character, had entered the house of Marie-Anne Lacheneur, and taken advantage of her absence to mingle poison with her food."

The report added that: " Said Chupin had been himself assassinated, soon after his crime, by a certain Balstain, whose whereabouts were unknown."

But this affair interested the community much less than the visits which Martial was paying to Mme. Blanche.

It was soon rumored that the Marquis and the Marquise de Sairmeuse were reconciled, and in a few weeks they left for Paris with the intention of residing there permanently. A few days after their departure, the eldest of the Chupins announced his determination of taking up his abode in the same great city.

Some of his friends endeavored to dissuade him, assuring him that he would certainly die of starvation.

"Nonsense!" he replied, with singular assurance; "I, on the contrary, have an idea that I shall not want for anything there."

CHAPTER XLIX

Time gradually heals all wounds, and in less than a year it was difficult to discern any trace of the fierce whirlwind of passion which had devastated the peaceful valley of the Oiselle.

What remained to attest the reality of all these events, which, though they were so recent, had already been relegated to the domain of the legendary?

A charred ruin on the Reche.

A grave in the cemetery, upon which was inscribed: "MARIE-ANNE LACHENEUR, DIED AT THE AGE OF TWENTY. PRAY FOR HER!"

Only a few, the oldest men and the politicians of the village, forgot their solicitude in regard to the crops to remember this episode.

Sometimes, during the long winter evenings, when they had gathered at the Bœuf Couronne, they laid down their greasy cards and gravely discussed the events of the past years.

They never failed to remark that almost all the actors in that bloody drama at Montaignac had, in common parlance, " come to a bad end."

Victors and vanquished seemed to be pursued by the same inexorable fatality.

Look at the names already upon the fatal list !

Lacheneur, beheaded.

Chanlouineau, shot.

Marie-Anne, poisoned.

Chupin, the traitor, assassinated.

The Marquis de Courtornieu lived, or rather survived, but death would have seemed a mercy in comparison with such total annihilation of intelligence. He had fallen below the level of the brute, which is, at least, endowed with instinct. Since the departure of his daughter he had been cared for by two servants, who did not allow him to give them much trouble, and when they desired to go out they shut him up, not in his chamber, but in the cellar, to prevent his ravings and shrieks from being heard from without.

If people supposed for awhile that the Sairmeuse would escape the fate of the others, they were mistaken. It was not long before the curse fell upon them.

One fine morning in the month of December, the duke left the château to take part in a wolf-hunt in the neighborhood.

At nightfall, his horse returned, panting, covered with foam, and riderless.

What had become of its master?

A search was instituted at once, and all night long twenty men, bearing torches, wandered through the woods, shouting and calling at the top of their voices.

Five days went by, and the search for the missing man was almost abandoned, when a shepherd lad, pale with fear, came to the château one morning to tell them that he had discovered, at the base of a precipice, the bloody and mangled body of the Duc de Sairmeuse.

It seemed strange that such an excellent rider should have met with such a fate. There might have been some doubt as to its being an accident, had it not been for the explanation given by the grooms.

"The duke was riding an exceedingly vicious beast," said these men. "She was always taking fright and shying at everything."

The following week Jean Lacheneur left the neighborhood.

The conduct of this singular man had caused much comment. When Marie-Anne died, he at first refused his inheritance.

"I wish nothing that came to her through Chanlouineau," he said everywhere, thus calumniating the memory of his sister as he had calumniated her when alive.

Then, after a short absence, and without any apparent reason, he suddenly changed his mind.

He not only accepted the property, but made all possible haste to obtain possession of it. He made many excuses; and, if one might believe him, he was not acting in his own interest, but merely conforming to the wishes of his deceased sister; and he declared that not a penny would go into his pockets.

This much is certain, as soon as he obtained legal possession of the estate, he sold all the property, troubling himself but little in regard to the price he received, provided the purchasers paid cash.

He reserved only the furniture of the sumptuously adorned chamber at the Borderie. These articles he burned.

This strange act was the talk of the neighborhood.

"The poor young man has lost his reason!" was the almost universal opinion.

And those who doubted it, doubted it no longer when it became known that Jean Lacheneur had formed an engagement with a company of strolling players who stopped at Montaignac for a few days.

But the young man had not wanted for good advice and kind friends. M. d'Escorval and the *abbé* had exerted all their eloquence to induce him to return to Paris, and complete his studies; but in vain.

The necessity for concealment no longer existed, either in the case of the baron or the priest.

Thanks to Martial de Sairmeuse they were now installed, the one in the presbytery, the other at Escorval, as in days gone by.

Acquitted at his new trial, restored to the possession of his property, reminded of his frightful fall only by a very slight lameness, the baron would have deemed himself a fortunate man, had it not been for his great anxiety on his son's account.

Poor Maurice! his heart was broken by the sound of the clods of earth falling upon Marie-Anne's coffin; and his very life now seemed dependent upon the hope of finding his child.

Assured of the powerful assistance of Abbé Midon, he had confessed all to his father, and confided his secret to Corporal Bavois, who was an honored guest at Escorval; and these devoted friends had promised him all possible aid.

The task was very difficult, however, and certain resolutions on the part of Maurice greatly diminished the chance of success.

Unlike Jean, he was determined to guard religiously

the honor of the dead; and he had made his friends promise that Marie-Anne's name should not be mentioned in prosecuting the search.

"We shall succeed all the same," said the *abbé*, kindly; "with time and patience any mystery can be solved."

He divided the department into a certain number of districts; then one of the little band went each day from house to house questioning the inmates, but not without extreme caution, for fear of arousing suspicion, for a peasant becomes intractable at once if his suspicions are aroused.

But the weeks went by, and the quest was fruitless. Maurice was deeply discouraged.

"My child died on coming into the world," he said, again and again.

But the *abbé* reassured him.

"I am morally certain that such was not the case," he replied. "I know, by Marie-Anne's absence, the date of her child's birth. I saw her after her recovery; she was comparatively gay and smiling. Draw your own conclusions."

"And yet there is not a nook or corner for miles around which we have not explored."

"True; but we must extend the circle of our investigations."

The priest, now, was only striving to gain time, knowing full well that it is the sovereign balm for all sorrows.

His confidence, which had been very great at first, had been sensibly diminished by the responses of an old woman, who passed for one of the greatest gossips in the community.

Adroitly interrogated, the worthy dame replied that

she knew nothing of such a child, but that there must be one in the neighborhood, since it was the third time she had been questioned on the subject.

Intense as was his surprise, the *abbé* succeeded in hiding it.

He set the old gossip to talking, and after a two hours' conversation, he arrived at the conclusion that two persons besides Maurice were searching for Marie-Anne's child.

Why, with what aim, and who these persons could be the *abbé* was unable to ascertain.

" Ah! rascals have their uses after all," he thought. " If we only had a man like Chupin to set upon the track! "

But the old poacher was dead, and his eldest son— the one who knew Blanche de Courtornieu's secret— was in Paris.

Only the widow and the second son remained in Sairmeuse.

They had not, as yet, succeeded in discovering the twenty thousand francs, but the fever for gold was burning in their veins, and they persisted in their search. From morning until night the mother and son toiled on, until the earth around their hut had been explored to the depth of six feet.

A word dropped by a peasant one day put an end to these researches.

" Really, my boy," he said, addressing young Chupin, " I did not suppose you were such a fool as to persist in hunting birds' nests after the birds have flown. Your brother, who is in Paris, can undoubtedly tell you where the treasure was concealed."

The younger Chupin uttered the fierce roar of a wild beast.

"Holy Virgin! you are right!" he exclaimed.
"Wait until I get money enough to take me to Paris,
and we will see."

CHAPTER L

Martial de Sairmeuse's unexpected visit to the Château de Courtornieu had alarmed Aunt Medea even
more than Blanche.

In ten seconds, more ideas passed through her brain
than had visited it for ten years.

She saw the *gendarmes* at the château; she saw her
niece arrested, incarcerated in the Montaignac prison,
and brought before the Court of Assizes.

If this were all she had to fear! But suppose she,
too, were compromised, suspected of complicity,
dragged before the judge, and even accused of being
the sole culprit!

Finding the suspense intolerable, she left her room;
and, stealing on tiptoe to the great drawing-room, she
applied her ear to the door of the little blue *salon,* in
which Blanche and Martial were seated.

The conversation which she heard convinced her
that her fears were groundless.

She drew a long breath, as if a mighty burden had
been lifted from her breast. But a new idea, which
was to grow, flourish, and bear fruit, had just taken
root in her brain.

When Martial left the room, Aunt Medea at once
opened the communicating door and entered the blue
salon, thus avowing that she had been a listener.

Twenty-four hours earlier she would not have
dreamed of committing such an enormity.

"Well, Blanche, we were frightened at nothing,"
she exclaimed.

Blanche did not reply.

She was deliberating, forcing herself to weigh the probable consequences of all these events which had succeeded each other with such marvellous rapidity.

"Perhaps the hour of my revenge is almost here," murmured Blanche, as if communing with herself.

"What do you say?" inquired Aunt Medea, with evident curiosity.

"I say, aunt, that in less than a month I shall be Marquise de Sairmeuse in reality as well as in name. My husband will return to me, and then—oh, then!"

"God grant it!" said Aunt Medea, hypocritically.

In her secret heart she had but little faith in this prediction, and whether it was realized or not mattered little to her.

"Still another proof that your jealousy led you astray; and that—that what you did at the Borderie was unnecessary," she said, in that low tone that accomplices always use in speaking of their crime.

Such had been the opinion of Blanche; but she now shook her head, and gloomily replied:

"You are wrong; that which took place at the Borderie has restored my husband to me. I understand it all, now. It is true that Marie-Anne was not Martial's mistress, but Martial loved her. He loved her, and the rebuffs which he received only increased his passion. It was for her sake that he abandoned me; and never, while she lived, would he have thought of me. His emotion on seeing me was the remnant of the emotion which had been awakened by another. His tenderness was only the expression of his sorrow. Whatever happens, I shall have only her leavings— what she has disdained!" the young marquise added, bitterly; and her eyes flashed, and she stamped her foot

in ungovernable anger. " And shall I regret what I
have done? " she exclaimed; " never! no, never! "

From that moment, she was herself again, brave and
determined.

But horrible fears assailed her when the inquest began.

Officials came from Montaignac charged with investigating the affair. They examined a host of witnesses,
and there was even talk of sending to Paris for one of
those detectives skilled in unravelling all the mysteries
of crime.

Aunt Medea was half crazed with terror; and her
fear was so apparent that it caused Blanche great anxiety.

" You will end by betraying us," she remarked, one
evening.

" Ah! my terror is beyond my control."

" If that is the case, do not leave your room."

" It would be more prudent, certainly."

" You can say that you are not well; your meals
shall be served in your own apartment."

Aunt Medea's face brightened. In her inmost heart
she was enraptured. To have her meals served in her
own room, in her bed in the morning, and on a little
table by the fire in the evening, had long been the ambition and the dream of the poor dependent. But how
to accomplish it! Two or three times, being a trifle
indisposed, she had ventured to ask if her breakfast
might be brought to her room, but her request had
been harshly refused.

" If Aunt Medea is hungry, she will come down and
take her place at the table as usual," had been the response of Mme. Blanche.

To be treated in this way in a château where there

were a dozen servants standing about idle was hard indeed.

But now——

Every morning, in obedience to a formal order from Blanche, the cook came up to receive Aunt Medea's commands; she was permitted to dictate the bill-of-fare each day, and to order the dishes that she preferred.

These new joys awakened many strange thoughts in her mind, and dissipated much of the regret which she had felt for the crime at the Borderie.

The inquest was the subject of all her conversation with her niece. They had all the latest information in regard to the facts developed by the investigation through the butler, who took a great interest in such matters, and who had won the good-will of the agents from Montaignac, by making them familiar with the contents of his wine-cellar.

Through him, Blanche and her aunt learned that suspicion pointed to the deceased Chupin. Had he not been seen prowling around the Borderie on the very evening that the crime was committed? The testimony of the young peasant who had warned Jean Lacheneur seemed decisive.

The motive was evident; at least, everyone thought so. Twenty persons had heard Chupin declare, with frightful oaths, that he should never be tranquil in mind while a Lacheneur was left upon earth.

So that which might have ruined Blanche, saved her; and the death of the old poacher seemed really providential.

Why should she suspect that Chupin had revealed her secret before his death?

When the butler told her that the judges and the

police agents had returned to Montaignac, she had great difficulty in concealing her joy.

" There is no longer anything to fear," she said to Aunt Medea.

She had, indeed, escaped the justice of man. There remained the justice of God.

A few weeks before, this thought of " the justice of God " might, perhaps, have brought a smile to the lips of Mme. Blanche.

She then regarded it as an imaginary evil, designed to hold timorous spirits in check.

On the morning that followed her crime, she almost shrugged her shoulders at the thought of Marie-Anne's dying threats.

She remembered her promise, but she did not intend to fulfil it.

She had considered the matter, and she saw the terrible risk to which she exposed herself if she endeavored to find the missing child.

" The father will be sure to discover it," she thought.

But she was to realize the power of her victim's threats that same evening.

Overcome with fatigue, she retired to her room at an early hour, and instead of reading, as she was accustomed to do before retiring, she extinguished her candle as soon as she had undressed, saying:

" I must sleep."

But sleep had fled. Her crime was ever in her thoughts; it rose before her in all its horror and atrocity. She knew that she was lying upon her bed, at Courtornieu; and yet it seemed as if she was there in Chanlouineau's house, pouring out poison, then watching its effects, concealed in the dressing-room.

She was struggling against these thoughts; she was

exerting all her strength of will to drive away these terrible memories, when she thought she heard the key turn in the lock.   She lifted her head from the pillow with a start.

Then, by the uncertain light of her night-lamp, she thought she saw the door open slowly and noiselessly. Marie-Anne entered—gliding in like a phantom.   She seated herself in an arm-chair near the bed.   Great tears were rolling down her cheeks, and she looked sadly, yet threateningly, around her.

The murderess hid her face under the bed-covers; and her whole body was bathed in an icy perspiration. For her, this was not a mere apparition—it was a frightful reality.

But hers was not a nature to submit unresistingly to such an impression.   She shook off the stupor that was creeping over her, and tried to reason with herself aloud, as if the sound of her voice would reassure her.

" I am dreaming! " she said.   " Do the dead return to life?   Am I childish enough to be frightened by phantoms born of my own imaginations? "

She said this, but the phantom did not disappear.

She shut her eyes, but still she saw it through her closed eyelids—through the coverings which she had drawn up over her head, she saw it still.

Not until daybreak did Mme. Blanche fall asleep.

And it was the same the next night, and the night following that, and always and always; and the terrors of each night were augmented by the terrors of the nights which had preceded it.

During the day, in the bright sunshine, she regained her courage, and became sceptical again.   Then she railed at herself.

" To be afraid of something that does not exist, is

folly!" she said, vehemently. "To-night I will conquer my absurd weakness."

But when evening came all her brave resolution vanished, and the same fear seized her when night appeared with its *cortége* of spectres.

It is true that Mme. Blanche attributed her tortures at night to the disquietude she suffered during
the day.

For the officials were at Sairmeuse, then, and she
trembled. A mere nothing might divert suspicion
from Chupin and direct it toward her. What if some
peasant had seen her with Chupin? What if some
trifling circumstance should furnish a clew which
would lead straight to Courtornieu?

"When the investigation is over, I shall forget," she
thought.

It ended, but she did not forget.

Darwin has said:

"It is when their safety is assured that great criminals really feel remorse."

Mme. Blanche might have vouched for the truth
of this assertion, made by the most profound thinker
and closest observer of the age.

And yet, the agony she was enduring did not make
her abandon, for a single moment, the plan she had
conceived on the day of Martial's visit.

She played her part so well, that, deeply moved, almost repentant, he returned five or six times, and at
last, one day, he besought her to allow him to remain.

But even the joy of this triumph did not restore her
peace of mind.

Between her and her husband rose that dread apparition; and Marie-Anne's distorted features were ever
before her. She knew only too well that this heart-

broken man had no love to give her, and that she
would never have the slightest influence over him.
And to crown all, to her already intolerable sufferings
was added another, more poignant than all the rest.

Speaking one evening of Marie-Anne's death, Martial forgot himself, and spoke of his oath of vengeance.
He deeply regretted that Chupin was dead, he remarked, for he should have experienced an intense delight in making the wretch who murdered her *die*
a lingering death in the midst of the most frightful tortures.

He spoke with extreme violence and in a voice vibrant with his still powerful passion.

And Blanche, in terror, asked herself what would
be her fate if her husband ever discovered that she was
the culprit—and he might discover it.

She now began to regret that she had not kept the
promise she had made to her victim; and she resolved
to commence the search for Marie-Anne's child.

To do this effectually it was necessary for her to be
in a large city—Paris, for example—where she could
procure discreet and skilful agents.

It was necessary to persuade Martial to remove to
the capital. Aided by the Duc de Sairmeuse, she did
not find this a very difficult task; and one morning,
Mme. Blanche, with a radiant face, announced to
Aunt Medea:

"Aunt, we leave just one week from to-day."

CHAPTER LI

Beset by a thousand fears and anxieties, Blanche had failed to notice that Aunt Medea was no longer the same.

The change, it is true, had been gradual; it had not struck the servants, but it was none the less positive and real, and it betrayed itself in numberless trifles.

For example, though the poor dependent still retained her humble, resigned manner; she had lost, little by little, the servile fear that had showed itself in her every movement. She no longer trembled when anyone addressed her, and there was occasionally a ring of independence in her voice.

If visitors were present, she no longer kept herself modestly in the background, but drew forward her chair and took part in the conversation. At table, she allowed her preferences and her dislikes to appear. On two or three occasions she had ventured to differ from her niece in opinion, and had even been so bold as to question the propriety of some of her orders.

Once, Mme. Blanche, on going out, asked Aunt Medea to accompany her; but the latter declared she had a cold, and remained at home.

And, on the following Sunday, although Blanche did not wish to attend vespers, Aunt Medea declared her intention of going; and as it rained, she requested the coachman to harness the horses to the carriage, which was done.

All this was nothing, in appearance; in reality, it was monstrous, amazing. It was quite plain that the humble relative was becoming bold, even audacious, in her demands.

As this departure, which her niece had just announced so gayly, had never been discussed before her, she was greatly surprised.

"What! you are going away," she repeated; "you are leaving Courtornieu?"

"And without regret."

"To go where, pray?"

"To Paris. We shall reside there; that is decided. That is the place for my husband. His name, his fortune, his talents, the favor of the King, assure him a high position there. He will repurchase the Hôtel de Sairmeuse, and furnish it magnificently. We shall have a princely establishment."

All the torments of envy were visible upon Aunt Medea's countenance.

"And what is to become of me?" she asked, in plaintive tones.

"You, aunt! You will remain here; you will be mistress of the château. A trustworthy person must remain to watch over my poor father. You will be happy and contented here, I hope."

But no; Aunt Medea did not seem satisfied.

"I shall never have courage to stay all alone in this great château," she whined.

"You foolish woman! will you not have the servants, the gardeners, and the _concièrge_ to protect you?"

"That makes no difference. I am afraid of insane people. When the marquis began to rave and howl this evening, I felt as if I should go mad myself."

Blanche shrugged her shoulders.

"What _do_ you wish, then?" she asked, in a still more sarcastic manner.

"I thought—I wondered—if you would not take me with you."

"To Paris! You are crazy, I do believe. What would you do there?"

"Blanche, I entreat you, I beseech you, to do so!"

"Impossible, aunt; impossible!"

Aunt Medea seemed to be in despair.

"And what if I should tell you that I cannot remain here—that I dare not—that I should die!"

A flush of impatience dyed the cheek of Mme. Blanche.

"You weary me beyond endurance," she said, rudely.

And with a gesture that increased the harshness of her words, she added:

"If Courtornieu displeases you so much, there is nothing to prevent you from seeking a home more to your taste. You are free and of age."

Aunt Medea turned very pale, and she bit her lips until the blood came.

"That is to say," she said, at last, "you permit me to take my choice between dying of fear at Courtornieu and ending my days in a hospital. Thanks, my niece, thanks. That is like you. I expected nothing less of you. Thanks!"

She raised her head, and a dangerous light gleamed in her eyes. There was the hiss of a serpent in the voice in which she continued:

"Very well! this decides me. I entreated you, and you brutally refused to heed my prayer, now I command and I say: 'I will go!' Yes, I intend to go with you to Paris—and I shall go. Ah! it surprises you to hear poor, meek, much-abused Aunt Medea speak in this way. I have endured in silence for a long time, but I have rebelled at last. My life in this house has been a hell. It is true that you have given me shelter—that you have fed and lodged me; but you have taken my entire life in exchange. What servant ever endured what I have endured? Have you ever treated one of your maids as you have treated me, your own flesh and blood? And I have had no wages; on the contrary, I was expected to be grateful since I lived by your tolerance. Ah! you have made me pay dearly for the crime of being poor. How you have insulted me—humiliated me—trampled me under foot!"

She paused.

The bitter rancor which had been accumulating for years fairly choked her; but after a moment she resumed, in a tone of intense irony:

"You ask me what *I* would do in Paris? I, too, would enjoy myself. What will you do, yourself? You will go to Court, to balls, and to the play, will you not? Very well, I will accompany you. I will attend these *fêtes*. I will have handsome toilets, I—poor Aunt Medea—who have never seen myself in anything but shabby black woollen dresses. Have you ever thought of giving me the pleasure of possessing a handsome dress? Yes, twice a year, perhaps, you have given me a black silk, recommending me to take good care of it. But it was not for my sake that you went to this expense. It was for your own sake; and in order that your poor relation should do honor to your generosity. You dressed me in it, as you sew gold lace upon the clothing of your lackeys, through vanity. And I endured all this; I made myself insignificant and humble; buffeted upon one cheek, I offered the other. I must live—I must have food. And you, Blanche, how often, to make me subservient to your will, have you said to me: 'You will do thus-and-so, if you desire to remain at Courtornieu?' And

I obeyed—I was forced to obey, since I knew not where to go. Ah! you have abused me in every way; but now my turn has come!"

Blanche was so amazed that she could not articulate a syllable. At last, in a scarcely audible voice, she faltered:

"I do not understand you, aunt; I do not understand you."

The poor dependent shrugged her shoulders, as her niece had done a few moments before.

"In that case," said she, slowly, "I may as well tell you that since you have, against my will, made me your accomplice, we must share everything in common. I share the danger; I will share the pleasure. What if all should be discovered? Do you ever think of that? Yes; and that is why you are seeking diversion. Very well! I also desire diversion. I shall go to Paris with you."

By a terrible effort Blanche had succeeded in regaining her self-possession, in some measure at least.

"And if I should say no?" she responded, coldly.

"But you will not say no."

"And why, if you please?"

"Because——"

"Will you go to the authorities and denounce me?"

Aunt Medea shook her head.

"I am not such a fool," she retorted. "I should only compromise myself. No, I shall not do that; but I might, perhaps, tell your husband what happened at the Borderie."

Blanche shuddered. No threat was capable of moving her like that.

"You shall accompany us, aunt," said she; "I promise it."

Then she added, gently:

"But it is unnecessary to threaten me. You have been cruel, aunt, and at the same time, unjust. If you have been unhappy in our house, you alone are to blame. Why have you said nothing? I attributed your complaisance to your affection for me. How was I to know that a woman as quiet and modest as yourself longed for fine apparel. Confess that it was impossible. Had I known— But rest easy, aunt; I will atone for my neglect."

And as Aunt Medea, having obtained all she desired, stammered an excuse:

"Nonsense!" Blanche exclaimed; "let us forget this foolish quarrel. You forgive me, do you not?"

And the two ladies embraced each other with the greatest effusion, like two friends united after a misunderstanding. But Aunt Medea was as far from being deceived by this mock reconciliation as the clear-sighted Blanche.

"It will be best for me to keep on the *qui vive*," thought the humble relative. "God only knows with what intense joy my dear niece would send me to join Marie-Anne."

Perhaps a similar thought flitted through the mind of Mme. Blanche

She felt as a convict might feel on seeing his most execrated enemy, perhaps the man who had betrayed him, fastened to the other end of his chain.

"I am bound now and forever to this dangerous and perfidious creature," she thought. "I am no longer my own mistress; I belong to her. When she commands, I must obey. I must be the slave of her every caprice—and she has forty years of humiliation and servitude to avenge."

The prospect of such a life made her tremble; and she racked her brain to discover some way of freeing herself from her detested companion.

Would it be possible to inspire Aunt Medea with a desire to live independently in her own house, served by her own servants?

Might she succeed in persuading this silly old woman, who still longed for finery and ball-dresses, to marry? A handsome marriage-portion will always attract a husband.

But, in either case, Blanche would require money—a large sum of money, for whose use she would be accountable to no one.

This conviction made her resolve to take possession of about two hundred and fifty thousand francs, in bank-notes and coin, belonging to her father.

This sum represented the savings of the Marquis de Courtornieu during the past three years. No one knew he had laid it aside, except his daughter; and now that he had lost his reason, Blanche, who knew where the hoard was concealed, could take it for her own use without the slightest danger.

" With this," she thought, " I can at any moment enrich Aunt Medea without having recourse to Martial."

After this little scene there was a constant interchange of delicate attentions and touching devotion between the two ladies. It was " my dearest little aunt," and " my dearly beloved niece," from morning until night; and the gossips of the neighborhood, who had often commented upon the haughty disdain which Mme. Blanche displayed in her treatment of her relative, would have found abundant food for comment had they known that Aunt Medea was protected from the possibility of cold by a mantle lined with costly fur, exactly like the marquise's own, and that she made the journey, not in the large Berlin, with the servants, but in the post-chaise with the Marquis and Marquise de Sairmeuse.

The change was so marked that even Martial remarked it, and as soon as he found himself alone with his wife, he exclaimed, in a tone of good-natured raillery:

"What is the meaning of all this devotion? We shall finish by encasing this precious aunt in cotton, shall we not?"

Blanche trembled, and flushed a little.

"I love good Aunt Medea so much!" said she. "I never can forget all the affection and devotion she lavished upon me when I was so unhappy."

It was such a plausible explanation that Martial took no further notice of the matter, for his mind just then was fully occupied.

The agent, whom he had sent to Paris in advance, to purchase, if possible, the Hôtel de Sairmeuse, had written him to make all possible haste, as there was some difficulty about concluding the bargain.

"Plague take the fellow!" said the marquis, angrily, on receiving this news. "He is quite stupid enough to let this opportunity, for which we have been waiting ten years, slip through his fingers. I shall find no pleasure in Paris if I cannot own our old residence."

He was so impatient to reach Paris that, on the second day of their journey, he declared if he were alone he would travel all night.

"Do so now," said Blanche, graciously; "I do not feel fatigued in the least, and a night of travel does not appall me."

They did travel all night, and the next day, about nine o'clock, they alighted at the Hôtel Meurice.

Martial scarcely took time to eat his breakfast.

" I must go and see my agent at once," he said, as he hurried off.   " I will soon be back."

He reappeared in about two hours, pleased and radiant.

" My agent was a simpleton," he exclaimed.   " He was afraid to write me that a man, upon whom the conclusion of the sale depends, demands a bonus of fifty thousand francs.   He shall have it in welcome."

Then, in a tone of gallantry, which he always used in addressing his wife, he said:

" It only remains for me to sign the paper; but I will not do so unless the house suits you.   If you are not too tired, I would like you to visit it at once.   Time presses, and we have many competitors."

This visit was, of course, one of pure form; but Mme. Blanche would have been hard to please if she had not been satisfied with this mansion, one of the most magnificent in Paris, with an entrance on the Rue de Grenelle, and large gardens shaded with superb trees, and extending to the Rue de Varennes.

Unfortunately, this superb dwelling had not been occupied for several years, and required many repairs.

" It will take at least six months to restore it," said Martial; " perhaps more.   It is true that they might in three months, perhaps, render a portion of it very comfortable."

" It would be living in one's own house, at least," approved Blanche, divining her husband's wishes.

" Ah! then you agree with me!   In that case, you may rest assured that I will expedite matters as much as possible."

In spite, or rather by reason of his immense fortune, the Marquis de Sairmeuse knew that a person is never so well, nor so quickly served, as when he serves himself, so he resolved to take the matter into his own hands. He conferred with architects, interviewed contractors, and hurried on the workmen.

As soon as he was up in the morning he started out without waiting for breakfast, and seldom returned until dinner.

Although Blanche was compelled to pass most of her time within doors, on account of the bad weather, she was not inclined to complain. Her journey, the unaccustomed sights and sounds of Paris, the novelty of life in a hotel, all combined to distract her thoughts from herself. She forgot her fears; a sort of haze enveloped the terrible scene at the Borderie; the clamors of conscience sank into faint whispers.

The past seemed fading away, and she was beginning to entertain hopes of a new and better life, when one day a servant entered, and said:

"There is a man below who wishes to speak with Madame."

CHAPTER LII

Half reclining upon a sofa, Mme. Blanche was listening to a new book which Aunt Medea was reading aloud, and she did not even raise her head as the servant delivered his message.

"A man?" she asked, carelessly; "what man?"

She was expecting no one; it must be one of the laborers employed by Martial.

"I cannot inform Madame," replied the servant. "He is quite a young man; is dressed like a peasant, and is perhaps seeking a place."

"It is probably the marquis whom he desires to see."

" Madame will excuse me, but he said particularly that he desired to speak to her."

" Ask his name and his business, then. Go on, aunt," she added; " we have been interrupted in the most interesting portion."

But Aunt Medea had not time to finish the page when the servant reappeared.

" The man says Madame will understand his business when she hears his name."

" And his name? "

" Chupin."

It was as if a bomb-shell had exploded in the room.

Aunt Medea, with a shriek, dropped her book, and sank back, half fainting, in her chair.

Blanche sprang up with a face as colorless as her white cashmere *peignoir*, her eyes troubled, her lips trembling.

" Chupin ! " she repeated, as if she hoped the servant would tell her she had not understood him correctly; " Chupin ! "

Then angrily:

" Tell this man that I will not see him, I will not see him, do you hear? "

But before the servant had time to bow respectfully and retire, the young marquise changed her mind.

" One moment," said she; " on reflection I think I will see him. Bring him up."

The servant withdrew, and the two ladies looked at each other in silent consternation.

" It must be one of Chupin's sons," faltered Blanche, at last.

" Undoubtedly; but what does he desire? "

" Money, probably."

Aunt Medea lifted her eyes to heaven.

" God grant that he knows nothing of your meetings
with his father! Blessed Jesus! what if he should
know."

" You are not going to despair in advance! We
shall know all in a few moments. Pray be calm.
Turn your back to us; look out into the street; do not
let him see your face. But why is he so long in coming?"

Blanche was not deceived. It was Chupin's eldest
son; the one to whom the dying poacher had confided
his secret.

Since his arrival in Paris he had been running the
streets from morning until evening, inquiring everywhere and of everybody the address of the Marquis de
Sairmeuse. At last he discovered it; and he lost no
time in presenting himself at the Hôtel Meurice.

He was now awaiting the result of his application at
the entrance of the hotel, where he stood whistling,
with his hands in his pockets, when the servant returned, saying:

" She consents to see you; follow me."

Chupin obeyed; but the servant, greatly astonished,
and on fire with curiosity, loitered by the way in the
hope of obtaining some explanation from this country
youth.

" I do not say it to flatter you, my boy," he remarked,
" but your name produced a great effect upon madame."

The prudent peasant carefully concealed the joy he
felt on receiving this information.

" How does it happen that she knows you?" pursued the servant. " Are you both from the same
place?"

" I am her foster-brother."

The servant did not believe a word of this response; but they had reached the apartment of the marquise, he opened the door and ushered Chupin into the room.

The peasant had prepared a little story in advance, but he was so dazzled by the magnificence around him that he stood motionless with staring eyes and gaping mouth. His wonder was increased by a large mirror opposite the door, in which he could survey himself from head to foot, and by the beautiful flowers on the carpet, which he feared to crush beneath his heavy shoes.

After a moment, Mme. Blanche decided to break the silence.

"What do you wish?" she demanded.

With many circumlocutions Chupin explained that he had been obliged to leave Sairmeuse on account of the numerous enemies he had there, that he had been unable to find his father's hidden treasure, and that he was consequently without resources.

"Enough!" interrupted Mme. Blanche. Then in a manner not in the least friendly, she continued: "I do not understand why you should apply to me. You and all the rest of your family have anything but an enviable reputation in Sairmeuse; still, as you are from that part of the country, I am willing to aid you a little on condition that you do not apply to me again."

Chupin listened to this homily with a half-cringing, half-impudent air; when it was finished he lifted his head, and said, proudly:

"I do not ask for alms."

"What do you ask then?"

"My dues."

The heart of Mme. Blanche sank, and yet she had courage to cast a glance of disdain upon the speaker, and said:

" Ah! do I owe you anything? "

" You owe me nothing personally, Madame; but you owe a heavy debt to my deceased father. In whose service did he perish? Poor old man! he loved you devotedly. His last words were of you. ' A ter-rible thing has just happened at the Borderie, my boy,' said he. ' The young marquise hated Marie-Anne, and she has poisoned her. Had it not been for me she would have been lost. I am about to die; let the whole blame rest upon me; it will not hurt me, and it will save the young lady. And afterward she will re-ward you; and as long as you keep the secret you will want for nothing.' "

Great as was his impudence, he paused, amazed by the perfectly composed face of the listener.

In the presence of such wonderful dissimulation he almost doubted the truth of his father's story.

The courage and heroism displayed by the marquise were really wonderful. She felt if she yielded once, she would forever be at the mercy of this wretch, as she was already at the mercy of Aunt Medea.

" In other words," said she, calmly, " you accuse me of the murder of Mademoiselle Lacheneur; and you threaten to denounce me if I do not yield to your de-mands."

Chupin nodded his head in acquiescence.

" Very well! " said the marquise; " since this is the case—go! "

It seemed, indeed, as if she would, by her audacity, win this dangerous game upon which her future peace depended. Chupin, greatly abashed, was standing there undecided what course to pursue when Aunt Medea, who was listening by the window, turned in affright, crying:

" Blanche! your husband—Martial! He is coming!"

The game was lost. Blanche saw her husband entering, finding Chupin, conversing with him, and discovering all!

Her brain whirled; she yielded.

She hastily thrust her purse in Chupin's hand and
dragged him through an inner door and to the servants'
staircase.

" Take this," she said, in a hoarse whisper. " I will
see you again. And not a word—not a word to my
husband, remember!"

She had been wise to yield in time. When she re-
entered the *salon*, she found Martial there.

His head was bowed upon his breast; he held an
open letter in his hand.

He looked up when his wife entered the room, and
she saw a tear in his eye.

" What has happened?" she faltered.

Martial did not remark her emotion.

" My father is dead, Blanche," he replied.

" The Duc de Sairmeuse! My God! how did it
happen?"

" He was thrown from his horse, in the forest, near
the Sanguille rocks."

" Ah! it was there where my poor father was nearly
murdered."

" Yes, it is the very place."

There was a moment's silence.

Martial's affection for his father had not been very
deep, and he was well aware that his father had but little love for him. He was astonished at the bitter grief
he felt on hearing of his death.

" From this letter which was forwarded by a messenger from Sairmeuse," he continued, " I judge that everybody believes it to have been an accident; but I— I——"

" Well? "

" I believe he was murdered."

An exclamation of horror escaped Aunt Medea, and Blanche turned pale.

" Murdered ! " she whispered.

" Yes, Blanche; and I could name the murderer. Oh! I am not deceived. The murderer of my father is the same man who attempted to assassinate the Marquis de Courtornieu——"

" Jean Lacheneur ! "

Martial gravely bowed his head. It was his only reply.

" And you will not denounce him? You will not demand justice? "

Martial's face grew more and more gloomy.

" What good would it do? " he replied. " I have no material proofs to give, and justice demands incontestable evidence."

Then, as if communing with his own thoughts, rather than addressing his wife, he said, despondently:

" The Duc de Sairmeuse and the Marquis de Courtornieu have reaped what they have sown. The blood of murdered innocence always calls for vengeance. Sooner or later, the guilty must expiate their crimes."

Blanche shuddered. Each word found an echo in her own soul. Had he intended his words for her, he would not have expressed himself differently.

" Martial," said she, trying to arouse him from his gloomy revery, " Martial."

He did not seem to hear her, and, in the same tone he continued:

" These Lacheneurs were happy and honored before our arrival at Sairmeuse. Their conduct was above all praise; their probity amounted to heroism. We might have made them our faithful and devoted friends. It was our duty, as well as in our interests, to have done so. We did not understand this; we humiliated, ruined, exasperated them. It was a fault for which we must atone. Who knows but, in Jean Lacheneur's place, I should have done what he has done? "

He was silent for a moment; then, with one of those sudden inspirations that sometimes enable one almost to read the future, he resumed:

" I know Jean Lacheneur. I alone can fathom his hatred, and I know that he lives only in the hope of vengeance. It is true that we are very high and he is very low, but that matters little. We have everything to fear. Our millions form a rampart around us, but he will know how to open a breach. And no precautions will save us. At the very moment when we feel ourselves secure, he will be ready to strike. What he will attempt, I know not; but his will be a terrible revenge. Remember my words, Blanche, if ruin ever threatens our house, it will be Jean Lacheneur's work."

Aunt Medea and her niece were too horror-stricken to articulate a word, and for five minutes no sound broke the stillness save Martial's monotonous tread, as he paced up and down the room.

At last he paused before his wife.

" I have just ordered post-horses. You will excuse me for leaving you here alone. I must go to Sairmeuse at once. I shall not be absent more than a week."

He departed from Paris a few hours later, and Blanche was left a prey to the most intolerable anxiety. She suffered more now than during the days that immediately followed her crime. It was not against phantoms she was obliged to protect herself now; Chupin existed, and his voice, even if it were not as terrible as the voice of conscience, might make itself heard at any moment.

If she had known where to find him, she would have gone to him, and endeavored, by the payment of a large sum of money, to persuade him to leave France.

But Chupin had left the hotel without giving her his address.

The gloomy apprehension expressed by Martial increased the fears of the young marquise. The mere sound of the name Lacheneur made her shrink with terror. She could not rid herself of the idea that Jean Lacheneur suspected her guilt, and that he was watching her.

Her wish to find Marie-Anne's infant was stronger than ever.

It seemed to her that the child might be a protection to her some day. But where could she find an agent in whom she could confide?

At last she remembered that she had heard her father speak of a detective by the name of Chefteux, an exceedingly shrewd fellow, capable of anything, even honesty if he were well paid.

The man was really a miserable wretch, one of Fouché's vilest instruments, who had served and betrayed all parties, and who, at last, had been convicted of perjury, but had somehow managed to escape punishment.

After his dismissal from the police-force, Chefteux founded a bureau of private information.

After several inquiries, Mme. Blanche discovered that he lived in the Place Dauphine; and she determined to take advantage of her husband's absence to pay the detective a visit.

One morning she donned her simplest dress, and, accompanied by Aunt Medea, repaired to the house of Chefteux.

He was then about thirty-four years of age, a man of medium height, of inoffensive mien, and who affected an unvarying good-humor.

He invited his clients into a nicely furnished drawing-room, and Mme. Blanche at once began telling him that she was married, and living in the Rue Saint-Denis, that one of her sisters, who had lately died, had been guilty of an indiscretion, and that she was ready to make any sacrifice to find this sister's child, etc., etc. A long story, which she had prepared in advance, and which sounded very plausible.

Chefteux did not believe a word of it, however; for, as soon as it was ended, he tapped her familiarly on the shoulder, and said:

" In short, my dear, we have had our little escapades before our marriage."

She shrank back as if from some venomous reptile.

To be treated thus! she—a Courtornieu—Duchesse de Sairmeuse!

" I think you are laboring under a wrong impression," she said, haughtily.

He made haste to apologize; but while listening to further details given him by the young lady, he thought:

" What an eye! what a voice!—they are not suited to a denizen of the Saint-Denis! "

His suspicions were confirmed by the reward of twenty thousand francs, which Mme. Blanche imprudently promised him in case of success, and by the five hundred francs which she paid in advance.

"And where shall I have the honor of addressing my communications to you, Madame?" he inquired.

"Nowhere," replied the young lady. "I shall be passing here from time to time, and I will call."

When they left the house, Chefteux followed them.

"For once," he thought, "I believe that fortune smiles upon me."

To discover the name and rank of his new clients was but child's play to Fouché's former pupil.

His task was all the easier since they had no suspicion whatever of his designs. Mme. Blanche, who had heard his powers of discernment so highly praised, was confident of success.

All the way back to the hotel she was congratulating herself upon the step she had taken.

"In less than a month," she said to Aunt Medea, "we shall have the child; and it will be a protection to us."

But the following week she realized the extent of her imprudence. On visiting Chefteux again, she was received with such marks of respect that she saw at once she was known.

She made an attempt to deceive him, but the detective checked her.

"First of all," he said, with a good-humored smile, "I ascertain the identity of the persons who honor me with their confidence. It is a proof of my ability, which I give, gratis. But Madame need have no fears. I am discreet by nature and by profession. Many ladies of the highest ranks are in the position of Madame la Duchesse!"

So Chefteux still believed that the Duchesse de Sairmeuse was searching for her own child.

She did not try to convince him to the contrary. It

was better that he should believe this than suspect the truth.

The condition of Mme. Blanche was now truly pitiable. She found herself entangled in a net, and each movement far from freeing her, tightened the meshes around her.

Three persons knew the secret that threatened her life and honor. Under these circumstances, how could she hope to keep that secret inviolate? She was, moreover, at the mercy of three unscrupulous masters; and before a word, or a gesture, or a look from them, her haughty spirit was compelled to bow in meek subservience.

And her time was no longer at her own disposal. Martial had returned; and they had taken up their abode at the Hôtel de Sairmeuse.

The young duchess was now compelled to live under the scrutiny of fifty servants—of forty enemies, more or less, interested in watching her, in criticising her every act, and in discovering her inmost thoughts.

Aunt Medea, it is true, was of great assistance to her. Blanche purchased a dress for her, whenever she purchased one for herself, took her about with her on all occasions, and the humble relative expressed her satisfaction in the most enthusiastic terms, and declared her willingness to do anything for her benefactress.

Nor did Chefteux give Mme. Blanche much more annoyance. Every three months he presented a memorandum of the expenses of investigations, which usually amounted to about ten thousand francs; and so long as she paid him it was plain that he would be silent.

He had given her to understand, however, that he should expect an annuity of twenty-four thousand

francs; and once, when Mme. Blanche remarked that
he must abandon the search, if nothing had been discovered at the end of two years:

"Never," he replied: "I shall continue the search
as long as I live." But Chupin, unfortunately, remained; and he was a constant terror.

She had been compelled to give him twenty thousand francs, to begin with.

He declared that his younger brother had come to
Paris in pursuit of him, accusing him of having stolen
their father's hoard, and demanding his share with his
dagger in his hand.

There had been a battle, and it was with a head
bound up in a blood-stained linen, that Chupin made
his appearance before Mme. Blanche.

"Give me the sum that the old man buried, and I
will allow my brother to think that I had stolen it. It
is not very pleasant to be regarded as a thief, when
one is an honest man, but I will bear it for your sake.
If you refuse, I shall be compelled to tell him where I
have obtained my money and how."

If he possessed all the vices, depravity, and cold-
blooded perversity of his father, this wretch had inherited neither his intelligence nor his *finesse*.

Instead of taking the precautions which his interest
required, he seemed to find a brutal pleasure in compromising the duchess.

He was a constant visitor at the Hôtel de Sairmeuse.
He came and went at all hours, morning, noon, and
night, without troubling himself in the least about
Martial.

And the servants were amazed to see their haughty
mistress unhesitatingly leave everything at the call of
this suspicious-looking character, who smelled so
strongly of tobacco and vile brandy.

One evening, while a grand entertainment was in progress at the Hôtel de Sairmeuse, he made his appearance, half drunk, and imperiously ordered the servants to go and tell Mme. Blanche that he was there, and that he was waiting for her.

She hastened to him in her magnificent evening-dress, her face white with rage and shame beneath her tiara of diamonds. And when, in her exasperation, she refused to give the wretch what he demanded:

"That is to say, I am to starve while you are revelling here!" he exclaimed. "I am not such a fool. Give me money, and instantly, or I will tell all I know here and now!"

What could she do? She was obliged to yield, as she had always done before.

And yet he grew more and more insatiable every day. Money remained in his pockets no longer than water remains in a sieve. But he did not think of elevating his vices to the proportions of the fortune which he squandered. He did not even provide himself with decent clothing; from his appearance one would have supposed him a beggar, and his companions were the vilest and most degraded of beings.

One night he was arrested in a low den, and the police, surprised at seeing so much gold in the possession of such a beggarly looking wretch, accused him of being a thief. He mentioned the name of the Duchesse de Sairmeuse.

An inspector of the police presented himself at the Hôtel de Sairmeuse the following morning. Martial, fortunately, was in Vienna at the time.

And Mme. Blanche was forced to undergo the terrible humiliation of confessing that she had given a large sum of money to this man, whose family she had known, and who, she added, had once rendered her an important service.

Sometimes her tormentor changed his tactics.

For example, he declared that he disliked to come to the Hôtel de Sairmeuse, that the servants treated him as if he were a mendicant, that after this he would write.

And in a day or two there would come a letter bidding her bring such a sum, to such a place, at such an hour.

And the proud duchess was always punctual at the rendezvous.

There was constantly some new invention, as if he found an intense delight in proving his power and in abusing it.

He had met, Heaven knows where! a certain Aspasie Clapard, to whom he took a violent fancy, and although she was much older than himself, he wished to marry her. Mme. Blanche paid for the wedding-feast.

Again he announced his desire of establishing himself in business, having resolved, he said, to live by his own exertions. He purchased the stock of a wine merchant, which the duchess paid for, and which he drank in no time.

His wife gave birth to a child, and Mme. de Sairmeuse must pay for the baptism as she had paid for the wedding, only too happy that Chupin did not require her to stand as godmother to little Polyte. He had entertained this idea at first.

On two occasions Mme. Blanche accompanied her husband to Vienna and to London, whither he went charged with important diplomatic missions. She remained three years in foreign lands.

Each week during all that time she received one letter, at least, from Chupin.

Ah! many a time she envied the lot of her victim! What was Marie-Anne's death compared with the life she led?

Her sufferings were measured by years, Marie-Anne's by minutes; and she said to herself, again and again, that the torture of poison could not be as intolerable as her agony.

CHAPTER LIII

How was it that Martial had failed to discover or to suspect this state of affairs?

A moment's reflection will explain this fact which is so extraordinary in appearance, so natural in reality.

The head of a family, whether he dwells in an attic or in a palace, is always the last to know what is going on in his home. What everybody else knows he does not even suspect. The master often sleeps while his house is on fire. Some terrible catastrophe—an explosion—is necessary to arouse him from his fancied security.

The life that Martial led was likely to prevent him from arriving at the truth. He was a stranger to his wife. His manner toward her was perfect, full of deference and chivalrous courtesy; but they had nothing in common except a name and certain interests.

Each lived their own life. They met only at dinner, or at the entertainments which they gave and which were considered the most brilliant in Paris society.

The duchess had her own apartments, her servants, her carriages, her horses, her own table.

At twenty-five, Martial, the last descendant of the great house of Sairmeuse—a man upon whom destiny had apparently lavished every blessing—the possessor of youth, unbounded wealth, and a brilliant intellect, succumbed beneath the burden of an incurable despondency and *ennui*.

The death of Marie-Anne had destroyed all his hopes of happiness; and realizing the emptiness of his life, he did his best to fill the void with bustle and excitement. He threw himself headlong into politics, striving to find in power and in satisfied ambition some relief from his despondency.

It is only just to say that Mme. Blanche had remained superior to circumstances; and that she had played the *rôle* of a happy, contented woman with consummate skill.

Her frightful sufferings and anxiety never marred the haughty serenity of her face. She soon won a place as one of the queens of Parisian society; and plunged into dissipation with a sort of frenzy. Was she endeavoring to divert her mind? Did she hope to overpower thought by excessive fatigue?

To Aunt Medea alone did Blanche reveal her secret heart.

"I am like a culprit who has been bound to the scaffold, and then abandoned by the executioner, who says, as he departs: 'Live until the axe falls of its own accord.'"

And the axe might fall at any moment. A word, a trifle, an unlucky chance—she dared not say "a decree of Providence," and Martial would know all.

Such, in all its unspeakable horror, was the position of the beautiful and envied Duchesse de Sairmeuse. "She must be perfectly happy," said the world; but she felt herself sliding down the precipice to the awful depths below.

Like a shipwrecked mariner clinging to a floating spar, she scanned the horizon with a despairing eye, and saw only angry and threatening clouds.

Time, perhaps, might bring her some relief.

Once it happened that six weeks went by, and she heard nothing from Chupin. A month and a half! What had become of him? To Mme. Blanche this silence was as ominous as the calm that precedes the storm.

A line in a newspaper solved the mystery.

Chupin was in prison.

The wretch, after drinking more heavily than usual one evening, had quarrelled with his brother, and had killed him by a blow upon the head with a piece of iron.

The blood of the betrayed Lacheneur was visited upon the heads of his murderer's children.

Tried by the Court of Assizes, Chupin was condemned to twenty years of hard labor, and sent to Brest.

But this sentence afforded the duchess no relief. The culprit had written to her from his Paris prison; he wrote to her from Brest.

But he did not send his letters through the post. He confided them to comrades, whose terms of imprisonment had expired, and who came to the Hôtel de Sairmeuse demanding an interview with the duchess.

And she received them. They told all the miseries they had endured " out there; " and usually ended by requesting some slight assistance.

One morning, a man whose desperate appearance and manner frightened her, brought the duchess this laconic epistle:

" I am tired of starving here; I wish to make my escape. Come to Brest; you can visit the prison, and we will decide upon some plan. If you refuse to do this, I shall apply to the duke, who will obtain my pardon in exchange of what I will tell him."

Mme. Blanche was dumb with horror. It was impossible, she thought, to sink lower than this.

" Well! " demanded the man, harshly. " What reply shall I make to my comrade? "

" I will go—tell him that I will go! " she said, driven to desperation.

She made the journey, visited the prison, but did not find Chupin.

The previous week there had been a revolt in the prison, the troops had fired upon the prisoners, and Chupin had been killed instantly.

Still the duchess dared not rejoice.

She feared that her tormentor had told his wife the secret of his power.

" I shall soon know," she thought.

The widow promptly made her appearance; but her manner was humble and supplicating.

She had often heard her dear, dead husband say that madame was his benefactress, and now she came to beg a little aid to enable her to open a small drinking saloon.

Her son Polyte—ah! such a good son! just eighteen years old, and such a help to his poor mother—had discovered a little house in a good situation for the business, and if they only had three or four hundred francs——

Mme. Blanche gave her five hundred francs.

" Either her humility is a mask," she thought, " or her husband has told her nothing."

Five days later Polyte Chupin presented himself.

They needed three hundred francs more before they could commence business, and he came on behalf of his mother to entreat the kind lady to advance them.

Determined to discover exactly where she stood, the duchess shortly refused, and the young man departed without a word.

Evidently the mother and son were ignorant of the facts. Chupin's secret had died with him.

This happened early in January. Toward the last of February, Aunt Medea contracted inflammation of the lungs on leaving a fancy ball, which she attended in an absurd costume, in spite of all the attempts which her niece made to dissuade her.

Her passion for dress killed her. Her illness lasted only three days; but her sufferings, physical and mental, were terrible.

Constrained by her fear of death to examine her own conscience, she saw plainly that by profiting by the crime of her niece she had been as culpable as if she had aided her in committing it. She had been very devout in former years, and now her superstitious fears were reawakened and intensified. Her faith returned, accompanied by a *cortége* of terrors.

" I am lost ! " she cried; " I am lost ! "

She tossed to and fro upon her bed; she writhed and shrieked as if she already saw hell opening to engulf her.

She called upon the Holy Virgin and upon all the saints to protect her. She entreated God to grant her time for repentance and for expiation. She begged to see a priest, swearing she would make a full confession.

Paler than the dying woman, but implacable, Blanche watched over her, aided by that one of her personal attendants in whom she had most confidence.

"If this lasts long, I shall be ruined," she thought. "I shall be obliged to call for assistance, and she will betray me."

It did not last long.

The patient's delirium was succeeded by such utter prostration that it seemed each moment would be her last.

But toward midnight she appeared to revive a little, and in a voice of intense feeling, she said:

"You have had no pity, Blanche. You have deprived me of all hope in the life to come. God will punish you. You, too, shall die like a dog; alone, without a word of Christian counsel or encouragement. I curse you!"

And she died just as the clock was striking two.

The time when Blanche would have given almost anything to know that Aunt Medea was beneath the sod, had long since passed.

Now, the death of the poor old woman affected her deeply.

She had lost an accomplice who had often consoled her, and she had gained nothing, since one of her maids was now acquainted with the secret of the crime at the Borderie.

Everyone who was intimately acquainted with the Duchesse de Sairmeuse, noticed her dejection, and was astonished by it.

"Is it not strange," remarked her friends, "that the duchess—such a very superior woman—should grieve so much for that absurd relative of hers?"

But the dejection of Mme. Blanche was due in great measure to the sinister prophecies of the accomplice to whom she had denied the last consolations of religion.

And as her mind reviewed the past she shuddered, as

the peasants at Sairmeuse had done, when she thought
of the fatality which had pursued the shedders of innocent blood.

What misfortune had attended them all—from the
sons of Chupin, the miserable traitor, up to her father,
the Marquis de Courtornieu, whose mind had not been
illumined by the least gleam of reason for ten long
years before his death.

" My turn will come ! " she thought.

The Baron and the Baroness d'Escorval, and old
Corporal Bavois had departed this life within a month
of each other, the previous year, mourned by all.

So that of all the people of diverse condition who
had been connected with the troubles at Montaignac,
Blanche knew only four who were still alive.

Maurice d'Escorval, who had entered the magis-
tracy, and was now a judge in the tribunal of the Seine ;
Abbé Midon, who had come to Paris with Maurice,
and Martial and herself.

There was another person, the bare recollection of
whom made her tremble, and whose name she dared
not utter.

Jean Lacheneur, Marie-Anne's brother.

An inward voice, more powerful than reason, told
her that this implacable enemy was still alive, watching for his hour of vengeance.

More troubled by her presentiments now, than she
had been by Chupin's persecutions in days gone by,
Mme. de Sairmeuse decided to apply to Chefteux in
order to ascertain, if possible, what she had to expect.

Fouché's former agent had not wavered in his devotion to the duchess. Every three months he presented
his bill, which was paid without discussion ; and to ease
his conscience, he sent one of his men to prowl around
Sairmeuse for a while, at least once a year.

Animated by the hope of a magnificent reward, the spy promised his client, and—what was more to the purpose—promised himself, that he would discover this dreaded enemy.

He started in quest of him, and had already begun to collect proofs of Jean's existence, when his investigations were abruptly terminated.

One morning the body of a man literally hacked in pieces was found in an old well. It was the body of Chefteux.

" A fitting close to the career of such a wretch," said the *Journal des Debats,* in noting the event.

When she read this news, Mme. Blanche felt as a culprit would feel on reading his death-warrant.

" The end is near," she murmured. " Lacheneur is coming ! "

The duchess was not mistaken.

Jean had told the truth when he declared that he was not disposing of his sister's estate for his own benefit. In his opinion, Marie-Anne's fortune must be consecrated to one sacred purpose ; he would not divert the slightest portion of it to his individual needs.

He was absolutely penniless when the manager of a travelling theatrical company engaged him for a consideration of forty-five francs per month.

From that day he lived the precarious life of a strolling player. He was poorly paid, and often reduced to abject poverty by lack of engagements, or by the impecuniosity of managers.

His hatred had lost none of its virulence ; but to wreak the desired vengeance upon his enemy, he must have time and money at his disposal.

But how could he accumulate money when he was often too poor to appease his hunger ?

Still he did not renounce his hopes. His was a rancor which was only intensified by years. He was bid-
ing his time while he watched from the depths of his
misery the brilliant fortunes of the house of Sairmeuse.

He had waited sixteen years, when one of his friends
procured him an engagement in Russia.

The engagement was nothing; but the poor come
dian was afterward fortunate enough to obtain an interest in a theatrical enterprise, from which he realized
a fortune of one hundred thousand francs in less than
six years.

"Now," said he, "I can give up this life. I am rich
enough, now, to begin the warfare."

And six weeks later he arrived in his native village.

Before carrying any of his atrocious designs into
execution, he went to Sairmeuse to visit Marie-Anne's
grave, in order to obtain there an increase of animosity,
as well as the relentless *sang-froid* of a stern avenger
of crime.

That was his only motive in going, but, on the very
evening of his arrival, he learned through a garrulous
old peasant woman that ever since his departure—that
is to say, for a period of twenty years—two parties had
been making persistent inquiries for a child which had
been placed somewhere in the neighborhood.

Jean knew that it was Marie-Anne's child they were
seeking. Why they had not succeeded in finding it, he
knew equally well.

But why were there two persons seeking the child?
One was Maurice d'Escorval, of course, but who was
the other?

Instead of remaining at Sairmeuse a week, Jean
Lacheneur tarried there a month; and by the expira-
tion of that month he had traced these inquiries con-

cerning the child to the agent of Chefteux. Through him, he reached Fouché's former spy; and, finally, succeeded in discovering that the search had been instituted by no less a person than the Duchesse de Sairmeuse.

This discovery bewildered him. How could Mme. Blanche have known that Marie-Anne had given birth to a child; and knowing it, what possible interest could she have had in finding it?

These two questions tormented Jean's mind continually; but he could discover no satisfactory answer.

"Chupin's son could tell me, perhaps," he thought. "I must pretend to be reconciled to the sons of the wretch, who betrayed my father."

But the traitor's children had been dead for several years, and after a long search, Jean found only the Widow Chupin and her son, Polyte.

They were keeping a drinking-saloon not far from the Château-des-Rentiers; and their establishment, known as the Poivrière, bore anything but an enviable reputation.

Lacheneur questioned the widow and her son in vain; they could give him no information whatever on the subject. He told them his name, but even this did not awaken the slightest recollection in their minds.

Jean was about to take his departure when Mother Chupin, probably in the hope of extracting a few pennies, began to deplore her present misery, which was, she declared, all the harder to bear since she had wanted for nothing during the life of her poor husband, who had always obtained as much money as he wanted from a lady of high degree—the Duchesse de Sairmeuse, in short.

Lacheneur uttered such a terrible oath that the old woman and her son started back in affright.

He saw at once the close connection between the researches of Mme. Blanche and her generosity to Chupin.

"It was she who poisoned Marie-Anne," he said to
himself. "It was through my sister that she became
aware of the existence of the child. She loaded Chupin
with favors because he knew the crime she had committed—that crime in which his father had been only
an accomplice."

He remembered Martial's oath at the bedside of the
murdered girl, and his heart overflowed with savage
exultation. He saw his two enemies, the last of the
Sairmeuse and the last of the Courtornieu take in their
own hands his work of vengeance.

But this was mere conjecture; he desired to be assured of the correctness of his suppositions.

He drew from his pocket a handful of gold, and,
throwing it upon the table, he said:

"I am very rich; if you will obey me and keep my
secret, your fortune is made."

A shrill cry of delight from mother and son out-
weighed any protestations of obedience.

The Widow Chupin knew how to write, and Lacheneur dictated this letter:

"MADAME LA DUCHESSE—I shall expect you at my
establishment to-morrow between twelve and four
o'clock. It is on business connected with the Borderie.
If at five o'clock I have not seen you, I shall carry to
the post a letter for the duke."

"And if she comes what am I to say to her?" asked
the astonished widow.

"Nothing; you will merely ask her for money."

"If she comes, it is as I have guessed," he reflected.

She came.

Hidden in the loft of the Poivrière, Jean, through an opening in the floor, saw the duchess give a bank-note to Mother Chupin.

" Now, she is in my power ! " he thought exultantly. " Through what sloughs of degradation will I drag her before I deliver her up to her husband's vengeance ! "

CHAPTER LIV

A few lines of the article consecrated to Martial de Sairmeuse in the " General Biography of the Men of the Century," give the history of his life after his marriage.

" Martial de Sairmeuse," it says, there, " brought to the service of his party a brilliant intellect and ad-mirable endowments. Called to the front at the moment when political strife was raging with the utmost violence, he had courage to assume the sole responsibility of the most extreme measures.

" Compelled by almost universal opprobrium to retire from office, he left behind him animosities which will be extinguished only with life."

But what this article does not state is this : if Martial was wrong—and that depends entirely upon the point of view from which his conduct is regarded—he was doubly wrong, since he was not possessed of those ardent convictions verging upon fanaticism which make men fools, heroes, and martyrs.

He was not even ambitious.

Those associated with him, witnessing his passion-ate struggle and his unceasing activity, thought him actuated by an insatiable thirst for power.

He cared little or nothing for it. He considered its burdens heavy; its compensations small. His pride was too lofty to feel any satisfaction in the applause that delights the vain, and flattery disgusted him. Often, in his princely drawing-rooms, during some brilliant *fête*, his acquaintances noticed a shade of gloom steal over his features, and seeing him thus thoughtful and preoccupied, they respectfully refrained from disturbing him.

"His mind is occupied with momentous questions," they thought. "Who can tell what important decisions may result from this revery?"

They were mistaken.

At the very moment when his brilliant success made his rivals pale with envy—when it would seem that he had nothing left to wish for in this world, Martial was saying to himself:

"What an empty life! What weariness and vexation of spirit! To live for others—what a mockery!"

He looked at his wife, radiant in her beauty, worshipped like a queen, and he sighed.

He thought of her who was dead—Marie-Anne— the only woman whom he had ever loved.

She was never absent from his mind. After all these years he saw her yet, cold, rigid, lifeless, in that luxurious room at the Borderie; and time, far from effacing the image of the fair girl who had won his youthful heart, made it still more radiant and endowed his lost idol with almost superhuman grace of person and of character.

If fate had but given him Marie-Anne for his wife! He said this to himself again and again, picturing the exquisite happiness which a life with her would have afforded him.

They would have remained at Sairmeuse. They would have had lovely children playing around them! He would not be condemned to this continual warfare—to this hollow, unsatisfying, restless life.

The truly happy are not those who parade their satisfaction and good fortune before the eyes of the multitude. The truly happy hide themselves from the curious gaze, and they are right; happiness is almost a crime.

So thought Martial; and he, the great statesman, often said to himself, in a sort of rage:

"To love, and to be loved—that is everything! All else is vanity."

He had really tried to love his wife; he had done his best to rekindle the admiration with which she had inspired him at their first meeting. He had not succeeded.

Between them there seemed to be a wall of ice which nothing could melt, and which was constantly increasing in height and thickness.

"Why is it?" he wondered, again and again. "It is incomprehensible. There are days when I could swear that she loved me. Her character, formerly so irritable, is entirely changed; she is gentleness itself."

But he could not conquer his aversion; it was stronger than his own will.

These unavailing regrets, and the disappointments and sorrow that preyed upon him, undoubtedly aggravated the bitterness and severity of Martial's policy.

But he, at least, knew how to fall nobly.

He passed, without even a change of countenance, from almost omnipotence to a position so compromising that his very life was endangered.

On seeing his ante-chambers, formerly thronged

with flatterers and office-seekers, empty and deserted,
he laughed, and his laugh was unaffected.

"The ship is sinking," said he; "the rats have deserted it."

He did not even pale when the noisy crowd came
to hoot and curse and hurl stones at his windows; and
when Otto, his faithful *valet de chambre*, entreated him
to assume a disguise and make his escape through the
gardens, he responded:

"By no means! I am simply odious; I do not wish
to become ridiculous!"

They could not even dissuade him from going to a
window and looking down upon the rabble in the
street below.

A singular idea had just occurred to him.

"If Jean Lacheneur is still alive," he thought, "how
much he would enjoy this! And if he is alive, he is undoubtedly there in the foremost rank, urging on the
crowd."

And he wished to see.

But Jean Lacheneur was in Russia at that epoch.
The excitement subsided; the Hôtel de Sairmeuse was
not seriously threatened. Still Martial realized that it
would be better for him to go away for a while, and
allow people to forget him.

He did not ask the duchess to accompany him.

"The fault has been mine entirely," he said to her,
"and to make you suffer for it by condemning you to
exile would be unjust. Remain here; I think it will be
much better for you to remain here."

She did not offer to go with him. It would have been
a pleasure to her, but she dared not leave Paris. She
knew that she must remain in order to insure the silence
of her persecutors. Both times she had left Paris be-

fore, all came near being discovered, and yet she had Aunt Medea, then, to take her place.

Martial went away, accompanied only by his devoted servant, Otto. In intelligence, this man was decidedly superior to his position; he possessed an independent fortune, and he had a hundred reasons—one, by the way, was a very pretty one—for desiring to remain in Paris; but his master was in trouble, and he did not hesitate.

For four years the Duc de Sairmeuse wandered over Europe, ever accompanied by his *ennui* and his dejection, and chafing beneath the burden of a life no longer animated by interest or sustained by hope.

He remained awhile in London, then he went to Vienna, afterward to Venice. One day he was seized by an irresistible desire to see Paris again, and he returned.

It was not a very prudent step, perhaps. His bitterest enemies—personal enemies, whom he had mortally offended and persecuted—were in power; but he did not hesitate. Besides, how could they injure him, since he had no favors to ask, no cravings of ambition to satisfy?

The exile which had weighed so heavily upon him, the sorrow, the disappointments and loneliness he had endured had softened his nature and inclined his heart to tenderness; and he returned firmly resolved to overcome his aversion to his wife, and seek a reconciliation.

" Old age is approaching," he thought. " If I have not a beloved wife at my fireside, I may at least have a friend."

His manner toward her, on his return, astonished Mme. Blanche. She almost believed she saw again the Martial of the little blue *salon* at Courtornieu; but the realization of her cherished dream was now only another torture added to all the others.

Martial was striving to carry his plan into execution, when the following laconic epistle came to him one day through the post:

"MONSIEUR LE DUC—I, if I were in your place, would watch my wife."

It was only an anonymous letter, but Martial's blood mounted to his forehead.

" Can it be that she has a lover? " he thought.

Then reflecting on his own conduct toward his wife since their marriage, he said to himself:

" And if she has, have I any right to complain? Did I not tacitly give her back her liberty? "

He was greatly troubled, and yet he would not have degraded himself so much as to play the spy, had it not been for one of those trifling circumstances which so often decide a man's destiny.

He was returning from a ride on horseback one morning about eleven o'clock, and he was not thirty paces from the Hôtel de Sairmeuse when he saw a lady hurriedly emerge from the house. She was very plainly dressed—entirely in black—but her whole appearance was strikingly that of the duchess.

" It is certainly my wife; but why is she dressed in such a fashion? " he thought.

Had he been on foot he would certainly have entered the house; as it was, he slowly followed Mme. Blanche, who was going up the Rue Grenelle. She walked very quickly, and without turning her head, and kept her face persistently shrouded in a very thick veil.

When she reached the Rue Taranne, she threw herself into one of the *fiacres* at the carriage-stand.

The coachman came to the door to speak to her; then nimbly sprang upon the box, and gave his bony horses one of those cuts of the whip that announce a princely *pourboire*.

The carriage had already turned the corner of the Rue du Dragon, and Martial, ashamed and irresolute, had not moved from the place where he had stopped his horse, just around the corner of the Rue Saint Pares.

Not daring to admit his suspicions, he tried to deceive himself.

" Nonsense ! " he thought, giving the reins to his horse, " what do I risk in advancing ? The carriage is a long way off by this time, and I shall not overtake it."

He did overtake it, however, on reaching the intersection of the Croix-Rouge, where there was, as usual, a crowd of vehicles.

It was the same *fiacre;* Martial recognized it by its green body, and its wheels striped with white.

Emerging from the crowd of carriages, the driver whipped up his horses, and it was at a gallop that they flew up the Rue du Vieux Columbier—the narrowest street that borders the Place Saint Sulpice—and gained the outer boulevards.

Martial's thoughts were busy as he trotted along about a hundred yards behind the vehicle.

" She is in a terrible hurry," he said to himself. " This, however, is scarcely the quarter for a lover's rendezvous."

The carriage had passed the Place d'Italie. It entered the Rue du Château-des-Rentiers and soon paused before a tract of unoccupied ground.

The door was at once opened, and the Duchesse de Sairmeuse hastily alighted.

Without stopping to look to the right or to the left, she hurried across the open space.

A man, by no means prepossessing in appearance, with a long beard, and with a pipe in his mouth, and clad in a workman's blouse, was seated upon a large block of stone not far off.

" Will you hold my horse a moment? " inquired Martial.

" Certainly," answered the man.

Had Martial been less preoccupied, his suspicions might have been aroused by the malicious smile that curved the man's lips: and had he examined his features closely, he would perhaps have recognized him.

For it was Jean Lacheneur.

Since addressing that anonymous letter to the Duc de Sairmeuse, he had made the duchess multiply her visits to the Widow Chupin; and each time he had watched for her coming.

" So, if her husband decides to follow her I shall know it," he thought.

It was indispensable for the success of his plans that Mme. Blanche should be watched by her husband.

For Jean Lacheneur had decided upon his course. From a thousand schemes for revenge he had chosen the most frightful and ignoble that a brain maddened and enfevered by hatred could possibly conceive.

He longed to see the haughty Duchesse de Sairmeuse subjected to the vilest ignominy, Martial in the hands of the lowest of the low. He pictured a bloody struggle in this miserable den; the sudden arrival of the police, summoned by himself, who would arrest all the parties indiscriminately. He gloated over the thought of a trial in which the crime committed at the Borderie would be brought to light; he saw the duke and the duchess in prison, and the great names of Sairmeuse and of Courtornieu shrouded in eternal disgrace.

And he believed that nothing was wanting to insure the success of his plans. He had at his disposal two miserable wretches who were capable of any crime; and an unfortunate youth named Gustave, made his willing slave by poverty and cowardice, was intended to play the part of Marie-Anne's son.

These three accomplices had no suspicion of his real intentions. As for the Widow Chupin and her son, if they suspected some infamous plot, the name of the duchess was all they really knew in regard to it. Moreover, Jean held Polyte and his mother completely under his control by the wealth which he had promised them if they served him docilely.

And if Martial followed his wife into the Poivrière, Jean had so arranged matters that the duke would at first suppose that she had been led there by charity.

" But he will not go in," thought Lacheneur, whose heart throbbed wildly with sinister joy as he held Martial's horse. " Monsieur le Duc is too fine for that."

And Martial did not go in. Though he was horrified when he saw his wife enter that vile den, as if she were at home there, he said to himself that he should learn nothing by following her.

He, therefore, contented himself by making a thorough examination of the outside of the house; then, remounting his horse, he departed on a gallop. He was completely mystified; he did not know what to think, what to imagine, what to believe.

But he was fully resolved to fathom this mystery; and as soon as he returned home he sent Otto out in search of information. He could confide everything to this devoted servant; he had no secrets from him.

About four o'clock his faithful *valet de chambre* returned, an expression of profound consternation visible upon his countenance.

"What is it?" asked Martial, divining some great misfortune.

"Ah, sir, the mistress of that wretched den is the widow of Chupin's son——"

Martial's face became as white as his linen.

He knew life too well not to understand that since the duchess had been compelled to submit to the power of these people, they must be masters of some secret which she was willing to make any sacrifice to preserve. But what secret?

The years which had silvered Martial's hair, had not cooled the ardor of his blood. He was, as he had always been, a man of impulses.

He rushed to his wife's apartments.

"Madame has just gone down to receive the Countess de Mussidan and the Marquise d'Arlange," said the maid.

"Very well; I will wait for her here. Retire."

And Martial entered the chamber of Mme. Blanche.

The room was in disorder, for the duchess, after returning from the Poivrière, was still engaged in her toilet when the visitors were announced.

The wardrobe-doors were open, the chairs were encumbered with wearing apparel, the articles which Mme. Blanche used daily—her watch, her purse, and several bunches of keys—were lying upon the dressing-table and mantel.

Martial did not sit down. His self-possession was returning.

"No folly," he thought, "if I question her, I shall learn nothing. I must be silent and watchful."

He was about to retire, when, on glancing about the room, his eyes fell upon a large casket, inlaid with silver, which had belonged to his wife ever since she was a young girl, and which accompanied her everywhere.

"That, doubtless, holds the solution of the mystery," he said to himself.

It was one of those moments when a man obeys the dictates of passion without pausing to reflect. He saw the keys upon the mantel; he seized them, and endeavored to find one that would fit the lock of the casket. The fourth key opened it. It was full of papers.

With feverish haste, Martial examined the contents. He had thrown aside several unimportant letters, when he came to a bill that read as follows:

"Search for the child of Madame de Sairmeuse. Expenses for the third quarter of the year 18—."

Martial's brain reeled.

A child! His wife had a child!

He read on: "For services of two agents at Sairmeuse, ——. For expenses attending my own journey, ——. Divers gratuities, ——. Etc., etc." The total amounted to six thousand francs. The bill was signed "Chefteux."

With a sort of cold rage, Martial continued his examination of the contents of the casket, and found a note written in a miserable hand, that said: "Two thousand francs this evening, or I will tell the duke the history of the affair at the Borderie." Then several more bills from Chefteux; then a letter from Aunt Medea in which she spoke of prison and of remorse. And finally, at the bottom of the casket, he found the marriage-certificate of Marie-Anne Lacheneur and

Maurice d'Escorval, drawn up by the Curé of Vigano and signed by the old physician and Corporal Bavois.

The truth was as clear as daylight.

Stunned, frozen with horror, Martial scarcely had strength to return the letters to the casket and restore it to its place.

Then he tottered back to his own room, clinging to the walls for support.

" It was she who murdered Marie-Anne," he murmured.

He was confounded, terror-stricken by the perfidy and baseness of this woman who was his wife—by her criminal audacity, by her cool calculation and assurance, by her marvellous powers of dissimulation.

He swore he would discover all, either through the duchess or through the Widow Chupin; and he ordered Otto to procure a costume for him such as was generally worn by the *habitués* of the Poivrière. He did not know how soon he might have use for it.

This happened early in February, and from that moment Mme. Blanche did not take a single step without being watched. Not a letter reached her that her husband had not previously read.

And she had not the slightest suspicion of the constant espionage to which she was subjected.

Martial did not leave his room; he pretended to be ill. To meet his wife and be silent, was beyond his powers. He remembered the oath of vengeance which he had pronounced over Marie-Anne's lifeless form too well.

But there were no new revelations, and for this reason: Polyte Chupin had been arrested under charge of theft, and this accident caused a delay in the execution of Lacheneur's plans. But, at last, he judged that all would be in readiness on the 20th of February, Shrove Sunday.

The evening before the Widow Chupin, in conformance with his instructions, wrote to the duchess that she must come to the Poivrière Sunday evening at eleven o'clock.

On that same evening Jean was to meet his accomplices at a ball at the Rainbow—a public-house bearing a very unenviable reputation—and give them their last instructions.

These accomplices were to open the scene; he was to appear only in the *dénouement*.

"All is well arranged; the mechanism will work of its own accord," he said to himself.

But the "mechanism," as he styled it, failed to work.

Mme. Blanche, on receiving the Widow Chupin's summons, revolted for a moment. The lateness of the hour, the isolation of the spot designated, frightened her.

But she was obliged to submit, and on the appointed evening she furtively left the house, accompanied by Camille, the same servant who had witnessed Aunt Medea's last agony.

The duchess and her maid were attired like women of the very lowest order, and felt no fear of being seen or recognized.

And yet a man was watching them, and he quickly followed them. It was Martial.

Knowing of this rendezvous even before his wife, he had disguised himself in the costume Otto had procured for him, which was that of a laborer about the quays; and, as he was a man who did perfectly whatever he attempted to do, he had succeeded in rendering himself unrecognizable. His hair and beard were rough and matted; his hands were soiled and grimed with dirt, he was really the abject wretch whose rags he wore.

Otto had begged to be allowed to accompany him; but the duke refused, saying that the revolver which he would take with him would be sufficient protection. He knew Otto well enough, however, to be certain he would disobey him.

Ten o'clock was sounding when Mme. Blanche and Camille left the house, and it did not take them five minutes to reach the Rue Taranne.

There was one *fiacre* on the stand—one only.

They entered it and it drove away.

This circumstance drew from Martial an oath worthy of his costume. Then he reflected that, since he knew where to find his wife, a slight delay in finding a carriage did not matter.

He soon obtained one; and the coachman, thanks to a *pourboire* of ten francs, drove to the Rue du Château-des-Rentiers as fast as his horses could go.

But the duke had scarcely set foot on the ground before he heard the rumbling of another carriage which stopped abruptly at a little distance.

"Otto is evidently following me," he thought.

And he started across the open space in the direction of the Poivrière.

Gloom and silence prevailed on every side, and were made still more oppressive by a chill fog that heralded an approaching thaw. Martial stumbled and slipped at almost every step upon the rough, snow-covered ground.

It was not long before he could distinguish a dark mass in the midst of the fog. It was the Poivrière. The light within filtered through the heart-shaped openings in the blinds, looking at a distance like lurid eyes gleaming in the darkness.

Could it really be possible that the Duchesse de Sairmeuse was there!

Martial cautiously approached the window, and
clinging to the hinges of one of the shutters, he lifted
himself up so he could peer through the opening.

Yes, his wife was indeed there in that vile den.

She and Camille were seated at a table before a large
punch-bowl, and in company with two ragged, leering
scoundrels, and a soldier, quite youthful in appearance.

In the centre of the room stood the Widow Chupin,
with a small glass in her hand, talking volubly and
punctuating her sentences by copious draughts of
brandy.

The impression produced upon Martial was so terrible that his hold relaxed and he dropped to the ground.

A ray of pity penetrated his soul, for he vaguely
realized the frightful suffering which had been the chastisement of the murderess.

But he desired another glance at the interior of the
hovel, and he again lifted himself up to the opening and
looked in.

The old woman had disappeared; the young soldier
had risen from the table and was talking and gesticulating earnestly. Mme. Blanche and Camille were listening to him with the closest attention.

The two men who were sitting face to face, with their
elbows upon the table, were looking at each other; and
Martial saw them exchange a significant glance.

He was not wrong. The scoundrels were plotting " a
rich haul."

Mme. Blanche, who had dressed herself with such
care, that to render her disguise perfect she had encased
her feet in large, coarse shoes, that were almost killing
her—Mme. Blanche had forgotten to remove her superb
diamond ear-rings.

She had forgotten them, but Lacheneur's accomplices had noticed them, and were now regarding them with eyes that glittered more brilliantly than the diamonds themselves.

While awaiting Lacheneur's coming, these wretches, as had been agreed upon, were playing the part which he had imposed upon them. For this, and their assistance afterward, they were to receive a certain sum of money.

But they were thinking that this sum was not, perhaps, a quarter part of the value of these jewels, and they exchanged glances that said:

" Ah ! if we could only get them and make our escape before Lacheneur comes ! "

The temptation was too strong to be resisted.

One of them rose suddenly, and, seizing the duchess by the back of the neck, he forced her head down upon the table.

The diamonds would have been torn from the ears of Mme. Blanche had it not been for Camille, who bravely came to the aid of her mistress.

Martial could endure no more. He sprang to the door of the hovel, opened it, and entered, bolting it behind him.

" Martial ! "

" Monsieur le Duc ! "

These cries escaping the lips of Mme. Blanche and Camille in the same breath, changed the momentary stupor of their assailants into fury; and they both precipitated themselves upon Martial, determined to kill him.

With a spring to one side, Martial avoided them. He had his revolver in his hand; he fired twice and the wretches fell.

But he was not yet safe, for the young soldier threw himself upon him, and attempted to disarm him.

Through all the furious struggle, Martial did not cease crying, in a panting voice:

" Fly! Blanche, fly! Otto is not far off. The name —save the honor of the name!"

The two women obeyed, making their escape through the back door, which opened upon the garden; and they had scarcely done so, before a violent knocking was heard at the front door.

The police were coming! This increased Martial's frenzy: and with one supreme effort to free himself from his assailant, he gave him such a violent push that his adversary fell, striking his head against the corner of the table, after which he lay like one dead.

But the Widow Chupin, who had come downstairs on hearing the uproar, was shrieking upon the stairs. At the door someone was crying: " Open in the name of the law!"

Martial might have fled; but if he fled, the duchess might be captured, for he would certainly be pursued. He saw the peril at a glance, and his decision was made.

He shook the Widow Chupin violently by the arm, and said, in an imperious voice:

" If you know how to hold your tongue you shall have one hundred thousand francs."

Then, drawing a table before the door opening into the adjoining room, he intrenched himself behind it as behind a rampart, and awaited the approach of the enemy.

The next moment the door was forced open, and a squad of police, under the command of Inspector Gevrol, entered the room.

" Surrender!" cried the inspector.

Martial did not move; his pistol was turned upon the intruder.

"If I can parley with them, and hold them in check only two minutes, all may yet be saved," he thought.

He obtained the wished-for delay; then he threw his weapon to the ground, and was about to bound through the back-door, when a policeman, who had gone round to the rear of the house, seized him about the body, and threw him to the floor.

From this side he expected only assistance, so he cried:

"Lost! It is the Prussians who are coming!"

In the twinkling of an eye he was bound; and two hours later he was an inmate of the station-house at the Place d'Italie.

He had played his part so perfectly, that he had deceived even Gevrol. The other participants in the broil were dead, and he could rely upon the Widow Chupin. But he knew that the trap had been set for him by Jean Lacheneur; and he read a whole volume of suspicion in the eyes of the young officer who had cut off his retreat, and who was called Lecoq by his companions.

CHAPTER LV

The Duc de Sairmeuse was one of those men who remain superior to all fortuitous circumstances, good or bad. He was a man of vast experience, and great natural shrewdness. His mind was quick to act, and fertile in resources. But when he found himself immured in the damp and loathsome station-house, after the terrible scenes at the Poivrière, he relinquished all hope.

Martial knew that Justice does not trust to appearances, and that when she finds herself confronted by a mystery, she does not rest until she has fathomed it.

Martial knew, only too well, that if his identity was established, the authorities would endeavor to discover the reason of his presence at the Poivrière. That this reason would soon be discovered, he could not doubt, and, in that case, the crime at the Borderie, and the guilt of the duchess, would undoubtedly be made public.

This meant the Court of Assizes, prison, a frightful scandal, dishonor, eternal disgrace!

And the power he had wielded in former days was a positive disadvantage to him now. His place was now filled by his political adversaries. Among them were two personal enemies upon whom he had inflicted those terrible wounds of vanity which are never healed. What an opportunity for revenge this would afford them!

At the thought of this ineffaceable stain upon the great name of Sairmeuse, which was his pride and his glory, reason almost forsook him.

" My God, inspire me," he murmured. " How shall I save the honor of the name? "

He saw but one chance of salvation—death. They now believed him one of the miserable wretches that haunt the suburbs of Paris; if he were dead they would not trouble themselves about his identity.

" It is the only way! " he thought.

He was endeavoring to find some means of accomplishing his plan of self-destruction, when he heard a bustle and confusion outside. In a few moments the door was opened and a man was thrust into the same cell—a man who staggered a few steps, fell heavily to the floor, and began to snore loudly. It was only a drunken man.

But a gleam of hope illumined Martial's heart, for in
the drunken man he recognized Otto—disguised, almost unrecognizable.

It was a bold ruse and no time must be lost in profiting by it. Martial stretched himself upon a bench, as if
to sleep, in such a way that his head was scarcely a
yard from that of Otto.

" The duchess is out of danger," murmured the faithful servant.

" For to-day, perhaps. But to-morrow, through me,
all will be known."

" Have you told them who you are? "

" No; all the policemen but one took me for a vagabond."

" You must continue to personate this character."

" What good will it do? Lacheneur will betray me."

But Martial, though he little knew it, had no need to
fear Lacheneur for the present, at least. A few hours
before, on his way from the Rainbow to the Poivrière,
Jean had been precipitated to the bottom of a stone
quarry, and had fractured his skull. The laborers, on
returning to their work early in the morning, found him
lying there senseless; and at that very moment they
were carrying him to the hospital.

Although Otto was ignorant of this circumstance, he
did not seem discouraged.

" There will be some way of getting rid of Lacheneur," said he, " if you will only sustain your present
character. An escape is an easy matter when a man has
millions at his command."

" They will ask me who I am, whence I came, how I
have lived."

" You speak English and German; tell them that you
have just returned from foreign lands; that you were a

foundling and that you have always lived a roving life."

" How can I prove this? "

Otto drew a little nearer his master, and said, impressively:

" We must agree upon our plans, for our success depends upon a perfect understanding between us. I have a sweetheart in Paris—and no one knows our relations. She is as sharp as steel. Her name is Milner, and she keeps the Hôtel de Mariembourg, on the Saint-Quentin. You can say that you arrived here from Leipsic on Sunday; that you went to this hotel; that you left your trunk there, and that this trunk is marked with the name of May, foreign artist."

" Capital! " said Martial, approvingly.

And then, with extraordinary quickness and precision, they agreed, point by point, upon their plan of defence.

When all had been arranged, Otto pretended to awake from the heavy sleep of intoxication; he clamored to be released, and the keeper finally opened the door and set him at liberty.

Before leaving the station-house, however, he succeeded in throwing a note to the Widow Chupin, who was imprisoned in the other compartment.

So, when Lecoq, after his skilful investigations at the Poivrière, rushed to the Place d'Italie, panting with hope and ambition, he found himself outwitted by these men, who were inferior to him in penetration, but whose *finesse* was superior to his own.

Martial's plans being fully formed, he intended to carry them out with absolute perfection of detail, and, after his removal to prison, the Duc de Sairmeuse was preparing himself for the visit of the judge of instruction, when Maurice d'Escorval entered.

They recognized each other. They were both terribly agitated, and the examination was an examination only in name. After the departure of Maurice, Martial attempted to destroy himself. He had no faith in the generosity of his former enemy.

But when he found M. Segmuller occupying Maurice's place the next morning, Martial believed that he was saved.

Then began that struggle between the judge and Lecoq on one side, and the accused on the other—a struggle from which neither party came out conqueror.

Martial knew that Lecoq was the only person he had to fear, still he bore him no ill-will. Faithful to his nature, which compelled him to be just even to his enemies, he could not help admiring the astonishing penetration and perseverance of this young policeman who, undismayed by the obstacles and discouragements that surrounded him, struggled on, unassisted, to reach the truth.

But Lecoq was always outwitted by Otto, the mysterious accomplice, who seemed to know his every movement in advance.

At the morgue, at the Hôtel de Mariembourg, with Toinon, the wife of Polyte Chupin, as well as with Polyte Chupin himself, Lecoq was just a little too late.

Lecoq detected the secret correspondence between the prisoner and his accomplice. He was even ingenious enough to discover the key to it, but this served no purpose. A man, who had seen a rival, or rather, a future master, in Lecoq had betrayed him.

If his efforts to arrive at the truth through the jeweller and the Marquis d'Arlange had failed, it was only because Mme. Blanche had not purchased the diamond ear-rings she wore at the Poivrière at any shop, but from one of her friends, the Baroness de Watchau.

And lastly, if no one at Paris had missed the Duc de Sairmeuse, it was because—thanks to an understanding between the duchess, Otto, and Camille—no other inmate of the Hôtel de Sairmeuse suspected his absence. All the servants supposed their master confined to his room by illness. They prepared all sorts of gruels and broths for him, and his breakfast and dinner were taken to his apartments every day.

So the weeks went by, and Martial was expecting to be summoned before the Court of Assizes and condemned under the name of May, when he was afforded an opportunity to escape.

Too shrewd not to discern the trap that had been set for him, he endured some moments of horrible hesitation in the prison-van.

He decided to accept the risk, however, commending himself to his lucky star.

And he decided wisely, for that same night he leaped his own garden-wall, leaving, as a hostage, in the hands of Lecoq, an escaped convict, Joseph Conturier by name, whom he had picked up in a low drinking-saloon.

Warned by Mme. Milner, thanks to a blunder on the part of Lecoq, Otto was awaiting his master.

In the twinkling of an eye Martial's beard fell under the razor; he plunged into the bath that was awaiting him, and his clothing was burned.

And it was he who, during the search a few minutes later, had the hardihood to call out:

"Otto, by all means allow these men to do their duty."

But he did not breathe freely until the agents of police had departed.

"At last," he exclaimed, "honor is saved! We have outwitted Lecoq!"

He had just left the bath, and enveloped himself in a *robe de chambre,* when Otto handed him a letter from the duchess.

He hastily broke the seal and read:

" You are safe. You know all. I am dying. Farewell. I loved you."

With two bounds he reached his wife's apartments. The door was locked: he burst it open. Too late!

Mme. Blanche was dead—poisoned, like Marie-Anne; but she had procured a drug whose effect was instantaneous; and extended upon her couch, clad in her wonted apparel, her hands folded upon her breast, she seemed only asleep.

A tear glittered in Martial's eye.

" Poor, unhappy woman!" he murmured; " may God forgive you as I forgive you—you whose crime has been so frightfully expiated here below!"

END OF PART SECOND.

EPILOGUE

THE FIRST SUCCESS

Safe, in his own princely mansion, and surrounded by an army of retainers, the Duc de Sairmeuse triumphantly exclaimed:

"We have outwitted Lecoq."

In this he was right.

But he thought himself forever beyond the reach of the wily, keen-witted detective; and in this he was wrong.

Lecoq was not the man to sit down with folded hands and brood over the humiliation of his defeat.

Before he went to Father Tabaret, he was beginning to recover from his stupor and despondency; and when he left that experienced detective's presence, he had regained his courage, his command over his faculties, and sufficient energy to move the world, if necessary.

"Well, my good man," he remarked to Father Absinthe, who was trotting along by his side, "you have heard what the great Monsieur Tabaret said, did you not? So you see I was right."

But his companion evinced no enthusiasm.

"Yes, you were right," he responded, in woe-begone tones.

"Do you think we are ruined by two or three mistakes? Nonsense! I will soon turn our defeat of today into a glorious victory."

" Ah! you might do so perhaps, if—they do not dismiss us from the force."

This doleful remark recalled Lecoq to a realizing sense of the present situation.

They had allowed a prisoner to slip through their fingers. That was vexatious, it is true; but they had captured one of the most notorious of criminals—Joseph Conturier. Surely there was some comfort in that.

But while Lecoq could have borne dismissal, he could not endure the thought that he would not be allowed to follow up this affair of the Poivrière.

What would his superior officers say when he told them that May and the Duc de Sairmeuse were one and the same person?

They would, undoubtedly, shrug their shoulders and turn up their noses.

" Still, Monsieur Segmuller will believe me," he thought. " But will he dare to take any action in the matter without incontrovertible evidence? "

This was very unlikely. Lecoq realized it all too well.

" Could we not make a descent upon the Hôtel de Sairmeuse, and, on some pretext or other, compel the duke to show himself, and identify him as the prisoner May? "

He entertained this idea only for an instant, then abruptly dismissed it.

" A stupid expedient! " he exclaimed. " Are two such men as the duke and his accomplice likely to be caught napping? They are prepared for such a visit, and we should only have our labor for our pains."

He made these reflections *sotto voce;* and Father Absinthe's curiosity was aroused.

"Excuse me," said he, "I did not quite understand you."

"I say that we must find some tangible proof before asking permission to proceed further."

He paused with knitted brows.

In seeking a circumstance which would establish the complicity between some member of the duke's household and the witnesses who had been called upon to give their testimony, Lecoq thought of Mme. Milner, the owner of the Hôtel de Mariembourg, and his first meeting with her.

He saw her again, standing upon a chair, her face on a level with a cage, covered with a large piece of black silk, persistently repeating three or four German words to a starling, who as persistently retorted: "Camille! Where is Camille?"

"One thing is certain," resumed Lecoq; "if Madame Milner—who is a German and who speaks with the strongest possible German accent—had raised this bird, it would either have spoken German or with the same accent as its mistress. Therefore it cannot have been in her possession long, and who gave it to her?"

Father Absinthe began to grow impatient.

"In sober earnest, what are you talking about?" he asked, petulantly.

"I say that if there is someone at the Hôtel de Sairmeuse named Camille, I have the proof I desire. Come, Papa Absinthe, let us hurry on."

And without another word of explanation, he dragged his companion rapidly along.

When they reached the Rue de Grenelle, Lecoq saw a messenger leaning against the door of a wine-shop. Lecoq called him.

"Come, my boy," said he; "I wish you to go to the

Hôtel de Sairmeuse and ask for Camille. Tell her that her uncle is waiting her here."

"But, sir——"

"What, you have not gone yet?"

The messenger departed; the two policemen entered the wine-shop, and Father Absinthe had scarcely had time to swallow a glass of brandy when the lad returned.

"Monsieur, I was unable to see Mademoiselle Camille. The house is closed from top to bottom. The duchess died very suddenly this morning."

"Ah! the wretch!" exclaimed the young policeman.

Then, controlling himself, he mentally added:

"He must have killed his wife on returning home, but his fate is sealed. Now, I shall be allowed to continue my investigations."

In less than twenty minutes they arrived at the Palais de Justice.

M. Segmuller did not seem to be immoderately surprised at Lecoq's revelations. Still he listened with evident doubt to the young policeman's ingenious deductions; it was the circumstance of the starling that seemed to decide him.

"Perhaps you are right, my dear Lecoq," he said, at last; "and to tell the truth, I quite agree with you. But I can take no further action in the matter until you can furnish proof so convincing in its nature that the Duc de Sairmeuse will be unable to think of denying it."

"Ah! sir, my superior officers will not allow me——"

"On the contrary," interrupted the judge, "they will allow you the fullest liberty after I have spoken to them."

Such action on the part of M. Segmuller required not a little courage. There had been so much laughter about M. Segmuller's *grand seigneur,* disguised as a clown, that many men would have sacrificed their convictions to the fear of ridicule.

"And when will you speak to them?" inquired Lecoq, timidly.

"At once."

The judge had already turned toward the door when the young policeman stopped him.

"I have one more favor to ask, Monsieur," he said, entreatingly. "You are so good; you are the first person who gave me any encouragement—who had faith in me."

"Speak, my brave fellow."

"Ah! Monsieur, will you not give me a message for Monsieur d'Escorval? Any insignificant message—inform him of the prisoner's escape. I will be the bearer of the message, and then— Oh! fear nothing, Monsieur; I will be prudent."

"Very well!" replied the judge.

When he left the office of his *chef,* Lecoq was fully authorized to proceed with his investigations, and in his pocket was a note for M. d'Escorval from M. Segmuller. His joy was so intense that he did not deign to notice the sneers which were bestowed upon him as he passed through the corridors. On the threshold his enemy Gevrol, the so-called general, was watching for him.

"Ah, ha!" he laughed, as Lecoq passed out, "here is one of those simpletons who fish for whales and do not catch even a gudgeon."

For an instant Lecoq was angry. He turned abruptly and looked Gevrol full in the face.

"That is better than assisting prisoners to carry on a surreptitious correspondence with people outside," he retorted, in the tone of a man who knows what he is saying.

In his surprise, Gevrol almost lost countenance, and his blush was equivalent to a confession.

But Lecoq said no more. What did it matter to him now if Gevrol had betrayed him! Was he not about to win a glorious revenge?

He spent the remainder of the day in preparing his plan of action, and in thinking what he should say when he took M. Segmuller's note to Maurice d'Escorval.

The next morning about eleven o'clock he presented himself at the house of M. d'Escorval.

"Monsieur is in his study with a young man," replied the servant; "but, as he gave me no orders to the contrary, you may go in."

Lecoq entered.

The study was unoccupied. But from the adjoining room, separated from the study only by a velvet *portière*, came a sound of stifled exclamations, and of sobs mingled with kisses.

Not knowing whether to remain or retire, the young policeman stood for a moment undecided; then he observed an open letter lying upon the carpet.

Impelled to do it by an impulse stronger than his own will, Lecoq picked up the letter. It read as follows:

"The bearer of this letter is Marie-Anne's son, Maurice—your son. I have given him all the proofs necessary to establish his identity. It was to his education that I consecrated the heritage of my poor Marie-Anne.

Those to whose care I confided him have made a noble man of him. If I restore him to you, it is only because the life I lead is not a fitting life for him. Yesterday, the miserable woman who murdered my sister died from poison administered by her own hand. Poor Marie-Anne! she would have been far more terribly avenged had not an accident which happened to me, saved the Duc and the Duchesse de Sairmeuse from the snare into which I had drawn them.

"JEAN LACHENEUR."

Lecoq stood as if petrified.

Now he understood the terrible drama which had been enacted in the Widow Chupin's cabin.

"I must go to Sairmeuse at once," he said to himself; "there I can discover all."

He departed without seeing M. d'Escorval. He resisted the temptation to take the letter with him.

———

It was exactly one month to a day after the death of Mme. Blanche.

Reclining upon a divan in his library the Duc de Sairmeuse was engaged in reading, when Otto, his *valet de chambre,* came to inform him that a messenger was below, charged with delivering into the duke's own hands a letter from M. Maurice d'Escorval.

With a bound, Martial was on his feet.

"Is it possible?" he exclaimed.

Then he added, quickly:

"Let the messenger enter."

A large man, with a very florid complexion, and red hair and beard, timidly handed the duke a letter.

Martial broke the seal, and read:

" I saved you, Monsieur, by not recognizing the prisoner, May. In your turn, aid me! By noon, day after
to-morrow, I must have two hundred and sixty thousand francs.

" I have sufficient confidence in your honor to apply
to you.

" MAURICE D'ESCORVAL."

For a moment Martial stood bewildered, then,
springing to a table, he began writing, without notic-
ing that the messenger was looking over his shoulder:

" MONSIEUR—Not day after to-morrow, but this
evening. My fortune and my life are at your disposal.
It is but a slight return for the generosity you showed
in retiring, when, beneath the rags of May, you recognized your former enemy, now your devoted friend,

" MARTIAL DE SAIRMEUSE."

He folded this letter with a feverish hand, and giving
it to the messenger with a louis, he said:

" Here is the answer, make haste! "

But the messenger did not go.

He slipped the letter into his pocket, then with a
hasty movement he cast his red beard and wig upon
the floor.

" Lecoq! " exclaimed Martial, paler than death.

" Lecoq, yes, Monsieur," replied the young detective.
" I was obliged to take my revenge; my future depended upon it, and I ventured to imitate Monsieur
d'Escorval's writing."

And as Martial made no response:

" I must also say to Monsieur le Duc," he continued, "that on transmitting to the judge the confession written by the Duke's own hand, of his presence at the Poivrière, I can and shall, at the same time, furnish proofs of his entire innocence."

And to show that he was ignorant of nothing, he added:

" As madame is dead, there will be nothing said in regard to what took place at the Borderie."

A week later a verdict of not guilty was rendered by M. Segmuller in the case of the Duc de Sairmeuse.

Appointed to the position he coveted, Lecoq had the good taste, or perhaps the shrewdness, to wear his honors modestly.

But on the day of his promotion, he ordered a seal, upon which was engraved the exultant rooster, which he had chosen as his armorial design, and a motto to which he ever remained faithful: *Semper Vigilans.*

www.ingramcontent.com/pod-product-compliance
Lightning Source LLC
Chambersburg PA
CBHW032252020726
47495CB00001B/81